To My Fr [barcode] CW01081653

Now retired, the author has turned to her lifelong interest in history and coupled it with her own imagination. She likes to imagine what famous characters might have said and done at important times in their lives. She has a vivid imagination and utilises it to the full but it is her 'people observations' that bring the people from history to life. Her main challenge is to hold the readers' interest in both historical fact and fictitious stories, putting words into the mouths of people from the past, most of whom are known to us. She varies the historical stories with completely fictitious scenarios where the characters 'do their own thing' – that is, both good and bad things. Over the past three years, she has had four books published – all containing new and unusual short stories. She hopes the readers will enjoy them and keep coming back for more.

Please Enjoy

J B Pritchard

X

This book has been written for my four grandchildren. Their very existence in my life has prompted and encouraged me to complete the book. They provide me with hope for the future. These stories are for you kids – Abbie, Holly, James and Oliver – my best little friends.

Joan B. Pritchard

MYSTERY, HISTORY AND IMAGINATION

20 Short Stories

AUSTIN MACAULEY PUBLISHERS™

LONDON • CAMBRIDGE • NEW YORK • SHARJAH

A CIP catalogue record for this title is available from the British Library.

ISBN 9781398416406 (Paperback)
ISBN 9781788230155 (ePub e-book)

www.austinmacauley.com

First Published (2021)
Austin Macauley Publishers Ltd
25 Canada Square
Canary Wharf
London
E14 5LQ

Table of Contents

A New Start in a New Land

She sat at the water's edge and watched the waves lapping against the bottom of the large rock. She visualised the Pilgrims stepping onto it and then down onto the actual ground of the new land. A hundred had lived through the two-month's journey from England and now they looked tired and bedraggled, having spent so much time in the crushed confines of the ship, the Mayflower. Five of the initial Pilgrims had died on the voyage – William Button died 6 November 1620, Edward Thompson died 14 December 1620, Jasper More died 16 December 1620, Dorothy Bradford died 17 December 1520 and James Chilton died 19 December 1620. They were all laid to rest on Coles Hill which became the cemetery in the new Plymouth colony. One baby – Oceanus Hopkins – had been born on board and was even now with his mother in the makeshift tent made by the men of the group. The journey to the new continent had started off smoothly but the ship soon encountered wild and rough seas, splitting one of the main masts. Consideration was given to turning back but they used 'a great iron screw' to hold the mast together and went on their way regardless. At the outset of the expedition, there had actually been two ships – the Mayflower and a smaller ship called the Speedwell, but it was discovered that the latter was not seaworthy and so, only the Mayflower set sail for New England. The girl had experienced the confusion of the ships and for a while, thought she would be able to stay in England – but it was not to be, so here she was sitting by the great rock which would become known as Plymouth Rock. She was thinking about the old country. She was 15 years old and missed the land of her birth. Her name was Eleanor and she was the Puritan daughter of Michael and Mary Crawford. She'd been happy in her life at home and had many friends there but this new and strange country was to be her home now. There were no buildings and the trees and bushes were everywhere – the land was rough with no welcoming signs at all. She felt sorry for herself – what would her future be and how would she deal with it? No answer was the cry!

The background as to why she found herself in this foreign land was mostly unknown to her. She was a simple person and didn't know very much about England's political matters.

King James I of England and VI of Scotland had given a group of Puritans permission to travel to the New World and set up a second colony there. Several years before, 1585 to be exact, Sir Walter Raleigh had attempted to establish a colony in North Carolina, all in the name of Queen Elizabeth I and he was given the credit for bringing back to England, both tobacco and potatoes. He also named the land of Virginia for the virgin queen. The colony at the time was Roanoke Island (now North Carolina), but it failed as did the second attempt to form a similar colony two years later. But he spent five years helping to build the colony and, in the end, it was successful. He was knighted for his part in this and it was the reason the Pilgrim Fathers knew of the native Indians and of course, why the native Indians themselves were aware of the white men. The saddest thing was that Walter Raleigh was later accused of being a traitor by James I and subsequently executed, but not before he'd changed England for the better.

In England, a few years before 1620, the Pilgrims or Separatists/Brownists, had broken away from the main church and formed a religion of their own. At first, many of them travelled to Holland in the Netherlands, where the Dutch were more tolerant of differing religions – believing more in puritan Calvinistic theories – but eventually, they decided to form a new colony in the new world. They sought out investors who thought they'd make a lot of money through such a venture. The Pilgrims went on to establish the second successful colony, the first being Jamestown, Virginia in 1607. (This was named after James I of England.)

The Pilgrims were strongly Protestant and hated the way the church in England appeared to be favouring traits of the Catholic church and they believed there were too many Roman Catholic fripperies still attached to what should have a purely Protestant country. In effect, they believed that Catholicism was creeping back into Britain. King James was the Head of the church – and not the Pope – as Henry VIII had decreed at the end of the previous century, when he desperately wanted to marry his second wife, Anne Boleyn. The main reason therefore, that the Pilgrim Fathers left England in 1620 was because they didn't like what the Church of England was becoming. The increasing fripperies of Catholicism had to be avoided at all costs and also, when any Puritans failed to attend services in the Church of England, they were fined one whole shilling for each missed service. The penalties for conducting a service, other than the C of E, could be imprisonment, much higher fines, or even execution. There was no room for compromise it seemed.

Of course, the wish to form the colony was also because wealthy merchants wanted to make their fortunes in the New World and other investors were also only too willing to help finance the expedition. It wasn't all about the Pilgrims being not allowed to practice their own style of religion – although it formed a big part of it, but there were also financial aspects in their decision to leave England.

Most of this was unknown to Eleanor – all she knew was that she'd been swept up in the changes at the time. Her father and mother were strong Protestants and so was Eleanor herself – but they knew that many sacrifices had to be made! Having saved up a few shillings, they applied for places on board the Mayflower and were lucky enough to get them.

Eleanor stood up and shook out her skirts. Climbing onto the rock, it was easy to imagine she could hear the sounds of the Pilgrims' feet as they jumped, one by one, onto the shore of the new country. They came from the small boat or shallop which had brought them from the Mayflower. The imagined sounds made a sound that reverberated around her head and she knew she'd remember it for ever. The rock was special and seemed perfectly positioned to help the tired and hungry people to disembark. It was part of the welcome to the new land – and it certainly made it easier for them. The Mayflower was still out there, harboured in the bay but she would be going nowhere until the people were a bit more settled in the new land. The ship's captain and crew were there to help them do that.

It was the beginning of the month of January and they'd only been here for the past few days. They had actually landed on 26 December in the Year of our Lord, 1620 and were still bringing supplies from the mother ship to their makeshift camp. Without the ship, they would have died, so it was very comforting to see it standing proudly on the waves in the distance. The ship's captain, Christopher Jones, was working hard with the Pilgrims, bringing rowing boats full of goods and provisions to shore, where the men were waiting for their tools, saws, axes to begin the building of huts for their families. Captain Jones owned one quarter of the Mayflower and had volunteered to bring the people to the New World, in the hope he'd make a large fortune for himself. In fact, he'd already invested most of his money in the venture. The worst of winter was still to come and some protection was imperative – the tools that came from England were being used every day and through most of each night – it was necessary if anyone was to survive the next few months of winter.

Eleanor could smell the cooking fires of the camp and got up quickly. She ran past the trees and slipped into her tent. Before anyone had spotted that, she'd been gone. She wasn't supposed to wander outside the camp as no one yet knew what dangers existed there. They had been told there were Indians in the area – as well as bears – who might not welcome the newcomers and this was something everyone feared. They understood how strange they might appear to the indigenous tribes, whose home it had been for about ten thousand years. The Indians were part of the Wampanoag people and were already watching the newcomers from behind the trees and trying to judge how dangerous they might prove to be. Fearing such people, they were obviously prepared to take whatever lives were necessary, but probably only if they felt under attack. Eleanor had seen nothing of the Indians so far but she was curious as to what they looked like and she knew that soon, they would have to show themselves.

She went out the tent towards the large fire over which a haunch of what looked like venison hung, but it was probably wildcat, something they'd managed to hunt down in the short time since their arrival. It was suspended on a pole over the fire and was making everyone's mouths water with hunger. The smell was incredible and the Pilgrims were slowly approaching the fire, leaving off their chores for a little while. The smell drew them into the warmth of the fire – they were cold, stiff, and ready for something to eat.

"Eleanor, fill those flagons with beer, ready for the workers to slake their thirst. What a good thing there's still plenty of the beer we picked up at Cape Cod." The Pilgrims were suspicious of the water here, as the water in England had been undrinkable – and it might be the same here. Her mother was busy getting some ships' biscuits, of which they still had plenty – mainly because people didn't really like them and the supply had dwindled very little. Eleanor did as she was told and offered Captain Christopher one of the flagons and an empty tankard.

"Why thank you, Miss Eleanor, I am most grateful and very thirsty." He accepted the beer from the young girl and sat down with the other men in the circle around the fire. The Chief Elder, William Brewster, was sitting next to him and they discussed what work was required the next day – the carpenters were working every minute there was daylight and were proud of what they'd achieved so far.

Suddenly, two of the men jumped up and reached for their muskets. Two Indians, covered in bright paintings, stood at the edge of the trees. They wore different coloured feathers in their hair and had axes and knives tucked into their waistbands. A bow and arrows were swung over their shoulders. Pointing the muskets at the Indians, the two men moved slowly forward but young Eleanor picked herself off the ground and fetched a piece of venison on a wooden platter. Some instinct told her that an offering with such delicious aroma would please anyone – she hoped Indians were the same as her own people. She took tentative steps towards the strangers and held out the meat saying, "Please take this. You are welcome."

One of the Indians made to grab the platter but his companion held his arm back and said something none of the Pilgrims could understand. He chose to ignore his friend and bit into the savoury meat, pulling off a piece and giving it to the other Indian. Both men chewed and swallowed quickly, eying the rest of the meat roasting on the fire. Once swallowed, both Indians touched their foreheads and bowed their heads – it was their way of saying thank you.

"Well done, Eleanor – that was a good move. They look ferocious and dangerous – but you've shown that perhaps they're not as bad as they look. Maybe we're just very strange to them – we certainly look very different, don't we?" He spoke to all the Pilgrims grouped around the fire and the muskets were lowered. One of the Indians took a step forward and pulled a feather from his headband – he offered it to Eleanor, whose father pulled her back, but she shook off his hand and walked towards the Indian. She took the yellow feather and smiled at him. She hadn't yet learned that to be given a feather by an Indian was a great honour and only given to those who were special. Both Indians turned and disappeared into the trees, with steps so soft, no one could hear them.

The Chief Elder, William Brewster, whistled and said, "Well, what do you make of that?" And puffed deeply on his pipe.

Another man said, "I don't know what to make of it but at least nothing bad happened. I can't imagine how we're going to communicate with them."

"Well, the girl managed it, didn't she?" the Elder tried to be positive. "They managed to say thank you to her and she didn't seem afraid." William Bradford, the leader of the expedition, nodded his head in agreement.

Next day, the whole community was up early – the men working on the frames of at least three houses and the women working on the land, planting seeds of onions, cabbages and carrots. (Potatoes were not part of the Pilgrims' diet, as although Walter Raleigh had brought them from America, they had not then reached the ordinary people of England. One had to be wealthy to eat potatoes in the 17th Century!) They planted the seeds and tubers with their fingers crossed, hoping that the soil in the new land would be kind to them. Lots of water would be needed and they'd have to find a river somewhere close by. The women's heavy skirts dragged as they worked but at least the digging kept them warm. They'd brought chickens with them and the birds were strutting around without a care in the world, but then they didn't know their feed could run out any day. Two men, who'd bragged about their fishing skills, had been sent off with makeshift rods and a large basket, which they hoped they'd fill before the day was over. Once they got to know the country, they'd be able to hunt down the wild turkeys which seemed numerous in the area. Their food might not be as at home, but at least they wouldn't starve.

Although it was January and the winter months loomed ahead, there was a feeling of optimism in the air and the group found pleasure in the hard work. Eleanor worked alongside her mother and hitched her skirts up around her waist.

"Eleanor, drop your skirts at once. You're a young lady now and need to act like one." Her mother was a very proper lady.

"But it's much easier to work, Mother – you should try it." Eleanor laughed at her mother's shocked expression and left the rough ground to go back to the large tent where provisions were stored. More seeds and tubers were needed and she rummaged in the biggest sack there. She tidied her long, brown hair into the cap she wore – it helped make the work easier. As she turned to leave the tent, she spotted a young Indian staring at her from behind a tree in the clearing. She walked towards him but he turned and ran away. She ran after him, saying, "Come back – I'm not going to hurt you." He stopped and turned around. She thought he smiled but maybe it was just a grimace.

"How?" he said quite clearly and she repeated his word back to him. It was the start of a communication between the two. He did smile this time and then turned away, but this time, he didn't run, just walked back through the woods. Eleanor ran back to her mother.

"Mother, I've just met an Indian boy and he said 'How' to me – I think it was his way of saying hello."

"You've been told before not to go out of the camp. You're a very naughty girl. He could have killed you – they carry all those sharp weapons and you have nothing." Her mother really was cross. "And where's the seed plants you went to fetch?" Eleanor ran back to fetch them, but she felt good – it was almost like making a new friend. In fact, she had made a friend; she was sure.

After a month – and many chilblains – the first village house was ready for occupation. Initially, it would house two families and a partition made of blankets hung across the room to give some privacy. The plan was as more houses were built; families would have one of their own – but this was still a way ahead. The house was timber framed and the women were given the task of covering it with a 'wattle and daub' mixture, which they gathered from around the countryside and mixed it with mud, chicken droppings, water and when possible, with urine. It was the grandest house they'd ever seen and even, some Indians joined them to admire the creation. They were amazed at how strong the walls seemed and was easy to see that they might attempt to copy it.

Two families with young children were the first to live in the completed house and people were obviously vying for the next one. Eleanor's family would have to wait for some time, as they were healthy, young and quite independent. It wasn't a problem and they waited their turn patiently. It became quite normal for small parties of men to go out into the wilds to see what was possible and what was not. They found a spring which was full of the sweetest water and this was great for the camp – they hunted as well, bringing back some animals which were a welcome addition to the cooking pot. Amazingly, on one of their trips from the camp, they found an old European style house with an iron kettle inside, probably abandoned by some ship's crew who'd stayed on shore for a short time. Beside it, there were two or three cultivated fields, clearly showing corn stubble. So, someone had been there before them. They moved further on and found several mounds of earth in the dunes by the shore. They dug the first one and found it was an Indian grave, then they found more mounds of soil and realised they were in a graveyard. Inside each mound, they found corn which had been buried with the bodies – probably to feed the dead in the next world. They scooped as much of the corn as they could and brought it back to the camp to use as seed for planting. They also came across two Indian houses, covered with mats and inside, there were some tools and bags of more corn – but the Indians had run away and the Pilgrims couldn't find them. They had to take some of the corn without asking but did leave at least half.

15

On one of their expeditions, Christopher Jones and Myles Standish, who was an English soldier chanced upon a lone Indian fishing quietly in a stream. He looked at them but didn't smile and said nothing. What they didn't know at that time was that this man was going to be their saviour and yet they'd almost walked straight past him.

Then they heard. "How are you today, gentlemen?" The Indian called after them and stopped them in their tracks. "I am called Tisquantum but most people call me Squanto – I belong to the Patuxet tribe and if you are going to be friendly, then so will I." He flicked his rod from the water and grabbed at the fish that hung there. He had long dark hair which was caught back in a pony tail and he wore buckskin trousers. His chest was bare with strange markings – just like the other Indians they'd seen in the camp. It made him look quite ferocious.

Captain Christopher lowered his musket and smiled at the Indian. "We certainly intend to be friendly – as I hope you do. Where did you learn to speak such good English?"

"I was captured by some trading slavers who took me from my village and sold me to some monks beside your other colony and tried to make a Christian of me – but I was too cunning for them and after one year, I escaped and came home. I learned English from them – I felt they owed me that much as I'd worked hard in that year. I am a Christian now but decided to do this myself and not because they told me to."

"Escaping must have been quite a feat," Christopher said, "I can't imagine how you managed it. Will you come and see us at our camp? We're building homes as fast as we can, but it's a slow business and we'd welcome your advice about some things, particularly about the cultivation of the land and the best crops to plant. Our food will soon run out so we must plant as much as we can – and soon." Squanto agreed and shook hands with the two men before disappearing into the trees. His English really was amazing and the Pilgrim men knew it was going to prove very useful to them in setting up the village.

The weather was turning bad and there'd been more than one snowfall. Some of the Pilgrims and the crew from the Mayflower fell sick, coughing violently. They suffered from scurvy too and were seriously ill. Many of them died that first winter, although Squanto and the other Indians tried to help by offering food and some blankets.

Eleanor's father, Michael, was one of the men who fell ill. At least by the time this happened, they had a small house built, so his wife and daughter were able to look after him as best they could. He was burning up with fever and Mary was very worried – what if he died – how would she and Eleanor survive without him? Eleanor bathed his head and kept putting the blankets over him when he threw them off. She left the house very early one morning and without telling her mother, she made her way to where she'd once met the young Indian boy. She was going to ask him if the Indians had any medicine that might help her father. She found him, gathering wood for a fire and, using the Indian words Squanto had taught her, she asked him the question. He didn't understand at first but then realised what she was trying to ask. He led her to his mat-covered home and showed her inside. Eleanor was frightened but tried not to show it. A very old man sat on a straw mat, legs crossed and smoking a long-stemmed pipe. He was rocking to and fro at the same time and seemed really very old. His long, straggly hair was pure white and his skin was wrinkled and dark brown but his eyes were kind and she could see a resemblance to the boy in his face.

He listened to what his grandson had to say and pointed to a bag hanging at the top of a long stick. The boy fetched it and the old man poured some of the contents into a smaller bag, which he gave to Eleanor. It looked like some sort of seed but she took it gratefully. The boy indicated she should soak the mixture in water and make her father drink it – as often and as much as he could.

It took the best part of a week and Michael seemed to get worse before he got better – but one morning, it was all over and he was sleeping peacefully with no trace of a fever. The medicine had worked and Eleanor would never forget the boy and his grandfather.

Although it had worked for Michael, there were many others who weren't so lucky and before the first winter was over, 45 Pilgrims and members of the Mayflower crew had died. Only half of those who'd set off from England were alive to face the second year in the New World. The sad thing was that diphtheria and smallpox had come to the new land with the Pilgrims and this was partly what killed them. Unfortunately, they gave some of their infected blankets to the Indians as gifts for their help and within a few months, a great number of them had died from the diseases, which they'd never encountered before and had no knowledge of.

During their expeditions, the Pilgrims met with other tribes of Indians – many not so friendly as the Patuxet tribe and there were many skirmishes between the parties. The Indians shot with their bows and arrows and the

Pilgrims used guns, to much better effect. It was inevitable that this happened and something the Pilgrims had expected.

Whilst this was going on, the women back at base camp were working flat out – digging, ploughing and planting. It was cold and stormy and sometimes they had to stop and stay huddled within their shelters. The builders were however, getting on with erecting properties and had started work on a church-cum-schoolhouse. Eleanor was chosen to be the first teacher and she relished the thought. It wouldn't be easy as they had brought no supplies for such a thing, but she was determined to manage. She was sixteen years old now and after the sea journey and the hardships of the first winter, she felt really grown up.

The building the men were working on just then was extralong and wide and was to be used as a temporary hospital for the Pilgrims who were falling sick every day and needed some protection. There were patients lying on mats at the same time as the walls were going up – a hardship for all concerned.

One day, Eleanor and her friend, Humility Brown, had set off for a forage amongst the trees and bushes, looking for edible berries. They knew they were edible – and very tasty – because Squanto had told them so, and he was becoming the Wise Man of their village. They started up an incline towards the top of a small hill – the best berries were to be found there. They had a bucket each which they intended to fill, thinking of all those pies to come. In fact, the juice of the berries was also good for dying cloth and gave a wonderful taste to cold water from the spring.

"Look over there, Humility. What are those strange mounds of earth all in a circle?" Eleanor knew it was something they'd not seen before. Outside the large circle of mounds, there were trees also in a wide circle. It all looked quite deliberate and was obviously made by human hand.

Humility said, "It could be some sort of monument built by the Indians – that's what I think it is. We can ask Squanto when we get back." She wasn't as curious as Eleanor.

The sun, which had been quite bright, suddenly clouded over and an eerie darkness fell onto the hill. The girls looked at each other and Humility said, "I think we should go back to camp, Eleanor – don't you?"

"Just before we do, let's go a little nearer to the circle – there looks like some signs carved on the trunks of the trees." A reluctant Humility followed her daring friend higher up the hill. The top was very flat and the circles were even more distinctive there. They saw a figure move. He was sitting under one of the trees

18

and was obviously distressed. It was the young Indian boy who'd helped Eleanor in the past. Very slowly, the girls walked towards him, carefully avoiding stepping on the mounds of earth. Something told the girls it wouldn't be right to step on them.

Eleanor said, "How," as he'd taught her and Squanto had told her it was the Indian greeting for 'Hello'.

The boy looked up and brushed away the tears from his eyes. An Indian boy shouldn't ever be caught crying and he was embarrassed. After all, he would soon be a young warrior.

"What is this place?" Eleanor asked, looking around.

"Place of death – ancestors lie here for ever," the boy answered. He had had several lessons from Squanto and had learned some of the white man's words.

He was holding a strange looking object and Humility asked straight out, "What is that – it's almost pretty – but not quite."

The boy smiled at her, "It not meant to be pretty – it a Dream Catcher – to protect my grandfather – he lies here now." And he pointed at one of the mounds. Fresh tears began to trickle down his face.

Eleanor thought it was a lovely tradition. "It's almost like us putting flowers on a grave – we're quite similar, you see."

She smiled at the boy, who stood up and said, "I go now. Goodbye." His new language was very good.

The girls started to collect berries and there were plenty around this place. Both buckets were nearly full and they agreed it was time to go home but just before she left, Eleanor turned to look at the Indian graveyard and saw standing under the trees, many Indian men and women and even some children. They all looked rather grey but were dressed in brightly coloured garments, probably their burial clothes. There was no question about it, they were the ghosts of the local tribe's ancestors – and they just stood there as though, waiting for something to happen. She would speak to Squanto about it – she knew he wouldn't laugh at her. The two girls ran down the hill and returned to the village. The next day, however, Eleanor chose to visit the small – but getting bigger – Pilgrim cemetery. Spring was in the air and she found some wild flowers to take along and leave on the graves. The boy had made her conscience prick and she remembered all those poor souls who'd never made it through the harsh winter. Their graves numbered forty-five and were unmarked – they sat on a similar hill to that chosen by the Indians. They were unmarked for a reason. Not being sure how the Indians would act towards them in that first year, they didn't want to advertise that half of those who'd arrived on the Mayflower, had actually perished in the first couple of months. It would quite rightly imply they were less strong than before with dwindled numbers – so the grass was allowed to grow over the graves in an attempt to conceal their numbers. It made the cemetery look sad and uncared for, but Eleanor knew nothing could be further from the truth. Everyone had lost a relative or friend and would never forget them.

Eleanor went back to the village and approached William Bradford who had been voted the governor of the new colony. This followed the death at the beginning of March of the first governor, John Carver. Braford had just signed a Peace Treaty with the Massasoit Indians of the Wampanoags tribes and went on to be re-elected again and again until his death in 1657. He was regarded as a great man by the rest of the Pilgrims.

"Well, how can I help you, young lady? I saw you up on Coles Hill amongst our dead – a sombre visit for such a lovely morning." He was busy working with the other men, digging a well in the middle of the square. Squanto had advised where to dig – he'd used some sticks in the shape of the letter 'Y' to find the underground water. It was called Dowsing and Bradford had heard of it before but knew only certain people had the gift and luckily, Squanto was one of them.

Eleanor explained to the governor that she'd been having dreams about the five people who had died on the sea journey and they seemed to be telling her that although their last resting place couldn't be marked with their names, they would like an inscription somewhere to record that they'd once been alive – and not be forgotten.

"And what do you propose we do, Eleanor?" he asked the girl.

"I would like for us to find a big, suitable rock or boulder and use sharp nails to inscribe their names and dates of birth and death. We can place it on Coles Hill, alongside the others – and as it's only five names, it won't give the Indians a wrong indication of how many people we lost in the winter. Does that seem possible, sir?" She was enthusiastic now and knew it was the right thing to do. She hadn't really had bad dreams about it but it was just a little, white lie.

"I think that's an excellent idea, Eleanor, and something we can all take part in. Thank you for suggesting it. At the next town meeting, I shall bring it up and we can get the wheels moving very soon." He smiled at the young woman and thought what a good choice they'd made in appointing her as the teacher of the first school.

Eleanor's family had a lodger living with them in their small house. It had been decided at the last town meeting that all the single men must choose a family with whom to live – at least until more houses were built. It would take a little of the pressure off the builders and free them for other tasks that needed doing.

On the first day of summer, the school opened – having already been opened as the church – and Eleanor was busy collecting all things needed for her task. Of course, the teaching utensils were minimal – but it was amazing how ingenious she could be in finding useful things. Ahady helped her. His name meant 'Walks in the Woods' and he was the Indian boy who'd become her friend. He could speak a little English and she could manage a few Indian words. Her mother and father weren't too happy about the friendship and frequently reminded her that 'Protestant Pilgrims and Pagan Indians' should never get too close to each other.

"He is my friend." Was all Eleanor would reply. The new school was a success and even two of the Indian children attended classes there. There were only a very few children in the Plymouth colony but more children would eventually be born and the school would be needed more than ever.

The big boulder – much smaller of course than the Plymouth Rock – was in place – the men had dragged it from near the shore and care had been taken over the inscriptions for the four men and one woman who'd died at sea. Now, they would be remembered forever. The woman had been Dorothy, Governor Bradford's own wife, and he was proud to see her name on the great stone. The intention was that, as soon as sufficient time had passed and they knew they had nothing to fear from the Indians, an individual stone would be placed at every grave. No one would be forgotten.

The crops in the small, cultivated fields were coming along nicely and their shoots were visible above ground. Although it had been such a cruel winter, somehow the crops thrived and would soon be ready for eating. When this happened, the Pilgrims planned to have a Day of Celebration to say thank you to God for protecting them this far. It would be called The Forefathers Day and would stay that for a number of years, but then 'Thanksgiving Day' would take over and it has remained so ever since. It would be a Holy Day but there would be food and enjoyment as well.

Eleanor had returned only once to the Indian graveyard and decided not to go back because she felt like an intruder – she was sure the ghostly figures of the

Indians were there still and she felt they would look at her accusingly – as indeed they might, knowing what was to come for their people in the future. The Indians in Squanto's tribe were friendly and even shared their food with the newcomers, but there were many other tribes around and who could tell how they would act in the future.

Eleanor was happy with her lot in life but she wasn't so sure about her parents, Mary and Michael. They still spoke of the old country with great nostalgia and often spoke of what it would be like to return home. Eleanor didn't join in these conversations as she was quite happy. Life was hard, it was true, but even little achievements gave a lot of pleasure. She was a good baker and helped her mother a lot – but the flour was precious and soon, more would be needed. A second ship, with more Pilgrims was promised in the autumn of the following year and fresh supplies would be brought then. Christopher Jones told them he intended to return to England in early summer and anyone who wanted to return to the old country would be welcome to join him. This caused considerable consternation amongst the Pilgrims. It must have been a tempting proposition for some of them.

That week, a great bear came into their village. He was hungry and tired, and therefore pretty ferocious. Luckily, Squanto was around and he held out a piece of meat from the fire and the bear sniffed it and then followed it quickly into the trees, where Squanto had thrown it. Strangely enough, he didn't come back for more.

"We don't want to kill him unless we have to, but if he comes back, we may have to do it." He kept one of the Pilgrim's muskets close by, just in case. She didn't understand why, but Eleanor felt sorry for the bear. She soon discovered she had a great affinity with the wild animals – as did the Indians. Ahady and she became good friends and he tried to explain how he felt about the animals. "Perhaps it's because my name means 'Walks in the Woods' that I feel so close to them." She'd even been to his village and met his mother and father – of course they could speak no English but their son helped with the conversation. Eleanor really felt she was becoming part of the New World.

On ninth of May that year, the Mayflower set off on its return journey to the homeland – and on it, were Eleanor's own mother and father. Their parting was very emotional and the young girl cried a lot. She'd had to decide whether to go with them, but in the end, she decided she couldn't. This was her home now and she would soon be seventeen so she must act like a grownup. But she did feel like an orphan – but knew she was no worse than many others. She watched her closest family cross from the Plymouth Rock down onto the shallop boat which would take them to the Mayflower. They had struggled with the dilemma – whether to stay in the new country or return to what they'd always known – and in the end, familiarity won the day. They were the only ones from the original group of Pilgrims who decided to leave – although many had been tempted.

Ahady took her hand and held it. He wanted to comfort her but didn't know how. The months passed and she was kept busy with the school, her baking and trying to learn as much as she could about the Indians. The Harvest was good and the Indians helped to reap the crops alongside the Pilgrims. They worked well together and the language barrier didn't stop them from becoming friends. Governor William Bradford thanked the Indian Chief for his people's help. The corn had done particularly well and the Indians showed their new friends how to make it into a nourishing porridge, which could have different flavours added, depending on which berries were available at the time. It proved to be an invaluable addition to their diet – good for children and old folk alike.

Eleanor began to bake a new bread and used crushed corn to enhance its flavour. It was a great success in the colony and people began to bring their rations to her house, asking that she make the bread for them. Soon, she wasn't only the colony's school teacher but their baker as well. She was a very busy young woman and didn't have time to miss her parents too much. Governor Bradford announced that there was to be a celebration to thank the Lord for the good harvest they'd had – and the Indian village was invited to join on the day. It was the first Thanksgiving and was a feast day even then – the governor even sent two men on an expedition to hunt for several wild turkeys, fish and any other potential meal that might cross their paths. They were successful and returned to the colony with cartloads of food, which the women immediately began to pluck and skin – and generally prepare it for cooking. There was great happiness in the atmosphere and everyone was looking forward to the special day.

Suddenly, on the horizon, a ship was sighted and as it came closer, it was seen to resemble the Mayflower itself. It was called The Fortune and it had come from Leiden in the Netherlands, where the original Pilgrims had tried to settle before coming to New England. There were thirty-five Pilgrims on board and many were English. The swollen number of the colonists made the special day even more special. It really was a time for giving thanks to the Lord.

On the morning of the celebration day on November 1621, Ahady led his people into the Plymouth colony, each one bearing gifts of food which had been made specially for the Pilgrims. They were welcomed by Governor Bradford and the Chief Elder, the latter opening the Day by saying a prayer to God. The Indians stood politely by and then the Indian Chief began to chant in his own language, probably saying the same thing as the Elder had, but dancing in a circle as well. Everyone stood patiently by and then great tables of food were uncovered in the open space in front of the houses. The laughter and singing filled the air and there was so much excitement around that Eleanor had to escape for a few moments to calm herself down.

She walked towards Coles Hill where the Pilgrim dead lay. She had an unexplained need to include them in the celebration – after all, they should have been part of it. Indeed, they were part of it as many of them had helped set up the original camp and many had living relatives who would not have been there, but for those who'd gone too soon.

Ahady had seen her leave the celebration and followed her to the Pilgrim Cemetery. As he joined her, they both looked around and a heavy mist had come down and enveloped them in a cloud. Not only were there figures of the dead Pilgrims but amongst them, there were also Indian figures, dressed in their bright costumes. It was a wonderful moment – full of pathos and promise for the future. It gave a very clear message to the young folk.

Ahady said, "Can we marry please, Eleanor? I know we have different backgrounds, cultures and religion, but I love you and would like you to become my wife. I know it will not be easy but you – so young – have already faced much worse in life. Is it possible, dear Eleanor?" He looked sad, fearing her answer.

"I have been expecting you to ask me that, Ahady and I'd be happy to 'walk in the woods' with you – we've already learned a lot about each other and we will have a lot more to learn, but I am willing if you are." Eleanor spoke without hesitation – she'd been expecting this and knew what she would answer.

All the ghostly figures disappeared slowly and left the couple alone on the hill. It was as though all the spirits had come together to show that the white and red man could mix – and it had worked. Ahady and Eleanor had understood their message.

There would be two weddings – one Christian and one Indian. Ahady had decided to convert to Christianity but there would still have to be an Indian wedding for his people.

And so, preparations were made in the Indian camp – the Pilgrims were invited to attend the ceremony, which was quite simple. Eleanor had to wear red – as that was the colour all brides wore to their wedding, but no guests could wear the colour or that would be bad luck. Eleanor asked her friends to help gather berries for the dying of a simple dress – they did this with great enthusiasm. At the ceremony, two baskets were produced, filled with gifts of seeds, fruit, bread and woven cloth. The groom offered one to the bride and the bride did likewise – and the ceremony was over but the celebration was still to be enjoyed. Both parties returned to their respective homes and next day, a Christian ceremony was conducted by the Chief Elder William Brewster of the colony. Rings were exchanged and the groom returned with his new wife to her small house, where he would set up home with her. This was the Indian custom – the man must live with his wife's family, but as Eleanor's family were far away in England, this caused no problem.

The English Pilgrims had really integrated with the native Indian people now, and memories of the dreadful journey on the Mayflower paled into insignificance when compared with the new happiness and hope that was part of village life for the Pilgrims. Neither Eleanor nor Ahady ever saw the ghosts of the dead again – their deed was done and they'd helped encourage two nations to become one.

Ahady and Eleanor had seven children and between them, those seven children had twenty children and between those twenty children, another fifteen children were born…and so it went on and with the passage of time, AMERICA itself was born and eventually became the most powerful country in the world.

A few Pilgrims who survived great hardships and were brave and determined enough to survive that first harsh winter created the foundation of a great country. And Plymouth Rock still stands there today and its concept is, even now, built into the initial Senate Declarations in Washington.

From a small acorn, a great oak tree can grow. And it did!

Beware the Ides of March

"What – go and stand in the market square, like any lowly prostitute? Rashida, what are you thinking of? I could never allow that!" Her mother was pummelling the bread and making it into a round shape. "Wipe your hands and help me finish these loaves. Do it girl and do it quick." Rashida quickly ran to the table and grabbed a lump of dough. She was very light-fingered and her bread was usually good.

"Well, mother, you can say what you like, but I want to try and make my life better. I don't want to be like you and look after a husband and family, I just know there's better things out there. I'm now sixteen years of age and you can't stop me from leaving home." She banged the bread on the table and reached for a baking mould from the corner. She slapped the dough into the mould and put it alongside the others, all waiting to go into the big oven. She finished off several more and left them for her mother to fill the oven.

She went into the shop next to her own and called out for her friend, Heba. She understood where Rashida was coming from and knew standing in the market place was not only for prostitutes but for people, looking for general work. They were free to come and go and need only accept employment if they found the employer acceptable.

"When are you going then?" Heba came in from the laundry and kissed her friend's cheek. "I heard your mother shouting at you – in a way, you can't blame her – she doesn't understand modern ways and how young people want to do things differently. Just be patient with her, I'm sure you'll win her around in the end." Heba helped her parents in the shop. It was a shop where people brought their dirty clothes and collected them when they'd been washed. It made good money, as did Rashida's own shop with the sale of bread and rolls.

"Can I come along with you and see what happens?" Heba was really interested but not enough to do it herself. She was less confident than her friend.

"Of course you can – in fact, I wish you would. I'm only a little bit brave myself. Can I borrow your blue silk dress to wear on the day – it's so pretty?" And that was that. The decision was made.

One week later, Rashida looked lovely in her friend's blue dress and with her dark-brown curls caught up in a bunch, with just a few tendrils escaping down the sides. There were red glints in her hair that shone when the light hit them. She knew she looked her best and Heba confirmed it. The market square in Alexandria, Egypt's capital, was crammed full of people, it being a Friday and the busiest day of the week. The girls walked around and took in the atmosphere – it was all loud, exciting and quite scary but they loved it. There were stalls selling everything imaginable and wild animals and birds for sale in wire cages. They stopped at one of the stalls and Rashida explained to the woman there that she was looking for work and knew there was a place she could put herself up for employment. The woman pointed across the square. "You mean over there, I think – now don't get into the wrong queue. One's for ladies of the night and one's for job seekers." She turned away to serve a customer.

It was easy to pick the right queue – the ladies of the night were pretty obvious – and Rashida stood in the line of men and women looking for work. There was a man walking up and down the line. He was carrying a gold-topped cane and looked important – he had a young man following him and carrying a ledger of sorts and a stylus pen. He stopped in front of a couple of men and told them to stand straight – he also asked to see their teeth – before moving on up the line. He stopped at Rashida and asked to see her teeth – and she smiled at him, thinking what an odd question it was. He tapped the pretty young woman on the shoulder with his cane and the young man darted forward and asked her name, which he then wrote in his ledger. He started to speak, "The position that Master Alim is offering you is that of a handmaiden to the Pharaoh – it is a lowly position and you would be expected to support the higher servants above you. There will be some hard work but also some leisure time. Do you wish to accept his offer of work?" He was obviously in a hurry to catch up with his master. When Rashida nodded her head in agreement, he moved quickly on, telling her to report to the palace kitchens the next day. He called over his shoulder, "My name's Amenei by the way."

"Good Heavens, Rashida, I didn't think it would be that quick, did you?" Heba was astonished and took her friend's arm to help her down from the stool she'd used in the line.

"It was your beautiful dress, Heba, I'm sure of it." And they wandered back to their homes, Heba to work and Rashida, to tell her mother the news. She wasn't looking forward to it.

The odd thing was, that when her mother heard where her daughter would be working, she seemed to accept the fact that she planned to leave home. The word Pharaoh obviously had magical powers.

"Well, as long as you're a good girl and come home to see your parents now and then, I shall allow it. You can go with my blessing. I suppose." And it was settled as easily as that.

Next morning, Rashida used several back streets and crossed the main square to reach the Pharaoh's palace, which was an enormous building sitting on the edge of the Nile River. There were many pathways around it and it took her several attempts to reach one of the doors. Guards stood by the side of the entrance, but she knew she must not speak to them – they were on duty. She smoothed her plain linen dress over her hips and tentatively stepped forward past the guards, who didn't challenge her, so she knew it was all right. Inside, she was in a long corridor with stone pillars stretching as far as the eye could see and, in the distance, she saw the Scribe, Amenei. He was walking quickly towards her, so she asked him where she should report. At first, he didn't recognise her but when she smiled at him, he remembered where he'd seen her before.

"Go to the kitchens, girl, and they'll point you in the right direction." Rashida followed his pointing finger and found herself in a large square room with several people rushing to and fro and the most delicious smell of food she'd ever experienced.

"Are you new, girl? Well then, do you know anything about making bread?" A big man in a white apron asked her. "If you do, start mixing that grain with the salt and water and shape it into balls of dough for baking." He didn't even wait to see if she did know anything about bread – he just rushed off to oversee the meat that was roasting in a huge fireplace against the wall. Rashida felt lonely and wanted to cry – not one person had been nice to her since she'd got here, but she continued to shape the bread rolls and then painted their tops with oil another man had given her. He showed her how to use a paintbrush for the job and she felt a little better. He had spoken to her quite nicely and she began to feel happier in the strange place. The kitchen was steamy and misty and sometimes it was difficult to see properly but she persevered and in due course, another young girl brought her a tankard of honey mead and some broken bits of cooked bread. She realised hours had passed since she'd arrived and she hadn't noticed. The other girl asked her name and told her she was called Sara.

"You'll be all right in a few days – it just takes a while to get used to it. No one's cruel in the kitchen, at least we've got that." And she carried away Rashida's dishes and left the girl to continue making balls of dough for the Head Cook.

There were so many people to feed in the palace that she was given the same job for the next few days. In fact, truth to tell, she was getting tired of making bread – she may as well have stayed at home with her mother and made bread there. After another week, the Master Alim with the gold-topped cane came into the kitchen. She could see he didn't do this very often with the way everyone jumped out of his way and lowered their eyes. He had come to check on the menu for some great feast that was due and at which, the Pharaoh herself would be attending – so nothing could be left to chance. Master Alim made to leave and walked past Rashida, then turned around and stared at her.

"What are you doing here, girl? You weren't meant for the kitchen – although I can see you work hard with your bread. I told Amenei that you were to be handmaiden to the Pharaoh – well, at least to the Pharaoh's personal handmaidens. You shouldn't be here – I'm going to find Amenei now and clip his ear before telling him to sort things out. Just keep on with what you're doing and he'll come to fetch you soon." And he swept from the kitchen, with everyone still bowing and dropping their eyes as he passed.

Amenei did come, with a very red cheek where the Master had struck him. "I knew you were going to be trouble as soon as I saw you. Come on, I've got to take you upstairs to the handmaidens' room. Wash your floury hands first, though, or you won't be made welcome."

Rashida did as she was told and then followed the boy. He took her upstairs and stopped outside a very tall and wide door, knocking politely. A woman opened the door and asked what his business was. Rashida was invited inside and he was sent on his way. The room was beautiful with many voile curtains draped across the open windows and with velvet footstools and small chairs dotted around; everything was in a soft peach colour and there were several chaise longue around the walls with fur rugs strewn on top. There were two or three ladies who looked very lovely and wore dresses of soft material in bright colours, that fell elegantly to the floor. Rashida's little linen dress looked quite out of place and she felt herself squirming under the ladies' gazes. One took pity on her and crossed the room.

The woman held out her hand and smiled. "Don't look so afraid, I'll help you. My name is Charmain and I am one of the personal handmaidens to the Pharaoh, Cleopatra. Suddenly, the air was filled with loud music and all the ladies hurried out of the room. Their mistress needed them. Rashida very cheekily followed them – she didn't want to be left by herself. She pressed herself against the door whilst the other handmaidens gathered around the most beautiful lady Rashida had ever seen. She was lying on a bed in the middle of the room and the bed was covered with soft white sheets and honey-coloured cushions and pillows. The vision spoke. "Ladies, I hear the music that heralds Mark Antony's approach – come, make me look beautiful and then be gone and leave us alone."

Rashida thought, *How could she be made more beautiful than she already was?* But the handmaidens knew what to do and brushed Cleopatra's hair whilst spraying her with perfume and exchanging her green dress for one of pure white. The woman was a dream.

The door was thrown open and a Roman soldier came into the chamber. The handmaidens scurried out, lowering their eyes in humility and collecting Rashida as they did so. Cleopatra and Mark Antony were left alone together. Mark Antony, or Marcus Antonius, had been a friend of Julius Caesar, the declared Dictator of Rome now and one of the most powerful men in the world. As his friend, Mark Antony had the ear of Cleopatra as well, he was very powerful in his own right. Cleopatra knew she had to seduce him, just as she'd done with Caesar when they'd first met. When he first arrived in her city, she dressed as Venus, Goddess of Love and completely overwhelmed him. They travelled together to Syria where they spent a most enjoyable time and then, he returned to Rome where he married Octavia in an attempt to placate her brother. In the next few months, he remained in Rome with his wife and in Egypt, Cleopatra bore him twin babies, one boy and one girl. She had played her cards well. He returned to Alexandria on the birth of the twins and married the Pharaoh although this was frowned upon by Rome, not only because he already had a wife, but because it was illegal for a Roman to marry a foreigner. He had committed a double Whammy!

She had had one son with Caesar, but they'd never married. The boy was called Caesarion and he was a fine healthy boy. In 44 BC, members of the Senate in Rome had taken it upon themselves to assassinate the dictator by stabbing him over and over again – actually in the Senate room itself. This brought forth Caesar's famous last words, *'Et tu Brute'* as he recognised one of the conspirators as Brutus, whom Caesar had always thought of as his good friend and supporter. He had recently been warned by a soothsayer to 'Beware the Ides of March – the middle day in the month of March, but as he didn't know what to watch out for, he did nothing about the warning. That was something he would live to regret – if indeed he did live, but he didn't and it turned out to be the actual day of his death. 'Beware the Ides of March' indeed – it wasn't just Caesar's death but all the resulting disasters that occurred following it. Rome had lost its dictator and soon would be a Republic.

When he died, Cleopatra was living in Rome with him and after the assassination, she fled back to Egypt for safety. For one still quite young, she'd already had a complex and dangerous life, fraught with many problems. She was a clever woman and tried to hedge her bets when appeasing Rome and her own people at the same time. She had much experience in dangerous times as all through her father Ptolemy's reign – and in the times before his – there were several famines due to the falling levels of the Nile's River. The dry, parched soil failed to produce crops and the people went hungry. They blamed whoever was ruling at the time and they revolted again and again. The throne throughout the Ptolemaica period in Egypt faced precarious and repeated challenges from the people. Ptolemy and his family, including Cleopatra, were forced to flee the country. This was why Cleopatra needed the help of Rome to secure and win back her throne.

Egypt was in the midst of famine and plague and Cleopatra realised she had to find some way to feed her own people – but this was complicated by the grain she had agreed to ship to Italy and to Rome itself in particular. She took grain from the royal provisions and gave it to the people of Alexandria, who had begun to rebel against the authorities. She had no choice, as she had to be seen doing something to help – and she told Rome she couldn't manage to sell them grain because her country was in the grip of the plague and a famine. The River Nile was responsible for the food crisis in Egypt as for three consecutive years, it had failed to flood the plains along its banks and without the parched land benefitting from the flooding, the healthy, lifegiving grain was non-existent.

To add to her problems at this time, the great city of Rome was also having problems. Control of the country was being pulled in two directions one side headed by Mark Antony, who had been a friend to both Caesar and Cleopatra and who was a well-respected Army General – and the other led and controlled by Octavian, who was a great nephew of Julius Caesar and who'd been named as his successor in his uncle's will. The two men actually hated each other on both a personal and political level. Mark Antony was married to Octavian's sister but had chosen to be with Cleopatra – not a very good position for anyone. Octavian sincerely believed was a challenge to his position as the highest-ranking official in the Senate. Not to mention his being named as Caesar's successor and anyway, he absolutely hated Mark Antony who was making a fool of his sister by deserting her.

This then is the situation in which Cleopatra found herself when she met with Mark Antony in her chamber. Which way does she go – to her lover and father of two children or to Octavian, who was very powerful. Her mind was in great turmoil – her people were still suffering from the plague and were again running out of grain: the River Nile's level of water was still too low to flood the plains – and now she was torn between the two warring factions in Rome. All of this was happening whilst she also had to keep an open eye on what Rome intended – they'd always had their eye on Egypt, which was known as the Bread Basket of the world – and very valuable.

"Oh my beloved, what are we to do? I want you to be the next leader but how do we make sure that's what will happen? You were Caesar's friend and I love you for that alone." She leaned across and rang a small bell. "Whatever we decide, we must eat and I'm sure you are famished after your long sea voyage." Her handmaidens hurried to her side and were sent off to collect victuals from the palace kitchen.

Rashida tried to help them but they shooed her away, saying, "Not now, Rashida. Your time will come." So she settled down outside the door of the Pharaoh's bedroom and almost fell inside the room when Mark Antony opened the door suddenly. He helped her up from the floor and asked, "What are you doing child – do you want to speak to your mistress?"

"I am sorry, Lord – I don't mean to be a nuisance, I just wondered if I could do anything to help."

An imperious voice cut through the air. "Come in – whoever you are, there is something I need." Cleopatra rose from the pile of cushions. "I want my hair brushed – I have a headache and it always helps. Where are my handmaidens?

Although, I suppose you'll do – even if your robes are not acceptable for waiting on such as I."

Rashida crossed the room and took the hairbrush from the Pharaoh's hand. Gently and with soft strokes, she brushed Cleopatra's hair which was oiled and beautifully dark in colour. Her skin was the colour of honey and she smiled with a set of perfect teeth. She leaned back in her chair by the window and closed her eyes. "Your brush strokes are so gentle that I fear I will fall asleep." Cleopatra purred her words in pleasure.

The two chief handmaidens – one called Iras and the other, Charmain – came into the room to say the kitchen staff were bringing the food. The sight that met their eyes was astounding – as attending to the Pharaoh's personal needs was something they normally did.

"Would your Majesty like me to take over brushing your hair?"

Charmain asked but Cleopatra stirred from her reverie and said, "No, allow the child to continue – she is doing well. But I do not like how she is dressed – when I am finished with her, take her away and dress her in silks, such as you wear." Rashida couldn't believe her ears but knew anything was possible, if the Pharaoh so demanded.

The kitchen staff came into the room with sumptuous food and drink – plenty of meat and fresh fruit with wine too, both white and red. It really was a meal fit for a queen. Mark Antony came back into the room – he had changed his soldier's uniform for white robes, ready to feast and rest in that order. The Pharaoh told Rashida to cease brushing her hair – she was now ready to eat – but felt much better than before, her headache having gone. The two senior handmaidens took Rashida away from the room in a rather brusque way, as they both believed she'd reached beyond what was expected of her. Who was she after all? She had made her mark on Cleopatra, who now called for her when she wanted her hair brushed and dressed. The two women gave Rashida a pretty tunic and flowing robes, but also reminded her she was very junior at the palace and shouldn't reach beyond her station.

"Of course, ladies, I shall be more careful in future – it was just that neither of you were there when she asked for help, so I didn't know what to do." They accepted her explanation and then tended to ignore her.

Mark Antony and Cleopatra were both replete with food and lay, stretched out on the soft cushions. He started to talk about how large the army was at his disposal and how he could easily deal with Octavian, but she shushed him and said, "My Lord, it's too soon after food – let's just rest for a while. He was disappointed but knew he mustn't pressure her until she was good and ready. She turned onto her side and whispered in his ear, "I am with child again, my Lord – what do you think of that?"

"I think it's wonderful news and babies can only cement our two great powers together – the might and power of Rome and Alexandria and the two great countries that support them. What a future we will have and next in line following your son with the great Gaius Julius Caesar – Caesarion – our own child will govern both great countries." He was very excited at the prospect and leaned over to kiss her on the lips. She sighed and relaxed but sat up quickly when he asked her, "Did you really have yourself delivered to Caesar in a rolled-up rug?"

"Yes, I did and it worked. I had to show humility and ask that he help me hold on to the throne of Egypt. You may recall how my father and I were expelled from the country and some upstart placed his daughter, Bernice, on the throne. We needed Rome's help to undo this and Caesar was the man in control. Everything was in a mess for me and I needed his help – he was after all the most powerful man in the world. My own family were against me at that time and I had to have my sister killed as she was not to be trusted." She thought for a moment about her sister, Arsinoe – perhaps regretting the act – whom she still missed, but it had had to be done. "I even had to marry my brother Ptolemy when father died in order to become the co-ruler of Egypt. Everything was at its worst then – and there were plagues and famine in my country. Having myself delivered in a carpet was a small price to pay, I assure you. Anyway, it appealed to his vanity."

She was wide-awake now. "I've had many disasters since coming to the throne, but I've survived them all – and I intend to do so again with my current problems – your help is needed of course. Try to remember, I am from the Ptolemaic Dynasty of Persian, Syrian and Egyptian blood, who have governed Egypt for thousands of years – and, with the help of the Goddess Isis, I'm sure I'm not going to be the last." As she uttered these last words, the great woman looked suddenly vulnerable.

"You'll have all the help I can give, my darling – don't worry about that." Mark Antony refilled both wine glasses but she told him to ring for her handmaidens, as she wanted to retire to bed. He rang for the maids, but added, "We'll have even more children, Cleopatra – to help secure our hold on the throne of Egypt and hopefully of Italy as well – try not to worry, it's bad for the baby!" And he left the room. In the end, they had three children together – a set of twins and one son.

Young Rashida had been given a small room as her sleeping quarters. It was close to the Pharaoh's own rooms, so she could be summoned when necessary. She had become her mistress' pet, almost like a dog and she now helped with the ritual bathing and dressing of the lady, but when Mark Antony was present, she kept her gaze lowered to show her humility. The baker's daughter was learning the ways of court quickly. As a potential leader of Rome, Mark Antony had to return frequently to Alexandria to oversee his business and to keep a close eye on Octavian, who was always trying to secure his own support in the Senate – he believed strongly he should be the leader following Caesar and meant for it to happen.

At least two years passed with the struggle for power between the two men and Rome was a very troubled place to live. Rashida had grown up a lot and was now one of her mistress' favourites. Periodically, she went home to visit her parents – and of course, to see Heba. To them, she looked more like a great lady than a handmaiden. She now dressed in silks and flowing robes and was carried in a litter by slaves, all the way across Alexandria to her former home. She enjoyed playing the great lady, especially as her mother had been against her leaving home in the first place. She brought them gifts, especially food as they too were suffering from the famine in the country, their ability to provide bread to the people was much diminished. They did benefit, however, from living in the city and not the country, as Cleopatra had opened the palace's grain stores to the local people. She'd had no option but to do this as citizens had to blame someone for their starvation and that person could only be the ruler, the Pharaoh. So, her decision wasn't altogether an act of Philanthropy – more of necessity. She was after all a shrewd woman.

How is your Mistress, Rashida? We hear she is quite a lady and very free with her favours?" Rashida's mother couldn't conceal her criticism of the Pharaoh. She'd always thought the Republic of Rome was a better way of living than Egypt's autocratic policy. Her father, however, was a more practical man and stopped the conversation there, before his wife said too much. He changed the subject of the conversation.

"What about all the changes with the River Nile – more than I can ever remember before? The word is that they only started when Julius Caesar was assassinated in Rome by his fellow Senators. Someone obviously upset the gods and we know they would have the power to affect nature itself. Where are the rains these days? Mind you, Rome is suffering as well as Egypt, they'd always bought a lot of our grain – and now there is none for them and therefore, no money for us. A punishment indeed!" Rashida's father had always been a deep thinker and interested in politics.

"Oh father, what a load of rubbish. You listen too well to the chatter in the market. How can a volcano erupting affect the Nile? You're allowing your imagination to run away with you. I suppose you'll try to tell me the three suns seen in the sky at the one time really did occur – imagine three suns! It's not possible!" Rashida felt rather superior to her humble parents, now that she was a great lady. She tucked a few loose tendrils of hair behind her ears and called for her slave to bring the litter. Her long robe caught on a broken basket and the silk threads were torn, but she said, "Don't worry, there's plenty more at the palace." She really had changed since she helped her mother with the bread.

Back in the palace, politics were afoot! Mark Antony was strutting up and down the throne room, where Cleopatra sat imperiously on a dias. "I have done the deed, Cleopatra. I have divorced Octavia and so angered her brother. I am happy that he is angry, as I am eager to do battle with him and hopefully put an end to his life." Mark Antony was a handsome man and Cleopatra admired him greatly, but she was very concerned for his safety.

"Take care, my Lord – these are dangerous times and Octavian has a strong force behind him. He has many supporters in Rome who will rally to his cause when he asks it. He is pressuring me to provide more grain to Rome – but the famine continues here at home and I have none to spare. The malnutrition of my people has increased as has the spread of the plague which now reaches across the land. Have you heard what is being said, Mark?" she asked.

"And what rubbish is that, my dear?" He was scathing of the peoples' opinions.

"They do say that three suns have been seen in a purple sky and that the failure of the Nile's flooding began two years ago when Caesar was assassinated in the Senate. They claim the gods are blaming this region for his death and so, this is our punishment. Mind you, it was the Romans who murdered him and not the Egyptians. We are, however, a superstitious race and so, it is not surprising that signs in the sky tell of foreboding. I am very frightened, Mark – it is as though everything is suddenly beyond my control." She must have been very worried indeed, as nature's cruel treatment of the people was something she'd not had to deal with before.

He tried to reassure her. "Really, you are much smarter than to believe that. Although it's now more important than ever that we sort out the problems we have with Octavian and I too, have many loyal supporters awaiting my command. We will take him, I promise you!" He had just been victorious in a battle with Armenia and to celebrate the victory, he staged a triumphal procession through the streets of Alexandria. Both he and Cleopatra sat on golden thrones and their children were given imposing royal titles. Unfortunately, this spurred on the people in Rome to interpret the spectacle as a sign that Mark Antony intended to deliver the Roman Empire into alien Egyptian hands. A frightening prospect to the people of Egypt.

And so, Cleopatra combined her forces with those Roman supporters of Mark Antony's, but before anything else happened, Octavian – so angry with his sister's divorce and abandonment at Mark Antony's hands – declared war on Egypt and on Cleopatra in particular – not on Mark Antony but on the Pharaoh herself. The year was 32 BC and she was a woman still only in her thirties.

"Madam, please have some refreshments – we have had a supply of pineapples delivered and I can fetch you a glass with crushed ice. Have you a headache and would you like for me to brush your hair?" Rashida came quietly into the room and found her mistress alone.

"Yes, Rashida, that would be lovely – something refreshing and cold will serve me very well."

And she leaned back in her chair and rested her head. Not particularly interested, she asked, "Is your family home far from here, child? Do you see your parents anymore?"

"I do, madam, but when I visit, I have to listen to my father's ridiculous tales about the state of Egypt – and I don't want to hear them. He talks such rubbish about more than one sun in the sky – about the fact that Caesar was murdered as the reason famine has visited our land. It really is all 'pie in the sky' and he doesn't know what he's talking about." Rashida put down the hairbrush and reached for the large fan that rested against the wall. She wafted the cooler air over her mistress and offered her a bowl of sweetmeats and nuts.

"Don't write your father off so much, Rashida, he is your father and deserves your respect – something of what he says may be true. The story about more than one sun in the sky confuses me greatly and I cannot see how it could affect the flow of the River Nile, but then, there's many a thing we know nothing about, isn't there?" Cleopatra was feeling unusually humble. "By the way, Rashida, don't forget to tell Charmain and Iris that my son, Caesarion, is dining with me tonight – I haven't seen much of him lately and I need to know if he has any problems that trouble him."

"I won't forget, madam, in fact I'll do it now, of you so wish." Cleopatra told her to go with a wave of her hand, and crossed to a large desk covered in maps and papers. Mark Antony had been working on it, working out strategy for the upcoming battle with Octavian. It was going to be a bloody affair but she had confidence in his military ability. He joined both her and Caesarion that evening for dinner but his head was so full of battle matters that she had to tell him to stop talking about it. Caesarion was getting too excited. He was after all his father's son and would have preferred Egypt to join with Rome and his mother rule over them both.

"Will I be able to accompany you, sir? I know how to handle a sword and could be of use to you." He pleaded with the Roman General, who was just about to agree to the boy's request, when she intervened, telling her son not to be ridiculous.

"You are far too young and too precious to me. I cannot allow that. You are the heir to my throne and I cannot place you in danger." She was quite adamant.

The day of the Battle of Actium arrived. Cleopatra's troops and those of Mark Antony were joined together against Octavian. Preparations took many weeks until at last, both sides were ready. Cleopatra led her own troops into battle and sailed with Mark Antony's ships to the West of Greece. The battle took place in the Ionian Sea on 2 September 31 BC.

Cleopatra's three closest handmaidens waited together, dreading the news in case it was bad. The women were close, despite their earlier different stations in life. In fact, they were almost friends – as long as they didn't forget who their mistress was and treat her accordingly. But then, no one could ever forget who and what she was. There was wine and fruit and beautifully baked bread – there was nothing else to do but eat and drink, so they did. The whole palace was in a state of impatience – as their personal futures also depended on the outcome of the battle – not just those of Egypt.

Octavian had on his side, a military genius for a Commander – Agrippa, who seemed able to do no wrong. The battle must have been an amazing site, one of the most major battles of the time. Agrippa won many skirmishes at the start but the battle became so intense that Cleopatra broke away from it with sixty of her ships and successfully pushed through the enemy's lines. Although the battle continued with much depleted numbers, especially on Mark Antony's side, he soon realised that all was lost and charged at the enemy lines to force a break through. He headed as far away from the battle site as he could.

It was all over and Octavian had won. What was left of the other side's ships went on fighting but there were too few to do much damage and Octavian chased them away with their tails between their legs.

News soon reached Alexandria and the palace itself where the handmaidens comforted each other through their tears. Rashida innocently asked, "What does it all mean – surely if the mistress is on her way back, all will be fine.

The two women looked at each other and Iras said, "You don't understand, do you? It could mean the end of the Pharaoh's reign and therefore the end of us. Go out into the corridors and you'll see many people already deserting their places and running away. They just don't know what else to do."

"Will we run too then?" she asked. "But I don't know where to run. I don't want to go home to my parents' house – not now I've lived here."

"You may have no option, Rashida – just be grateful that you have some place." Charmain snapped at the girl. "We must prepare for our mistress's arrival – she will need our help."

"Aren't you going to run away as well?" Rashida wouldn't let it drop.

"We will most certainly not run away – our mistress will need us more than ever now, but you can do what you want." The two women began laying out fresh clothes on Cleopatra's bed. "We will run a bath for her as soon as there is word of her return – that she will need." And they set about their duties, ignoring Rashida as they did so.

Cleopatra returned to her palace but she knew all was lost. When the leaders had left the battle, the disheartened ships that were left, surrendered to Octavian and one week later, all of Mark Antony's land forces surrendered too. Rome's Republican days were over and the victor would take control of Rome and of Italy – and as it turned out, of Egypt as well. It took Octavian several months to finally enter Alexandria where he had to do battle again with Mark Antony – but it was just a skirmish this time and he won easily.

Following yet another defeat at Octavian's hands, Cleopatra took refuge in a mausoleum she'd had built for herself. Word was carried to Mark Antony telling him that she was dead, by her own hand. He took his sword and stabbed himself, just moments before further news arrived saying she was still alive. His dying body was carried to her retreat so he could say goodbye, and before he died, he begged her to make her peace with Octavian and save herself. She told him 'never' but he smiled – he thought he knew her better than that.

When the triumphant general finally arrived at her retreat, she did try to seduce him, after all, it had worked before, but he was too wily for her and resisted her charms. He left her then, having learned where she kept her secret hoards of treasure. This money, he used to pay off his army veterans in gratitude for their loyal service. Incredibly therefore, her enemies were paid by Cleopatra herself, the very enemies she'd recently fought against.

Cleopatra's retreat was as comfortable as her palace and her handmaidens were there with her. They pandered to her and cossetted her. She was after all the Pharaoh and perhaps the last of the ruling Ptolemy line – and they truly loved her. Rashida was still with them, too afraid to make the decision to leave.

"My loyal handmaidens, I will be honest with you." She was dressed all in white with even her head covered. She was only thirty-nine years of age but suddenly, looked much older. "Charmain, I want you to go and find Master Alim who should still be in the palace. You must say that you come on my instructions to ask that he obtain a snake – an Asp – which should be placed in a basket and brought back to me. Can I trust you to do that for me, Charmain?"

"Oh Madam, for what purpose do you need a snake – and a poisonous one at that?" Charmain was distressed.

"Once you have brought it, you may all go free as I shall not need you again. I am sorry that I'm unable to give you much of value but you see how my situation has changed." She almost smiled at this understatement. "Now go and do as you are bid. It is the last thing you can do for me." Charmain couldn't argue more with the Pharaoh. "Iras, you may pour me some wine." Iras rushed to do as she was told.

Little Rashida stepped forward and asked, "Madam, would you like me to brush your hair. I shall be most gentle."

"Yes please, Rashida – I would like that." And she drank the wine Iras had given her.

Charmain soon returned with the small, round basket that she put down on the floor by her mistress. She looked how she felt. She loved Cleopatra and always had. Iras had always felt the same and they had both been with their mistress for a very long time.

"Rashida, you may stop brushing my hair now. I am finished with life. Ladies, come and kiss your Pharaoh goodbye, you have been good and faithful since I first met you and I am sad at saying goodbye to you." She removed heavily jewelled rings from her fingers and gave them one each. "I have none for you, Little Rashida – but you have not been with me as long as the others have, so I hope you will forgive me."

As she was talking, she opened the basket and waited. The snake's head slowly emerged from the basket and she put her hand towards it. There was a rasping sound and it clearly bit into her wrist. She sighed and fell back onto the soft bed linen. Several drops of blood fell onto the white cover and she closed her eyes – those lovely eyes that had seen so much. The Pharaoh was no more and neither was Caesar nor Mark Antony in whose lives, she'd played such a big part. And now, they were all gone.

Charmain lifted the snake and looked at Iras and Rashida. Iras came towards her, "Me first Charmain – I want to go first. She kissed Charmain who held the snake's head over her friend's arm – and then turned it on her own. Both women were bitten by the snake and they curled up at their mistress's feet but didn't offer the snake to Rashida – they knew she didn't want it.

In the mausoleum, the three bodies lay together. They now knew what the After Life was about and they welcomed it. It was good that Cleopatra didn't know then what happened in the next few days. Caesarion succeeded his mother as Pharaoh of Egypt – Caesarion I – but it only lasted a short time, as Octavian had the young man executed. He felt it would be too dangerous to allow him to live. The very last of the Ptolemaic line was gone.

Rashida left the mausoleum and ran through the streets of Alexandria – she ran to the home she'd shared with her mother and father. They were both working in the bakehouse, kneading the dough for tomorrow's bread. Her mother looked up. Her daughter was still dressed as a great lady but she was crying and obviously distressed. She told them both what had happened and why she'd come home.

"I have nowhere to go, mother – can I come back here and stay with you? I promise to work hard for you – you won't regret it."

The man and woman looked at each other, "What do you think, mother – shall we let her come back to us?"

But he was smiling and Rashida threw herself into his arms. "Oh father, what a time I've had. I have much to tell you."

Her mother spoke at last. "I warned you not to leave home in the first place, didn't I? I knew it wasn't a good thing, but you're back now and I suppose we'll have to clothe and feed you, as well as ourselves. We'll just have to make our meagre earnings stretch further." Her mother had never been as nice as her father. "What is that you're clutching in your hand?"

She placed two amazing objects on the table. They were gorgeous rings – one a large ruby and one a stone she didn't recognise, but they were obviously of great value. "We can sell these and that'll pay for my keep – for a while at least. The Pharaoh gave them to her two older handmaidens but they committed suicide alongside her – and so nobody wanted the rings. It would have been silly to leave them there for the next person who came along to pick up. I didn't do wrong, did I?"

"You certainly did not. We'll be able to buy fresh grain tomorrow – we've almost run out. And now, the grain situation is getting better, there's grain to buy. It seems the Nile has turned a corner and the levels of water are rising, to flood the plains again. Hooray!"

Her father was feeling pretty pleased with the turn of recent events.

Rashida was never to forget her time at the palace and after going home, she kept the promise made to her parents and made bread alongside her mother. In the end, the family had to move to bigger premises, so successful were they that the money obtained when Cleopatra's rings were sold left them with a little cushion of money and they ended up with two shops. The River Nile was flooding the plains again and there was grain enough to feed Egypt and Italy – this was especially good news for the people in the baking trade.

One day, a man came into the shop when Rashida was serving behind the counter. She looked at him and thought she knew him but couldn't place where she'd seen him before. Then it struck her – it was Amenei, the young boy who had met her when she first applied for a job.

"Don't you recognise me, Amenei? I met you once when you were with Master Alim. I was looking for employment at the time and you helped me. What are you doing now?" She chose two well-shaped loaves and put them in his bag.

"Of course, I remember you – you were the pretty one. I am still at the palace and working as a scribe for the lawyers. The palace is quite different nowadays, you wouldn't know it. It is really nice to see you again." He turned to leave the shop but turned back. "Would you like to see the palace once more – I could take you there, if you like."

"I would like that very much." And next day, they met in the market place. They walked together and came to the mausoleum where Cleopatra had ended her life. Neither of them said anything, but when Rashida looked back, she saw some figures under the stone porch. She looked closer and recognised the two handmaidens, standing with a young boy between them. She touched Armenei's shoulder and crossed to the figures. How could it be the handmaidens? They'd died on the same day as Cleopatra.

Charmain spoke, "Ah Rashida, we've been waiting for you to come this way – and here you are."

The figures were misty and obviously not of this world – Iras spoke then, "You are a bad woman – you stole from the dead. You took the rings Cleopatra had given to us before she died. How could you steal from dead people – it was an evil thing to do."

"But you were both gone, by your own hands. If I'd left the rings, someone else would have come along and taken them – surely you see that." Rashida felt very low and looked at the boy, "Why have you waited for me – I did nothing to hurt you."

"I am here to tell you we forgive you. What you did was wrong but some good has come from it, as your parents have benefitted in their business. My mother sent me here to say it was okay for you to take the rings and if she'd had more at the time, she would have given you something too – but Octavian left her with nothing when he left Egypt."

"Thank you, Caesarion – it is Caesarion, isn't it? I recognise you." Amenia came up behind her.

"Why are you talking to yourself, Rashida?" he asked.

"Can't you see them there?" But when she turned, they'd all gone. It seemed she still had a conscience for what she'd done and it was pricking her then.

Looking around the corridors in the palace, she saw great changes. There were still grand rooms and beautiful furniture, but it looked more like offices and formal staterooms. The atmosphere was different too – and no pleasant smells, just everyday odours. There was nothing of Cleopatra, Julius Caesar nor Mark Antony here. It felt all wrong.

"We must go now, Rashida – I have much to do before the Emperor Augustus, he who was Octavian, arrives this evening. He is coming on one of his periodic visits – just to check on us. Rome is our master now and we pay hefty taxes to the city. Egypt is now an annex of Italy and no more than that."

"It all sounds so sad. Don't you find it so" Her tears were very close.

"No, not really, in fact I am better now than I ever was. The country is wealthy again, we have grain for all and Rome is our protector – we now have nothing to fear from them. Augustus is a good Emperor – do you remember him as Octavian perhaps? He seems to be a decent man who oversees our country in a fair way."

"That is not how I remember him. He was feared greatly by my mistress and he is the reason Cleopatra killed herself." She could never forgive him that.

They both went their separate ways, both feeling rather nostalgic, but knowing too that they were better off than they'd ever been under Cleopatra's autocratic rule. What a troublesome time it had been. As can be imagined, they went on meeting and Amenei continued to buy his bread at her shop, but did they ever marry? No, it never came to that and Rashida went on baking the bread for the rest of her life and eventually became quite a wealthy woman.

Author's Note

Cleopatra has been blamed by History for the downfall of Egypt and for binging about the end of the Ptolemaic line of Pharaohs. Accusations have been flung at her, saying she was promiscuous all her life and her country suffered the consequences. However, we now recognise she had a difficult reign with many problems, not of her own making. During her father's reign – and that of many of her earlier ancestors – Egypt had had many famines due to Mother Nature. In fact, the entire Ptolemaic period of rule had been fraught with problems. Cleopatra had been chased out of Egypt by the people revolting when still a young woman and to regain her country, she'd had to turn to Rome for help. Caesar was her saviour in this respect, followed by Mark Antony. Her people revolted and clamoured at the palace gates, asking for grain – of which she had none. She'd even been forced to have her sister murdered when she tried to take the throne of Egypt – something which pricked her conscience for the rest of her life.

The Emperor Augustus lived until the age of 75 and ruled peacefully over Rome and all its annexes, including Egypt. It was a very peaceful time in that part of the world. It looked as though Julius Caesar knew what he was doing when he named this man, his great nephew – as his heir, but in the end, Augustus really had to fight for it.

As for Cleopatra and what History said of her:

Could she really be blamed for the Nile ceasing to flood the plains by the riverbanks, resulting in no grain being harvested and the people starving?

NO.

Could she be blamed for the plague which spread through her land like hot fire, killing many of her people? It is now believed that they suffered from Bubonic Plague, for which there was no cure at the time?

NO.

Could she be blamed for Caesar's assassination in 44 BC by the Senators in Rome, so bringing an end to the Republic that existed in Rome and sparking off a Civil War between Octavian and Mark Antony. Both wanted to be Emperor?

NO.

Could she be blamed for people seeing the three suns in the sky at the same time as the skies were completely dark for many days – so in their eyes, prophesying a future disaster? This too was in the year 44 BC.

NO.

Could she be blamed for choosing the wrong side in the Roman Civil War? After all, she had no foreknowledge as to who would win. She was brave enough to fight in the sea battle at Actium alongside Mark Antony – but couldn't face the battle in the end.

NO.

Could she be blamed for the Volcanic Eruption that took place in Ethiopia in the year Caesar was assassinated – 44 BC? It was 7,000 miles from Egypt and in recent investigations in Greenland, scientific results now show that masses of sulphates blew all around the world as the fallout – these sulphates affected the waters in Ethiopia that had always fed the Nile and so drench the plains with life-giving harvests. The rainfall dried up completely in 44 BC. The Volcanic eruption so far away did affect the Nile – it had nothing to do with Cleopatra.

NO.

Could she even be blamed for taking her own life when the only other prospect she had was being dragged in chains through the streets of Alexandria by Octavian – and her head would be shaved? She was the failed Pharaoh after all and it would have been her punishment.

NO.

These are just my thoughts, but what do you think? Was Cleopatra a wicked and shallow floosy who liked the men too much, or was she an astute and brave politician who suffered the consequences of a Volcano erupting 7,000 miles from her home – and inevitably affecting her whole life? And one last thought.

How would events in Egypt and therefore for Cleopatra herself have unfolded, had Caesar listened to the old soothsayer, who warned him to 'BEWARE THE IDES OF MARCH'. If anyone ever tells you this, you should listen – JUST IN CASE.

(By the way, the Ides is the middle day of each month.)

We'll Meet Again

Jenny Mundy was late for school again. It was the second time this week, and she could already hear Miss Turner saying, "Ah, the late Miss Mundy, is it?" to the class who would laugh politely. They had heard her saying it many times before but knew too that she expected them to laugh. Anyway, better Jenny Mundy facing the sarcasm than any one of them. There were four rows with ten desks in each row – the cleverest child sat at the top of row one and then, one by one around the class, the other children sat in order of their assumed intelligence. It could of course be more likely to be the 'Teachers' Pets' who claimed the first desks. Jenny took her seat at the bottom of row four. She'd known her place for a long time. Miss Turner was not yet finished with her and asked loudly, "Did you have time to get some breakfast, Jenny?"

"Yes, Miss, thank you." Jenny kept her eyes lowered in the hope that she'd be left alone.

"And what exactly did you have?" Miss Turner was on a roll and enjoying herself.

"Two cream cakes, Miss – the ones with jam and cream in them." Even as she said it, Jenny knew she'd gone too far. Her answer was obviously a lie and sounded cheeky.

Miss Turner looked at the class and raised her eyebrows. Some laughed and some coughed but it wasn't really funny anymore. The teacher could be cruel and they knew it. The little scenario had been played out so many times before, but always with the poorest children in the class.

The children attended what was called a Ragged School. It was for children who, firstly, wanted to learn but who came from the poor part of town where money was scarce and they had had no chance of an education before these schools were opened. They had been created originally for children who were destitute with no one to care for them but with the passage of time, other children joined the school, as formal education was hard to find. The poorest children

47

tended to live in the town's Poor Houses, and so were always sent to the Ragged School. It was 1850 and the throne had a relatively new monarch – Victoria. The education comprised of basic subjects, such as reading, writing and even more basic arithmetic, but the great thing was that, as well as being educated, the poorest pupils were given some bread and cheese for their lunch at no cost. They were lucky, especially as they were also given clothing to wear – but the clothing was all the same so they looked like children from the Ragged School. Well-off people had private tutors and governesses of course but for the poor in Victorian England, there was no money for such things. The Ragged Schools and Sunday Schools were all that was available but even children from better-off homes attended them, as the basic education was good – but they all had to pay a penny a day for the privilege.

Jenny Mundy belonged to the poorest class and she knew it. She had a nice friend at school however, called Catriona Campbell and although coming from opposite sides of the track, they gelled almost as soon as they met. Catriona had to pay a penny a day unlike Jenny, who got everything for nothing. But the two girls were kindred spirits and bosom buddies both at once, although one was dressed in neat, darned clothing and the other in scrappy torn garments, issued by the school. Catriona was an only child and Jenny had six brothers and sisters. One lived in a flat in a stone-built tenement and the other in a two-up/two-down terrace house with no running water and sanitation. The differences were apparent but the girls didn't notice and were genuinely fond of each other.

Christmas was the next week and Miss Turner was showing the class how to make decorations from sticky, coloured paper. It was a good time in class and the cocoa and bun the children were given at midday went down a treat. While they paused for their break, Catriona said quietly to her friend, "Would you like to come home with me one day and we could have tea. It won't be very fancy, but it would be a treat for both of us."

Jenny didn't know what to say. She'd never been invited into anyone's home before and she looked down at her ragged clothes and wondered what Catriona's parents would say when they saw her. "I really would like that but I'd never be able to invite you to my home. It's too cramped and there's so many of us, but if you like, I'll ask my mum if I can visit you."

"Then, let's do that, Jenny – you ask your mum and I'll ask mine." And that's how their friendship continued for the next couple of years.

The first Christmas they spent together was quite jolly and all the children were given a small present taken from a rather straggly tree. The presents were only paper mottoes, a bit small but very religious and the colours were bright and pretty. Jenny thought hers was especially pretty – the baby Jesus lying in his mother's arms and against the blue of Mary's dress, he seemed to glow from the paper.

Walking out of the school gates on the day they'd been given the mottoes, Catriona asked, "How many brothers and sisters do you have?"

"Six of them – and we're all so crammed against each other, there's no room to do much – just sit there and annoy each other. Mum makes us girls work and do housework but the boys don't have to do anything. It's not fair."

"What about your dad – what does he do? Where does he work?" Catriona was intrigued.

"He doesn't go to work regularly, only the odd day when he can pick up some work down at the docks. He helps load things onto boats and sometimes, when he's very lucky, he can bring home scraps of food that people throw away."

Catriona looked at her friend and wondered how she survived, but knew not to say that. The next Wednesday, Jenny went home with her. The flat was amazing – real curtains at the windows and chairs all over the place. There was even a flush toilet outside on the landing of the tenement. Jenny's eyes were round with disbelief. There were soft cushions on the chairs and a lovely table with two plates of sandwiches and a small iced cake. She thought Buckingham Palace must look like this. Catriona's home made her aware of how poor she was – she was one of the few who was given bread and cheese for school dinner and her friend wasn't. She went to a Ragged School, wore ragged clothes and was fed by the school as one of the poorest pupils, but she told herself she could only go upwards in life and she would be patient 'till that happened.

Catriona offered her a sandwich which she took gratefully, saying, "Thank you, you're very kind." The mother was pleased with her manners, she could see that, although she didn't know how she knew about manners but it just came naturally to her. Unfortunately, she then wiped her nose on her sleeve causing Mrs Campbell to produce a fresh handkerchief for her. "Keep that for yourself." She told her and made a mental note to go through Catriona's old clothes for something to fit this child.

It was snowing when she left the house and walked home. Her feet were freezing, but then that was normal. Just in front of her, she spotted Michael

Wilson who went to the same school as the girls. He was shovelling snow from the pavement outside one of the houses. He looked up and smiled. "I get threepence for doing this. Good, ain't it?" And he went on shovelling. She liked Michael. He was one of the nicer boys in her class and he'd always treated her well, although some of the other boys enjoyed teasing her and pulling her hair. She reached her own house and didn't want to go inside – but then the heavy snow soon changed that.

"Get in here, you lazy good-for-nothing but bring logs with you for the fire. I think there's a few left in the backyard." Jenny had to turn and go back outside and her chilblains burnt into her skin leaving large red swellings on her face, fingers and feet. She always suffered from chilblains in the cold. She brought in the three logs that were left and put one of them on the fire. Her brothers and sisters pushed their way forward – the room was very cold. They had had some cabbage soup, peppered heavily and a chunk of stale bread. It wasn't a bad supper but Jenny kept thinking of the plateful of sandwiches that Catriona's mum had served that night.

Next day at school, Jenny was on time for a change and Miss Turner couldn't pick on her. She did ask where the red marks on the girl's arms and face had come from. "Hm – a few logs shouldn't have done that. Are you telling the truth, Miss Mundy? It looks more like chilblains to me." Jenny nodded and sneaked a glance around the classroom. The teacher continued, "Now children, I want you to do a coloured drawing of the" Virgin Mary and Baby Jesus. The best pictures will go on the wall for Christmas.

The next hour was spent peacefully. The children enjoyed such a task and worked diligently on their work. In her mind's eye, Jenny remembered in detail the picture on the moto she'd been given. In fact, her picture was lovely – the shade of blue she used was just right and the baby was wrapped tightly in a shawl. Walking around the classroom, Miss Turner silently came up behind her and whacked her fingers with a wooden ruler.

"You've copied that, Jenny Mundy – you were not told to do that. Your picture was to be an original. Bad girl, that's cheating." And she raised her ruler again over her head and made to whack Jenny again. The strangest thing happened then – Catriona, who was quite tall for her age, reached up and grabbed the teacher's ruler.

"Please don't hit her again, Miss Turner – she has very bad chilblains and they bleed sometimes. Please don't hit her again." Catriona stared at the teacher and waited for herself to be struck instead of her friend, but it never happened. Miss Turner turned away and went to her desk.

"Catriona Campbell, you will wait behind when it's home time and the rest of the class leave." She was breathing hard and her nostrils were flared.

"Yes, Miss," Catriona answered," I will stay behind after school." She knew she was in for a beating. Miss Turner was famous for that.

Suddenly, there was a loud scraping of chairs and shuffling of feet. A great number of boys and some girls had got to their feet and Michael Wilson said, "We'll all stay behind then, Miss Turner. If you're going to punish Catriona for standing up for her friend, then you'd better punish all of us." The teacher looked at Jenny with round, staring eyes. She obviously blamed the girl for what had just happened. The pupils were obviously all behind Michael's words, as they stood there quite stoically. The silence was almost deafening. Miss Turner left the room and told one of her favourites to watch the class in her absence.

On the way home, the two girls whispered to each other, "I'll never forget what you did, Trina – you were very brave."

Catriona laughed and said, "Not as brave as Michael Wilson."

"Well, I think you were." Jenny insisted and took her friend's hand. "I'll do something like that for you some day – just you see if I don't." And the girls hurried home out of the freezing wind.

As the months passed, Jenny began to look a little smarter. She wore her Ragged School uniform during the week but at the weekends, she dressed in some of the clothes Mrs Campbell had given her. The girls were growing up and would soon be leaving school.

"What are you going to do with your life, Jen? I've decided when I'm old enough, I'm going to get a job in a hospital."

"So am I, Trina – perhaps we'll be able to work together. You never know." And both of them had dreamy looks in their eyes.

The following year, however, they were told to dress neatly and have a good wash. There was a gentleman coming to visit the school and he wanted to talk to some of the children. "Who can he be?" they all asked each other.

"Well, it's definitely not the queen – she's a woman – but I suppose it might be her husband, Prince Albert." And that was how word got around that the prince was coming to visit.

Next morning, all the pupils arrived early and the classroom was as neat as a new pin. "Sit up straight and don't slouch," Miss Turner ordered and took out her little mirror to look at herself. The classroom door opened and the Headmaster came in, followed by a well-dressed gentleman, carrying a notebook and pencil. Catriona mouthed to Jenny, "That's not Prince Albert." Nor was it, it was a man called Charles Dickens who was apparently a famous writer, known to lots of people. He told the children he was particularly interested in Ragged and Sunday Schools and asked them if they were happy and what were the best things about the school. The headmaster left the room and Miss Turner sat down at her desk. Charles Dickens asked everyone to pull their chairs into a circle so he could talk to them. Much scuffling later, they were all there, waiting expectantly.

He talked to them about their homes and families and asked if any of them had any particular friends in the school. Jenny put her hand up and pointed to Catriona, "That's my best friend, sir." He looked at the 'friend' and smiled.

"How long have you been friends?" he asked, all the time scribbling in his notebook.

"Two years now, sir," Catriona replied.

He asked them what they planned to do when they left school and they told him they wanted to be nurses. "Very worthwhile, with the medical world learning all the time and although the hospitals are still very basic, it's much better than we've ever had before." He went on to ask if anybody wanted to write stories and perhaps become a journalist. Several pupils raised their hands and he looked pleased. "Well, to do that, you must work hard at your lessons and learn as much as you can about words and their meanings – that's what magic is, to put your thoughts down on paper and share them with the rest of the world."

The class never forgot that day. The man had an air about him that spoke of success – he encouraged them to make their lives better – and said, if ever they needed anything to help them do that, they could call on Mr Charles Dickens and he wrote his address on the blackboard. He also wrote about them in the newspapers of the day, telling people how the children lived and how hard it was for them. Dickens had actually started work as an office boy and now he owned his own newspaper. He stressed this to the class, that they could make life what they wanted – but they had to accept the knocks and just get on with the job in hand. It had been a very worthwhile visit and possibly the writings of Mr Dickens, helped move forward children's schooling in leaps and bounds.

The months passed and the last day of school dawned at last. The two best friends swore they'd keep in touch with each other in the future and held hands until they had to separate. In fact, they actually 'pinky swore' and pricked their fingers to mix their blood – to make their promise to each other even more definite. They held hands and kissed each other on the cheek, before parting and going their separate ways. It was the start of the rest of their lives and, as well as feeling sad, they also felt excited.

The truth was that they didn't keep in touch with each other at all. They both got jobs – one in the town mill and the other, in a bakery. As often happens, intentions don't always keep up with what actually takes place. When she reached seventeen, Catriona managed to join the local hospital, which was very basic in what it could offer patients, but at least she got some medical training – and she loved it. Cleanliness was an important basic in nursing. She worked hard and moved from home into one of the small rooms laid aside for nurses at the hospital. She was a good nurse, although most of her duties were washing patients' wounds and comforting them when they were in pain. Healing their problems wasn't something Victorian hospitals were yet ready to provide, but Catriona was sympathetic and kind and the patients loved her.

Jenny on the other hand still worked at the bakery but she was fed up with the heavy work and the getting out of bed in the early hours of the morning. She saw a notice in a shop window saying that a qualified nurse was putting together a team of nurses to go to help our wounded soldiers at Scutari in Turkey, known as The Crimean War – and would like any interested women to contact her – she would be holding interviews the following week at her home. Jenny made a note of her name – Florence Nightingale – and intended to contact her.

The Crimean Peninsula, the Baltic Sea, the Ottoman Empire, France, Great Britain, Sardinia and Turkey had all joined forces and taken on the might of Russia, who was obsessed with taking control of the Middle East and so, control half the world. Jenny made a point of reading the newspapers left behind by some of the shoppers to make herself aware of the Crimean problems. It was reported again and again in the newspapers that the allies were suffering badly, the British in particular – being so far away from home and with no one locally to support them. To date, the newspapers reported that 1,650,000 soldiers had taken part in this war and 900,000 of them had already died. For this reason, Florence Nightingale, who'd trained as a nurse and actually opened her own Nursing School, was to go to Turkey and help as many as she could. To do this, she needed a team of volunteers whom she could train to help the wounded men. The injured soldiers were apparently in desperate circumstances, in fact, really just being left to die in the worst possible conditions. Florence had approached the government and asked if she could do this – and they agreed. What did they have to lose? Her Training School for nurses was at St Thomas's hospital, which was far superior to the Workhouse Infirmaries where most people went – almost always just to die. Florence's name was becoming known across the whole country, in fact Queen Victoria herself was keeping an eye on the nurse's progress.

The following week, Jenny found her way to Florence's home and knocked timidly on the big front door. A little maid answered almost at once and Jenny told her she'd come to see Miss Nightingale. "I want to go to Scutari to help the wounded soldiers."

The maid smiled at her and said, "You just tell Miss Nightingale that's what you want to do, and she'll welcome you with open arms." She told Jenny to wait in a room and someone would come to fetch her. The room was quite dark and at first, she couldn't make out who was there, but she could hear sniffs and coughs, so she knew she wasn't alone.

Half an hour later, the little maid appeared and told Jenny Miss Nightingale would see her now. As Jenny made to follow her, she passed another young woman who was coming out of the office and paused for a moment, recognising Catriona, her old school friend. The two girls hadn't seen each other for about three years and were very surprised, but there was no time to stop and talk so they just smiled at each other and moved on. The maid showed Jenny into Miss Nightingale's room.

"Do sit down, Miss Mundy, and tell me why you're interested in coming with me to Turkey." The attractive woman could only have been in her early thirties but had a manner of someone much older. Jenny spoke of a difficult life and how much she wanted to help others – especially those who were ill or wounded. Miss Nightingale sat quietly and listened to the young woman. She obviously liked what she heard as she never interrupted once.

She did say however, "Do you understand the conditions won't be good – in fact they'll probably be very bad – and some of the wounds you'll be asked to dress will be worse than you've ever seen in your life. You will have to take responsibility for keeping your patients cheerful as well as comfortable – that way, they'll feel more secure and safe. Is that quite clear?"

"Ma'am, I hadn't really considered all of that but I'm not afraid of it. I am a hard worker and I can get used to anything when I try." Jenny thought her chances were slipping away and she looked down at her feet.

"I think you can plan ahead to be one of my nurses going to Turkey to help our boys there. You seem to be made of the right stuff." And she held out her hand to shake Jenny's. "Goodbye, Miss Mundy – get your things together and be ready to set sail on the 21 October this year, 1854. Our first stop will be Boulogne and then on to Marseilles where we will probably travel over land to Constantinople. That is our plan. I myself will have to stop my work at St Thomas's Hospital where I've been training the nurses. After that, I will train girls like you. Is all that clear? I like people to know what's in front of them." And she showed Jenny the door.

She left the house in a kind of dream. She'd only thought about it before, but now it was real. She was really going to be a nurse and go across the world to help wounded soldiers. She was scared and excited.

She never thought about her chance meeting with Catriona Campbell. There was too much to think about. She gathered together her meagre belongings and went to a pawn shop where she bought a small bag that would become her pride and joy. On the day in question, she made her way to the dock. There were many women wandering around the key, waiting for further instructions.

"Well, Jenny Mundy, fancy meeting you here after all this time." She recognised that voice and knew, before she turned around, that it was Catriona Campbell. She threw her arms around her friend's neck and kissed her on both cheeks.

"Oh, it's so good to see you again, Trina." And their friendship came alive again at that moment. They climbed the gangplank together and talked of what was ahead – although neither of them really knew what that would be. The ship was not as nice as they'd expected, there were rats below decks popping out from the least expected places, and there was a sickness developed amongst the nurses. It was a most unpleasant crossing and Miss Nightingale herself became ill and couldn't leave the ship at Boulogne.

"Girls, this is something we'll have to get used to, I'm afraid. Scutari will be much worse, but then, we knew that, didn't we?" The next ship – the Vectis – was even worse than the first and when it reached Malta, many of the passengers were ill and had trouble walking. They made their way overland to Constantinople and then on to Scutari, but they were all young and strong and soon recovered. However, what they saw when they first arrived was something else. They actually arrived on 4 November 1854 – just in time for the huge influx of wounded and dying soldiers from the battle, known as 'The Charge of the Light Brigade', which had just taken place. There had been 650 British soldiers all on horseback and, and although the Russians were more successful than the British, the accolade for courage and bravery, fell to the latter and the 'Thin Red Line' was established in History forever, mainly because of the poem Alfred Tennyson wrote just a few weeks after the battle. Lord Cardigan had led his men into battle and 40% of the soldiers fell almost immediately as casualties – a win for the Russians and a defeat for the British. It was only one of the battles however and overall, the allies beat the Russians and stopped their advancing all over Europe.

The hospital at Scutari was a converted barracks building and it was infested with giant cockroaches – not to mention rats – so before any nursing could begin, the nurses had to group together with a mountain of cleaning materials, which they'd bought at Marseilles on their journey to Turkey. They scrubbed and swept – but the blood and gore increased every day, as the wounded men arrived. Men died of their wounds, from Blood Poisoning, from Cholera and from the many amputations which went wrong. Things were much worse than Florence Nightingale had imagined – there was so much to do – and so few comforts for the men. The barracks looked more like a prison and the yard outside was a flowing sea of mud and excrement. The sick barracks had been full of prostitutes when the nurses arrived – they were all dying of malnutrition, scurvy, cholera and alcohol poisoning. They had to be cleared out to make room for the wounded. There were twenty chamber pots for a thousand men, which were emptied into larger pots outside the wards and dumped in the open. There was little furniture, very few beds and the woodwork was so rotten, it couldn't be scrubbed clean. Everyone had an allowance of one pint of water, both for drinking and washing and the Orderlies who had been drafted into the army for such duties, were all pensioners with no knowledge of hospitals whatsoever. It was an unbearable situation which had to be borne.

This is then what the 38 nurses had come to. Even the military doctors didn't have time to make them welcome as they hadn't wanted them in the first place. They believed women were useless in such situations. Time however – and the diligence of the nurses – would soon prove how wrong they'd been at first. The 40 people who had come with Miss Nightingale were given five small rooms and one kitchen. She was not welcomed at the hospital by the Army Medical Department and she seemed always to be fighting a battle just to get supplies and food for the patients, never mind her nurses.

Most of the nurses could face up to the dreadful conditions, but some couldn't and cried most of every day. Jenny and Trina shared a room with 10 others and both women looked shadows of their former selves. "Dear God, Trina, what have we let ourselves in for? Will we live to see our home again, do you think?"

"'Course we will, silly – we're tough and strong and we're certainly needed here." Catriona had always been the more positive of the two. Both girls were terribly thin and although they tried to stretch their daily pints of water as far as they could, they always felt very grubby.

Jenny felt they should be doing more for the wounded and the Army wasn't helping. "Did you know that Miss Nightingale and all the nurses have been refused entry onto the wards, unless a doctor requests their presence?"

"Yes," Trina replied, "but that will pass when they realise how useful we can be. Poor Miss Nightingale – she had to fight to get here, fight to clean the foul place, fight the Army Medics to look after the patients. She's had to fight on all sides, hasn't she?"

"You're right of course – come on, let's go outside and see if there's anything we can do to cheer her up." Jenny felt more positive now and said, "I'll race you to the kitchen to see if there's any spare scraps of food – I'm starving." They ran into Miss Nightingale however who chastised them for running in the corridors and told them to straighten their caps. There was no question but that she was a very strict leader.

That night, when the hospital quietened down, Jenny slipped out of her narrow bunk. To reach the small room used for the chamber pots at the very end of the corridor was quite a walk, and she hated having to creep around in the dark to reach it. Tonight was no different and she held her candle high to see the way ahead but what was surprising on this night was the atmosphere seemed quite heavy and threatening. Along both sides of the corridor there were several stretchers on the floor that hadn't been there during the day. She cautiously cupped the light of the candle and approached the stretchers. The men who lay there were all very grey in colour – in fact, they were almost white – and they were covered by blankets that were soaked in blood. None of them was moving but there was a soft moaning emanating from their lips and Jenny suddenly realised the men were dead – and not dying – but already dead, and somehow able to emit a sound. Her walk was through two rows of the dead and she was petrified. She scurried between the stretchers and reached the chamber pot room but had no idea how she was going to get back to her room.

Florence Nightingale appeared at the end of the long corridor and Jenny became aware there were no stretchers now and definitely no dead men. Miss Nightingale was carrying a glowing lamp which flickered up and down the corridor. She looked like a ghost herself, standing there very still.

"Come along, Jenny, I'll see you to your room." And the frightened girl quickly ran towards the glow of the lamp.

"Oh, Ma'am, such terrible things I saw – did you not see them yourself? Lots of men in the last throws of death? I've never seen them here before."

"Oh Nurse – if you walked these corridors as I do – in the dead of the night – you would see them all the time. Some soldiers are still only boys and they were killed so soon and so quickly that their young lives were snuffed out so suddenly that, even their corpses take a while to completely die." Florence took the girl to her door and put her inside. "Get some sleep now, tomorrow we're expecting a large number of wounded from a recent battle, which unfortunately the British lost – I'll be expecting you to work even harder than you have already." And she closed the room door.

Next morning, the nurses were all wakened by an early gong and they had a hasty breakfast of oats and milk in the kitchen. The trucks were beginning to arrive in the yard and Jenny and Catriona were two of the first to stand ready to receive the wounded. It really was a pitiful sight, with so many blood-soaked bandages and moaning men. The orderlies brought the stretchers into the hospital and Florence was already organising her team. The doctors were waiting there too and knew that they had to include the nurses as they now realised they were needed to help the men. Their attitude had changed somewhat from when the women first arrived. In fact, they found they could work faster and more efficiently with a nurse beside them

"Follow me, nurse." One doctor bellowed at Jenny who ran over to join him. He was bending over a young man on a stretcher, whose head was covered in bandages – as was his left leg. The man was unconscious which must have been a blessing to him. "Let's get him onto the ward," the doctor continued, "and I need you to wash him first so I can see what damage has been done. Can you do that for me?"

"I'll do it immediately, Sir." And she did. She began to gently wash her old school friend, Michael Wilson. It felt surreal but it was the first thing that had to be done. He was in a bad way, but she washed him carefully and slowly unwound the bandages that were around his head. His eyes were closed but very bloody. He didn't even know she was there. 'Wait till I tell Catriona.' She thought and got on with her job.

Both the friends were responsible for nursing Michael. Florence split the duties between several of the nurses – to look after the wounded soldiers who'd arrived that day. It was exhausting work and that night the nurses just dropped into bed – except for the unfortunate ones who were on night duty.

Miss Nightingale had brought some of her own kitchen supplies, which she'd picked up in Marseilles and she had the orderlies and the nurses set them all around the kitchen. She began to arrange for the one cook she had, to teach a couple of the orderlies to cook tasty but healthy recipes of invalid food. She knew from experience that the quality of ingredients was as important as the nursing and medicines.

Catriona was on duty the day Michael Wilson asked for water through very parched lips. She carefully raised his bandaged head and touched his lips with water. "Come on, Michael – just a little sip." He did as he was told and almost smiled – but it was more like a grimace. She couldn't wait to find Jenny to tell her he was starting to come around. Jenny laughed and said, "And don't you start flirting with him before I get the chance – I remember how much you liked him at school." Catriona had liked the boy but this was a man and she wasn't sure how she felt about him now. Still, time would tell. He still had a long road to travel before he could think about things like that.

Jenny never went up the long corridor again in the middle of the night, even when she was desperate to use the toilet. That experience would never leave her and she felt no inclination to experience it again.

The running of the wards was beginning to take shape and now at least the nurses knew their presence was appreciated by both patients and doctors.

"Trina, why are there biscuits on Michael's bedside table." Jenny knew she hadn't put them there so it must have been Trina.

"I'm sure I don't know, Jenny. I can't know everything that goes on in the hospital, can I?"

Jenny didn't pursue the matter as she had done the same thing for him the previous day. In fact, between them, the two girls could have been accused of spoiling Michael Wilson. They told themselves it was only for old time's sake – and went right on doing it. He'd been at the hospital for about three weeks and his leg was healing well. He was able to take a few steps with the help of crutches but he couldn't go far because he still had no sight. Still, it was early days.

Jenny asked him if he'd like a head massage, something Miss Nightingale favoured. "It's all part of the healing process, girls." And she demonstrated the best way to do it.

"Yes, please," Michael responded, "are you Jenny or Catriona. I still can't tell, you know – you both sound alike." He was sitting on a chair beside the bed and was beginning to get some colour in his face.

"It's Jenny, Michael. Do you remember me from school?" And she started to smooth his temples with cream softened hands. "Do you remember that horrible Miss Turner who always managed to punish someone every day? She was a real monster, wasn't she?"

"Of course I remember her. Who could forget her?" But he was falling asleep in the chair, so comforting were Jenny's hands. She went on massaging but after a few minutes, he sat up screaming – he'd been dreaming.

"What is it, Michael?" she asked him.

"I thought I was back in the thick of the battle – and a Cossack was just about to thrust his long spear into my stomach. I pushed him away but he came at me again and I must have screamed. Did I startle you? I'm sorry." She could see tears running down his cheeks, making his bandages wet.

"Oh, Michael, it's all right, you're quite safe and nowhere near the battle field – you're in the hospital at Scutari and we're all here to look after you."

Catriona suddenly appeared. "What's wrong with him, Jenny? You haven't upset him, have you?" And the two nurses stared defiantly into each other's eyes.

"Don't be silly, Trina? I've done nothing to hurt him." Jenny felt very angry with her friend. And, where Michael was concerned, Trina felt the same. After that, he had many nightmares but on waking, there was soon a nurse on hand to calm him down. The nurse couldn't always have been one of the two friends – other nurses had ward duties as well. Another two weeks passed and he could walk a little better every day – but his sight was another thing and although the bandages had been removed, he could see nothing. Everything was still black. In his sleep, he kept calling out comrades' names and talking to them as if they were there, but in the cold light of day, he knew that would never be so again.

The army doctor stood by Michael's bed, reading a clipboard. He smiled at the patient. "Well, young man, it's time for you to go back to Britain so we can arrange for a specialist to help with your eyes. We don't have the facilities here – nor the skills – to deal with your problem. Your leg has healed nicely but I'm afraid you can't go back to duty – there'll always be a bit of a limp so your soldiering days are over." He stared into the young man's eyes and added, "I said your soldiering days are over but certainly not your life. I'm sure our surgeons will know what to do with you." He walked away, calling over his shoulder, "In about a week's time, we'll start you on your journey home."

Catriona was on duty that afternoon and she heard everything. She touched Michael's hand and asked if he was all right. "Is that you, Jenny?" And he tightened his grasp of her hand.

"Did you hear that, dear girl, I'll soon be back home – away from this dung-ridden country. The only thing I'll really miss, is you, but you must know that already. You do know, don't you, Jenny?" He waited for her reply, but none came.

Catriona said nothing but gently smoothed the hair from his forehead. "Ssh now, be quiet – you'll overstretch yourself." And she kissed his cheek, knowing that might be the only time she ever did it. She straightened his bed covers and drifted quietly away. She knew now that he loved Jenny and not herself, although she thought she had always loved him, since those early days at school. She felt lower than she'd ever felt in her life and needed to get out of the hospital for some fresh air. She went into the yard, filled her water bottle from the pump and splashed some of it on her brow and cheeks. A few sips and she went back into the hospital.

When she heard about Michael's good news, Jenny was not surprised. She had known it was inevitable and was sad that Michael would be leaving the hospital, but happy for him as well. Catriona seemed rather disinterested which wasn't like her at all, especially where her old school friend was concerned. She seemed more lethargic than usual and had developed a strange grey-blue pallor to her skin. In fact, she seemed to spend most of her time in the latrine and she was losing weight fast. Miss Nightingale herself called Catriona to come to her office and made her sit down opposite her desk.

"Now then young lady, what ails you? Tell me exactly what is wrong." As she spoke, she poured two cups of tea and moved one towards Catriona. "While you're so far away from home, I am responsible for your well-being – remember

I am a nurse too." She really was a gentle, warm person and Catriona felt safer already.

She sipped her tea and shyly said, "I don't know what's wrong – really I don't. I am sick all the time and I mean vomiting – I have to run to the latrine almost every hour and I think I am becoming dehydrated; my mouth is as dry as sandpaper." Not surprisingly, she began to cry and Miss Nightingale came around the desk and put her arms around the girl.

"Tell me, dear, do your limbs ache – and do your muscles feel weak?" Catriona nodded and looked pleadingly at the woman.

"What is it, Ma'am? What's wrong with me?"

"We'll have to do some tests but I believe the results will show that somehow you've contracted Cholera. Have you drunk any water away from the hospital?" The girl shook her head and then remembered.

"Actually, I did fill a water bottle from the well in the yard – it was so hot and I felt exhausted. "Was that it? Do you think I drank contaminated water?"

"I'm afraid you could have, my dear." And she led Catriona back to her own bed and made her get under the covers. "Now I'm going to fetch some boiled water for you to drink. It's only that that's safe until we get you on the mend." She left the room in a hurry. In the short time she'd been talking to the girl, Catriona's pallor had become worse and even more blue. Cholera was commonly known as 'The Blue Death'. She knew she had to hurry.

Catriona died the next day and Miss Nightingale felt as though she'd failed the girl, but it was too late by the time she'd heard of her illness. Jenny was broken-hearted and found it hard even to leave her bed. *How had Trina contracted Cholera? Had she drunk water from outside the hospital – that had to be it. Cholera was deadly and came from contaminated water. But Trina knew that, so how did it happen?* Her mind raced and she couldn't have felt more miserable had she tried. The irony was that Trina's body was taken back to her parents on the same boat on which Michael returned home. What a sad day that was for Jenny! She made and remade beds, emptied chamber pots that didn't need emptying and generally fussed over patients until they were fed up with it. She had to keep busy and keep her mind off what was happening outside the wards. She heard the hospital truck's engine and knew the two people she thought most of in the whole world were leaving Scutari, although one of them didn't know it.

Jenny stayed in Scutari for another year and then, as most of the patients were moved to the bigger hospital nearby, Miss Nightingale's angels with their famous night lamps were to return home, their vital work done. The allies had beaten the Russians and Europe settled down for a while.

"Well, Jenny, have you enjoyed your time here? Actually, enjoy is perhaps the wrong word to use but you must feel valued. You've done a sterling job here and become a very proficient nurse. When you get home and if I carry out my plans for better hospitals, you must come and see me and I'll certainly have a job for you." She had been invited to take tea with the Head Nurse – as had all the nurses one by one – but somehow, Miss Nightingale's words made her feel special and she fully intended to carry on her nursing work back in Great Britain.

"It's been a great honour, Ma'am." She managed to mumble the words. "And I feel I have learned so much from you. What will you do first when you reach home?"

"After a rest, Jenny, I shall start up another hospital, but before doing that, I have been invited to meet Queen Victoria at Buckingham Palace. I too, feel very honoured at that."

"It's no more than you deserve, Ma'am. I can't imagine how many soldiers owe their lives to you."

Jenny finished her tea and stood up but not before the other woman said, "And you deserve recognition nurse – as do all your dedicated colleagues."

And that was that. One month later, they all began the long and uncomfortable journey home. Jenny often wondered how Michael was now and she often thought of her old, school friend Trina. Why couldn't they have been returning home together – life could be so cruel. Trina had been too young to die and it had all happened so quickly. She knew she'd have to go and see Mr and Mrs Campbell and tell them how wonderful their daughter had been in Scutari. She didn't want to make that visit, but she knew she must and she wiped tears from her eyes, thinking about it.

On arriving home, she found some digs, as she couldn't face going back to the small and overcrowded house, she'd left almost two years before. It hadn't been very nice then and she doubted it was any better now. They probably hadn't missed her much – they'd never written to her although she'd sent several letters home at the beginning. *Blood isn't always thicker than water,* she thought. She slept for days it seemed although of course it wasn't – only hours really, but she needed that rest and she had some wages still in her purse, so she would be okay for a little while. On waking at last, she stared at herself in the mirror and realised how thin she'd become and how lank her once lovely hair had become. Oh well, she could do something about the hair.

Two weeks later, she came out of the hairdresser's, looking completely different and feeling better than she had for a long time. She knew it was now or never, so she worked her way across town to where Trina's parents lived. She had with her, her friend's special nursing badge awarded to the nurses at Scutari by a grateful wounded officer and she'd planned to keep Trina's safe for Mr and Mrs Campbell. As she neared the tenement where they lived, she turned the badge over and over in her pocket, feeling nervous at what was to come about. Mrs Campbell opened the door and gasped when she saw Jenny standing there. "Come in, dear," she stuttered and beckoned the girl into the sitting room, where Mr Campbell was sitting in an armchair with an opened newspaper on his lap. He stood up and held out his hand to her and that's what did it. Jenny just crumpled and fell down onto her knees.

"I'm sorry, so sorry – but seeing you both as it always was, brought everything back and I thought Trina would come into the room at any minute." Mrs Campbell wrapped her arms around the girl and smoothed the hair from her forehead.

"There, there now, Jenny – you're safe here and we're so pleased to see you."

They spent the next two hours talking about their Catriona and Jenny was able to add bits about when they'd served together in Scutari. Little funny things and many sad things came into her mind and she shared them with the man and woman and saw them smile and even laugh at some of her stories. She even told them about the wounded soldier, who attended the same school as they had and turned up badly hurt and blinded and how Trina and herself had cared for him on the ward.

"I think I remember him – Catriona had a crush on him, didn't she?" Mrs Campbell smiled and offered Jenny anther slice of cake. "Let me top up your tea, dear."

Jenny left the tenement, first giving Trina's badge to the mother of her friend. She stepped out onto the street and looked up at the window to wave goodbye, but she saw quite clearly, her friend Trina standing in the window. Jenny felt it was only right to wave to her, and she did just that. Trina lifted her arm slightly and smiled down into the street, before disappearing completely. It had been her friend; she was sure and she was safe at home where she belonged – in spirit at least. Jenny walked on down the street and pulled her coat collar around her neck to try to keep out the cold. She looked up at the sky and saw the snow begin to fall. It reminded her of that night so long ago when she'd just had tea at her friend's house. Funny how times changed and yet, also stayed the same. She went on her way and her feet turned in the same direction as they had once before, when she came across Michael sweeping the snow from his front yard.

Suddenly, through the light snowflakes, she saw a man brushing the snow from where it was beginning to settle on the bonnet of a car. There was something familiar about the way he held his head and as he walked around the car, she noticed he walked with a limp. She realised it was Michael – he looked a bit different but there was little doubt it was him. "Hello, Michael." She spoke softly, not wishing to make him jump, and she remembered he hadn't been able to see anything the last time she saw him. The man straightened up and came towards her. Through the falling snow, he peered into the night and she knew his sight was fine now.

'*Was it a ghost?*' was his first thought but then he realised it was a real, live person, but a person he believed had accompanied him on his journey back from Scutari. Jenny had died of Cholera during the Crimean War where he'd been injured. He felt sure about that and yet, here she was standing a few feet away.

"I don't understand…you're real, aren't you? I thought you died in Scutari…"

He came closer to her and reached out towards her. She knew he could see her and she smiled. "It's me, Michael…Jenny Mundy. I didn't die in Scutari…Trina did and when you returned home, her body was taken on the same journey."

His eyes were the same, lovely blue colour she remembered from when he was a little boy and then, when he was a wounded soldier in the hospital. She'd always liked him and so had Trina, she thought.

"I told you once in the hospital that you were the only thing I'd miss when I came home, but you didn't answer and left me there feeling awkward and embarrassed. I realise now…I must have been talking to Trina and that's why she didn't answer me."

"I didn't know, Michael. Trina never told me." She felt let down by her good friend but knew Trina also had carried a torch for him, so she understood.

"Let's not stand here in the snow. Come on in and have a hot drink, we've got a lot of catching up to do, haven't we?" He took her arm and guided her up the path. "I thought you were dead, Jenny, and it broke my heart. It was always you, even when we were still at school. Of course, I liked Catriona too – or Trina, as you always called her – but you were the one for me. I loved you then and I love you now, I think. We'll have to get to know each other again, won't we?"

In the lights inside, she looked at him properly. He was the same as she remembered but he still walked with a limp. His eyes, however, were unblemished and she thanked God for the surgeon who'd helped him. He lived on his own now as his mother had recently died and he had found work in the railway offices in the town. It wasn't the best job in the world but at least he received a regular income and could sit down most of the day. They settled down on the sofa in front of a blazing fire and he made them cups of steaming hot chocolate.

"What are you going to do now, Jenny?" he asked, passing over a plate of digestives.

"I plan to go and see Miss Nightingale who promised to help me get a job. I know she'll keep her word – I just hope my nursing skills are good enough. She was a wonderful leader in Scutari and I learned so much from her." She helped herself to a biscuit.

They chatted away, rekindling their friendship and neither noticed the figure standing on the front path, holding a bright lamp above her head. She was dressed in a nurse's uniform and wore a woollen cloak around her shoulders. She crossed over to the window and looked inside. She smiled at the pair, staring so intently into each other's eyes, and slowly turned away and faded into the falling snow. Soon, only the glow of her lamp could be seen – and then nothing. Trina had visited them and given her blessing to their growing friendship.

That friendship did grow over the next few months and in the month of May, they married at a small service in the local church. Mr and Mrs Campbell were guests at the wedding and gave the couple a very generous present of £20, which was a fortune to the nurse and the railway clerk. They'd managed to rent a room and kitchen in a tenement building as Michael had to leave his council house which had really belonged to his mother. The wedding service was drawing to a close and the music was soft now, played on the gramophone which Mr and Mrs Campbell were lucky enough to own. Mr Campbell stood up and tinkled his glass with a spoon. Everyone looked up expectantly.

"My wife and I just wanted to thank you all for coming and to wish Jenny and Michael all the luck in the world. They both knew our daughter, Catriona, and were her friends. May I say, God Bless the happy couple and bless our dear Catriona, whom I know is here in spirit, if not in person." Everyone raised their glasses and said 'to Jenny and Michael' and after a pause, added 'And to Catriona who should have been here in person.'

No one knew but she was there, living in the hearts of the people who had loved her – and hidden in a corner of the room, a nurse in uniform smiled in the darkness and was happy for her two friends in her own special way.

A Good Boy Really

He munched his popcorn and drank his cola – but never took his eyes off her – whenever she laughed at something on the screen, he felt himself smiling too. He was sitting in the row just behind her – in fact, he couldn't have got much closer to her, if he'd tried. She was with her friend – a blond girl with a harsh laugh – not the kind he liked. He'd seen his favourite at the cinema before and knew roughly where she'd sit. He felt he knew her but had to get to know her better. Her friend lived in a different direction – he'd seen her on previous nights, and knew he could follow her quite safely, something he'd done several times before. Following her made him very excited. He loved the chase. In fact, the stalking of a victim was the most enjoyable part of the whole thing

The film was over and the audience began to leave – her name was Liz – he'd heard her friend say goodnight as they kissed each other's cheeks and talk about what they'd do tomorrow. Very slowly, he started to walk behind her, quite a bit behind her, as he didn't want to alert her. She had lovely, long, brown hair and was wearing a sky-blue coat. Her hair swung from side to side as she walked and he could almost feel the silkiness of it. He crossed the street onto the other pavement so she wouldn't notice him. She walked towards the park and pulled her hood further over her head. He kept up with her but was careful to stay several yards behind. He was sweating now as he already knew what he was going to do – and perspiration and a dry mouth was all part of the excitement. *The thrill of the chase,* he thought and smiled. He'd built up in his mind how good this 'incident' was going to be – the final moments were what he enjoyed most.

She suddenly stopped walking and turned around – but of course, there was no one there. She continued along the pavement but there was only a little light – only a few street lamps standing quite far apart. She could hear very faint footsteps – perhaps a little distance away, but they were regular and seemed to stop when she stopped. A couple of seconds later, she stopped again. It was very dark now and the rain was getting heavier. He removed his shoes for silence and felt the wetness seep into his socks. He crossed back again to the other side of the road where she was, only made his way several yards in front. Luckily, the whole road was empty and the rain seemed to be keeping people indoors. Now he was facing her and looked as if coming from the opposite direction. She began to speed up and soon came face to face with him. She paused and so did he. "Can I help you, miss?" he asked softly. "Is there something wrong?"

She too was sweating and she reached out as though to touch his shoulder for reassurance, before blurting out, "I think someone's following me – could you please walk with me – I live quite near – it's just I'm scared. I know I'm being cheeky, but I really need your help."

She was a pretty woman and of course he agreed to walk her home. "No problem," he said and they walked on in silence. He noticed she wore quite the wrong shoes for the weather – they were white and her bare toes peeped out. The nails were painted a bright red. *Not for her,* he thought – *too cheap and bold. She should have worn a soft, pink colour.*

"Just a few yards ahead now – I live over there." And she pointed ahead. He was watching her closely now but she didn't look at him. "I'll just get my key." She rummaged in an oversized handbag and fished out a key. "Just here," she said, and turned into a pathway that led to a blue front door. There were no lights in the building and that helped build his confidence.

"Thank you so much – you made my walk home easier." She reached up to put the key in the lock but never quite made it. She was wearing a chiffon scarf – it was lilac and very pretty. He grabbed the scarf from behind and pulled her around to look into her face. The scarf was made of strong material and the sharpness of the chiffon bit into her neck.

She looked petrified and he smiled and said, "You really shouldn't be out on your own on a night like this." She couldn't speak but just stared into his eyes, which were round and shining in the darkness. He twisted the scarf around and around and clasped it in his hands. He squeezed hard until her beautiful, blue eyes glazed over and her tongue began to loll out of her mouth. The last thing he saw in those eyes, was an image of himself, smiling in satisfaction. She went limp in his hands and he let her fall onto the wet path. He looked at her lying there and felt exhilarated. He had done a good job – he hadn't let her cry out and the rain and wind had kept the street quiet – she had come home but would never do so again. She had died quite quickly and looked so lovely lying there in the puddles as if she was just asleep, her long, brown hair covering one side of her face. *A good death,* he thought and congratulated himself again. Her red toenails sparkled pitifully with rain drops.

He could hear her phone ringing inside the flat and he knew he'd have to move quickly – someone might be curious if she didn't answer – maybe it was the friend from the cinema, checking if she'd got home all right. Well, she did get home – he'd seen to that. He bent down and pulled the lilac scarf from her neck. It left red welds on her skin and had actually cut into her neck in places. He liked to take a souvenir when he'd done something like this – and he was certainly proud of the way he'd dispatched her – quietly and efficiently. The 'incident' was over and he quickly whipped his smart phone from his pocket and angled it so that her whole length was captured – he liked to have a photograph of his victims although he kept them hidden under a password. That was one for the album, as people said.

Stealthily, he left the path and checked if the street was empty, before walking home. The lilac scarf was safely tucked into his anorak pocket and he walked quickly, reliving those wonderful moments when she went limp in his arms. Arriving home, he had a stiff drink, as was his usual practice after 'an incident' and went into his Trophy Room, as he liked to call his spare bedroom. He opened the bottom drawer of a bureau and looked at the six – quite miscellaneous objects – that lay there side by side. There was a small handbag, a perfume bottle, one odd shoe amongst several other things. Each one brought him a clear memory and he relished the thought of all those lives he'd ended. He placed the lilac scarf in the drawer and quietly closed it again. *Mother would like that scarf,* he thought.

"Supper time," he said to no one in particular, "I think pizza would be rather tasty." And he ate it all, followed by a custard tart – his favourite cake. His food actually seemed to taste better after an 'incident'. "I'll wash the dishes in the morning." Again, said to no one and off he went with a book tucked under his arm and enjoyed a good night's sleep. His conscience was clear because he'd ended her life painlessly and with care – just the way he always did. Just think of all the misery and sadness she might have had to experience in her life – he'd saved her from that. A good job!

His phone woke him in the morning. "Peter, Peter – where are you? You've got a viewing at nine o'clock – and it could be a good one." The voice hung in the air until he'd shaken himself awake.

"All right, all right – I'm coming. Make them a cup of coffee until I get there." And it only took him ten minutes to dress and arrive at the shop. He didn't even look dishevelled. He was impeccably dressed, as an estate agent should be.

"Good morning, I'm Peter and I'm delighted to meet you. Ah good, you've had your coffee – shall we make a start?" And he ushered them out of the shop, raising his eyes at Jennifer, the receptionist, as he did so. She just smiled – he always got off with everything.

He'd seen that girl before – looking out of the window of the house next door to the sale house. She was rather pretty and had her hair tied in a ponytail. *Must find out who she is,* and he made a mental note. He showed the middle-aged couple around the house, pointing out all the good things and failing to mention the bad ones. They were very interested, he could tell. He was good at his job and within a week, he had their deposit in his hand and their signatures on paper. He wandered back to the house he'd just sold. The girl wasn't there but the milkman was just going in the garden gate.

"Does anyone live at that house?" He pointed at the blond girl's house. He was carrying a camera and a briefcase, so he looked like a businessman on a mission.

"Oh yes, sir – Young Lilly lives there but she won't be home at this time of day. She teaches at the local school." The milkman laughed at Peter's crestfallen look. "She only wants one pint today – her parents are away." And he went whistling on his way, already having told the stranger too much.

The sun was quite blinding and Peter closed the shop blinds. Jennifer looked up from her work and said, "You're not supposed to do that, Peter – the window should always look welcoming for customers."

"My, what a goodie-goodie you are. I'm also supposed to be able to see what I'm doing – as should you, miss." He was about ten years older than she was and he liked working with her. She was a pretty girl of about twenty-five. He'd asked her out a couple of times but she'd always turned him down so he was careful now not to show his interest. He shouldn't have pushed his luck asking her out more than once – but he had to try, didn't he?

He said, "I've got a valuation to do, Jennifer – I'll see you later." And he was off. It was time for the Secondary Schools to come out and he liked ogling the girls in their school uniforms. He was well dressed and looked respectable, so the one girl sitting on a park bench, wasn't bothered when he sat down beside her. She glanced at him and then turned back to reading her book. She must have been fifteen or sixteen so old enough for him to be interested. He could see she was the studious type so he started a conversation about literature and would move on to another subject once he learned more about her.

"Good story?" he asked innocently as a squirrel crept closer to his feet and the girl suddenly looked interested. "Tame little chaps, aren't they?" He fumbled in his pocket and fished out a crumbled biscuit which the squirrel grabbed and ran away. "Do you like animals?" he asked her and she responded enthusiastically.

"Oh, I do – all sorts of animals, really." She was still watching the squirrel.

He asked, "I don't suppose you have any spare time either today or tomorrow? I'm thinking about going to the zoo and perhaps you'd like to come with me?"

"Oh no, I couldn't – I don't even know you." She seemed quite shocked at his suggestion.

"Oh do go on – I'm quite harmless – just lonely. I'll meet you here tomorrow if you'd rather?" He was careful not to pressure her.

She hesitated and then said, "All right, but I have no money – you'll have to pay." She stood up and put the book in her satchel. "See you tomorrow, then." And she was gone. *As easy as that*, he thought. Too easy in fact – she'll deserve all she gets was his first thought. And he went off whistling to do his fictitious valuation.

"Another valuation?" Jennifer asked the next day, as he reached for his smart phone. She was obviously curious about the fact that he went out nearly every day at the same time. "Well, it is my job, you know." He spoke rather more sharply than usual.

"It's just that I knew nothing about it, that's all – and I am the receptionist you know and you should log all your appointments through me." She liked to be as professional as she could.

"Good bye, smart ass." And he banged the door closed. At the park, there sat his little friend, reading as usual. He scooped her up and they made their way to the zoo, which wasn't very far.

"What do you want to see first?" he asked and they spent what turned out to be an enjoyable hour wandering around the grounds. They both had an ice cream which attracted a nuisance of bees.

He asked her, "Why do you have so much free time? You seem to be able to come and go as you please. Don't your parents get worried about where you are?"

"They don't care where I am or what I'm doing." She shrugged her shoulders and looked rather sad. *Ah*, he thought, *a neglected child – all the better.*

"Let's finish off with the monkeys, they're always good for a laugh." And they strolled over to the monkey enclosure. It was at the edge of the zoo and there must have been about ten or fifteen monkeys jumping around, stretched out on tree branches or just grooming each other. She fished some nuts from her pocket and held them out through the fence. One big monkey came over – he wasn't cautious at all – it was as though he knew her.

"I've fed him before," she explained, "my dad used to bring me here before he left us." She put her hand over her mouth – she hadn't meant to say that, but Peter was already going around to the back of the enclosure.

"Come on, there's more of them around here." And she followed him. There were no people around but then the light was fading and the zoo would soon close. "Come on, Molly." He'd managed to learn her name – not an easy task, as she was very guarded, especially about her family life.

"Look at that little family in the corner there." He pointed at a cute group of monkeys and noticed the big monkey had followed them towards the back of the enclosure. Peter realised that, if he moved quickly, he would have enough time for an 'incident'. He stood behind her and looked at her young, slim neck – he thrust both hands around it and found it didn't take much force to finish her off. She was quite frail. His fingers almost touched each around her neck, so slim was she. A delicate, young girl on the brink of womanhood, but who'd never get there now, and all thanks to him. She slipped from his hands and he pulled her up against the fence as though she was talking to the monkeys. She was such a young girl – he almost felt some pity for her – but not enough to stop him getting his phone out of his pocket. He took her picture for his collection. He also emptied her satchel and took her pencil case before going back to the front and walking smartly – but not too quickly – towards the exit. Strangely enough, the big monkey seemed to be watching him, as though he understood what had just happened. But of course he hadn't – he was a monkey after all.

Next morning, before work, he sorted out the Trophy Room, carefully lying Molly's pencil case close beside the lilac scarf. It all looked so tidy and as it should be. He then got ready for Church every Sunday, he met his mother there and then had lunch with her. It had become a regular thing – a ritual in fact – as he'd been doing it since he was a schoolboy. There she sat, in her usual pew near the front of the Church – she believed herself to be very important and as such, chose her seat carefully. She nodded when she saw Peter and he made his way up the aisle. The Vicar was just climbing into the pulpit and people were having their last coughs – they hoped – before the service began. The sermon was all about loving your neighbour and honouring your father and mother – not very original, he thought. Mother leaned forward and actually told him to sit up straight, "You're in Church, young man, behave as though you are." God, he hated his mother and yet, at the same time, he believed he loved her. He'd always had this dilemma – one day he hated her and next day, he didn't.

Following lunch, which was the same menu as all other Sundays, Peter said he'd have to leave early as he had a viewing that afternoon. "Really, Peter – it's Sunday. You shouldn't be working today." She was in a bad mood now and tutted loudly.

He had formed the habit of returning to the scene of the 'incidents'. He'd read somewhere that a killer always did that and so he did. There was a police presence at the zoo and they were questioning everyone. There were 'Do Not Cross' barriers around the monkey area and the back of the enclosure was completely shut off. At the main entrance, there were two policemen, talking to some people as they came through. A zoo worker was standing by the fence and Peter asked what had happened. The man told him a young girl had been found murdered that morning and the police were looking for clues. He obviously knew no more than that.

Suddenly, Molly's big monkey came rushing over to Peter as though he knew him. He reached behind his back and fouled into the palm of his hand. The smell was abominable. He came close to the fence and threw the excrement through the wire right at Peter. It went all down his Sunday suit and dripped onto the ground. The monkey was staring at Peter and was wailing and making screeching sounds. He was banging his chest. *What a disgusting thing to happen*, he thought but he couldn't even get his handkerchief out of his pocket. The monkey's eyes were round and staring and there was such hatred in them, that, could he have spoken, he would have said 'I know it was you'. Peter felt very ill at ease.

"I've never seen that before – and I've been their keeper for twenty years, Well, I never did. I can only apologise on his behalf, sir. What a bad boy," he shouted at the monkey and rattled the fence with a stick.

74

Peter fled the scene as quickly as he could. God the smell was dreadful. Luckily, he reached home without meeting anyone he knew, although even strangers gave him a curious look.

As usual, the following Sunday, Peter left for Church. As he went through the great wooden door, he saw the building was already half full. Near the front, he saw the girl with the blonde ponytail standing before the glorious stained-glass window. Reds, royal blues, yellows and greens were all reflected around the walls and the girl stood there in rapt concentration, staring at the beauty of the colours. She didn't have a ponytail today – her long, pale blond hair framed her pretty face and hung in soft folds to below her shoulders. The red and blue sparkled like jewels on her hair and made her hair look even more alive. She looked so beautiful, he could hardly take his eyes off her but then she moved slightly and only the red was reflected in the hair – in fact, it covered the whole girl for a few seconds and he saw a distorted version of a woman, like a red devil standing on holy ground. He shivered and the hairs on the back of his neck stood on end – it was like a premonition of something bad emanating from her towards him. He told himself not to be silly and then his mother's shrill voice broke the spell and she called him over to her pew. The girl too walked in the same direction and settled in the pew in front of Peter's own. His mother obviously had met her before, as she said, "Good morning, Lilly – how nice to see you." He had the same need to watch her as he had with most of his victims and when the service was over, he managed to leave the church at the same time as she did – and his mother joined them of course.

"Would you care to come for some lunch – only salad, I'm afraid – but it's so warm today." Lilly said she'd love to come and Peter moved to the outside of the pavement to walk beside the ladies. They ate the limp salad in the sunny garden and when mother went indoors to fetch some trifle, Peter took the opportunity of asking Lilly if she'd like to go to the cinema with him the next night. He wasn't a particularly sexually motivated man – he had never raped his 'incidents' but the beauty he liked in his victims, gave him enormous pleasure. Unfortunately, Lilly said she couldn't but thanked him for his kindness. *Damn it,* was Peter's reaction.

When mother came back with the sweet, she began her usual way of discussing Peter as though he wasn't there. "He was a difficult boy to live with and he was most unhappy at school. He never managed to make any friends; you know – no one ever wanted to play with him. A thoroughly miserable child – and he's not much better now, to tell the truth." She was on her favourite subject now, condemning her only child.

A cringing Peter and an embarrassed Lilly fidgeted in their seats – but mother didn't notice. She always rubbished her son and ended the tirade by adding, "I really think that's why his father left us – such a miserable child." The miserable child was contemplating how it would feel to put his hands around that sagging neck and squeeze as hard as he could. But he just smiled in apology to Lilly. "Mother really is the limit, I'm afraid," he said.

"May I walk you home, Lilly? Unless of course, you'd like to stay longer?" He was desperate to get away from his damned mother. Luckily, she was ready to go home and he did indeed walk with her, knowing full well where she lived. He left her there and returned home to an evening in front of the television. Other than his job, he led a quiet life and indulged himself with a couple of hobbies. He had many lead soldiers which he used to plan battle strategies – on this occasion, some were British and some were French from Napoleon Bonaparte's main battle with the Duke of Wellington. This may seem strange when coupled with his serial killings but it was something in which he'd always been interested since childhood, in fact he and his dad used to play a lot with them, taking sides and discussing strategies. He actually involved his Trophy Drawer in the game now and whichever side won the skirmish of the moment, was awarded one of his precious victims' souvenirs. He got a lot of pleasure from this – it seemed as though he was killing the victims all over again, with less excitement perhaps but them he didn't give them the award to keep – after all, they belonged to him. When he was younger, he'd had to play by himself once his dad had left the family home, so he was used to taking on both sides of the battle. His mother had no interest whatsoever in his hobbies but then she had no interest in anything about him.

He continued to follow women about the streets – any woman would do, but they had to be reasonably good looking although not always young. He loved the thrill of the chase and he couldn't keep track of the number of women who might have been 'incidents' if things had gone to plan – but of course, they didn't always. He was a good stalker he thought, as they never spotted him, or if they did, they never showed it. Poor Peter, he just couldn't find a girlfriend in the normal way – but then, he was probably too good for most of them. In fact, if he had had a girlfriend, he wasn't sure what he'd do with her. Being in love wasn't something he particularly wanted. Possession and power were more to his liking.

One afternoon, going back to the shop for a few minutes' respite, he found Jennifer chatting to a young woman, who turned out to be an old school friend. "Come and meet Rosie, Peter – she was a real tomboy at school." Rosie laughed and told him not to believe her.

"Hello, Rosie, can I interest you in a house for sale perhaps?" He joked and went to switch on the kettle. "Or maybe a cup of coffee instead?"

"Coffee would be lovely – but not the house at this time, I'm afraid." He watched her surreptitiously as she chatted with Jennifer. She wasn't his type at all – she was short and had bright ginger curly hair and a very freckled face. She seemed a nice person though – happy and cheerful. He gave her the cup of coffee and offered her a Ginger Nut biscuit – but was careful not to mention the pun about the ginger.

"Do you live far from here, Rosie?" And he settled down to have a chat with the girls. It was odd but he always felt more comfortable in the company of women – men always seemed to be judging him and finding him wanting. "I know where that is – not too far from here really," he said. Rosie nodded and helped herself to another biscuit.

When she finally left the shop, Jennifer asked him, "Well, did you like her? She's always been a nice girl."

"She seems okay but I don't much like her hair colour." He couldn't resist saying. However, he began to hang around outside her house – she lived in a downstairs flat of a much bigger house and although he didn't find her attractive, he liked her as a person. His pleasure came from watching women when they weren't aware of his presence. One day, however, she spotted him across the street from her house and opened the window to call out his name.

"Come on in and have a drink, if you like," she shouted and innocently saw no danger in inviting him inside where she'd be alone with him. She was that sort of friendly girl who had no idea she might be moving towards the end of her life.

"Tell me about yourself, Rosie – what work do you do?" He felt very comfortable and at ease. He wasn't used to being alone in a woman's house with no one else around but she was open and friendly so he felt himself relaxing against the comfy armchair. She'd brought out a china teapot and some buttered scones from the small kitchen. *A very polite girl,* he thought, *pity about the hair.* She told him she taught kindergarten children and that she loved her job.

"They're all so cute and loving – of course we have the odd 'pee-pee' accident but that's easy to deal with." She held out the scones to her visitor.

"Those are lovely pearls you're wearing, Rosie – they really suit you." He was still on his best behaviour. "Are you expecting anyone else today – or are you having a rest day?"

"No – no one else and I actually have two days off work now, so I'm feeling pretty good." He found himself thinking, *I'll soon put a stop to that.* He'd already made up his mind that an 'incident' was going to take place in the very near future.

He leaned forward on the chair and asked, "Did they call you carrots at school by any chance – or were there other names as well?"

"Oh they called me carrots all right and many other names besides – but always derogatory, spiteful ones. Children know how to hurt you, don't they? And they don't hold back." Rosie actually looked upset at the memory.

"I know all about that. They used to call me 'Mummy's Boy' until I reached sixteen and managed to stop my mother coming to meet me after school. The other boys never considered how much it hurt and when I explained to mother to try to stop her meeting me, she just laughed and told me I'd have to get a thicker skin. She never understood anyone else's problems – just her own." He was on his feet by this time and had crossed to the window behind the sofa where Rosie was sitting. He imagined how the pearls would feel, biting into her neck and turned around slowly, gently touching her cheek. His big hands closed round her neck and it took only a few moments for her to pass out. Her head fell forward, the string that held the pearls broke and all the little beads rattled across the floor. The broken necklace didn't stop him – he just went right on squeezing until he knew for sure, she'd stopped breathing. She went a blue colour which didn't go well with her red hair. The poor little, curly-haired girl was just a crumpled heap now, hanging over the sofa edge.

"Well, carrots, no one will ever call you that again, well not that you'll know anyway." He poured himself a fresh cup of tea and helped himself to another scone, before settling back on the chair and crossing his legs. At least Rosie wasn't staring at him – she was just a sagging bundle. He laid her down on the floor and straightened her legs. She was wearing large, hooped earrings, one of which he yanked from her ear and caused a trickle of blood to run down her cheek. He stared at her for a while and then had a good idea – the earring would be his souvenir but some red curls would look great in his Trophy Drawer. He fetched some scissors from the kitchen and snipped off some of her ginger curls from the crown of her head. The colour didn't look so bad when it wasn't attached to a face covered in freckles. Yes, she looked better now. He'd helped her already.

"Well Rosie, I'm going to love you and leave you – well not that exactly but I am going to leave you." And he put the curls into a small plastic bag that he'd had with him. "Bye, carrots – nice to have met you." And he left her place as cautiously as he'd entered it. He wandered along the wet streets and bought some fish and chips for supper. He loved that smell, but then so did everyone else.

Afterwards, he very carefully laid his most recent souvenir in the Trophy Drawer – it looked rather odd, compared to the others, but that was a good thing because it made it more interesting. In fact, next time he had a battle between his soldiers, he'd award the curly red hair as a medal to whoever won. A nice touch.

A week later, he was astonished when he opened his front door to find two policemen standing on his doorstep. "Hello, gentlemen, and what can I do for you?" He was as smooth as ever. "Do come inside, would you like a cup of tea perhaps?"

"No thank you, sir, we just have a few questions to ask and then we'll be out of your hair." The older one had white stripes on his sleeve so he must be in charge. They came into the sitting room and sat down on the sofa. "Now. sir, we need you to tell us where you were a week ago today – sometime in the afternoon?"

Peter bristled. "How can you expect me to remember something like that? Which day was that? My works diary may be able to help." And he left the room to fetch it. The two policemen looked at each other.

"He got a bit angry rather easily, didn't he?" One said to the other.

Peter came back into the room, "Yes, I can tell you where I was that afternoon. I was doing one of my usual inspections of properties that have been on the market for some time – on the market with other estate agents, that is. I call in and courteously ask if they'd ever considered having a valuation done by another agency. We can pick up quite a bit of business by doing that. I was in Fore Street, Forrester Green and Berwick Road that day – I didn't pick up any new business. It's the way it pans out sometimes."

"Have you anything to prove that's where you were – any notes of people you spoke with or who perhaps said they might be interested in your agency taking over their sale?" the second policemen asked.

"Unfortunately not. As I said, I didn't manage to pick up any new business that day. By the way, do you mind telling me why you're asking these questions?" Peter realised he should have asked that at the beginning of the conversation. But, better late than never.

"No, sir, we don't mind at all. Have you read about the young girl who was murdered in her home on the day in question?" And Peter said he'd read something vague about it but he didn't pay it too much attention.

"Your receptionist hasn't said anything to you about the murder? The dead girl was an old school friend of hers and she's very upset about it."

"That's unusual. Jennifer usually talks to me about most things and strangely, I only met an old school friend of hers a couple of weeks ago. It wasn't that girl who was murdered, was it? I remember her vaguely – a short girl with very red curly hair – I think her name was Rosie or something like that." He began to sweat rather a lot.

"Yes, I'm afraid it was her sir – Rosie Smith. She died in her own home. She was strangled and some of her hair was cut off." They were watching him closely but he didn't bat an eye lid.

"Sorry, gentlemen, I only met her once – when Jennifer introduced her to me. I've never seen her since that day. Did Jennifer tell you about that meeting – well, obviously she did or you wouldn't be here now. Poor little girl – what a dreadful thing to happen. Well, is there anything else I can help you with before you leave?" The policemen said there wasn't but also that they might have to come back at a later date. They asked him if, in the meantime, he could check and see if he had any evidence to confirm his movements on the day in question.

He agreed and saw the policemen out the door. He really was sweating now and fetched himself a stiff drink – he really needed that. He sat for a while, going over in his mind what he'd said about the murdered girl. He didn't think he'd said anything out of place – he could hardly deny that he'd met Rosie – Jennifer would have told them even if he hadn't. He put his glass down, went into the trophy room and was glad that his toy soldiers were still spread out on the table. A good battle was what he needed and he stood up several of them – the ones who'd died in the previous battle. *And the award for winning will be Little Rosie's red curls – a suitable medal if ever there was one.* He was angry with Jennifer – she had to bring his name into it, didn't she?

He'd been very lucky so far. When he considered how many women he'd killed, he knew he'd been pretty lucky. This was the first time he'd been questioned by the police. Amazing when one thought of how small the radius was where the victims were found. Still, that wasn't his problem – that was up to the police. Jennifer, however, was another matter – she could be dangerous for him. *Think, think,* he told himself, *what can I do to silence her?* He knew the answer to that but that would be too risky so soon after Rosie's death. He'd have to be patient and calm down – tomorrow was Sunday so he'd be going to mother's for lunch. Although she was a blasted nuisance, he seemed calmer after he'd heard more of her gibbering. He sat down to work out who the two sides in the battle would be. The First World War was always a good time for his battles – lots of death and blood. Yes, the First World War it was – in France of course and just to make things more interesting, he'd have the Germans win this one, making sure that all of the Brits never went home again. That was the power he had – just like after an 'incident', it made him feel great to change what happened in history – sort of like God really. Patriotism didn't enter his head. Their victory at WW1 didn't affect him – it suited him to believe that.

The next day in the office was awkward. Jennifer seemed to know the police had been to see him and asked how he'd got on with them.

"All right really, they were pretty reasonable. I explained the only time I met Rosie was here with you and they were quite happy with that." Peter was watching her expression closely.

"Funny that, 'cause I spoke with Rosie the day after her visit here and she mentioned that she'd seen you in her street. What were you doing there – we've got nothing for sale around there, have we?"

"Exactly the reason I may have been there. I don't remember going there but I do try to wander the streets at least once a week to keep my eye on potential properties. When you're a real estate agent, you'll do the same. You've always got to keep your eyes on the open market. Are you going to make some coffee now that you've interrogated me – perhaps you're a special policeman?" He felt some sarcasm was needed to shut her up.

"No, I'm not that – just a curious person who lost an old friend after introducing her to you. That's all. I'm sorry if it sounds as though I'm accusing you of something – I don't think I am." And she got up to make the coffee. Yes, he'd have to keep an eye on her.

That week at Church, blond Lilly wasn't there and he was disappointed. He mentioned it to mother who didn't even bother to reply. She started on him instead. "Really Peter, you seem to be losing weight and it's not very attractive. Do you feed yourself properly?"

He reassured her that he did and went on to say, "Mother, I can't come home for lunch today – instead, could I come for tea on Wednesday? It's just that house sales are picking up now and there's one or two things I have to do. Would that be all right?"

"I suppose so," she said, "it doesn't really make much difference to me when you come. I know if you had your way, you'd stop coming all together – but I'm not going to make that easy for you." She never ceased to amaze him, the way she managed always to turn things around so that he was the bad one, doing something to hurt her. He left her as soon as the service was over and hurriedly made his way home. His mind had already worked out a plan and going to his mother's on Wednesday was part of that. He secured a sleeping draught from the doctor, complaining that he couldn't sleep lately and his work was suffering because of it. The doctor swallowed it.

"Only take this for three nights – as it's quite strong – and you shouldn't need it for longer than that to change your sleeping pattern." The doctor had no reason to doubt what Peter was saying, as he hadn't needed a doctor much in the past.

"Okay, doc – many thanks for listening to me." And he left with the sleeping draught safely in his pocket. Needless to say, he didn't take any of it as he had another purpose for it all together.

The next couple of days in the office were quiet and he and Jennifer hardly spoke. "Is there something wrong with you?" he asked the receptionist, not really caring whether there was or not.

"Nothing whatsoever but I need to take Thursday off – it's Rosie's funeral – perhaps you'd like to attend with me?" She watched his face.

"Why on earth should I – I only met her once? She was your friend, not mine. Oh by the way, I need you to do a property valuation on Wednesday but the owner won't be available until six o'clock in the afternoon. Unfortunately, it's right on the edge of the town and you'll have to get a train there and back again. I'm really sorry, Jennifer – but I can't do it myself. I have another valuation in the exact opposite part of town."

"Oh, Peter – that's a bit of a drag and so far out of town. Can't you change the time?" She plonked his coffee in front of him, spilling it on the paper he was working on.

"No, can't do, I'm afraid – it's the only time they can make it. Come on, Jennifer, I don't ask you to do this sort of thing very often, do I? And it would help me out a lot." He mopped up the spilt coffee with a tissue.

She agreed reluctantly and told him he owed her one. "Oh, don't worry, I'll be sure to pay you back in some other way." Of course, she never picked up on the sarcasm.

On the day in question, he had to remind her to leave in time to catch the train. She grabbed her bag and coat and rushed into the street. "See you tomorrow, Peter." And she was gone.

The night was darkening already – it had been cloudy all day. He left the shop within minutes of her going and made his way to his mother's home. There she was as usual, watching one of her favourite programmes on the telly. "Hello, mother – what's for tea?" he called from the lobby. He still had a key of his own so could let himself in when necessary. "Don't get up, mother, watch the rest of your programme. I'll make us a nice cup of tea." And he did that. She let him of course – she'd always been a lazy woman. He put a whole packet of the sleeping draught into her china mug and put two of her favourite biscuits on a plate. "Here you are, mum – drink it while it's sweet and hot." And she grabbed the biscuits from the plate and gulped the tea down. "I'd like a second cup, Peter, and some more of those biscuits." No please or thankyou – just as normal. He took her cup and went back into the kitchen – but when he returned, she was fast asleep, her head leaning back against the sofa and her mouth wide open. *Not a pretty sight,* he thought and washed and tidied away the cups before going into his bedroom where he kept a jogging suit, trainers and a woollen hat. He'd been a keen cyclist some time back and he kept these things at mother's along with his speed cycle. From the garage, he got out the cycle and off he went. It was rainy so he had to be careful of skidding.

He cycled for a good half an hour before reaching the road where he'd sent Jennifer. He hid the bike in an open gateway and jogged along to the house he'd told her was to be valued. He could see her silhouette through the glass panel of the front door – she was talking to someone. The door opened and he could hear her voice. "I am so dreadfully sorry; my boss must have got his wires crossed. I've disturbed your evening and I hope you'll forgive me."

Sounds of a man's voice making soothing noises. "Oh don't let it worry you, my dear" and "It really doesn't matter" and "Safe journey home" came floating towards Peter. She walked down the garden path and he hid behind a handy hedge. She walked quickly, clutching her notebook to her chest. He followed at a safe distance, catching up with her a few moments later but not too close to the house she'd just left.

He reached out and put a stranglehold on her – his strong, right arm tightly around her neck. He'd chosen the spot well as there was a very tall and thick hedge of bushes along the nearside of the pavement. He dragged her into the hedge and squeezed her neck even tighter. She was crying out – luckily not too loudly, so he slapped her across the face with his other hand. "Pipe down, you little interfering bitch." She managed to look into his eyes and knew exactly who he was and what he was planning to do.

"Please, Peter…" She managed to get out but of course, he just laughed.

"You shouldn't have interfered, Jennifer – you've got to pay the price now." And he jerked her neck abruptly to one side and heard it crack. Her neck was broken and she slipped from his grasp onto the ground. He looked down at her and felt no pity at all. *No one had asked her to interfere, had they? She'd brought this on herself.* He pulled her gold locket from her neck and took out his camera. That was all he wanted – just his usual souvenir and photo. He dragged her body deeper into the bushes and left her there on the wet grass. "Goodbye, Miss Jennifer, parting is such sweet sorrow." And he went back to the gateway where his bike was.

Going back the way he'd come took a lot less time than coming had done – the mass exodus from peoples' work had ceased and the roads were clearer. He soon reached his mother's house and quietly put the bike back into the garage. He used his key and got into the house, relieved to find his mother still asleep on the sofa, mouth still hanging open. In his bedroom, he hung the jogging suit on the outside of the wardrobe to dry and put his trainers away. His work suit that he'd left on the bed, was waiting for him and in shirtsleeves, he went into the kitchen to boil the kettle and make some cheese sandwiches. As was usual after an 'incident', he was hungry and thirsty and carried the tray into the sitting room, turning down the TV sound as he did. He didn't want to wake her with a fright.

"Mother – Mother – time to wake up. You've been asleep for a long time." He took the newspaper from her lap and reminded himself to check what programmes she would have been watching, as he would be claiming he had watched them with her. "Mother – time to wake up – look there's fresh sandwiches and a pot of tea for you."

She stirred but in a very groggy way, she slurred. "Peter, is that you?" And she sat up slowly. "I've been asleep Peter, haven't I?"

"Yes, you have – but you must have needed it or you wouldn't have slept at all." He poured her tea and put a couple of sandwiches on a plate. "Oh dear, you were tired, weren't you? What on earth have you been doing today?"

She got up and staggered towards the door. "Must spend a penny first, Peter." And when she came back, she was much more awake and compos mentis. "Why did you let me sleep so long – really, you never do anything right. Turn the sound up on the telly, I can't hear it."

"By the way, mother, I was thinking of sleeping here tonight. It's so rainy tonight and so cosy in here. Is that okay?" He was desperate for her to agree but she could be so unpredictable sometimes – he never knew what she'd say.

"Do as you like." And she bit into the bread so greedily wondering why she was so hungry. Then she remembered she'd missed tea. "I'm going to have to go straight to bed as soon as I've finished this. I can't imagine why I'm so tired – but I am."

That suited him fine; he could look at his souvenir of Jennifer after mother had gone. "Goodnight, mother – I shan't disturb you when I leave in the morning." And he finished his tea before getting himself a real drink. Before getting into bed, he put his tracksuit back where it was kept and cleaned his trainers – just in case.

In the office next afternoon, the police arrived. He'd been expecting them. After all, Jennifer did work there. They told him about Jennifer being found dead at the other side of town – he swallowed hard and felt the tears come into his eyes. "You're sure it's Jennifer? I spoke with her just last night before she left to do a viewing. No...no...I can't believe it – yes, I admit she hasn't turned up for work today and that's unusual – I have tried to ring her twice but there's no answer. I was planning to go to her house at the end of the day – but now you're telling me I won't find her there. I thought she just had a cold or something – but not this." He sat down on his chair, ash grey and held his head in both hands. "Why would anyone want to kill Jennifer? She was such a lovely girl."

"That's what we hoped you'd tell us. We need to know your whereabouts last night and if you know of anyone who might want to hurt her. They were there for a whole hour and he had to put the 'Closed' sign on the door. He explained how he'd stayed at his mother's the previous night – she'd be able to confirm that – he had had tea with her, watched some telly and eventually went to bed. There was nothing exciting to tell them – nothing exciting ever happened around his mother.

"And as for someone hating Jennifer enough to kill her, no there's absolutely no one I can think of, everyone liked her." The police left him then but promised they'd be back with some more questions. In the meantime, they'd be going to see his mother.

Peter sat there for a while, feeling quite confident that he'd fooled the police. It was his and his mother's word against what they wanted to believe. Well, let them get on with it – it was their job after all. He fingered the locket in his pocket and felt some satisfaction that he'd been questioned by the police whilst he sat there with the murdered victim's gold locket in his pocket. Life was funny, wasn't it?

He got in touch with an agency who provided temporary staff – he couldn't manage everything on his own. She arrived two days later, a short, mousey girl who did nothing to get his adrenalin rising – but she was intelligent and soon picked up her duties. He contacted his mother to ask if the police had yet been to see her. They had but she told them the absolute truth, as she knew it. He'd been there all evening, had tea and slept there. She even confirmed he was still there in the morning as he left her some cereal on the kitchen table – very considerate, I'm sure, she told the police." Didn't take much effort to put out some cereal, did it?"

Towards the end of the week, he heard the shop doorbell jangle and looked up to see blond Lilly standing in front of his desk. "Now then, what can I do for you this fine morning?" He felt positive and cheerful. She told him she needed to talk to him and sat down, first removing her coat and scarf.

"I've been to see your mother this morning and she told me she was worried about you."

"Really?" He sounded disbelieving. "Mother never worried about me in her entire life. That I can confirm." He switched on the kettle to make them both a drink. *What was she saying then?* he wondered. Lilly was obviously very worked up about something and was tapping her heels in frustration. Peter remained jovial and said, "Well, spit it out then. What's the problem?"

"I heard about Jennifer this morning and was very shocked, especially after what happened to Rosie. I went straight to see your mother. I had to talk with a fellow-Church goer and she was the one who came to mind first – probably because she knows you so well. I suppose I've had my own suspicions about you for a while now, I found her in a confiding mood and she told me that she feared you've had something to do with the women who've been murdered over the last two or three years. Obviously, I didn't expect that and asked her why she thought that. She explained that the police had been to see her about you and that had scared her. She also told me about something she called a 'Trophy Drawer'." Lilly was crying and added, "She warned me to watch out, as you had your eyes on me and I could be next." Lilly fidgeted and wrung her hands before she went on, "Before I go to the police, I wanted to hear what you had to say." She looked expectantly at Peter who sighed deeply, stood up and came around to her side of the desk. He closed the blinds and put the 'Closed' notice in the window. Lilly got up quickly and started to reach for the door handle. He grabbed her hair and pulled her around to face him. His eyes were mad and staring and his face had actually changed almost beyond recognition – he clasped her neck and choked the life out of her. She went limp, slumped against the desk and breathed a heavy sigh, which turned out to be her last. He looked down at her, lying on the floor – her beautiful, golden hair loose and spread all over the floor. One minute, a lively beautiful girl and the next, a grotesque and twisted corpse. *All her own fault,* he told himself.

He felt very pleased with himself and tidied her dead body into a closet, first taking her coat belt as his souvenir and of course, a quick photo of her. Now he left the office, feeling on fire – he was on a killing spree and loving every minute of it. Now, to tackle Mother – how could she talk about him to a stranger and mention the 'Trophy Drawer'? Well, he'd soon find out.

Mother was in the kitchen preparing tea when Peter put his head around the door. "I didn't hear you come in. What do you want at this time of day?" She went on putting an omelette's ingredients together. He told her he wanted to talk with her. "Lilly came to see me earlier – did you know she was planning to do that?"

"Of course, I didn't – but from the way she was talking, I'm not surprised. I'm afraid, she's sussed you out, Peter – she believes you might have done the recent murders. I told her she was being ridiculous, but she did go on so."

"Maybe if you hadn't mentioned the 'Trophy Drawer' to her, I'd believe you tried to protect me – but she told me you were concerned that the murderer was me. That was pretty blatant, Mother, wasn't it?" He was being calm but he knew things were about to come to a head.

"On that subject, how's the 'Trophy Drawer' coming along these days? I hope you're keeping it nice and tidy, as I told you." She'd almost completed the preparation for the omelette.

"Oh yes, mother, the 'Trophy Drawer' is fine – filling up nicely, just as you instructed – each one representing the kind of woman Father probably went off with." Peter sat down at the table. "All except Jennifer, that is. You didn't want me to kill her, did you? You always liked her, but she became dangerous in the end and I had no option but to get rid of her. That was why I gave you the sleeping draught that night 'cause if you'd known what I was up to, you'd have tried to stop me, wouldn't you?"

"Yes, I would – she was too close to home for safety. I know you went to the other side of town to get her – but the girl in your office, really! Location-wise, you did the right thing – well away from this area – but the victim, oh no, that was particularly stupid."

He'd enjoyed carrying out his mother's wishes. Since his early twenties, she'd groomed him to murder miscellaneous women – the kind that made Father run away from them both.

"I'd like to see the 'Trophy Drawer', Peter – to see how it's coming along." She sat down opposite him and began to eat her meal, but she didn't get very far as her son leaped from his chair and came around behind her. He grabbed her head and twisted it almost all the way around. He'd always wanted to do this – he'd hated her all his life and was fed up doing things to please her. "You won't be seeing the 'Drawer', mother." And he relished looking into her bulging eyes – eyes that had never looked at him with love, just with disdain. He let her dead body drop under the table and sat down on her chair. The omelette looked good so he mustn't waste it. He ate every last crumb and wiped his mouth on the tablecloth. That would have upset her even more, he laughed and added, "You see, mother, I told you – I'm a good boy really."

Outside the house, he heard a police siren – it seemed to get louder until it stopped altogether. There was loud banging on the door and men's voices calling for the door to be opened. They burst in when he didn't move fast enough and grabbed hold of him. Heavy handcuffs were put on and one of the police said, "That's your mother, isn't it? You cruel bastard." And received an admonishing look from his colleague.

Peter was dragged into the street but he could see Lilly sitting in the back of the police car and he tried to walk over to her. He was stopped in his tracks by his captors and she shouted out the window, "You didn't quite manage it, Peter, did you? You didn't quite kill me – I phoned the police and told them you were coming here." She sat back against the leather and let the tears fall down her cheeks. The policewoman beside her put her arm around and tried to comfort her. Peter was thrown into the other car and whipped away just as the ambulance drew up to see to his mother.

"Too late for her," he called from the car window and was roughly pulled back inside.

"I wish I'd done a better job with the little blond. That was careless of me – to leave her still alive."

The day was over and Lilly – so close to death – was alive but with a very swollen neck. His mother however was declared dead and she hadn't even had her tea. *Poor old bitch,* her son thought.

The day of the trial dawned bright and sunny and the country as a whole, was interested in its outcome. The public part of the courtroom was packed with people who didn't even know Peter – but they knew what he'd done. A serial killer in their town and one who had killed even his own mother – was not something that happened every day. Peter was dressed in his best suit as he climbed the stairs into the dock, where he was flanked by two policemen. Everyone stood for the Judge's entrance and so it all began. The Prosecuting Barrister read the names of the deceased women and accused Peter of killing them one by one. He also produced the 'Trophy Drawer' and indicated the items it held and asked Peter if he recognised them. Peter said he did but added that he'd only been carrying out his mother's instructions.

"Mother told me to fill it up with souvenirs of the women – she told me they were the sort of women Father might have run away with – leaving his wife and me to fend for themselves." Peter looked directly at the Jury. "We worked well, mother and I – those women never suffered – we helped them out of what was probably an unhappy life." He looked genuinely concerned for their well-being.

The defending barrister took over at this point, asking, "Did you have to report to your mother after each death?" He was obviously attempting to make Peter a pitiful, dominated man who had to do everything his mother told him. "Did she check on your 'Trophy Drawer' often to see how it was filling up?"

"Oh yes, she always checked it – I had to keep it very tidy and she always liked to look at the photos I collected of the women – just to make sure I was telling the truth, you know." Peter looked proud at keeping his part of the agreement.

One by one, the victims' details were read out and Peter was asked on every occasion, if he had killed them and how exactly he had done it. He admitted to committing all of the murders – except that of his mother, of which he had no recollection. "I would never hurt mother," he said, "I loved her." The relatives of the victims were invited to make a statement from the Witness Box and the stories were heart breaking, each one coming from a close family member and causing some of the onlookers to break down in tears at what the man in the dock had done to all those families.

The trial was over after a few days and the Judge entered the courtroom to hear the Jury's verdict and to sentence the prisoner at the bar. There was little doubt as to the verdict. Peter was found guilty on all counts and before sentence was passed, the Judge spoke directly to the prisoner. "You are an evil man who committed atrocities such as I've not heard before – one by one, you murdered a series of women in a most barbaric way and for no reason whatsoever. You are a danger to humanity and to innocent women in particular. I have no option but to sentence you to a Full Life Sentence which means that you will die in prison. I cannot allow you to re-enter a society of innocent people. I realise that the Defence tried to paint you as a demented and pathetic man with no will of his own – other than his mother would allow – but that is a weak argument and not one I accept. You are not ill, just vicious." He turned to the guards then. "Take him down and let him begin his sentence." The Judge concluded and the courtroom cheered at his decision.

As Peter was led away, he turned and shouted, "But, I'm a good boy really – ask mother – she'll tell you." He disappeared down the steep flight of stairs to begin his life sentence.

He was shown his single cell and told he couldn't have his toy soldiers, something that hurt him more than being found guilty of murder. When he asked if his mother could come to see him, he was given a double blow on being told his mother was dead and he wouldn't see her ever again. Other than that, he quite liked his cell – it was his own after all – and he liked being allowed, and encouraged, to walk around the exercise yard every day. Now and again, he had conversations with his mother but he told her he couldn't have a 'Trophy Drawer' any more – the guards wouldn't let him. He did, however, walk in the exercise yard every day and got to know the prison building very well. He spotted a way to climb up some strong looking pipes and windowsills which would eventually reach the roof – that would be interesting – to look down on everything and everyone below.

He chose a dreary, wet day when not many prisoners were in the yard and he wrapped up well against the rain and walked around for a little while, before secreting himself in a corner where the pipes began. He had on his good trainers and so knew climbing would be easy. He started to climb upwards and did very well at first, but then it got a bit trickier as the pipe manifolds became further apart and he ran out of sills to grab onto. He managed though and despite the rain, he eventually reached the roof without anyone seeing him. He looked down and was amazed at how clearly he could see everything. He was careful not to stand too close to the edge in case he slipped. He sat down with his legs over the edge though and counted the only prisoners walking below – there were only three of them today.

Suddenly, there was a loud peel of thunder and a couple of minutes later, a huge flash of lightning. The noise was horrendous and the rain was pelting down now. It seemed as though the sky had opened. He looked down again but the men had run for shelter. Staring at the concrete below, he saw his two armies of soldiers lined up and facing each other. They had taken on a human form and wore different uniforms from each other and were carrying rifles and vicious looking spears. He wondered who the two sides were. They began to engage with each other, one side seemingly more powerful than the other and soon, there was a moving mass of bodies, fighting as though their lives depended on it – which of course they did.

Bodies were beginning to hit the ground. Peter watched closely, trying to decide the winning side when he suddenly noticed other figures amongst the armies. They were women – they were the women whom he'd murdered – all running around in the yard and shaking their fists at him. He covered his ears to try to shut out the screeching sounds they were making – but nothing could shut them out. He even saw there the big monkey from the zoo, beating his chest and snarling with big, uneven teeth. He was jumping up and down and shaking his fists at Peter. What on earth was he doing there – he hadn't been murdered? He had no right to be there. Then he spotted her, standing quite close to the monkey. His mother was one of them and she was as angry as all the others. Dressed in her Sunday best, she joined in the common cry and shouted, "Jump, jump. Damn you, Peter, jump." And the crowd shouted even louder.

91

His mother suddenly broke away from the others and stood alone in the middle of the crowd. There was another peel of thunder, followed by a ferocious flash of lightning that almost blinded Peter. Mother held her arms open to him and looked upwards into his eyes. "Come on now, Peter – you're a good boy really. You know what you have to do."

And he did. He stood up and stepped over the edge. As he crashed onto the concrete, all the figures disappeared – even the soldiers – and his brains spilled all across the ground. He could almost hear his mother's voice. "Now look at the mess you've made, Peter."

Had he been alive and witnessed this latest 'incident', he would have enjoyed it very much and would have said to his mother, "I did as I was told, mummy, you see I'm a good boy really."

But of course, he couldn't say it. The exercise yard was empty now and Peter was dead.

Identical but Not the Same

She'd managed to get a lower bunk at the Oxford Street tube station. She was very lucky as the station was full to the brim with people – businessmen, shop assistants, as well as shoppers in London for the day only, and people from some of the flats, houses and hotels dotted around the area. People from all walks of life, some very well off and some not well off at all. A varied mixture of humanity huddled together in the hope that they could escape the dreaded bombing of which the loud sirens were warning. German planes were above the city, their screaming drones drowning out ordinary conversations – although they were so far from the street level, deep in the bowels of the earth. The people knew, however, that they were safer there than in the buildings above.

The young girl on the bunk was screwed up in a tight ball, trying to stop the intense pain she was feeling. She was sixteen years old and very pregnant. She'd been sleeping rough in alleyways and shop door ways for a few nights recently so was grateful for the protection the roof of the station gave. She knew she was getting close to the moment her baby would be born and she was very frightened. She stuck her knuckles tightly into her mouth and bit down on her own hands. She could feel a wetness under her body and knew how close everything was. The unbidden thought came into her head. Where would she go after the birth? What would she do with the baby? How would she feed it and keep it warm? She pushed aside the unwelcome questions and focussed on the incredible pain she was experiencing.

Suddenly, a cool hand touched her forehead and a soothing voice asked, "What's your name, dear? Tell me your name and I'll try to help you."

Tracy looked around and saw a lovely face looking down at her. She tried to say her name but the pain stopped her from speaking. The woman wore a Red Cross band on her arm and wore a blue dress. On her head was a small white cap. She looked like an angel to Tracy, who suddenly lost the awful feeling of being alone. She was the nurse who attended any patients during an air raid and

93

she'd probably delivered more than one baby in her time. She asked the people closest to Tracy's bunk if they could move a bit further back and they did this quickly, the women in particular knowing full well the pain of giving birth to a child.

Needless to say, the word 'push' was soon heard and after a few moments, the first cry of a new born baby. "All right, my dear," the nurse said and wrapped the child in a towel she brought out of her medical bag, "now, you're going to have to be a brave girl and when I tell you, you must push again. They do say it never rains but it pours – so we're about to see your second baby. You're having twins, my dear." The nurse was on her knees and began to work with Tracy again, but not before she'd passed the baby to an onlooker to hold. Everyone standing nearby was speechless and tearful at the same time, all very relieved they were not the young girl on the bunk bed.

A new squalling sound erupted from a second child and the twin girls were born one minute apart, deep in the bowels of the earth and with bombs dropping from the sky overhead.

The mother never saw her daughters as she breathed her last within minutes after the second birth – as her lifeblood was seeping out of her young body.

By the next day, the scene was completely obliterated and the mattress from the bunk bed had been taken away, as had Tracy's body to the mortuary, to lie beside those people who'd been killed in the bombing raid that night. The kind nurse was catching a few hours' sleep before taking up her duty again in the tube station and the tiny twins had been taken to a local convent, where the nuns were looking after them as best they could. Newborn babies were not easy to look after without the mother but the nuns were competent at most things and if looking after the babies was what God wanted, then they'd get on with it. The firstborn girl was given the name Eve, after the first woman in the bible and the second, the name Maria, after the Lord's mother.

Discussed at the next meeting at the convent, it was agreed the babies could stay with the nuns until they became a little stronger. There was nowhere else they could go until an orphanage was found that wasn't already overflowing with children whose parents were dead. They realised great patience would be needed as well as some donated milk from kindly supporters who lived locally. In effect, the girls were brought up on tinned evaporated milk and the nuns were grateful for it.

They learned to walk and talk at about the same time although Eve, the first born, was just a bit bigger than her sister and of the two, seemed to be the leader. They were pretty little girls with shiny, straight, blond hair and vivid blue eyes. When either one of them looked at you, you had the feeling they could see right into your soul – so piercing were their eyes. There was no doubt they were identical twins – they were alike as two peas in a pod. Despite their start in life, they both survived and somehow grew, despite the poor rations the war made available. They helped the nuns by following them about the convent – each carrying a tiny duster in their pockets. They helped in the kitchens by bringing fresh vegetables from the garden and piling them onto the big wooden table in the middle of the room. They weren't allowed to touch any of the knives but they were each allowed a big wooden spoon, when it was pudding or cake day. Most of the nuns were very fond of them and would sneak little treats from any surplus ingredients – and the girls loved the nuns, well most of them anyway. It had to be said that Maria was just a little bit nicer than Eve, who had a bit of a temper and wasn't afraid to show it. There was a grudging edge to Eve's character – she always made sure she got the bigger half of everything. Maria never minded giving into her sister – and their relationship worked well.

It was unusual for the little girls to be allowed to stay at the convent but with the disruption of the war and the fact that no one knew if they'd even be alive the next day, rules were allowed to slip and the time passed without notice. The war was over and VE Day was celebrated by the nuns, just as it was by every person left alive in the country. On the morning of her fourth birthday, Maria woke up and looked across the room at Eve's bed. Unusually, it was stripped bare and there was no sign of her sister. Thinking, Eve had wet the bed in the night, Maria rubbed her sleepy eyes and slid out of bed. She cautiously opened the door and looked out into the corridor – there was no sign of Eve there – so she tiptoed along the cold floor looking for one of the nuns. Two nuns were in the kitchen preparing the other sisters' porridge and tea. Sister Angeline spotted little Maria and coughed loudly so the other nun was aware of her presence.

"Come and sit at the table, Maria – porridge is nearly ready." And she helped the little girl onto a stool and gave her a cup of milk.

"Where's Eve, Sister? She wasn't in her bed today." The nun looked embarrassed and began to cough nervously.

"Actually, Maria, Sister Clementine wants to have a word with you. As soon as you've finished breakfast, run along to her office but remember to knock before you go in." Sister Angeline studiously avoided the little girl's question and went on with her work.

As she'd been told, she knocked on the nun's office door and went in. "Hello Sister Clementine, you wanted to speak to me?" Maria was always polite, but couldn't help asking where Eve was.

"That's one of the things I wanted to talk to you about. Come and sit beside me on the sofa." And she held onto Maria's hand. She went on to explain that Eve had gone to live with another family and that they wouldn't be seeing her again. "She's got a new life now – and we mustn't grudge her that, must we? She had to leave very suddenly this morning and didn't want to wake you – you were still sound asleep." She could see the tears beginning to form in the child's eyes and she leaned forward and put her arms around the trembling shoulders. "But your life will continue here with us, except you'll soon be starting school in the classroom. You know Sister Antoinette teaches the local orphan children from around the convent – well, you'll be joining them as soon as you reach five. You'll enjoy that, won't you?" She gave the child a little squeeze before releasing her.

"Won't I see Eve again?" She knew the answer but had to ask the question again.

"That is correct, Maria – your room now belongs completely to you and we'll call it Maria's Room, shall we?"

"Yes please, Sister, may I go now?" The nun pointed to the door and the child went out into the corridor. With the passage of time, she became used to waking up with no Eve in the opposite bed.

She never really got over the way her sister was whisked away without a word of goodbye, but there was nothing she could do about it – and the sisters at the convent continued to look after her. She enjoyed attending lessons with other children although they all came from outside the convent. She was the only one lucky enough to live with the nuns.

One day, the class was being given a lesson about Adam and Eve – and of how the serpent told Eve to eat the apple from the Tree of Knowledge – and so began wickedness in the world.

"My sister is called Eve, you know," Maria told the little girl sitting next to her, but she didn't believe her.

"You don't have a sister."

"Sister, Sister, will you tell Margaret that I do have a sister, called Eve – same as in the bible?" Maria interrupted the lesson, something she wouldn't normally do.

"Really child, be quiet – yes, you did have a sister called Eve a long time ago, but you don't now." And the nun went on with the lesson

Maria thought about that for a very long time. If she once had a sister, then she must still have one. She wondered where Eve was and realised she still missed her.

The years passed and Maria became quite proficient in the convent's kitchen She was twelve years old now and had grown into an even prettier girl than when she was tiny. Sister Angeline had taught her all she could and Maria had begun to make some of her own recipes. The sisters appreciated some of the changes and praised the child they all treated as their own. She was like a daughter to them and in their turn, they continued to slip her some small treats they came across in carrying out their duties. She was a privileged girl, she knew. She'd been called to Sister Clementine's office again and told that now she was twelve, they'd have to discuss with her what she'd like to do when she had to leave the convent.

"Leave the convent – I don't want to leave the convent, Sister. This is my home and all the sisters are my friends." She felt quite distraught.

"When you reach age sixteen, Maria, you will have to leave the convent and make your way in the world. I merely need to know if there's anything you'd like to do as an adult, so I can help you prepare for whatever that may be. I want you to go away now and think over what I've said – think about the future – there is of course a chance you could stay in the convent but only if you became one of our student nuns – and went on to become a nun in your own right. But remember, you will have to live here at the convent for the rest of your life, without being able to go out into the world where you'd be able to learn many new things. You don't have to decide anything now – you have some time yet, but I want you to think about it. We would help you whatever you decide." She opened her desk drawer and brought out a small lace handkerchief. It was wrapped around a small object.

"I think you're old enough to have this now – you're clever enough to appreciate what it is. When you first came to us, there was a very kind nurse, who worked in the tube station underground, looking after people there. She gave me this to give to you when I thought you were ready." She unfolded the handkerchief and, lying side by side, were two shiny sixpences. "This was all your mother had when she died giving birth to you and Eve. Look in the corner there and you'll see the name 'Tracy' embroidered in blue silk – apparently, that was your mother's name but there was nothing that told us her second name – so it's all we have of your mother. The nurse said she'd been only sixteen – so very young – and she believed you and your sister should have one each, but when Eve left so long ago, no one thought of the sixpences. Please take them now and never forget it was all the money your mother had to her name – she must have been so frightened and alone. The nurse believed she might have been an orphan herself." And she rewrapped them in the handkerchief. Maria took them away, feeling very special – she had something of her mother's – she'd never had, nor known, anything about her mother before.

Soon, she was fifteen years old and leaving the convent was fast becoming a reality. She really was a very attractive young woman with waist-length blond hair and very pretty, blue eyes. She was of slender build and if any criticism could be made, perhaps it was that she was a bit shy and lacking in confidence, but other than that, she was a very nice, young girl and the nuns were proud of the girl they'd helped rear. A training course was set up for her by Sister Clementine and just as she reached sixteen, she started attending a college where she trained to be a Concierge 'cum Receptionist. Once she'd successfully completed the course, the convent even found her a position in a rather posh block of flats where she was a 'Jack of all Trades' and looked after all the home owners as best she could. The uniform she had to wear suited her very well as it was grey with a plain, white blouse – and sensible black shoes. It couldn't conceal her attractiveness though and she became very popular in her duties. It was the mid-sixties and her style of dress was very different at the weekends – she liked miniskirts and maxi coats. She liked modern clothes but always returned to her concierge 'grey' uniform on workdays.

"Hello, Mr Fotheringay, and how are you today?" she asked of an older gentleman whom she'd seen once or twice before.

"I am very well, Maria, thank you for asking. In fact, I'm really very happy as my daughter has told me she'll be coming home to live with me here. She's on the point of completing 'Being Finished' at a school in Switzerland. I'm sure you'll like her and to tell the truth, she's not unlike you in appearance." And he bounced towards the lift, too happy to walk normally.

The months passed and although she often enquired of Mr Fotheringay if his daughter would be coming home to him soon? He always told her 'yes' but it was a whole year since he'd first told her. One afternoon, she was at her reception desk checking her diary dates when she heard someone coming in the main door. She quickly went out to welcome whoever it was and had a momentary shock – she found she was looking at herself. The young visitor had her hair hanging loose and Maria's was tied back in a ponytail – their clothes were very different too – but other than that, they looked exactly the same. Neither spoke but just stared at each other. The main door came crashing open and Mr Fotheringay bounced into the hallway, carrying two large suitcases.

"Ah, you've met. Good. Good." And he rang for the lift. "Aren't you two young ladies alike? I told you so, Maria, didn't I? Come along, Evelyn, let's get you upstairs so you can unpack and settle." And he whisked his daughter quickly into the lift.

Maria stood there, open mouthed before returning to her office where her phone was ringing. She had to get on with her work no matter how shocked she felt. Mr Fotheringay's daughter had been dressed very glamorously in a gold mini dress and a cream feather boa. Maria's uniform seemed very dull by comparison. Her immediate thought was that she'd met her twin sister after all these years. The last time she'd seen her was when they were both four years old. Now she was nearly eighteen and the other girl looked much the same age.

She didn't see the girl for a whole week after that but when she did, a note was slipped to her, which asked her to meet across the street in a close-by smart and bijou café at four o'clock.

'My Treat', it ended. So Maria told the porter that she had to go out for a half hour or so – but that she'd be back. Evelyn was already there, sitting at a corner table well out of sight. "Oh there you are," she said in an impatient tone. "I thought you weren't coming."

She didn't give Maria a chance to answer but went on as though she was in a hurry. "You know who I am, don't you? I could tell from the moment we met – your eyes gave it away, but luckily, my father didn't notice. I don't want him to know who you are – not just yet anyway – obviously I'll tell him in due course." She paused, realising she was monopolising the conversation. "Well, in ten minutes, tell me what your life's been like and then I'll fill you in about mine."

Maria didn't know where to begin. It had to be the morning she woke to find Eve gone from her life. She started there and went on to the years that passed in the convent, how she was taught so much by the nuns and how they always looked after her. "I was happy there and I loved them all – I think they loved me too. They educated me and then sent me to a training school, after which I came here as a concierge. That's really it in a nutshell – not very interesting perhaps but happy. I never had much but then I never needed much."

"Oh Gawd." Evelyn drooled and lit up a cigarette. She didn't even offer her sister one. "How dreary that must have been. I did think of you once or twice throughout the years – but not that much, as I convinced myself someone would adopt you too, just as they did me. Obviously, that wasn't to be." And she crossed her silken legs to show off her expensive high-heeled stilettoes. She was dressed very elegantly and at great cost, Maria didn't doubt. "When the Fotherigays came to the convent looking for a little girl, I made sure they chose me. I told them you wet the bed all the time but that I didn't. I know it sounds trivial but it was enough to make their minds up about the two of us. There wasn't much between us – we were so alike – perhaps they flipped a coin to help them decide, I don't know. You were condemned to stay at the convent, whilst I have had a privileged life. They were a well-off couple and they made sure I had everything I wanted." She didn't even look embarrassed telling Maria this. She really had been spoilt as a child.

"Where is Mrs Fotheringay now?" was all Maria could think to say. She was upset by what Eve had admitted, especially the bit about telling the prospective adopters about the bedwetting, which wasn't true anyway.

"She died about five years ago and it's just been father and me since then. He has no relatives, except me and now that I've been 'finished' in Switzerland, he wants me to find a job. He's got pots of money – and could easily afford to keep me. He keeps going on about my learning to support myself. What's that all about, I ask you?" Evelyn gathered her things together ready to leave the café. "Can we meet here next week at the same time – there's something I want to ask you to do for me – but that can wait?"

And she swept out of the café in the blink of an eye, leaving Maria with the bill.

Two mornings later, Maria found a small, brown envelope beneath the blotter on her desk. Inside was a lovely, little locket, obviously made of gold. A small note said it was from Eve and promised to see her next week at the café. Maria was touched and put it on straight away. She admired herself in her small compact mirror.

The next week, Maria asked Eve if she'd like to see the convent again and some of the nuns.

"Certainly not, sister – I left all that behind long go." She was dressed in another outfit – a mini skirt with a box jacket and a matching clutch bag tucked under her arm – with a long silk scarf draped around her shoulders. Every inch an international model. Maria was, as always, dressed in her grey uniform and white blouse.

"Do you keep your uniform in the office, Maria, and change when you arrive in the morning?" Evelyn seemed genuinely interested.

"Yes, I come to work in my own clothes and go home the same way – why do you ask?" Maria was curious.

"Nothing really, dear – I just wondered. I see you're wearing your locket I gave you – very pretty, but I have many more like that. Perhaps I'll give you another one day."

"Actually, Eve, I have something for you today." And she searched in her shoulder bag and came out with a small, tissue parcel. Inside was a lace handkerchief with two silver sixpences inside. "This was our mother's, Eve – see her name embroidered there. Tracy was her name but I never knew her surname. It was given to Sister Clementine by the nurse who looked after our mother in the tube station – it was the only thing she had. I want you to have one of the sixpences although I'd like to keep the handkerchief. Is that all right?" And she spread it on the table, showing the embroidered 'Tracy' in pretty blue silk thread.

"Oh no darling – you must keep it all. I'm not really sentimental and I have no need for a sixpence, I assure you." Evelyn had no interest in it whatsoever.

Maria was very upset – she thought she was giving her sister something very special indeed, but apparently not. Evelyn pushed it back across the table towards her and Maria folded it carefully and put it back her bag. Her sister was even more callous than she'd thought.

About a month later, during which time the girls had often met in the café, Evelyn was going on about her mean father – a subject she regularly returned to and which she obviously enjoyed discussing with Maria. "But he is good to you, isn't he?" Maria asked.

"Reasonably, I suppose – but he has control of all the money and I just get an allowance." That allowance was as much money as Maria earned from her job in a month, but she refrained from pointing that out. "I wish he would hurry up and die – I'm his sole beneficiary, you know – I'll be a very rich woman then."

Maria just looked at her twin sister, whom she'd regularly thought of throughout the years and realised that she'd had a better upbringing at the convent and it had made her a better person. She was too shy to say this but thought it more every time she met Eve.

Later that week, it was almost seven o'clock and Evelyn knew for sure that Maria had left her office and gone home, so she went downstairs and into the office where Maria's uniform was on a hanger, neat as usual. She'd brought an old, pair of flat black shoes and left them under the desk. Upstairs, her father was getting ready to go out for the evening. He was going to his club in the city as was his routine and Evelyn said, "Travelling by tube as usual, Father? Anyone would think you couldn't afford a taxi."

"Look after the pennies and the pounds will look after themselves – never forget that daughter." And he left the flat. Evelyn followed him out and went into Maria's office where she quickly changed into her sister's uniform and slipped on the black shoes. She ran all the way to the station, making sure her father didn't see her. She reached the station just before he did and got a ticket from the automatic dispenser. She watched him arrive at the main door and purchase his ticket before getting on board the long escalator down to the right platform. She followed him and was glad to see quite a few people dotted along the platform. She stayed at the back of the people until she heard the tube coming in the distance. She moved forward until she was right behind him except for one person. As the tube came out of the tunnel, she could see its light in the darkness. Everyone was getting ready to board the train when she moved to just behind her father.

She took a deep breath and with all the strength she could muster, she pushed him right into the approaching train and he toppled over the edge of the platform onto the rail track. It all happened so quickly. The train screeched to a halt but of course, it was too late to avoid hitting the man. The passengers didn't know what to do or where to go – the station staff soon appeared and cleared them from the platform – but not before Evelyn had run off back to the 'Up' escalator and ran from the tube station. She knew some people would have seen her but she felt quite safe in Maria's grey uniform. She was back at the block of flats in the twinkling of an eye, hung Maria's uniform where it belonged and ran towards the building lift. She put the black shoes in the rubbish shoot to get rid of them – and then settled on the sofa with a gin and tonic to see how the evening would unfold.

She felt excited – but not nervous – everything had gone according to plan. She had done well.

Her description was in the newspapers the next day asking for people to contact the police if they'd seen a young girl, dressed in a grey suit and white blouse at the tube station the previous night. It would probably have been between seven and seven thirty. She had long, blond hair, tied back in a ponytail. Evelyn was delighted as it was exactly like Maria. The flat doorbell rang about nine o'clock the next morning and a detective stood there with a female police constable. He went through the normal formalities and then brought up the reason he was there. He explained what had happened to her father the previous night and that he'd been dead on arrival on reaching the hospital.

Evelyn broke down in tears and kept repeating, "No – no, that can't be. When he didn't come home last night, I just assumed he was staying at his club – he did that sometimes. Are you sure he's dead – have you had a second opinion? I've heard such weird stories of people waking up in the mortuary." The tears were running down her cheeks.

"I'm sorry, Miss, there's no doubt – first that it is your father and second that he is most certainly dead. I have to ask you a difficult question – will you be able to come back with us to the station to identify him – because of the way he died, we'll make sure you see nothing distressing. Will you be able to come with us now?"

She nodded her head and went into the bedroom to fetch her coat, emerging with no makeup on and just a slight whiff of delicate perfume. They took her down to the lobby and out into the street but not before the Detective's eye rested on Maria who had the newspaper spread open in front of her. He didn't ask who she was at that point as Evelyn was his first priority – but he knew he'd be back.

Identification complete, the young policewoman accompanied her back to the flat and made her a cup of sweet tea. The Detective had kept his word and her father had been completely covered by a white sheet and a white towel wrapped around half of his head – there was nothing dreadful to see, except of course for the corpse of the dead man. Strangely enough, she felt sad and upset but then it was what she wanted – and what she caused to happen. She had plenty of crocodile tears and let them fall from her eyes.

The policewoman asked her if there were any relatives she could contact – but was told, between sobs, that she had no one other than her father. The woman was very sympathetic and made the distraught girl go into her bedroom to lie on top of the covers. Evelyn knew she'd soon have to admit knowing the girl at the desk downstairs, but then her story was quite straightforward and only just a little unusual. Everything should be all right.

She asked, "Will the Detective be coming back to see me – there's something I want to tell him?"

"I'll make sure he does, don't you worry – now will you be all right if I leave you now – and you're sure there's no one you want me to contact?" On being reassured, she left the flat. Evelyn immediately got up, lit a cigarette and poured a gin and tonic. That was what she needed – not hot sweet tea. She did fall asleep on the sofa and sometime later, woke up to the sound of the doorbell ringing. It was the Detective and he was accompanied by another policeman.

"I'm here as you wanted. How can we help you now? Have you seen the newspaper yet – you know he didn't fall from the platform in front of the train – he was pushed by a young woman, whose description we already have. There were plenty of witnesses." He turned to his colleague. "Bob, go and make us a cup of tea please – there's a good chap." Bob did as he was asked.

Evelyn began to speak hesitantly as though she wasn't sure how to tell him. "Have you noticed the young concierge who works downstairs? The one who wears a grey uniform? I've had today's newspaper delivered now and I know the description of the person who pushed father. It sounds very like Maria, the concierge."

"Yes, I have actually and I think I know what you're going to tell me – do you suspect her of the crime?" He looked concerned.

Evelyn began. She told him of her sister and herself being born in the war and her mother dying at the birth – of how the twin babies were taken by a nurse to a local convent where they both lived until they were about four years old. She explained how she was adopted by Mr & Mrs Fotheringay whilst her sister, Maria, was left behind in the convent. She never saw her sister again until about two months ago when she joined her father. They recognised each other at once and met weekly to chat about the past and the present – Maria had been working for a couple of years when she learned the Fotheringays had chosen to leave her behind whilst taking her sister and giving her a rich and privileged life.

"She began to hate him at that moment. I tried to keep her calm, but she said she hated him and would kill him if she could. He had sentenced her to a life of drudgery with the nuns and no privileges whatsoever. She'd decided to hate him however and said she would pay him back one day – and I fear that day came a couple of days ago. I don't like telling you this – 'cause I've come to like her and feel mean telling you this. But what can I do – it's all true."

The hot tea arrived and the police tried their best to comfort her – but they couldn't cheer her up. "We'll have to go now, Miss, and do what's necessary. We'll have to question your sister and try to establish her side of the story, but I have to say your accusation seems quite likely."

The group separated and Evelyn was left alone again. When she next went down to the lobby, there was no Maria to be seen. The police had taken her away, the porter told her, "She wouldn't hurt a fly, Madam – she's a very good woman. I know 'cause I've had my problems and she always tried to help me." He looked upset. She patted his arm but got away quickly before he started to cry.

Maria was undergoing a terrible time at the police station. She was questioned and then questioned again. She was amazed to hear what Eve had told them and shocked that a sister could tell such lies. But then, she remembered how she'd lied about the bedwetting when she was only four – once a liar, always a liar. Of course, she denied she'd hated Mr Fotheringay – it hadn't been his fault that he chose the wrong twin, which is what she thought now. Why would she want to kill a man who'd done nothing but be nice to her since he'd moved to the apartment – but she realised Eve's story sounded quite feasible.

She was kept at the station and questioned again. Her grey suit was kept there too pending the trial. Witnesses were brought along and all recognised her and swore she was the woman they'd seen push the man onto the track. She was completely in a corner and had no idea which way to turn. Her trial was still a couple of months away and in the meantime, Evelyn had seen her lawyer several times and as she was the sole beneficiary of his will, the money and possessions he'd left would automatically go to her. Her plan had been so clever and with no other relatives in the picture, she would soon be a very rich woman. Her conscience didn't hurt at all and she'd managed to put Maria out of her mind – anyway she was languishing in jail.

Her lawyer had advised her to write her own will – although she was still so young – you never knew. So she did and left all her worldly goods to her only living relative, her sister Maria, if she outlived herself. Anyway, she was sure

Maria would die in prison – she would certainly be given a very long sentence for what she'd done and if her health was too good for that, she was sure she'd find some means of paying a prison inmate enough money to help Maria out of this world.

The time for the trial soon arrived and Evelyn was called as a witness for the prosecution. Two of the nuns from the convent were called as character witnesses for Maria – they were very keen to help as they remembered her with great affection. Her sweet nature and willingness to help everyone was told by the first nun and then repeated by the second. Evelyn avoided her sister's eyes as she stood in the stand – and told her story just as she'd told it to the Detective. Maria's own story was similar for the first few years of her life, but after her sister was adopted from the convent, her own life was very unexciting, but happy and comfortable, she told the court. The actual night of the murder, she'd been alone in her flat all night just watching television. The Prosecution Barrister pointed out that as she had no witnesses to confirm it, she could instead have had time to follow Mr Fotheringay to the tube station, push him over the edge and nip back to her office, discarding the grey suit there as was her pattern. The motive was most likely that she hated the man who'd rejected her as a child and chosen her sister for a life of luxury whilst she remained alone at the convent – a rejected twin.

The trial lasted only three days and because of the number of witnesses who had identified the young woman with the ponytail and the grey suit, there was little room for manoeuvre. The judge commented on the two women's identical looks but the way each was dressed was so different, it was easy to tell them apart. Maria was found guilty of murder – she had deliberately followed an innocent man to the tube station with every intention of making sure he never came back. It was a clear case of murder and she was given a sentence of twenty years in prison, with no prospect of early release or probation. It was a harsh sentence but then it had been a harsh murder.

Maria was taken down and immediately put into a prison van. She was in a daze and wasn't even sure what was happening. Evelyn on the other hand, knew exactly what was happening and looked forward to a huge payment from her lawyer. She planned to stay in the flat until she decided what was best to do. She had no conscience about it belonging to her father, whom she'd murdered – nor that there was a new girl on the desk downstairs. As far as she was concerned, she'd done what was necessary. She'd been taught at the Swiss Finishing School that self-preservation was the name of the game.

After a couple of days in prison, Maria asked if she could see her lawyer. Arrangements were made for him to visit her and he came, briefcase in hand. "Well, what can I do for you, Maria?" he asked gently. He felt sorry for her; she didn't seem the sort of girl who would commit a murder. But she'd been found guilty by twelve good and true citizens.

She unfolded a white piece of cloth and two silver sixpences fell out into her hand. She was close to tears as she offered him one of the coins. "You've always been kind to me so I want to ask you one last favour. Take this sixpence and give it to my sister, please – I did offer it to her once before but she refused, saying it was valueless. The sixpences belonged to our mother whom we never met but I had a dream the night of the trial when my mother came to me and told me that Eve's going to need some luck in the future now that her whole life will be based on a total lie." She stopped talking and looked at him closely. "You do know she lied, don't you? I never killed Mr Fotheringay so I can only surmise she did it, dressed as me. I just wanted you to know the truth. It makes me feel better. You should know this is the absolute truth – I have nothing else to lose now." She got up and held out her hand, which he took in both of his.

"The very best of luck, Maria – I was proud to defend you." And he called for the warder to let him leave. Maria just sat there waiting to be taken back to her cell.

In the swanky apartment, Evelyn was enjoying her freedom – the knowledge that her money meant she could have whatever she wanted in life. And yet, she had a strange melancholy feeling which she couldn't shake off. However, gin and tonic would help.

The doorbell rang and she opened the door to find Maria's lawyer on her doorstep. He promised to take up very little of her time and immediately held out the sixpence. She looked at it and said, "What's this?"

"Maria asked me to give it to you – it belonged to your mother and she wanted you to have it to bring you luck. Well, that's all I came for." She never held out her hand to take the coin so he placed it on the glass coffee table. "Goodbye, my dear – I hope some luck comes your way. I think you'll need it." And he left the flat, feeling stongly that he'd been in the presence of the real murderer.

She stared at the sixpence and then lifted it from the table. She shrugged her shoulders nonchalantly and wrapped the only contact from her birth mother in a tissue and went into the bathroom, where she threw it into the toilet pan and flushed twice. Looking into the pan, she saw the coin had gone – gone out of her life forever. Not much of an inheritance – she had much better from her adopted father. She poured another gin and tonic.

She met some friends for a drink that night and it was after midnight when she arrived home. She knew she was a bit tiddly, but not drunk and she flopped onto the sofa where she immediately fell asleep. She woke in the middle of the night by the lights flickering on and off. Maybe it was a thunderstorm, she thought and got up to look out of the window. In the corner of the room was an armchair usually used by her father and a figure was sitting there. It looked like a young girl with fair hair – a very young girl who slightly resembled Maria – and therefore herself she supposed. She moved towards the chair and the girl raised her head. "Do you know who I am?" she asked.

"No, I do not know who you are but you have no right to be here. Get out now before I ring the police." And she made to lift the phone.

"It won't work, Eve, I have control of you and of everything in the room." She fished some writing paper from the desk drawer and pushed it towards Eve.

"My name is Evelyn – not Eve." She was beginning to feel afraid, of what she didn't know.

"You are Eve, just as Maria is Maria. Come and sit down here at the desk. I want you to write something for me." And she moved the chair for her daughter to sit down. That's who she was and Eve feared it was so. "You helped me make up my mind as to what to do when you flushed my sixpence down the toilet. You are a girl with no heart; your sister has a heart big enough for both of you."

Eve felt as though she was being hypnotised and had no option but to obey the order. She sat at the desk and lifted the pen. "What do you want me to write?"

Tracy, for that's who she was, began to dictate:

'To Whom it may Concern'

It was I who killed my father and not Maria. I stole her uniform from the office and put it on, then I followed him to the tube station. It was I who crept up behind him and pushed him onto the track. He was mean to me and wouldn't give me the money I wanted – so I decided to get rid of him. You'd better let Maria go now– she's too much of a milksop to murder anyone.

I'm not sorry – and she signed the bottom of the page.

Looking up at the young ghost, she said, "Well, what do you want me to do now, 'mother'?"

"Oh you will do exactly as I tell you." And Eve moved uncontrollably as though in a trance and crossed the room towards the balcony window. The glass doors flew open and suddenly Tracy was out on the balcony. She beckoned to her daughter to follow her. With no will of her own, Eve did as she was told. She leaned on the balcony edge and looked down into the street so far away. The apartment was at the top of the very tall building. Again, she seemed to have no will of her own and she climbed onto the edge, swinging her legs free in the darkness.

"Now jump, daughter – jump. Do the one decent thing you've ever done and release your sister from wrongful punishment." She stood behind Eve and gently pushed her over the edge – she didn't have much strength but her will was strong enough. Eve didn't even scream, she just floated downwards and onto the hard ground below, where she lay spreadeagled on the concrete below.

The crushed body wasn't found 'till the next day and when the police broke into the apartment, they found the note she'd written the night before.

Everything was wrapped up very quickly after that and Maria was soon released from prison. She had nothing when she came out – not even a job or a place to live. She'd lost all of that. But the lawyer was waiting for her with a car and he helped her in.

"I knew that last time I saw you, that you were innocent, but there was nothing I could do at that stage. However, I do have some positive news for you. Before she killed herself, Eve made a will leaving all she possessed to you, so you are a very rich woman. I know this is a shock but you really do deserve some good luck. I can make all the arrangements for you and the money will soon be released, as you are her only living relative and beneficiary. She obviously had a conscience after all. Now, where would you like me to take you?"

"I've been thinking about that and I would like to go back to the convent and see if they could offer me a room there until I get myself sorted out. Do you think that would be all right?" Maria wanted the safety and comfort she associated with the nuns and the convent.

Sister Clementine was still there although quite old now. She was delighted to see Maria, knowing all about what she had been through. "Of course, we can find you a room here and you can stay as long as you like." The gentle, old nun was obviously pleased to see her again.

Maria did stay at the convent although this time, she paid them for the privilege. She soon had lots of money, half of which she gave to the convent and with the other half, she paid her own way in life. One thing that gave her more pleasure than she'd ever had in her life before was to set up and finance a Charity School affiliated to the convent and offer young, pregnant, single girls a temporary home until their babies were born. A job and a place to live was also found for them afterwards – something her own, sad mother had never had. She arranged for a new building to be added to the convent which included several dormitories for the women and one for herself. She helped as many women as she could and she named the Charity School 'Tracy's School' in memory of her mother.

'Tracy's School' became very well known in the years to come and Maria soon became known as Sister Maria like the nuns at the convent. She never left the convent nor the women who needed her help. She stayed there and became known for her good work and there were many new born babies called 'Maria' which pleased her enormously. One of those babies unfortunately lost its mother after a difficult birth and the nuns found a letter the mother had left, asking if Sister Maria would take the little baby and rear it as her own, something Maria was only too pleased to do. She made sure there were all the proper documents to make the child a real, official person – and not like Eve and herself. The baby must not grow up nameless and with no birth certificate.

She called the little girl Tracy and when she reached sixteen, she gave her the sixpence and told her it would bring her luck, because it had belonged to her grandmother. The child took it gratefully and had it pierced by a jeweller. She wore it as a necklace for the rest of her life and always felt there was a loving angel looking after her. Strangely enough, she believed the angel was called Tracy, just like her.

Where Does One Keep a Demon

Three young ladies were sitting in the upstairs parlour, all working on their embroidery. The different coloured silk threads shone in the early morning light – blues, pinks, crimson greens and all the other garden flower colours. They were pretty young ladies, all in their early twenties, dressed in the same gentle shades of the silk threads with which they were working. To the ladies, the year was 1860, one year after all three had died – and although their bodies left this world, their spirits stayed in their home to try to help their parents deal with the grief of losing three of their children to Typhoid. One of the sisters caught it first and then, a week later, her two sisters came down with it as well, but it never touched mother and father – nor any of the other people living in the house, except for Old Butler John, who died two weeks after the young women.

"May I have some pink please? I've run out, I'm afraid, Marigold."

She handed her sister the skein of thread and said, "You can't have used all the pink yet – Rosemary and I still need some to finish our pattern. You really do waste more than you use Eleanor – look at that – knots everywhere." Rosemary tutted in agreement with her sister and then crossed the room towards the big window.

"Sisters," she said, "there's more coming up the path with the same woman as before."

"Do you like the look of them?" Marigold asked and joined her sister by the window.

"No, I do not – they look stern and miserable and not the sort we want to live here. What shall we do this time?"

Eleanor spoke up, "Let's do our opening doors and curtains blowing into the rooms. That's always been enough in the past to send them all scuttling back outside. If it fails, we'll go to plan two." On being asked what was plan two, she responded, "Well, we've not had to think of it yet – plan one has worked quite well."

Downstairs, the Estate Agent opened the big front door with a key and ushered the middle-aged man and woman into the hall. "A remarkable house really it's been modernised to some extent but of course needs some more TLC. Its first recorded date – from the Polls records and old Church documents – is 1645, believe it or not. They certainly don't build them like this nowadays. Have a stroll around the place and any questions, just call on me and if I don't know the answer, I'll do my best to find out."

As the couple started upstairs, admiring the long, winding stairs as they went, bangs and thumps could be heard from upstairs. "Is there anyone else in the house?" the man asked and was reassured the three of them were all alone. As they reached the middle landing, the curtains that hung at the magnificent oriel window suddenly blew into the room – until they were almost parallel with the floor.

"Oh my God Victor, what was that?" His wife was getting agitated. The curtains in the first bedroom floated outwards as well and more loud bangs sounded in other parts of the house. The potential buyers turned quickly and fled out of the front door, apologising to the Estate Agent as they went.

Oh dear, the Agent said to herself, *I feared this would happen. Sometimes they're quiet as lambs but on other days, they behave very badly.* And she left the house as well, locking the door as she went.

"Told you so!" Eleanor said and danced around the room, tripping over her sisters' feet as she did so.

"Butler John helped with all that banging in the kitchen. I could hardly hear what the people were saying. He almost frightened me as well as them."

The parlour door suddenly flew open and the stable boy appeared as if from nowhere. He asked, "Was that more possible buyers?" And was reassured they'd been chased away.

"Well done, girls." Billy was only a boy but he thought he was a man. "I wonder when the next lot will come. Did plan one work all right?"

"Go away, Billy, and leave us in peace." Marigold spoke up, saying what her sisters were actually thinking. "Go and be a nuisance somewhere else."

"You can't boss me around – I was here before you. I was actually trampled by a horse in 1645 just when the house was first built – you lot didn't appear until much later Victorian times, same as Butler John. In fact, it was you who killed him – he caught the Typhoid from you and that finished him off."

"Yes, we've heard the story about the horse many times before. You may have been in the house before us, but that doesn't give you more rights than we have." Marigold was determined to have the last word.

There was a sudden rush of wind around the parlour and the Old Dowager appeared by the fireplace. "Really," she said, "such arguments again. Can't you lot ever get on together?" She was a very old lady with a crooked back and needed a bone-handled walking stick to help her get about. Everyone was in awe of her as she always assumed she was in charge in whatever room she was in. Rosemary stood up and offered her chair to the old lady – who immediately took it and sat there with no intention of moving.

She cleared her throat. "I hope none of you have forgotten the meeting in the downstairs sitting room – 8 o'clock tonight. We have to discuss the sort of people we might allow to live here with us – and the kind we would certainly not."

"Oh no Madam we haven't forgotten." Young Billy was always eager to please her. She scared him and kept reminding him he had been 'outside help' when he was alive and he must behave or he could be banned from inside the house.

"Are we going to allow 'the man in the cupboard' to come to the meeting?" Marigold said to everyone, but it was the Old Dowager who answered.

"No, we most certainly are not. He's not fit to understand what we'll be discussing. He's a moron – and has been locked away from society for a very long time. The General would be very annoyed if we let him come." She smoothed her heavy, black satin skirt and looked around the room, waiting for someone to disagree with her. Of course, no one did.

A loud voice was heard – a man's deep voice – saying the things he always said. The group in the room wondered who was facing his wrath this time. It could be Melissa, who came from the 1700s and who was very sweet and innocent. The General liked shouting at her because she never shouted back.

"Charles First is our rightful king and Parliament have no right to try him. Cromwell should be shot. He has no right whatsoever to take such decisions." He was dressed as a Royalist gentleman and had been a general when fighting for Charles. He wore a large feathered hat, silk stockings, a tunic and a long-sleeved shirt with a pointed collar – not a ruffle but a collar. He was every inch a follower of Charles and a hater of Oliver Cromwell, leader of the modern army. It was he who had built this house originally and his spirit had remained there ever since. He was always shouting about the King, Cromwell, Protestants and

Catholics – it was his one main topic and this was not surprising, as he had been executed in 1649 as a Royalist sympathiser. He was beheaded and could still remove his head from his body at will – but he rarely did it, as it seemed like showing off. He still felt the house belonged to him and not to all the usurpers, who'd subsequently lived there throughout the years. It had been he who had originally imprisoned the man in the upstairs cupboard and kept him there ever since. Some of the other ghosts had felt sympathy for him but the General was adamant that he stayed locked away. The cupboard door was securely locked and had a wooden cross nailed to it. A lot of trouble had been taken to keep him there.

Little Melissa had been a lady-in-waiting at the court of the German, George the First – a strict and insular man, who never troubled to learn English although he was the king of the country. Melissa had always been a quiet little thing and was scarcely noticed at court. She'd been travelling home one year and the carriage stopped for the night at the biggest house in the town, which happened to belong to her cousin. She dressed as they did at court and on arrival at the house, she wore a long, sky blue dress with a front split panel showing a white silk underskirt, stockings and a tri-cornered blue hat. Although approaching middle age, she looked attractive and like someone who'd come straight from the Georgian court – as indeed she had.

That night, as the carriage drew up at the house steps, she made her way out onto the boarding step but missed her footing and fell between the carriage and the high stone kerb. The two horses shied and struck at the air with their hooves, kicking out as they did so. Unfortunately, Melissa was struck with great force and quickly died at the side of the road. A very sad end for a woman who'd never done anyone harm in all her life. Her cousin was most upset and cried lots for the dear girl. Melissa was buried from this house.

"Woman, do stop snivelling – no one's going to hurt you. You know my bark's worse than my bite." Both he and Melissa walked upstairs to the parlour where all the other ghosts had gathered. The parlour was getting rather crowded by this time and the General told the others he'd just come to remind them about the meeting that evening. The Old Dowager almost spat at him. "Yes, we know – do you think we're stupid?" Needless to say, she didn't like him and she never hid it. She knew how important she actually was – he just thought he was.

"One thing I want to bring up tonight is that I think we should use the kitchen maid hanging herself in her bedroom a lot more than we've done in the past. That means Sally will have to perform again – and I do I know she's unwilling to keep on hanging herself – but if she wants to keep undesirables out of the house, then she has to do it." Eleanor avoided giving her opinion but the two sisters just giggled their agreement.

"We'll talk to her tonight," the Old Dowager said, "now I must go and have my afternoon nap. All that banging of doors and curtain blowing has quite tired me out." And she left the room with the same puff of wind she'd used on arrival. She liked to create an impression and she could certainly be relied upon to do that.

The old house actually had many ghosts from different periods in history and had been on the market for ten years now and no one had made an offer – mainly because the ghosts did their best to chase them away. Obviously, different people from different centuries had lived in the house, and even died in the house, but only a few of them had ceased to exist in such a way that their spirits could be retained where they'd died. Sudden and unexpected deaths, suicides, murders and for some reason, even deaths which had occurred away from the house but had a great longing to return home – their spirits could too stay if they so chose.

They were all gathering in the downstairs parlour – wearing a mixture of period costumes. The Old Dowager and the General took control of the meeting and they both sat in the middle of the ghosts. Before the meeting actually began, one young man, who was dressed in a World War One uniform, stood up and said he wanted to say something.

The soldier coughed nervously. He could only have been about twenty – one of the many casualties of the Great War. "I actually wonder if we have the right to make sure that no new owners move into the house. If people had done that to us, we wouldn't be here now, would we?" Polite coughs of agreement ran around the room, so he went on. "Why don't we allow the next potential buyers to actually buy the house and see how they fit in. We'd have to agree of course that we all liked them, or it wouldn't work." He sat down again having planted the thought in all their minds.

"We'll never all agree on anything, you know that." Young Billy spoke up and was immediately frowned at by the Dowager. The three Victorian ladies took the floor and said they agreed with the soldier, Jim.

"Why don't we try that and if it turns out they don't fit in, we start haunting with all our might. After all, many of us have had to break in new owners over the passing years and we've managed so far – ten years is a long time for the house to lie empty it would be terrible if it fell down through neglect, wouldn't it?"

They were all squashed into the parlour and were eager to spread themselves about more. "Okay, let's give it a go when the next people come to view – remember, we mustn't play any of our tricks on them, or they'll certainly never come here again." The General had spoken – and on that note, they all disappeared into the nooks and crannies of the old house.

One week later, the Estate Agent appeared with a young man and woman in tow. "Do come in," she said, "there's no one in the house." Her fingers were tightly crossed behind her back. *Please God, let them stay away today* was her one thought. She told the couple to wander around the house on their own and if there were any questions, just to come back to her. The house was quiet and she couldn't believe her luck – so far. But the viewing went smoothly and Tom and Lisa Middleton eventually made an offer to buy. There was rejoicing in the Estate Agent's office that day – the house had remained unsold for so long. The owner of the Agency, however, told them not to be too sure the ghosts had gone. "Don't count your chickens before they're hatched," he said mysteriously.

One month later, Tom and Lisa moved in. They'd been back to see the house a couple of times more – and found the whole place quiet and completely ghost free. In fact, truth to tell, they were disappointed as they'd been told about the haunted house and were looking forward to meeting its guests. Its reputation couldn't be concealed; however, the whole town knew about the haunted house, but kept well away from it. Tom and Lisa knew exactly what they were letting themselves in for and actually welcomed the challenge.

"Tom, you realise you won't be able to do as you planned." Lisa found the percolator and started to make some fresh coffee. They were surrounded by boxes, curtains and rugs.

"I know," her husband replied, "I was really looking forward to that, but what will be, will be. The ghosts are probably really here but are keeping a low profile – let's wait and see, shall we – our future payment depends on them, don't forget that." He said mysteriously, then paused for a moment. "Did you hear that?"

"Yes, I did. It sounded like a girl's laughter coming from the stairs – but of course, it couldn't have been that." Lisa looked concerned for a moment, but soon shrugged it off. The kitchen was so welcoming and comfortable that they knew this would always be their favourite room. Not all that much had actually changed – the construction of the house was intact and all the windows were original – even with the bubbles of air still in the very old glass – the fireplaces were still in situ although they must have been worked on throughout the years. The house wouldn't have been the same without them.

"I can just see us sitting here by the fire – with crisp white snow covering everything outdoors. Coffee's ready." Lisa was a romantic. There it was again, the gentle giggling floating in the air. "Someone's laughing at us, Tom – there's no mistaking it this time. There are ghosts – we were right."

The Old Dowager chased the young women from the stairs and hid herself in one of the upstairs bedrooms. Hiding was just a formality as not everyone could see ghosts anyway and could be in the same room as one of them, but knew nothing about it.

"Look, Tom, at the bottom of the garden. Can you see him?" Lisa was quite excited. She was staring down the overgrown garden from the kitchen window.

"I certainly can." Tom joined her, carrying his fresh coffee and a muffin. "Why don't we wander down there and try to introduce ourselves. Worth a try, isn't it?" And they both left the house, walking very slowly and quietly towards the figures of Billy and Jim the soldier, who were seated on a tree trunk, blown over many years before. They were chatting like friends, not ghosts at all and Tom coughed gently to get their attention.

"He can see us," Billy said, "and the woman, she can see us too." Billy was a cheeky little chap and wasn't at all bothered that the couple could see him. He stood up to his full height which wasn't very much and said ominously, "What do you want of us?"

Tom answered, "Don't be afraid of us – we'd like to help you. That's why we've come to this house – to try to help you and any other of your fellow ghosts. Can we speak with you for a while?" The soldier said they could but he couldn't see how they could help.

"Will you both meet Lisa and myself tonight in the downstairs parlour? We'll explain how we can help then." And that's what they did. At eight o'clock, Lisa and Tom made their way down the long stairs and tentatively opened the room door. There were three people in the room, all waiting expectantly. Billy in his jacket and muffler, stood by the fireplace, with Jim the soldier at the window and a third ghost called Percy who'd worked in the house kitchen in the seventeen hundreds but who'd cut himself badly one day and died of septicaemia at only fourteen years. All rather pitiful young men who stared at the new couple with interest. Lisa looked the same but Tom looked quite different. He was dressed in

117

a long, black cassock with a white 'dog-collar' around his neck. He had a long silver cross hanging from a chain around his waist. He was a vicar, minister or priest but definitely a holy man of some sort. Still the same Tom, however, he was smiling as he entered the room.

He sat down in an armchair and Lisa did the same. "Please don't be afraid of my clothes – these are what I wear on most days. I am a Preacher and my wife and I heard of this house a long time ago and I come here in the hope that I can be of service to you. Before deciding this, I need you to tell me your stories so that I can judge your present situation and suggest the way ahead. Let's start with Jim – how did you die in the war?"

Jim explained that he'd fought at the Somme and had stepped on a grenade. It hadn't killed him but he'd sunk into the deep field of mud and very slowly, knowing exactly what was about to happen, his face disappeared below the mud. "And that was that – my last thoughts were of this house, where I'd been a footman and very happy in my job. The next thing I knew, I was here again – but not really here – I was doomed to haunt the place forever, never knowing the peace that death can bring." He was very emotional and Tom could see how much he was hurting. Then it was Billy's turn.

"I was a stable boy when this was a great house. I had no money but at least I was given food for my labours. One afternoon, the mistress had returned from her ride and I was called to unbridle the horse. I left turning the spit over the great fire in the kitchen and went out to see to the mistress' horse. It was pawing the ground and almost growling and I found a big thorn was stuck under the saddle. When I pulled it out, the horse pawed the ground even higher and came down right on top of me. They took me into the kitchen but I died there and I've been haunting this place for more than three hundred years – me and the General started haunting at about the same time.

Tom intervened with Billy's story asking, "Have you been happy here, Billy?"

"Not always, Sir, and to tell the truth, I'm very tired of it. I would love to have a long rest, which I think must be due, but there seems to be no escape." Billy was obviously quite dejected at that thought.

"And you, Percy – can you tell me how you came to haunt in this house?" Tom was determined to hear them all.

Percy had a bad stutter but he could be understood. He explained how he'd been cutting up meat in the kitchen, when he brought the heavy gutting knife down on his arm – and it also slipped into his side. "They did try to help me, sir – they made me a fresh bed in the stable where I usually slept and the cook came to see me every day. But I developed something called septicaemia – or something like that – and that finished me off in a few days. I feel like Billy does – I'm always tired and am fed up with being here forever." His stuttering voice said the words with difficulty but Tom could sense the emotion.

Tom's task was to chase away the demon who had kept them on earth and invaded their spirits from the very moment they passed away. It meant that he must be around the house at the same time as them and know their individual stories – so he had a lot to learn from any other ghosts

"Before I rid you of your demon, I need you to tell me how to arrange meeting up with your fellow spirits who haunt this house." He was told the best place was the downstairs parlour – just where they were now.

The Reverend Tom held up the large silver cross and asked all three young men to kiss it and say the words 'I reject Satan and his fellow demons who have invaded my spirit for so long. Everything he stands for disgusts me and he entered my spirit without an invitation from me. I welcome Christianity into my soul and pray to the Father, Son and Holy Ghost and ask that I am welcomed into Heaven to sit alongside God'. The voice was strangely gruff and deep throated, as though it was an animal who was trying to speak. Tom stepped closer to Billy, then Jim and finally, Percy – three young souls who'd been wandering in the wilderness for so long. He placed his fingers in a cup of Holy Water and made the sign of the cross on each forehead, repeating, "Get you gone – you are not welcome here – and leave these young men in peace." The strain was beginning to show on Tom's face but he leaned forward and kissed the boys' foreheads. The air around the ghosts became misty and then the figures began shaking – then completely disappeared from the room. Tom fell onto a chair in a trancelike state and actually passed out. Lisa brought him a glass of water and held it to his lips.

"I'm all right, dear – and I know I've won. That's why it's taken so much out of me – those young people are now with God in his Heaven and I need to go to bed now. I haven't the strength to seek out someone else who needs exorcism. That can wait until tomorrow."

Two weary figures switched off the lights and made their way up the steep stairs.

Next morning however, Tom was up bright and early. Today really was a new day and he intended to achieve even more than the night before. The two were having breakfast in the kitchen when the telephone rang in the hall. It was the Estate Agent, just calling to find out how everything was going. A rather strange thing for an Estate Agent to do, but Tom put it down to customer services.

Meanwhile in the basement, several of the other ghosts had gathered. "Where is Billy and the other young men?" The three young ladies enquired of Melissa, who shook her head. The young maid who had hanged herself upstairs was sitting on the floor, cross legged but paying close attention. Her name was Sally and she had been just fourteen years old when she died.

Tom and Lisa had searched the house for ghosts and eventually arrived in the basement. Tom quietly turned the door handle and was pleased to find so many ghosts already there. As with the young men, he explained his dress, that he was a chaplain and had come to the house to help them. He stressed not to be afraid, as God had actually sent him. He explained about exorcism and asked if they would like to go to Heaven, where they should have gone a very long time ago. And that was it – the Victorian ladies told him about the Typhoid having killed them all in the middle of the nineteenth century. "And we stayed to comfort our parents who were very distressed. Somehow we've remained here ever since."

Tom had no reason to doubt what they said, but he though 'the demon' had more to do with their remaining here than they realised. He went through the exact procedure he'd gone through with the men and soon, the ladies began to fade away and all that could be heard was the tinkling tune of their girlish laughter. The mist that enveloped them shone with pinks and yellows and blues and exactly complimented their sad, young characters.

"It's good to think they're with their Heavenly Father and can rest at last." Tom looked at Sally, the little maid and crossed the stone floor to sit beside her on the ground. "Would you like to go to Heaven with the others and rest there – the place you should have gone before. It's no matter that you took your own life, God is all forgiving. Tell me your story though. What drove you to take such drastic action?"

Her lower lip was trembling and tears filled her lovely blue eyes, before trickling down her cheeks. She spoke at last. "You should know, sir – and I should tell you – that I am with child, a child I have carried around inside for many years now. I would greatly like to rest in Heaven and take my little child with me. It has never done harm to anyone and neither have I until I lost my way when I came to work in this house. It was the young master at the time, who came to my bedroom several times – and I ended up carrying his child. I honestly didn't know I was doing wrong and he reassured me I wasn't. He was older than I was, so I believed him. When the rest of the house learned about me, they told me to pack my bags and go – and never come back. I had nowhere to go and so I went to my room and did what I had to. I tied a rope from the garden around my neck and kicked away the stool I was standing on." She paused there as though trying to remember everything and added, "It didn't hurt me – one minute I was there and the next, I was outside my body and looking at it, hanging there. I must have become a ghost then, I suppose."

"You don't have to say more, Sally." And Lisa came over to the little ghost and tried to put her arms around her, but of course couldn't. Tom held the silver cross to her lips and told her to kiss it, saying as he did so, "Father, take this child into your care and look after her. She has been lost in the wilderness for so long now and is carrying a child of her own." His voice changed then and he challenged the demon who had held her prisoner in the house. "Get you gone, evil one – you are finished with this child. I forbid you to invade her spirit any more – in the name of the Father, Son and Holy Ghost."

The exorcism was complete and Sally was gone from the room. Tom was exhausted and told Lisa he had to rest for a while. "We're doing well though – soon the earthbound spirits will all be gone. And we can then reap our rewards from the Estate Agent." His wife nodded – she understood his meaning.

It took two days for Tom to track down Old Butler John and Melissa, the Georgian lady. They told him their stories and confirmed their wish to finally reach Heaven. Melissa and Butler John told him how they'd died – one of Typhoid like the young ladies and one crushed by a horse and carriage. Tom had no difficulties with this. They had been imprisoned in the house, through no fault of their own. He performed a service of exorcism on them both and released them to freedom and eternal rest.

"Now, there is only the Old Dowager and the General, according to the Butler – but they may prove to be more difficult than the others." As it turned out, however, the Old Dowager wasn't too difficult. She'd been telling people her story for years and now no one wanted to listen. They accused her of repeating herself. "Well really!" was her response. So when Tom met up with her one morning in the small breakfast room at the back of the house, she was very receptive to what he was saying. She told of her time alive in the house with her son and daughter-in-law and their seventeen-year-old daughter, Julia. For several weeks, there had been much confusion and consternation in the family because Julia had found herself a boyfriend with whom she wanted to be married. He was not of the same class as the family and Grandmother in particular, the Old Dowager, was completely against it. She was the matriarch of the family and still controlled the family's wealth.

"I told Julia that if she pursued her relationship with the young man, I would cut her off without a penny. She told me she didn't care what I did and so I told her I would also cut off her mother and father's inheritance, if they allowed the marriage to go ahead – and that would leave the whole family without a home and an income. Julia persisted however until one night, I couldn't sleep and went downstairs to get myself a drink of hot milk. It was something I often did. All the servants had already gone to bed and anyway, I was used to fending for myself. I was carrying a candle as I reached the top of the long staircase and I had only gone down one step when something bit into both my ankles and I fell, head over heels, all the way down to the bottom. I was bashed and bruised and couldn't see at all. Someone – and I don't know who, but I have my suspicions – had tied a strong twine across the stair, from one side to the other, held in place by nails – nails which were soon removed quickly. And that was how I met my end – killed by my own loving family. I didn't know at the time which one did it but I know it was one of them. When I had actually passed however, it was easy to listen into their conversation and to my surprise, I discovered my granddaughter had done it – and not my daughter-in-law, whom I had suspected. After all, it solved her problem as well as that of her father and mother, didn't it?"

She stopped talking and was breathless. Tom reached out his hand to her and she clasped it gratefully. "I was doomed to wander this house since then as I was murdered here. I had no option."

"Well, you do now," he said and pulled his chair over to hers and sat down next to her.

"I carry out exorcism to free earthbound spirits and allow them to go to their God. There was a demon in the house when you passed and he kept you here against your will. I've already freed several of your friends – would you welcome the same freedom?"

"I would welcome it – I never knew it was possible. How soon can you do it?" She was eager and impatient. "You mean I'll actually be free to go to Heaven, don't you? I wonder if I'll see any of my family there – not my granddaughter, of course."

He gave her the silver cross to kiss and then to hold and he spoke directly to the demon and told him to get away from this woman. "You have made this lady's time on earth far too long and God, her Father is waiting for her. Get you gone back to your friend, the Devil." He dipped his fingers in the holy water and made the sign of the cross on her forehead. She sighed deeply and swayed until after few moments, when she disappeared into a cloud of mist – then she was completely gone and Tom found himself alone. He slumped to the floor and sat against the wall, breathing heavily. This was proving to be quite a challenge.

On the following day, the couple visited the Estate Agent who'd helped them find the house in the first place. The owner was also there for the meeting and they all sat down. He and his assistant sat opposite and the lady offered a cup of coffee. Tom declined it and said, "We've come to discuss money and also to find out if you have any more houses where the ghosts are stopping the sale of the property. We've almost completed the current one and we need to be paid. Our agreement was five thousand pounds, wasn't it?"

"It was," the Estate Agent agreed, "but the house must be completely empty of ghosts. Are there any left?"

Tom explained about the General – the last one – but he was the toughest one. He pressed the point about any future work for him and his wife. "After all Mr Simpkins, we're doing a good job, aren't we?"

"You certainly are and I know you've been doing it for a long time now. My only problem is that I can't agree the job has been completed, until I visit the house and search for the ghosts myself. Only then can I part with the five thousand pounds. You understand, I hope." Mr Simpkins was an astute businessman and trusted no one without evidence.

"Come on Wednesday then – you and your assistant and you can see for yourself. We'll have got rid of the General by then." Tom stood up and as he left the room, he reminded Simpkins that he should come up with another property that couldn't sell because of ghosts – and for the same agreed price.

He and Lisa discussed how quiet the house was – how could ghosts have made so much noise – but they did. Now, it was only them and the General. It was actually a whole day before they tracked him down – in his full cavalier costume as usual – relaxing in the downstairs parlour. He stood up when they came in and removed his head, which he tucked under his arm. He made some ghostly noises before Tom stopped him saying, "Enough of that, General, we've already saved all the other ghosts' souls – your friends who shared this house with you. If you're trying to scare us, you're failing, I'm afraid."

"So, it's been you, has it? I wondered why it happened over just a few weeks." He placed his head back on his shoulders. "Well, there's no point trying to scare you two, is there – a waste of my time." He stood very straight and said loudly. "I have been given a very important job and I will always do my duty. You can't save my soul, I'm afraid, I am doomed to stay in this house for ever. So don't trouble yourselves. You can't budge me – and I can't go to your Heaven, anyway."

He did seem to understand what it was all about but Tom held up the silver cross and moved towards the General. "Why would you not want to join all those you knew in your time on earth – both when alive and dead."

"I have been placed here to protect the others who have lived here. I didn't manage to help them all but I assure you there would have been a lot more ghosts, if I hadn't been here. Have you ever noticed the cupboard beside the attic door – the one with the heavy chain and the big wooden cross?" He watched Tom and Lisa closely.

"Yes, I've noticed it," said Lisa, "but I never touched it. I don't know why but something about it scares me. What's in the cupboard, general?" Lisa already felt nervous just asking the question.

"A demon, my dear, one of Satan's own demons who came to me just before I had my head chopped off and told me if I gave him my soul, he would stop my execution from going ahead. I agreed but then he didn't keep his word and the executioner removed my head with one colossal blow. My spirit came back to this house – I had built it and lived in it and I was happy here, but my soul was then the devil's and my spirit was doomed to wander here ever since that time. However, I always managed to stop the demon from taking the souls of the ghosts who arrived later. And that became my job – and that's why the demon is still in the cupboard, held there by the holy cross – and with me standing guard over him."

"When you say Satan's demon, do you know which one he is?" Tom was interested in this strange tale. "How did you protect the other ghosts' souls from

Satan – because I know they're all now in Heaven with God – what did you do to stop the demon collecting the spirits one by one?"

"What did I do? What did I do? I tricked him as he'd tricked me. I lured him to this house, which I swore was full of ghosts – which of course it wasn't then, but they started to arrive soon after – and by that time, I had secured the demon in the cupboard and held him there with the big wooden cross. He couldn't do anything to me because he already had my soul – and Satan never bothered to help him escape because he had no time for failures. At first, there was only he and me here and we just ignored each other. I never went near the cupboard so I couldn't hear him moaning and cursing. No matter how much he begged, I never released him as I knew he would collect the ghosts' souls one by one as they arrived. I don't believe you General, you can't have managed to keep a demon in a cupboard for hundreds of years – he would have overpowered you." Tom was amazed.

"Not so young man – I outranked him; you see. He was one of Satan's lesser demons and I was after all a General, promoted in the Field." He looked thoughtful for a moment and then said, "Would you like to meet him? I've not seen him myself for many centuries – but he'll certainly know me."

Tom and Lisa looked at each other. Lisa was doubtful but Tom was eager. The swashbuckling General led the way upstairs with Tom and a hesitant Lisa in tow. If he could perform exorcisms satisfactorily, then Tom believed he could deal with a demon too.

The General smashed the wooden cross from the door and unlocked the cupboard with an ancient iron key. The heavy chains fell to the floor and the door creaked slowly open. He was grotesque – he looked like everyone's greatest fear. The General saw him as he really was but Tom saw him as an enormous snake crawling and curling his way across the floor. Lisa saw him as a gigantic rat with vicious sharp teeth and a long protruding tongue. He really portrayed their worst nightmares – what they both feared most in the world. He came out of the cupboard, saw the General and pounced on him, wrestling him to the floor. After much spitting and struggling later, the General was gone – to where, no one would ever know, except that it would be somewhere in Hell. The demon had obviously found a way around the fact that the General outranked him!

The rat turned to Lisa and grabbed her in his enormous mouth. He shook her whole body from side to side and finally spat her onto the floor, her head cracking loudly on the ground, where she writhed for a few moments and then lay very still. She was no more. The snake slid quickly towards Tom, who was already making his way towards the stairs – but to no avail – the long, curling tongue caught him before he reached the first step and threw him against the wall – a loud shrieking sound came from the reverend gentleman and then a heart-stopping thud. Tom's head took the full force of his fall and he, like Lisa, was no more.

Suddenly, there was no rat, snake or General to be seen. They had all disappeared into nothing and only Tom and Lisa's bodies lay there, dead to the world. The demon had obviously meant business. One good thing though, the house was now free of ghosts and demons – and at least the Estate Agent would be pleased. Maybe, it hadn't been a good idea to release the demon after all.

On Wednesday, Mr Simpkins and Audrey, his assistant, arrived at the house. Despite much ringing of the bell and knocking at the door, no one answered. Audrey still had the door key from when she was showing people around the house and so she fished it out and they went inside. It was a good opportunity to see if all the ghosts had really gone. They searched the house – every room proved to be empty – no ghosts appeared and they concluded that Tom had managed to do what he'd promised. To be thorough, they decided to go up to the topmost floor and there, they of course found Tom and Lisa in crumpled heaps on the landing. They lay beside a broken wooden cross and a heavy metal chain. An old cupboard had swung open but there was nothing inside. What on earth had happened?

The police and ambulance soon arrived and took the two bodies away. As they carried out Tom's body, his large, silver cross dangled from a tear in the black body bag.

Mr Simpkins and Audrey went into the kitchen where they made a cup of hot sweet tea for the shock. They sat at the table for a while, too dumbfounded to speak. At last, Audrey said, "Well, at least it's saved you five thousand pounds. I know it sounds callous but it's the truth, isn't it?"

Mr Simpkins sighed and got up to wash his cup. "Not only that Audrey but we've got the house back ready for the market and empty of all ghosts. It'll probably sell quite quickly as it's a beautiful property – it was only the ghosts that put people off." They both left the kitchen and went outside. They locked up securely.

Meanwhile, back in the kitchen, Lisa was making a cup of coffee and Tom was sitting by the table. "They're going to be very disappointed, aren't they, when they bring the first viewers to inspect the house – and they find us here in all our glory?" Tom couldn't help smiling. "We'll have to practice our haunting skills for that day. Wouldn't want to disappoint them now, would we?" And he accepted the coffee from his bemused wife.

Did She Do It – Or Didn't She

Lizzie Borden took an axe
And gave her mother forty whacks
When she saw what she had done
She gave her father forty-one

"Lizzie, for the fiftieth time, I have no money to give you for new boots." The richest man in Fall River, Massachusetts said in an exasperated tone. "There's nothing wrong with the ones you're wearing." He opened his newspaper, ready to enjoy his 'after breakfast' read.

"Pa, look at the soles – they're falling off these boots." Lizzie wasn't going to let it go. "Next time I'm in church, everyone will see and know how mean you are to your family. Mind you, they probably know that already." It was true, her boots were very old and the only place she could get money, was from her father, but he had to be handled carefully – the richer he'd become, the meaner he'd become too.

Her stepmother was still at the table, finishing her breakfast but there was no point in appealing to her, she'd just agree with her husband, and she'd always say, "Lizzie, don't talk back to your father – he always knows what's best." She was called Abby and wasn't liked by her two step daughters, Lizzie and Emma. Emma, however, was more long suffering than her sister and called the woman mother. Mind you, she had been at least twelve when her own mother, Sarah, had died whereas Lizzie had been only three. She hadn't understood what was happening. She called Abby 'The Gold Digger' when she married Andrew Borden and then 'Mrs Borden' after one particularly bad argument she had with her stepmother. She refused thereafter to call her mother.

The year was 1892 and Lizzie was 32 years old. It was the month of August and the day was incredibly hot – between 83% and 100%. Tempers in the Borden household were bound to be high as well and Andrew Borden and his daughter had similarly stubborn personalities, so the argument about the boots went on.

"Why don't you use your own money? You must have quite a bit put by now and I already give you two dollars each month, to do with what you want. What happens to it?" Andrew Borden was getting fed up with the argument and ended it by saying, "Leave me alone, daughter – I have no time for your theatrics just now. I have a sour stomach and feel as though I've been poisoned." He went on reading his newspaper.

Lizzie stood up and went towards the door. "You're a very unnatural father – you don't even care when your children need something. I wish my mother was still alive – she'd understand." Her mother had been dead for a long time now but Lizzie still missed her although she couldn't really remember much about her. Her father was a strange man, who seemed to like making enemies. No one in town liked him and tenants in the many houses he owned, positively hated him. In fact, that very morning, a sailor had visited him at home about receiving payment for work he'd done, but had been chased away by Andrew Borden.

"I have no money for you – when I have it, so will you," He told the man, who shouted back, "You have more money than anyone in the world – and you owe some of it to me." But he got nothing more than the door banged in his face.

"And another thing," Lizzie said before she left the room, "Mrs Borden has instructed me to darn the torn pillowcases and there are about ten of them. Surely, we're wealthy enough to buy some new ones. Anyone would think we're living on the poverty line – I'll hurt my eyes if I have to do that much sewing. Will you tell her it's not my job and that she has to buy some. Pa, are you listening to me?"

"I am listening, Lizzie, but I don't intend to do anything about it. Your stepmother is quite right – every cent we save goes towards a dollar. Think on that, girl, and get on with the sewing." Andrew Borden was not in a bending mood.

For a few days now, members of the household had been feeling sick. No one knew why, but even the maid was suffering from bad headaches. Mr and Mrs Borden both had stomach upsets and had kept their activities to a minimum. They felt sluggish and were prone to vomiting. Of course, they called the doctor but he could find nothing definite to help identify the illness. Mr Borden's brother-in-law was visiting at the time, but he hadn't mentioned feeling sick. As for Lizzie, she didn't tell anyone if she felt sick, but Abigail Russell, a friend of

Lizzie's, often took tea at the Borden house and she had been complaining of feeling ill too. Lizzie did actually visit the doctor's surgery and said that she thought she was being poisoned – but he told her not to talk so much rubbish and sent her away.

If her sister had been at home, Lizzie would have gone to see her, but Emma was away for a two-week holiday, so she had no option but to go upstairs to her room. She was seething with frustration. Her father was, if not the richest, then one of the richest men in the town of Fall River. In fact, it was often remarked on, that of the many arguments overhead between the sisters and their father, they were always about money. He was reputed to be parsimonious and totally disinterested in any form of charity. He was definitely not known for generosity. In fact, although the house on Second Street where they all lived was known to be an expensive property, and he was known as a very wealthy banker, Andrew Borden refused to have indoor plumbing and electricity installed as it would cost too much. This was at a time, when a great number of the well-to-do houses in Fall River had already carried out the work.

Lizzie lay on her bed and kicked off the rubbish boots. The heat was intense – almost unbearable. She stared at the net curtains on the window and there was no breeze whatsoever to move them. It made her feel even hotter. Maggie the maid, came into the room to tidy up and told Lizzie she should be outside enjoying the warm weather instead of languishing in a hot, sticky room like a sullen child.

"Really, Maggie – I'm trying to get away from the warm weather. Just because you have to do work you don't like; it doesn't mean I have to do the same. Go away and do something else, I need to rest. In fact, Mrs Borden wants you to wash all the house windows – inside and out. Has she told you yet? You'd better get started instead of coming in here and pestering me." Lizzie stretched out as much as she could. God, life wasn't easy and the heat was insufferable. Her petticoats clung to her legs and she tried to make herself think of snow, but it was no good.

Maggie, whose real name was Bridget Sullivan, did as she was bid. She went upstairs to do the master's room but as usual, it was as neat as a pin, and there was little to do, although woe betide her, if he found one speck of dust around the house. He liked to check her cleaning products every few weeks, just to make sure she was making them last and not wasting them. He was a hard taskmaster. The household chores were carried out in a strange way – Maggie was only

130

responsible for the daily cleaning of her room and the two sisters looked after their bedrooms. Even the main bedroom, occupied by Mr and Mrs Borden, was actually their responsibility – although Maggie did have to do the heavy cleaning, like sheet changing and sweeping the floor. She carried on cleaning and tidying and when finished, she started on the stairs up to the attic, which needed a good brushing. And she still had all the windows to wash.

Later in the morning, Lizzie left her room. She went through the kitchen and out across the yard towards the barn. She stopped by the old pear tree to gather some of the 'fallers' from the ground. It managed to produce masses of fruit which still tasted delicious, although the tree was as old as the house itself. In fact, once the pears hit the ground, they tasted even better than those still on the branches. She gathered three pears and realised her stomach was feeling a bit better. In the big barn, she settled down in the top most part of the loft – no one would bother her here and she began to leisurely munch her pears. She'd actually come to search for lead sinkers to go fishing, but couldn't find where they'd been put. Soon she dropped off to sleep and two pears slipped from her lap and rolled across the dusty floor. She woke with a start and sat up. What was that noise? It was like a groan and then a thump but there were no actual voices. Very cautiously, she climbed down from the loft and listened carefully. She could hear nothing now so she went into the downstairs hall – still nothing until she opened the sitting room door and saw her father spreadeagled along the sofa – dead as a doornail and with the most horrendous head injuries imaginable. She didn't know what to do. She couldn't help him, she knew that – and there was so much blood, she could hardly believe it. He was so cut about the head; he was almost unrecognisable and it looked like he'd even lost one of his eyes.

The time was about eleven o'clock and he'd not long come back from strolling around the town, checking on each bank where he kept money and on the tenants in his numerous properties. He had so many fingers in pies in Fall River, he had to keep a watchful eye on who might be cheating him. He must have been back in the house for a few moments only, when Lizzie screamed for Maggie, and had to scream a second time before being heard. Maggie took in the terrifying scene and wrapped her arms around Lizzie to stop her screaming. Then the maid ran out of the house to fetch the police, who turned up after only a few minutes. There was usually a policeman patrolling the suburban streets at most hours – and as soon as Maggie told him what was wrong, he blew his whistle to summon his colleagues from other beats. Lizzie and Maggie huddled together in the hall, too afraid to go back into the sitting room.

Soon, the house was full of policemen firing questions at Lizzie and Maggie for quite a long time and arranging for the body to be taken away. It had been photographed from all angles. The police photographer had arrived within minutes. "Where were you just before finding your father like this?" And Lizzie explained that she'd been looking for sinkers in the barn when she heard a sound coming from the house.

"Or was I coming down stairs from my room – no, I was definitely coming from the barn. And there he was, lying on the sofa with blood everywhere. "She looked around the room and asked, "Where is Mrs Borden, my stepmother – I haven't seen her all the morning." And she wrung her hands in despair. "It isn't like her to stay away for so long."

"I don't know where she is," Maggie said, "I spoke with her about nine o'clock this morning when she was going upstairs to check on the clean linen – she gave me my orders for the day then and I haven't seen her since. Where can she be?" Lizzie intervened at this point.

"Oh I remember, someone called at the house with a note for her, asking that she go and visit a sick friend in town. She must still be there."

Maggie looked puzzled and said, "I was working at the front of the house and I didn't see anyone."

Lizzie looked at her angrily. "I cannot help what you failed to see, can I, Maggie?"

The policeman nodded to his companion and beckoned him to follow him. "We want you two to stay here with this other officer until we search the rest of the house – in case there's still someone hiding somewhere."

Lizzie and Maggie looked scared out of their wits at the suggestion that some stranger might still be in the house, but the maid jumped up and said, "I'll go upstairs – I know where she might be." And she flew out of the room. Mrs Churchill, a neighbour and sister of Abby Borden's went with her – she'd come to the house to comfort Lizzie. The two scared women left together.

Shortly, the policeman ran upstairs after them and brought them back down. They'd been screaming loud enough to awaken the dead. "I'm afraid I have some more bad news for you, Miss Borden. Your stepmother is upstairs lying at the side of her bed and her head has been battered similar to Mr Borden's." Lizzie fainted clean away and lay there for some time. Maggie fetched smelling salts and the aroma soon brought her mistress around.

"How can that be, officer? I saw her just this morning? Do you think someone broke into the house and attacked them both? That must be what happened – but I never saw anyone else around the house today. Last night and the night before, I did see a man's figure running around the front of the house but it was dark and I couldn't make him out. It could have been him, couldn't it? I honestly thought Mrs Borden must still be with her sick friend."

Maggie was staring at her and said again, "I didn't see anyone with a note for Mrs Borden and I've been around all morning."

"I can't help what you miss seeing, Maggie – I took the note from the servant and passed it to Mrs Borden. And that's all there is to it." Lizzie was annoyed with Maggie again. "I'll not tell you again about contradicting me."

After several hours, the police left Number 92 Second Street. Lizzie and Maggie arranged for a telegraph to be sent to Emma Borden in New Bedford, telling her to come home and to cut her holiday short. The newspapers had got wind of the double murder and were around the house like flies. Lizzie's picture was on the front of all the local papers and a reader recognised her and reported to police that she'd seen that woman in a drug store in Fall River the day before the murders took place. The druggist confirmed that she been trying to buy the poison prussic acid but that he'd refused to sell it to her.

The police questioned her about this and she explained she'd wanted it to clean a seal skin jacket that she'd damaged. "It's quite normal to use prussic acid to remove such stains. I can't imagine what the stupid man thought I was going to do with it." The policeman just looked at her grimly and continued with his investigations. The strange thing was that later, when confronted with the druggist's accusation by the Prosecuting Barrister, Lizzie denied she'd ever been to the Drugstore at all. Another contradiction that didn't help her.

"I must contact the church to say that I won't be able to teach Sunday School this afternoon. Maggie, run along and tell Alice Russell what's happened here and ask her to tell the minister." Lizzie was a devout and devoted churchgoer and was highly thought of by the religious community, in fact she chaired several church committees which dealt with social and charitable issues. She'd always played a big part in such activities and had no intention of stopping. Alice Russell was her friend and neighbour, but when called as a witness at the subsequent trial, didn't help her friend at all.

Suddenly, the house was empty but she could still see the body of her father stretched along the sofa. She sat for a few moments before going upstairs to the room where her mother had been found. There was a bloodstain on the carpet but at least the body had been removed to the mortuary – and she didn't have to look at Mrs Borden. She felt guilty about always calling her Mrs Borden – but she'd never liked her and resented the place she'd filled in her father's life. "Poor Mrs Borden," she said to the empty room, "you really were hated, weren't you?" She wished her sister was there with her – she could talk to Emma.

Alice Russell decided to stay with her friend on the night of the murder – as did her uncle, John Morse, who'd been visiting Andrew Borden to discuss business matters. John said he'd concluded the business matters with his brother-in-law early in the morning of the day in question and had gone out to the town of New Bedford to buy some new oxen and visit some of his relatives there. He could add nothing to what had happened. He'd been absent for the whole day.

Emma Borden arrived in Fall River on the day following the murders and came straight to the house to see her sister. There were several people in the house – the neighbours had rallied around to comfort Lizzie – mostly from the church community. Mrs Churchill was there again and so was Alice Russell. There were police still there, scrutinising everything for clues. They'd found two axes and two hatchets in the cellar but one of the axes had no handle but its shape made the police think it could have caused the indentation on the head of Mrs Borden. There was no sign of any blood on the tools. Could the broken axe be the murder weapon, yet where was the blood? Lizzie said she didn't recognise it.

Next morning, before any visitors arrived, the two sisters sat in the kitchen together, with Maggie running in and out all the time, in case they needed something and because she was afraid to be alone for too long. Although there was almost eleven years between their ages, the sisters were very alike and could easily be recognised as such. Neither sister had ever married and seemed content to stay at home with their parents – despite their father's meanness. What else could unmarried ladies do in these days?

Emma took her sister's hand and said, "Now, Lizzie, tell me everything slowly. I am so shocked; I've hardly taken anything in – and you don't look too well either."

Lizzie looked thoughtful for a moment, then. "Do you remember the time Father gave Abby a house all of her own, to do with what she liked? I challenged him, saying what about us and was told, in no uncertain terms that he could do what he liked with his properties. But when he began to give other properties to Abby's relatives, it really was too much. What on earth was he doing? Don't forget that he'd even willed this house to Abby's sister, Mrs Churchill, on his death – he was quite willing to make us homeless. A strange kind of father, don't you think?"

"Of course I remember and what about the time last year when he gave the horse away because it ate too much. You loved that horse, didn't you? And used to enjoy riding him – but father wasn't interested in what you wanted. He could easily have afforded to keep a horse – he was just too mean. And this house – he refused point blank to have electricity and indoor plumbing installed – don't forget that." Emma was almost breathing fire. "I think we had every right to dislike the man, don't you?" She stopped talking and allowed herself to calm down.

"Mind you," she continued, "he did sell you and I a house for one dollar and then bought it back from us for five thousand dollars. I suppose that might have been a way of ensuring we would have a roof over our heads when he passed away – but a rather strange way to do it. Now, what was that all about? I bet it was some sort of cheat on taxes, you know how clever he was at not paying his way if he could avoid it."

The sisters were enjoying the conversation and Emma suddenly asked, "Lizzie, look at me straight in the eyes and tell me you had nothing to do with the murders."

"Don't be silly, sister – I was nowhere near either of them when they died. How can you even ask me that?" Lizzie was quite indignant. On being asked where she had actually been before discovering father's body, she replied she was in the kitchen doing some ironing. She had about ten hankies to launder. Then she changed it to 'I was on the stairs' and then again, 'I was in the barn looking for sinkers'. In fact, I must have been in all those places from one moment to the next but I can't remember where exactly I was just before finding his body. At this confusion, Emma became agitated and said, "Lizzie, you've got to straighten out your thoughts. If you start giving the police such contradictory answers when they question you, you'll become their main suspect. Are you listening to me, sister?"

Lizzie nodded and said she'd have to go to bed – she was so tired. She turned back at the door however and said, "One thing I do remember though was that I met Father when he came back from town that morning and I helped him by removing his boots and putting on his slippers. Then he lay down on the sofa to take a nap, so I suppose I must have been in the sitting room too." She looked confused and it turned out to be even more confusing when newspapers published the story on their front pages. It was alongside photos of Mr Borden lying dead on the sofa and he was clearly still wearing both boots. They were shiny and black. Her story about taking off his boots was even more confusing then. Lizzie was quite upset when she eventually saw this. Emma could only repeat her warning that she must get her thoughts together for when the police finally questioned her – or she would come across as very suspicious. Lizzie promised that she would.

Three days later, Lizzie Borden was charged with the murders of her father and stepmother and taken away to await questioning at the initial hearing, which was held in Fall River. Most of the Borden's friends and neighbours had, by this time, increasingly separated themselves from Lizzie. The police decision was based on the fact that no one, but Lizzie, was in the house when the unfortunate couple met their deaths. Unfortunately, when questioned about her whereabouts on that morning, Lizzie told them all the same options as she'd told Emma before. Maggie the maid also told yet another story to the police, saying that she'd heard Miss Lizzie upstairs when her father returned home from town and actually heard the two of them talking together in the sitting room. Then silence.

At the full trial in June 1893, it became public knowledge that the Borden House had been broken into and much stolen – just the previous year. The family actually suspected Lizzie herself as being the perpetrator – but there was no proof. She had also been accused of shoplifting in the same year but it couldn't be proven. She was an odd mixture of a religious, charitable churchgoer and someone suspected of being a thief – and now a murderer. At the Preliminary Hearing in Fall River, Judge Josiah Blaisdell had declared that Lizzie was probably guilty of the murders but that a full trial would be needed. Despite being found Not Guilty at the full Trial, the good churchgoers of Fall River never forgot Judge Blaisdell's declaration only a few days after the deaths, when the evidence was still fresh.

Her friend, Alice Russell, explained at the trial that the night before the murders, Lizzie had visited her at home and told her, "I really fear for my father's life. I'm sure someone will try to kill him – he is so mean and detested by many people. He could be a really dreadful man. Our conversation had taken an odd turn when Lizzie said this as we'd only been talking about food recipes. It was said right out of the blue, almost as though she desperately wanted to sow the seed in my mind." She went on to tell how she'd gone into the cellar the very next day and found Lizzie burning a pale blue dress in a brazier. "Because it had been covered in old paint," she'd explained. This was the same dress she'd been wearing on the day the murders occurred. Things were not looking good for Lizzie.

A discussion also took place at the Trial about pigeons, which didn't help her situation either. Apparently, there were a lot of pigeons in the area and Lizzie not only fed them, but built a nesting roost for them in the barn. She was very fond of the birds, but of course, her feeding them attracted not only large numbers of them, but also mice and rats. Her father objected but of course, Lizzie just ignored him. He got into the habit of going out into the barn each night and one by one, butchering them with an old, but very sharp axe. His daughter had hated him for doing this and she had to stop feeding and housing them in the barn, as they were dying in such great numbers. The actual butchery of the mice and rats didn't seem to bother her.

The Prosecuting Counsel had no difficulty in painting the accused in a bad light. Many people testified at the trial but all said, they'd seen no strangers around the house on the day in question. And even if any had seen someone, the house was always securely locked – even the inside doors – since the burglary the previous year. The Prosecuting Counsel called nine witnesses and the Defence Counsel only three.

The trial was held at New Bedford, opening on 5 June 1893 with the Jury's verdict declared on 20 June. The Jury took very little time to come to their decision. The verdict was Not Guilty. The Jury felt most of the evidence given against Lizzie Borden was circumstantial and not sufficient to justify a decision of Guilty. When the man in the Jury, said the words 'Not Guilty', Lizzie let out a loud shout of delight and fell forwards onto the banister of the stand, her head in her hands. She was jubilant and shouted out a second time.

In the course of the trial, it had also been established that, despite the very catchy chant which is still sung by children in modern times, there was only 29 fatal strikes on the bodies of Andrew and Abby Borden – but the numbers used in the chant rhymed so much better than the actual truth. Lizzie had been examined after the murders and found to have no blood on her or on any of her possessions, which helped in the finding of an innocent verdict.

When she returned home after the trial, friends and family ignored both Lizzie and by association, Emma as well. The town's people changed their direction if they saw either one of them coming and sat well away from them in church. Neither sister was 'a shrinking violet' and they immediately bought a large and beautiful house in the wealthiest part of Fall River. And why not? They were now worth Ten Million Dollars in today's money. The house was on 'The Hill' – the best of neighbourhoods in Fall River. In line with her new status and despite her infamous notoriety, Lizzie started to call herself Lisbeth. She felt the name had more dignity than Lizzie.

"I'll never be able to call you Lisbeth – it's not your name after all. Your name has always been 'Lizzie Andrew Borden' and that's what I'm going to call you." Emma was too old to change her ways. Just before they actually moved into the new house, the sisters visited their old home in Second Street to collect some personal possessions and some things they couldn't bear to part with. The house felt eerie indeed and the two women settled in the kitchen as it didn't seem right to go straight into the sitting room where Father had been found. "Don't you want more than you have there, Lizzie – there's lots of your things still around the place?" Emma was filling the kettle to make a cup of tea.

"At least, there's no rush, is there?" Lizzie agreed and said, "While you're doing that, Em – I'll go upstairs to my room and fetch a few of the old trinkets I've had for so long." She stood up and left the kitchen. Emma watched her go with a look of sympathy on her face. *Poor Lizzie*, she thought.

Lizzie tentatively stepped on to the stairs and very slowly started up the staircase. When she reached the middle of her climb, she looked upwards and saw there Mrs Borden her stepmother, her posture erects as it always had been. She was dressed all in black and wore a black veil. She stared down at Lizzie and slowly lifted the veil from her face, revealing clearly the smashed side of her head with the huge bloody scab that still encrusted her injuries.

Lizzie put her arm across her eyes and stumbled down a stair or two. Turning around, she intended to go back downstairs away from Mrs Borden and there, at the foot of the stairs with one hand resting on the banister, stood Mr Borden, her father. He was smartly dressed but had only half a face and one eye. His wounds were dreadful and Lizzie couldn't bear to look at him. He smiled crookedly but it was a sardonic smile and she could see his teeth shining white in the dried blood that clung to his face.

She screamed and screamed for Emma, who came rushing out of the kitchen, teapot in hand and shouting, "My God, Lizzie, what's wrong?" Lizzie just pointed to the top of the stairs and then the bottom.

"They're both there waiting for me." She was distraught.

"Lizzie, there's no one there – you're hallucinating, dear. Come on into the kitchen and have a hot, sweet cup of tea." She had to guide her sister down the rest of the stairs and her into the kitchen.

Lizzie never did get the trinkets from her old home. She left the house that day and never returned there for the rest of her life.

Following this incident, the women settled in the new house called 'Maplecroft' and as always, got on well together. Emma didn't change much but Lizzie did. She'd always been an outgoing person but it was mainly around church matters – now she became interested in the arts. She truly didn't care that none of her old friends came to see her and also that no one in the church would sit beside her – let them turn the other way when they saw her coming. She didn't care – she needed nothing from them and wouldn't miss their friendship. She became rather a Bohemian and started to visit New York and Boston where she became involved with actors and writers. She was very popular in their circles as she was a very rich woman, something poets and writers really appreciated. Emma didn't mix with them however – she had a much meeker personality and made no secret that she disliked her sister's new friends.

The women together, erected a ten-foot-high granite monument to their parents in Oakhill Cemetery, Fall River, two years after their deaths. Everyone in the town thought it was guilt on Lizzie's part and put it down to sheer bravado. It was costly bravado – it took Two Thousand Dollars to do it. Maplecroft didn't save them from the locals' prejudice. Lizzie's reputation was known worldwide – to be associated with such horrendous murders of a mother and father, brought onlookers in their droves to stare at the house and the children would run up and ring their doorbell in the middle of the night and then run away before anyone could get there. It was an old trick which children often indulged in, but usually at Hallowe'en. They also pelted the house with gravel and eggs – and chanted the verse over and over again:

'Lizzie Borden took an axe
And gave her mother forty whacks
When she saw what she had done
She gave her father forty-one'

They sang it as a dare to the murderess. Would she herself come to the door to chase them away? Every child in Fall River – and eventually in the whole of America and even the world – knew the chant off by heart. Although it wasn't actually accurate, it rhymed better and so, it caught on.

It was a horrible time for Emma but Lizzie chose to ignore it and went on even more of her visits to New York and Boston to meet her new Bohemian friends. On one occasion, she insisted on throwing a party for her new, very close friend, Nance O'Neill, an actress. The party was so wild that it made Emma come to the decision to leave her sister at Maplecroft and buy another house of her own. She did this and the two women were estranged for the rest of their lives. The Boston Sunday Herald asked for an interview with Emma and on asking why she'd left her sister after all this time, she told them. "I refuse to discuss the matter with you. I did not go until conditions became absolutely intolerable." It said it all really. Emma returned regularly to Fall River to visit her parents' grave – but she never went to see Lizzie, who never once visited the grave herself.

Emma made friends with the Gardner Family in New Market, New Hampshire and they became her good friends. She told them of her last wishes when she died and also where and how she was to be buried. Many people came to her funeral, as she was always liked. She died age 76 years old on 10 June 1927 of kidney inflammation – only nine days after Lizzie's own death at age 66 years. She died of pneumonia on 1 June 1927 and sadly, no one came to her funeral.

Both women were buried in Fall River, on either side of Andrew and Abby Borden and under the shadow of the 10 feet high blue, granite memorial stone. Sometimes, when the light is right and you squint your eyes just so, you think you can see three figures dressed in black. One is a man and two are women. It is Andrew Borden and on his one side is Abby, his wife and on his other side, Emma, his daughter – they can be seen quite clearly standing erect and side-by-side. There never has been a sighting of Lizzie.

There in could be the answer to the title of this story.

She Really is a Tough, Old Bird

Miss Blyth lived in the middle cottage in a row of terraced homes. She must have been at least eighty years old with a very slight build and snowy white hair. The village children were petrified of her and if they saw her coming along the street, they'd scurry off at great speed and tell their mothers that they'd just seen the village witch. Repeatedly, the mothers would scold them for calling her that and threaten punishment – but it never materialised. So her title of Witch stuck with her and the children continued to run away. She'd lived in the village all her life, never had children nor ever married. She'd looked after her mother and father until they passed away and she also taught at the village school for several years when she was younger. Her cottage had belonged to her father, and to his father before him, she'd been born there so it had always been a family home as long as anyone could remember.

It was Halloween and the children were even more excited than usual, running around and screaming to scare each other. The village always held a combined celebration – both for Halloween and for the burning of a bonfire with an effigy of Guy Fawkes on top. It was a strange tradition really, as the two incidents weren't connected but the dates fell so close to each other, it seemed a logical decision. It had been a few years since Miss Blyth had taken part in the village celebration but maybe this year, she would. It might make the children stop calling her 'witch', but she doubted it.

Today, she was walking to the village shop to collect a few groceries. She walked badly using a walking stick to steady herself and sometimes a small trolley on wheels. The weather today was bright but cold and the autumn leaves were lying all around – autumn was a lovely season, she thought, with everything going to sleep to be ready for the following Spring. She saw one of her neighbours coming towards her and prepared herself for a natter – Betty Smith could gossip for England, but she was a kind soul and meant well, so Miss Blyth put a smile on her face.

"Pop in for a cup of tea on your way home, I've got a few things to tell you." Betty lived next door and liked to think she looked after her elderly neighbour, but many times, it was the other way around.

"Very well, Betty, see you then." And Miss Blyth hobbled off up the street, the children watching her from the safe distance of the play park.

"Have you heard about Mr Jones at Number 5? They found him this morning lying in his kitchen, his head covered in blood and his home completely ransacked." Miriam was enjoying telling the story and could manage to fetch the requested goods from the shelves and gossip at the same time. "Are you listening, Miss Blyth? It's important. He was your neighbour, wasn't he?"

"I thought he still was until I came in here. You've shocked me beyond words." She had to sit down on the customers' chair by the door to catch her breath. *Mr Jones attacked. Who would ever do such a thing? Fred was not a young man but he wasn't as old as herself and she'd always thought of him as a youngster, although he must have been at least seventy. What was the world coming to?*

"Would you like the boy here to walk you home? You've obviously had quite a shock?" Miriam took great pleasure in the effect her story had had on the elderly woman. She liked to believe she was the 'News Source' of the village. Miss Blyth however, waved her hand in a refusal and began to pack her things into her trolley.

On her way home, a group of three boys approached her and asked if they could push her trolley for her. She thanked them but said no. They began to follow her and one asked, "Did you kill the old bloke, Witch? He lived close to you, didn't he?" The others made cackling noises and Miss Blyth felt afraid. Luckily, Betty appeared at her garden gate and shooed the boys away.

They ran, but not before shouting, "Watch her, Mrs – she's an old witch. You shouldn't be her friend."

"The kettle's boiling, Edwina, get yourself inside and sit down. Cheeky, young thugs – just ignore them." And Edwina Blyth did as she was told. "You've heard about Fred Jones then? I'm sure Miriam at the shop filled you in with the details. She'd enjoy doing that, I'm sure." And Betty laid out a newly baked Victoria Sponge, cutting her neighbour a good slice. She sat down opposite Edwina and clasped her chubby hands. "Apparently, it probably happened late last night or early this morning. He was already up and boiling the kettle in his kitchen when it must have happened. No one knows any facts yet, except whoever it was, was a thief as well as a murderer. He had a lot of old coins and medals, you know, he showed me them once and said they were very valuable. It'll be interesting to hear if they've all gone."

When Edwina went to her own house, she saw the police had put some kind of roped-off area in front of Fred's house and they were standing outside his front door. Edwina leaned over the hedge and asked if the two policemen would like a cup of tea. "I've just bought some ginger parkins." She added as an enticement.

"We'd really like that ma'am if you've got the time." She went inside and soon returned with a tray. She passed it over the hedge and said, "Enjoy." She folded her arms in front of her and breathed deeply. "What a to-do. Is Fred really dead?"

"He is unfortunately, ma'am, and his house has been wrecked by thieves. We'll be coming in to see you very soon to see if you can help us. You might have seen something, you never know." She told them he'd had a valuable collection of old coins and medals and asked if they'd been taken. "All in good time, ma'am." And they munched into their ginger biscuits as though they hadn't seen food for a week. Whilst talking to them, she had a good look into Fred's kitchen – looking for clues, she told herself. She noticed that the door hadn't been forced and no windows had been broken. Fred had obviously known whoever was at the door and invited them inside. Something she did notice however was that one side of the old brick fire had been knocked about and a few bricks were scattered over the floor. They looked like very old bricks – probably original and as old as the cottage itself. *Now what time had she got up this morning – did she see or hear anything unusual?* She went back indoors and sat at the kitchen table, where she always did her best thinking.

She remembered seeing some 'Trick and Treaters' going up his path last night, and then they'd come to her door as well. She told them she had no money and offered them a bag of Dolly Mixtures – but they refused, saying they only wanted money. "Sorry," she said and they disappeared. She didn't know how they'd got on with Fred but she knew he'd had them inside the house. He was – or had been – a nice man, had Fred.

Betty knocked Edwina's door after tea that night. "Are you coming down to the bonfire in the High Street – there's a barbeque and candy apples and goodness knows what else? Edwina hadn't been planning to go but as Betty had taken the trouble to call round for her, she decided she would.

Two old village women walking down the street together. They seemed innocuous and unimportant – but they were watching all around them and taking everything in. They'd become sleuths and they didn't realise it. The bonfire was already ablaze and the people were crowding around it, food in hand and Sparklers in the other. The effigy of a man was slowly disappearing as he sat on top of the flames. The Vicar approached them and asked if they'd like to sit down in the tent the Boy Scouts had provided. They followed him and he fetched them two glasses of cider. "Terrible business about Old Fred," he said, as he sat down, "I only saw him myself late yesterday afternoon when I called round to see him. Terrible business." He shook his head and stared at his hands.

"Was there something you wanted to talk to him about?" Edwina asked casually and listened to the answer with interest.

"He wanted to show me his coin collection and the medals his family had won. He was so proud of them and I'd promised to call round to see them many times before." A group of children ran past the tent, singing *Remember, remember the 5th of November, Guy Fawkes, Gun Powder and Plot.* They didn't know the rest of the rhyme and so they just kept repeating the same words. It was very irritating and almost threatening. The verse always intimidated Edwina although she knew it was just an old chant. The Vicar left them then and joined the group gathered around the fire. He was a sociable chap and liked to do his duty by his flock.

"Well then" – Edwina leaned closer to Betty – "that's several people who visited Fred in the last hours of his life. But it's not enough to know a little, we'll just have to keep on digging for more."

The women sat together drinking their cider and watching everything and everyone. Some of the children were dressed in amazing costumes and some of the grown-ups too. People went to such trouble to be better than their neighbours and friends. Two children were dressed as choirboys in white robes and carrying artificial candles that flickered like the real thing. With them, was a man dressed all in red like the Devil, with a long tail, a mask and a three-pronged fork. The group stood apart from the others and looked threatening – Good and Evil standing together. The two choirboys looked familiar to Edwina and she recognised them as part of the 'Trick and Treaters' who visited her house after having been at Fred's. One little boy in particular she recognised.

Betty and Edwina walked home together – two old friends but feeling and looking rather miserable. Betty put it in to words. "Remember to lock up tight tonight, Old Friend – we have to protect ourselves, the culprit's still at large."

"And you, Betty – see you tomorrow." And they went into their separate homes. Fred's house was in complete darkness of course. Edwina sat in the most comfortable armchair and found her mind was in turmoil. It was a real puzzle and she wanted to solve it. She'd always enjoyed puzzles and mysteries all her life and she was always searching for those type of books at the library. She realised she probably had seen the culprit hanging around in the last couple of days, yet nothing registered with her.

That night, something woke her and the clock said it was only 6.00 am and it was still very dark outside. She switched on the bedside lamp and got up – just to check everything was all right. The old house creaked and sighed as she went downstairs. The row of terrace cottages was very old; the first ones built reaching back to the seventeen hundred's – 1630 if the plaque on Number 1 was to be believed. Edwina's home had always made strange sounds because of its age so she climbed back upstairs to bed, feeling reassured. She managed to get another hour's sleep before the alarm clock woke her. She knew the postman had already been as she heard the letters plop onto the mat. A fresh pot of tea and a boiled egg later, she settled down with her mail.

There was a knock at the door – very early for anyone to call. When she opened the door, a child stood there with a small bunch of flowers in his hand.

"Hello, child, what can I do for you?" Edwina was pleasantly surprised to see a child there – and not calling her 'witch'. The child passed the straggly flowers to the old woman and then just stood there.

"Does your mummy know you're here?" And on being told that she did, Edwina asked him if he'd like to come inside. "You were at the bonfire last night, weren't you? I recognise you – one of the choir boys?" The little boy nodded. "Would you like some milk?" she asked.

With Edwina's tea and a glass of milk, the two settled at the kitchen table. "Now what made you come to see me?

The boy wiped his mouth on his sleeve before saying, "I wanted to tell you that I don't think you're a witch – all my friends do, but I don't. You're just a nice old lady who offered me Dolly Mixtures when I came to your door." Edwina was touched by his words and smiled.

"Will you be my friend then?" she asked.

"Yes please, my mummy told me to be your friend, so that's okay." He looked meaningfully at the bottle of milk and waited. "Can I ask you something else please?" And was told of course.

"Why is that lady lying on the ground next door, stretched out on the doorstop? She doesn't look well." And he slurped his second glass of milk.

Edwina moved fast – well as fast as she could and went up next door's garden path. There on the steps to the door, Betty was lying. She was still in her dressing gown and had a bleeding gash on her forehead. Edwina moved past her and rang for an ambulance. She also found a clean tea towel which she pressed on Betty's cut, putting gentle pressure on the cut. Good thing she still remembered her first aid lessons she'd had at the village hall.

"My God, Betty, what has happened? Did you trip over the door sill and hit your head on the step?" But Betty was concussed and couldn't speak properly. The ambulance arrived very quickly and took her friend to hospital. She remembered the little boy in her kitchen and returned to send him home. He'd been upstairs to use her toilet and was just coming down. He left her house then saying he'd be late for school if he didn't hurry. The police arrived and she had to give two statements – one about Fred and now, one about Betty, although she really didn't know what had happened to her.

"Her home has been ransacked in the same way as Mr Jones. Things have been thrown about and probably stolen. Are you aware if Mrs Smith kept any valuables in her home?"

Edwina nodded, "Well, I know she had some First Edition books she kept secreted away – could that be something worth stealing?"

"It most certainly could, Miss Blyth. Did she tell people about the books, do you know?" The young policeman was writing in his notebook as he spoke. "These things have happened very close together – may I ask that you keep your doors locked and if you hear – or see – anything out of the ordinary, you contact me immediately? They've thrown things around and strangely enough, pulled bricks out of her chimney wall – just the way they did in Mr Jones' kitchen. Proper mindless vandalism, if you ask me."

Edwina told him she'd been woken up about 5 or 6 o'clock in the morning by some strange sounds and she'd gone downstairs to investigate – but nothing had been disturbed, so she went back to bed. But she kept thinking about the strange vandalism. *Perhaps they were looking for something*, she thought. *It must have been Betty and her burglar I heard in the early hours.* She must remember to tell the police about the teenage boys who'd accosted her the other day – they could be possible suspects. Her curiosity was working overtime.

Betty soon recovered and came home. Edwina was delighted to see her, but wondered what was going on in this village – something had changed in the last few weeks, but what?

"Right, Betty, the tea pot is Old Fred, the sugar cubes the Trick and Treaters, the milk jug the Vicar, the salt seller, the postman and the pepper pot is the delivery boy from the shop. And she placed Fred in the middle with all the others in a circle around him. "Oh and also the pushy teenage boys who bothered me the other day" – she added several tea bags to the circle – "that can be them, although we don't actually know if they ever visited Old Fred."

"Why Edwina, that could be my own story with all the same people visiting me the day before I was attacked – even the Vicar who brought me some fresh carrots from his allotment. Use the vinegar bottle for yourself in the circle – and we've covered both incidents." Betty was getting quite excited and, in her haste, knocked over the postman. After throwing a pinch over her shoulder, she quickly stood the postman back up again.

Edwina fetched some scraps of paper. "Now, let's try to put the times each one called at Fred's – not exact times of course, but the best we can manage. Right – the day before Fred was found dead, the shop delivery boy brought some groceries about six o'clock and I saw the Halloween group go into his house about eight o'clock that night. They couldn't have hurt Fred and smashed his house 'cause they had young children with them. We don't actually know when the Vicar visited him so we'll just have to ask him tomorrow." As she was talking, she put the stickers with times by the salt seller etc. "The last person to see him was the postman and that was about seven o'clock the next morning – but he was already dead then, and of course, we don't know if the teenage boys even knew Fred." She touched the teabags but didn't move them.

Betty broke in with. "There could be someone else who visited him that we know nothing about."

"Yes, yes – that's true, Betty." Edwina fetched a cup from the shelf to be the possible 'new unknown person' in the group. Both women sat back on their chairs and clasped their hands on the table.

Next day, they hobbled off to see the Vicar at the manse and took him some freshly baked scones to butter him up. "Come in, come in, ladies, how pleasant to see you." He was an affable man and well liked in the village – but that didn't necessarily mean he couldn't murder. He liked talking about himself and was quite happy to tell the women about his movements before Fred died. "I'd been at the Town Museum and Library as I wanted to find a book about coins to take along for Fred. I love History, you see – I've always been a bit of an amateur historian and when I first came to the village, I set about searching through all the local records. This was quite an important area at one time and many famous incidents in history occurred here."

Despite the reason they'd originally come to the manse, Edwina and Betty were fascinated by what the Vicar was saying. "Your cottages are quite famous because of their past. After King Charles the First was executed by his own people and his son had fled to live in France, the new model army leader, Oliver Cromwell, actually lived in one of your homes. His men were billeted in all the others. The people were thrown out of their homes which were made available for the soldiers. Apparently, they stayed around here for quite some time.

The annoying thing is that we don't know which cottage he stayed in – but I'm still in the process of looking through several old records in the Library's Archives." He loved his subject and rattled on about it for quite a time. The two women eased their way out of the manse and went to the play park on their way home. They knew the 'rough boys' would be there after school and they had their question for them.

The group of boys saw them coming and formed a circle with their bikes. Edwina whispered to Betty, "Leave this to me – I know how to deal with them." And she pulled her long, black cloak tightly around her body. She pulled her hair loose and the long, straggly white hair blew all around her face. She looked more like a witch than ever before and her angular, haggard face looked very frightening.

The boys became quiet and watched her closely. She pointed a long, bony finger at them and said, "You all know who I am – and what I am. Make no mistake about, I am the witch you've always called me and I can do things you could never even imagine – and I don't care how many times I have to do them. Did any of you go near Old Fred's cottage on the day before he was murdered – or on the day he was found dead? This is no joke; I want the truth." Betty was staring at this new Edwina.

One of the more mouthy boys started to laugh and said, "You don't frighten us, you stupid old woman. So, you're a witch. That's your problem, not ours and you have no right to question us." He climbed onto his bike and was just about to ride off when the bike flew up in the air and came crashing down on the concrete, bending its frame quite badly.

"Now, who's next?" Edwina asked. "Or shall I just make it happen to all your bikes at once?"

"Oh no, Mrs, don't do that, we'll tell you what you want to know. We've never gone anywhere near the old man – we just heard that he'd died from listening to the village gossip. Honest that's the truth – and we'll stop shouting witch at you from now on."

Edwina pulled her cloak tighter and grabbed hold of Betty. They liked arms and walked out of the park without a backward glance. Mind you, as both the women were using walking sticks, it didn't do much for Edwina's witchlike appearance. "Well, Betty – now we've heard from two of the possible culprits – and I believe them, do you?"

Betty agreed and added, "Let's get you home, Edwina, and tidy you up. You really look like a witch. By the way, how did you do that trick with the bike?"

Edwina stared at her hard. "I don't know what you mean – I look like this more often than you realise and as for the bike, I did nothing. He was in such a hurry to get away, he did it himself." Having said that, however, she tidied herself as soon as she got home. "We can put the tea bags back into the caddy and the sugar bowl into the cupboard." She smiled grimly. "No point having them clutter up the other culprits, is there?"

Early next morning, her doorbell rang and when she opened the door, there stood the Vicar, a little bundle of books tied up with a leather belt under his arm. "Come in Vicar, do." And she hurriedly put the kettle on to boil as well as ringing Betty to say coffee would be two minutes. "Now what have you got to show me today?"

"You're never going to believe this, Miss Bligh, but I've been doing some more digging into local history – this very area where we live." He undid his bundle of books just as Betty arrived. He opened a couple of the books and held the pages open by using the pepper pot and the vinegar bottle.

"Oh no Vicar, you can't use those things, they're our props," Edwina said. He chose to ignore her, as he knew if he asked her why, she would take ages telling him.

"Look" – and he jabbed his forefinger on a page – "go on, read it."

"We'd rather you told us, Vicar – our eyesight's not what it used to be." Betty sipped her hot coffee carefully, waiting for him to speak.

"Oh very well." He tutted with impatience. "It's this cottage, Edwina – this very cottage you're living in. This was Oliver Cromwell's Headquarters, after Charles II was exiled to France." Edwina looked suitably surprised and Betty looked totally disinterested, seeing that it wasn't her own cottage in the limelight.

"It was just after the Battle of Naseby in Northamptonshire when Cromwell and General Fairfax beat the Royalists and King Charles I was beheaded. It had all started with an Irish Insurrection and ended with no monarch on the throne and an ongoing Civil War between the Cavaliers and the Roundheads. For a time, Cromwell had his headquarters right here. One of the books maintains there is a presence in your cottage, reaching back to his time. Have you ever sensed anything Miss Blyth? Anything unusual or strange?" The Vicar was carried away with his lecture and had to stand up for greater emphasis.

"Well, no, not really, although my mother and father always spoke of 'the lodger' – although we never had a lodger as far back as I can remember. I suppose that might fit with what you're saying." Edwina looked thoughtful now, trying to remember.

"Well, I've still got a couple of books to go through and see what else I can find. I'll be back soon with an update. By the way, Mrs Smith – have the police recovered your First Editions yet?"

"Not yet – but they say they're working on it." Betty didn't look hopeful.

"Yes, it's the same story with Mr Jones' coin and medal collection. I can always preach about the value of patience, but I personally find it difficult to be patient." He laughed as he gathered up his books.

When he'd gone, Edwina and Betty sat in companionable silence, sipping numerous cups of tea. Betty felt rather uncomfortable and searched the corners of the room for strangers.

"Stop it, Betty, you're being silly, there's no one here. By the way, on the day you were attacked, I had a visitor I wasn't expecting – a little boy who brought me a bunch of flowers. I meant to tell you about him but you were too busy being taken to hospital."

"Funny you should mention that, he came to see me the day before I was attacked – and he brought me flowers too. Strange that, I'd never met him before." And without speaking, Edwina added the salt seller to the circle of items – now it was the little boy with the flowers. Not that he could have carried out the burglaries, but it was very odd nonetheless.

That night, Edwina was late going to bed. She'd finished her cocoa but it wasn't having the same sleepy effect on her as it usually did. It was after midnight however and definitely time for bed. She changed into her voluminous nightdress and brushed her hair for 100 strokes, as she'd always done. The milky drink soon kicked in and before she knew it, she was fast asleep. A few hours passed and she woke with a start. Had she heard a bang coming from downstairs? Yes, there it was again. The clock said five and she got up slowly and went out onto the top landing. She could hear someone moving about in the sitting room and she tentatively opened the door. There was a man there, dressed all in black and wearing a balaclava. He was using a sort of screwdriver and inserting it between the bricks of the fireplace wall – as quietly as he could.

"I've already telephoned for the police – they'll be here soon." Her voice sounded weak but she was determined not to let him intimidate her. He dropped the screwdriver and turned to face her.

"What are you doing here, you Old Biddy – you should be sound asleep upstairs. I don't have time to waste on you." He made towards her but first grabbed his screwdriver from the floor and raised it above his head. "Go now and I'll not hurt you – go on, get back upstairs." But Edwina wouldn't move.

"You have no right to be here and I'm going nowhere until the police arrive." She hadn't really rung for the police. She hadn't had enough time, but he didn't know that. "Okay. If that's the way you want to play it." And he moved towards her, arm still raised. Suddenly, he stopped in mid-air and the screwdriver flew out of his hand and landed in the hearth. His arms were twisted back around his waist and he fell backwards into the fireplace – luckily for him, the fire had gone out. Jumping up, he was pushed to the door which miraculously opened in front of him and he fell onto the concrete path, face down and obviously hurt. He struggled to his feet and ran off down the garden path. The door closed behind him and the room was suddenly silent. Edwina fell backwards onto the armchair and said, "Where are you? I know you're here. Please show yourself, I just want to say thank you."

For many years, she'd suspected that she shared this cottage with someone else, but she'd never seen that person, nor mentioned it to anyone. Her mother and father used to tell her that they 'had a lodger' who'd lived there many centuries before and came back from time to time to visit. A deep voice broke into the quietness. "I'm here, Miss Blyth, in the corner." And there stood a soldier of Cromwell's New Model Army, still in uniform and carrying a round helmet under his arm.

"You've always been here, haven't you? I sensed your presence but never felt threatened by it."

"You had no reason to feel threatened. I have never intended you any harm." He came over to the fire and asked, "Do you know who I am?"

"I never knew in the past but I learned something only today that gave me a clue. Are you really Oliver Cromwell himself? The same one that helped run the whole country."

"I am that, ma'am – but also your friend I hope." He was certainly a gentleman. "I was very happy here all that time ago and I like to come back now and again just to visit. But I think you should go to bed now – you've had quite a shock and you need to rest. I am going now, but if you need me at any time, I'll come back. Good night, ma'am – one thing before I go, when you speak with the police and tell them what's happened, ask them to have a word with the little boy who visited you and your neighbour and brought flowers. I can say no more, but you'll benefit from my advice."

He was gone and so she hauled herself upstairs to bed. Oh, she felt her age tonight. However, in the morning, she felt fresh and wideawake. Had she been dreaming the night before? Surely, she had! But no, when she went downstairs, she saw that two or three bricks had been prised out of the chimney wall. But why? Now, what was it that the ghost had told her to do? She remembered and contacted the police to tell them she'd been burgled.

The police car drew up at the garden gate within 10 minutes and the young detective she'd met before, jumped out and hurried up the path. "The Forensic chaps are coming in a few minutes, hopefully to get some fresh clues as to who's doing this. You're now the third house he's broken into. Did he hurt you in any way, Miss Blyth? I think we should send for the doctor just to give you the once over, don't you?"

"Oh no, I'm really okay." He was amazed at the bravery of the eighty-year-old. *But then in her day, they had to be tough,* he thought. Despite her protestations, the doctor arrived half an hour later and gave her the proverbial onceover. She really was a tough old bird.

"Ah, Betty, there you are. Come on in, the kettle's just boiled and I have some fresh Parkin biscuits – the nice detective fetched them from the shop for me." And she bustled about in the kitchen. She told her friend all that had happened and Betty was relieved that he hadn't hurt the old lady. "Did he take anything? Have you had a chance to look yet?" And then, Edwina told her the rest of the story.

"You must have been dreaming, dear. You really must. You've always said there's nothing unusual in this house – no ghosts or witches, other than yourself of course." Betty couldn't help laughing at her little joke.

"If you don't believe me, there's nothing I can do about it. I thought you were my friend." Edwina decided not to press the point and changed the subject. "Betty, how can we find that little boy who gave us flowers – I want to speak to him."

"Well, if it's really important, we could always go to the village school and ask Miss Adams if she can help us. What do you think? By the way, have you seen the postman this morning – I waited for him but he never came and I'm waiting for something in the post?" Edwina hadn't seen him either and soon, both women wrapped up warmly against the chilly November day, were on their way to the village school. Both carried walking sticks and clung onto each other in case of a fall. Miss Adams saw them coming across the playground and came to meet them at the door.

"Of course, ladies – that won't be a problem. Come into the classroom and see if you can pick out the child. I'll have to stay with you whilst you talk as I have to look after all the children."

"That'll be fine, Miss Adams." And they followed the teacher along the corridor. In the classroom, they spotted the boy right away and Miss Adams asked Tommy to follow her out of the room. Edwina bent forward and said, "Hello, Tommy. Do you remember us?" and she pointed to Betty.

"Yes, Mrs – you're the ladies my mum told me to visit and take you some flowers." The boy spoke up well, Edwina thought.

"Why do you think she did that?" Betty asked him.

"She wanted me to see the insides of your homes and go back and tell her. I did that but I don't know why she wanted to know it." Tommy was getting bored now and just wanted to go back to the classroom. "Bye then, Mrs." He waved to the ladies and Miss Adams took him back to class. When she came back, Edwina asked the boy's name and was surprised to hear he was the son of their village postman.

On their way home, they bumped into the Vicar who invited them into the little teashop for a drink. After they'd told him all of their news, he said, "I've

153

got something to tell you as well and he brought a book out of his inside pocket. "By the way, did you ladies know that the postman's wife was an Oxford lecturer before she had her family? He's quite a new postman, only been in the village for about three months – and his wife's subject at Oxford was British History of the Middle Ages." The Vicar sat back in his chair and clasped his hands in front of him. "Are you following how my mind is working?"

The women said they were following and the Vicar returned to his book. "I've now discovered that, not only did Oliver Cromwell live in your cottage, Miss Blyth, but it was believed he hid a box of gold coins in the fabric of your house – the fireplace wall in particular. This small book from the Museum Archives is the only place I've ever read this and it would appear that not many people would ever have been aware of it. The even more interesting thing is that someone has studied the book at the Museum very recently – in fact about two months ago but they weren't allowed to take it from the building, it being so old. The hiding of the gold was only ever a rumour – and never taken seriously."

"Why have you been allowed to bring the book here and the other person wasn't?" Edwina asked.

"Well, I am the Vicar after all. If I can't be trusted, then who can?" He looked rather smug.

"Well, Edwina and I suspected you of being the burglar just a few days ago." Betty smirked. The Vicar's smug expression was replaced by a shocked one – and on that note, tea time was over.

"Vicar. Please will you come around to my home tomorrow morning – but very early, if you can, about 6.30 am – I think you'll be interested in what happens then," Edwina said curiously.

Very early next morning, Edwina woke from a restless and disturbed sleep. She felt nervous about what might happen today. She dressed carefully and tidied her hair into a bun, then slowly went downstairs. Immediately, she felt a presence and said boldly, "Show yourself, Mr Oliver Cromwell, I know you're here." She went into the kitchen then and there he was sitting at the breakfast table, still dressed in uniform and with his helmet under his arm. He stood up when she came in.

"I'm here only to protect you, should anything happen. I won't be seen by anyone else unless you want it." He really was a likeable and humble man. Although he'd allowed himself to be made Lord Chancellor of Great Britain, he'd refused to let Parliament crown him as the King, although that was what they wanted to do. He was a real man of the people – and she liked him.

There was a gentle knock on the kitchen window and in came Betty and the Vicar together. They couldn't see Cromwell as only Edwina could do that. "Come on in and have some coffee, but listen carefully for the postman to come. Sometimes he's very quiet and I miss him – but I don't want to miss him today." Edwina opened the door and the detective and a police constable came in. They all crowded around the table and waited. Edwina cleared away the teapot, the salt seller, the vinegar bottle and the china cup from the middle of the table – no need for them now. They heard a whistle outside and the constable looked at his watch. 6.45 am. The letterbox was lifted from outside and Edwina opened the door. "Hello, what have you done to your arm?" She looked meaningfully at the sling he had around his neck.

"Oh, I hurt myself knocking a ball about with my boy." He held out her post and made to turn away.

"I'd like you to come inside – and what is your first name? I never did learn it." She continued.

"I can't come in just now – I'm already late with my deliveries." Again, he turned away to leave, but she reached out and touched his good arm. "I'm afraid you have no option but to come inside. There's a few people here who would like to speak with you. Come in, Mr Postman." And Tom cautiously stepped over the door step.

The detective came forward and said, "Tom Matthews, I don't think you did get your injuries playing ball with your son. How did you sustain the injuries, Sir?"

"I don't have to tell you anything." But he looked at the warrant card being held in front of him and decided it was best to answer.

The detective asked again, "How did you get your injuries? Was it perhaps when you broke into this house and tried to hurt Miss Blyth?"

Edwina intervened at this point. "May I say something to him, Detective?" The detective nodded.

She looked towards Oliver Cromwell, who was still standing quietly in the corner. "Will you allow him to see you now?" And the postman's face turned grey. "This was my witness of last night, who twisted your arm up your back and stopped you from hurting me. He really is who you think he is – Oliver Cromwell himself."

155

The ghostly figure moved towards the postman and made to grab his injured arm, but the culprit screamed. "Don't let him touch me, please don't let him touch me. He hurt me last night and my arm might be broken."

Edwina smiled at Oliver who backed into the corner again and waited. The postman hung his head, knowing he'd given himself away. "Tom Matthews, I'm arresting you for the murder of Fred Jones and for breaking into Miss Blyth and Mrs Smiths' homes – and for injuring both of the ladies. Can I ask you why you did this, Sir?"

"I want a lawyer first." And the Vicar spoke up then. "I know why he did it. His wife, the Historian put him up to it. She recently discovered something in the Museum Archives, which could mean a lot of money for whoever discovered what was hidden – a bricked-up box." He went on, "After the Civil War in the 1650s, it turns out that Oliver Cromwell and his men were billeted in this row of cottages and this was the actual cottage Cromwell himself lived in – and I've found evidence in an ancient book in the Museum that he walled up a box of gold coins behind some brick work, but no one ever knew where the brick work was. The gold was never found and Cromwell never came back for the box." The Vicar looked pleased with himself and sat back down on a chair.

"You'll be going away for a long time for this, Matthews – as will your wife." The postman was shouting now.

"She had nothing to do with this. Honest, all she did was to tell me what she'd found in the Museum. I did everything else. It was all me." But the police just took him away.

The Vicar, Betty and Edwina were left in the kitchen, along with Oliver Cromwell of course. Edwina was still the only one who could see him but the sharp Vicar asked, "Who was your protector of last night, Miss Blyth? Who saved you from your attacker?"

Edwina looked at Cromwell and raised her eyebrows questioningly, "Well my friend, can we let them into our little secret?" And lo and behold, the Lord Protector himself sat down at the table. The Vicar didn't know what to say. This was totally against what he believed in but here was evidence right in front of his eyes. Edwina said nothing and got up to make some fresh coffee. As she filled the kettle, she called over her shoulder. "I really don't know what all the fuss is about. My grandfather had the chimneystack re-modelled over a hundred years ago and found the box of gold coins then. He spent a lot of it and left the rest for my mother and father. All my life, I've enjoyed the most wonderful holidays abroad with my parents – who left me a little of the money as well. It wasn't Treasure Trove as Oliver wasn't going to come back 300 years later to collect it, so there was never any need to report it to the authorities."

First of all, the Vicar laughed, then Betty and loudest of all, the Lord Protector himself joined in.

Edwina just looked puzzled, wondering why everyone was laughing. So she smiled too, not realising the significance of what she'd said. She'd already enjoyed the treasure Tom, the postman had been searching for.

History Called Her Bloody Mary – But Was She?

Not many people know the verse 'Mary, Mary quite contrary, how does your garden grow' is actually, about Mary Tudor, Henry VIII's daughter – or better known as Bloody Mary. The verse originated when she sat on the throne of England and Northern Ireland and was a popular ditty sung all over the country by children and adults alike. She became known as a cruel and unforgiving monarch who had great numbers of her own people put to death by execution – merely because they wanted to practise a religion that differed from her own.

But before you hear why this verse was written about her, perhaps you should look at her life story and better understand why she may have earned the rhyme, or indeed, should she have earned it at all:

'Mary, Mary quite contrary

How does your garden grow?

With silver bells and cockle shells

And pretty maids all in a row'.

She was born at the Palace of Placentia, Greenwich on 18 February 1516 and her parents Henry VIII and Katherine of Aragon had been married for seven years before she was born.

"I fear it's a girl, Majesty," the physician told the King, "but a bonny, healthy girl with a good, lusty cry, sound of limb with no problems whatsoever." He spoke to Henry and waited for an outburst of disappointment, but none came.

Henry just shrugged his shoulders and said, "Not to worry, it'll be a boy next time, I'm sure. I would like to see the lady Katherine now. She is well, I hope?"

"Very well, your Majesty, but it was a long labour and she is very tired." He was attempting to tell the King not to tire her, but he dared not say that to Henry.

Henry visited Katherine in her chamber and she was awake. "Well done, wife, she's a good, healthy girl, you have done well, but next time, make it a boy please." He spoke as if his wife had control of choosing the sex of a child. Rather unfairly, she thought. He patted her hand, kissed her cheek and went off with his gentlemen to celebrate being a father.

Initially, he liked the child and told anyone who would listen 'That child never cries, she is a wonder'. She was a pretty child with fair skin, blue eyes and reddish gold hair. She also had a ruddy complexion which she inherited from her father. She was a very well-educated young woman, as was to be expected – she studied Latin, Spanish, French, Music and Dance and when she was small, her parents were very proud of her. In particular, she was close to Katherine, her mother, who undertook most of her education.

"See how tall I have become, Mama." And she stood on her tiptoes to impress Katherine. "I am almost seven now and am growing stronger every day." Mary was indeed a straight and erect child, who looked every inch a princess.

Katherine smiled and hugged the girl. "You are certainly those things Mary but what else must you never forget you are?"

"Oh, I know what that is Mama. I am a Roman Catholic and look to the Holy Father in Rome as my spiritual leader. I shall never forget that and always be true to the faith, don't you worry."

They were both sitting in a sumptuous room which was the Queen's parlour at Hampton Court Palace. Everything was luxurious and comfortable; the King spared no expense in taking care of his wife and daughter, although as of late, he was not often in their company, preferring to dally with the ladies of court and in particular one raven haired beauty called Lady Anne Boleyn. She had been in the royal circles in France and only recently come to the court in England. Katherine looked out of the window and saw him, even now, speaking to the lady in question and bowing gallantly before her. The Queen sighed; he was such a philanderer but she did love him. She turned back to Mary and suggested they read one of their history books.

Katherine never bore a living child after Mary – and Henry resented that so much, he turned to a new queen, the same Anne Boleyn, to be his next wife. He uncaringly sent a sick Katherine of Aragon away from court and declared himself Head of the Church of England with no need for a Pope, who only interfered in English matters, particularly in turning down his request for an annulment from Katherine. The Pope had refused to agree to the annulment and declared Katherine as his true wife so Henry severed relations with Rome and took on the role himself as Head of the Church. This was the start of the Protestant religion in England. Also at the same time, he declared his daughter Mary illegitimate and sent her away from the Court. It must have been a humiliating experience for Mary but her life was precarious and she must have been afraid for much of the time. Without her own mother, whom she was forbidden to see, and the arrival of a new stepmother, she must have been a very lonely and unhappy child. Nonetheless, she was strong enough to keep going – and this she did.

Anne Boleyn, however, also failed to give Henry a male heir, and a charge was trumped up against her for adultery, even with her own brother. She was executed, although she claimed vehemently to be innocent. Henry immediately declared the one child they had had together to be illegal. The child was named Elizabeth. Two marriages, two daughters – and no male heir – Henry was frantic and Mary must have been confused as to her place in society – except that it was easy to lose that place for many reasons beyond her control. She had been born of Catholic parents and baptised a Catholic, so it was understandable that she believed this to be her true religion. She had been baptised in Greenwich three days after her birth at the Church of the Observant Friars and had several high-ranking Godparents, amongst whom was Cardinal Wolsey. In her eyes, her faith had been firmly established for the rest of her life.

As she grew, she spent a lot of time in Wales where Henry had actually given her many estates – but she visited his Court regularly – especially at Christmas. She remained an illegitimate child however as did her half-sister, Elizabeth. For a while, she had very disturbing dreams about Anne Boleyn. She had known she was a threat and also the reason her mother had been banished from court, but now she saw her as an evil woman who wished her nothing but bad. She took to moving regularly between houses, not staying at one for any length of time, in case the nightmare of Anne caught up with her, which it did on more than one occasion. After her execution, Anne's nightmare words were: 'Well, young Mary the bastard, what will the rest of your life be like? I can see it all now, you'll have to kneel at the block just as I did, you'll never be Queen. My daughter however, Elizabeth will become the best-loved monarch in history and take the throne from you.' The nightmare ran along similar lines every time.

Mary stuttered in her answer, muttering in her sleep. Had she been dreaming or was that really Anne Boleyn in the corner of the room. The apparition swept forward dressed in all her finery and wearing the Queen's crown. "You are not even a pretty girl and will never become a beautiful woman, such as I. Henry will turn on you, just as he did me. He loved me once and now has forgotten all

160

about me. He did this to your mother too and he will do the same to you eventually." Anne's beautiful face turned into a sneer and she leaned over Mary, her eyes closed in hatred. "Remember my visit and what I've said, you're not blessed and never will be." Mary never forgot that particular dream, if it was a dream, and continued to hate her half-sister for the rest of her life. Without a child of her own as heir however, she was well aware that after herself, Elizabeth would be next in line for the throne.

Her father's third marriage to Jane Seymour did however produce a son – but the birth labour took her life. She had been a gentle, more caring lady than Anne Boleyn and had persuaded Henry to bring his two daughters back to court. Once he had his son, she also entreated him to reinstate their 'Rights of Succession' to the throne – Mary first then Elizabeth. The newly born son would of course inherit the Crown.

When Henry told Jane to get up from her bed and attend the christening of her son, she pleaded with him, saying she felt too ill to get up, but Henry was not sympathetic.

"Madam, it is not a request but an order. The boy cannot be christened without his mother present – so you have no option." He turned to leave the chamber. Much as he was delighted to have a son, he was still King enough to expect his orders to be obeyed. And that was the end for Jane – she neither had the energy to do as she was bid, but neither did she have the energy not to. Her ghost is seen today quite regularly, in the small corridor outside her bedroom at Hampton Court and she wanders around as though looking for some place to rest – or to find the child she'd held in her arms only rarely.

Henry now had his male heir Edward but alas, no Jane. He was bereft with sadness and missed her greatly. She was very sickly after the birth but he had insisted she attend the baby's christening by his side, so proud was he of the male heir. Her exertions on that day caused a relapse and very soon afterwards, she died. He felt a degree of blame for making her rise from her sick bed to attend the ceremony. He really had loved her as a wife and it took him almost a whole year to mourn her death. For a time, he became a recluse and ignored his daughters. The loss of Jane caused him much broken sleep and she visited his dreams regularly, making his feeling of guilt even greater. However, these feelings passed too and Henry was soon on the lookout again for a new Queen.

As Jane Seymour had requested of him, he declared the two half-sisters to be his legal children – they would be Edward's heirs, the older first. So, Mary had prospects again.

When she was sixteen, she was engaged to marry Emperor Charles V who was sixteen years older. When she heard about this, she told her father, "I don't want to marry an old man. I am young yet and there is still plenty of time."

"You will marry whom I say, Madam – we Tudors are merely pawns in the marriage stakes. I myself, am subject to an unhappy life in order to get a male heir. You will follow my lead and do what is best for the country. The Tudor line as created by my father must continue and you will play your part in this. And that was the end of that conversation.

Before his death, Henry did allow Mary to return to live at court, but only if she signed a document to declare her father to be the Head of the Church of England and also agree that his marriage with her mother, Katherine of Aragon, had been illegal, her having been at his brother's wife first. She did agree to this but it lay heavily on her conscience for the rest of her life. She had never seen her mother again after the age of seven and was only now told of her death with no compassion or sympathy shown by her father. Although she pleaded with him to allow her to attend her mother's funeral, he denied her this and it broke her heart.

Mary did actually see her mother once more at the time of Henry's death. As his daughter, it was necessary for her to attend his own deathbed. She stood there and looked at the corpulent man who had so affected her life, and that of so many others. He was on the point of death and the doctor moved forward to reassure him. Something made Mary turn towards the back of the room and there, in the shadows, stood some figures, side by side. She knew who they were and moved towards them. She approached first the ghost of her mother Queen Katherine and fell to her knees in loving submission. A smile crossed the Queen's face and she beckoned her daughter to rise. Mary moved to the next figure and recognised the hated, ghostly figure of Anne Boleyn who was staring over at the bed where Henry lay. The disgust on her face was evident and she looked at Mary with contempt. Next in line, Mary recognised Jane Seymour, the kindest and sweetest of the wives. Jane's ghostly hand reached out and she stroked the younger woman's face. Mary couldn't resist whispering, "You were the best of them all, except my mother of course. You would have made a good Queen, had you lived but your husband's command for you to rise from your sick bed finished you for good. He didn't care that you were not a strong woman." Lastly, Mary moved to the final figure in the row and there was young Catherine Howard, whose eyes were filled with tears and she looked so very young, but that hadn't stopped Henry having her head cut off. She pitied Catherine more than anybody; she was just a child when she died, accused too of adultery with many – she hadn't had much of a life.

There were only four queens there. The four, in whose deaths he had been instrumental. For a moment, the king raised his head slightly and looked towards the women. He knew who they were and closed his eyes to make them disappear.

"Get them out of here." He gasped at the doctor, whereupon Mary returned to his bedside.

"They're waiting for you, Father. See how eagerly they wait for you." And she enjoyed his misery. He died then – and Henry VIII was no more.

Edward his son, lived only until he reached fifteen, when he developed tuberculosis and died. England was now very much Protestant following his father's rebellion against the Catholic Church but there were still large pockets of people faithful to the Catholic religion. Mary and her brother had fought continuously throughout his short reign – both staunch believers in their own 'true religion'. On one occasion when Mary had been invited to court, Edward chose the occasion to humiliate her in public for her 'religious ignorance'. She stood her ground however and faced up to the reigning monarch with impunity.

"I was chosen to be your Godmother and you should respect me for that. You are nothing but an uneducated brat who doesn't appreciate what went on before your birth. You call me ignorant – but it is you who have none of the facts about why we've ended up as we are today." And with that, she flounced out of the room and Edward disliked her even more.

She was instructed next morning to leave the court and go to one of the stately homes she'd received as a gift from her father. She never saw her brother again although he made decisions that affected her greatly. At this time in her life, she fell into ill health and had great difficulties with her menstruation, something she had trouble with for the rest of her life. Potential marriages came and went but none was successful. She was only twenty when it was reported to her that her mother had died. A very harsh message to receive from a royal messenger. She now had to turn her attention to a new Queen for her father. Henry married Anne of Cleeves in 1540. She was German and when Henry met her, he was most disappointed. Although he had had a miniature of her painted by his favourite artist, he declared it looked nothing like her or he wouldn't have sent for her to come to England. History actually records that Anne was a perfectly normal young woman and reasonably pretty, but Henry said she looked like a cow, smelt badly and possessed no social graces. The marriage was annulled as it was never consummated and Henry was able to sit back and relax again. Anne did well, in fact the best of all his wives. She made no fuss as she felt the same about Henry as he felt about her so she was given several houses and estates and a generous pension for life. She was a very wise woman. It was reputed that she almost became his sister and he became quite fond of her. From her side, she was kind and supported his daughters. She was often invited to court and Henry gave her many precious jewels as rewards for her acceptance of his rejection of her as a wife.

Henry now was with his fifth wife, Catherine Howard, whom he also accused of having several affairs with court officials, in fact very similar to the lines he took with Anne Boleyn. Catherine was very young when he chose her; she may have been only sixteen. She was happy and gregarious and he thought she was just what he needed, but he soon tired of her and as was his way, he had her beheaded. In effect, she was too lively for him and he couldn't keep up with her, so what was he supposed to do? It was very sad when the jailer found her the night before the execution, practising placing her head on a low stool, so that she'd 'get it right' on the actual day. She still haunts Hampton Court Palace where she was when the messenger came to her with the news that she was to be executed at the King's command. She ran along the long gallery, calling out for mercy – and can sometimes still be seen doing so today. The king was in the castle at the time, but chose to ignore her. Her ghost has been seen by many people – running along the long gallery. For Henry, it was an all-round practical solution. He didn't have the energy to keep up with her so she was accused of adultery and her head came off.

As simple as that.

The sixth and last wife was Catherine Parr, who, like Anne of Cleeves, turned out to be kind to Mary and Elizabeth, who were now of course, the King's heirs. Catherine was older than his other wives had been on marriage. She was in her thirties and did outlive him but she cared and nursed him through many illnesses, until he died. She was very kind and patient with him although his temper was not good. He was always in great pain, obese and with leg ulcers that wouldn't heal, he couldn't bear to be touched by anyone, other than his wife. She was also very kind to Mary and Elizabeth. She played cards and chess often with her stepdaughters and formed a good friendship with them. After his death, Catherine did, however, marry again to an existing sweetheart whom she'd known for a long time. She fared very well and did at least manage to live longer than four of his queens. She even had a child – but unfortunately only lived a very few years more.

On Edward VI's death, Mary Tudor took the throne at last – but she had to take it from Lady Jane Grey, who was the granddaughter of Henry VIII's younger sister. Edward wanted to declare Mary and Elizabeth as illegitimate again but his Ministers advised against this. He then declared in his will that Lady Jane Grey should rule the country after him. There was an uprising in the country supporting Jane's claim. It was led by Thomas Wyatt and was intended to dispense with Mary in favour of Jane but it failed, mainly because Mary gathered together an army of her own and managed to defeat the revolutionaries. Thomas Wyatt's rebellion was quite firmly put down and eventually he was executed on Tower Hill. He also had been against Mary's proposed marriage to Philip of Spain, a devout Catholic, who would have helped Mary bring Catholicism back to England. Many people in England were against their Queen's intention to marry such a devout Catholic.

In a way, therefore, it was her insistence to marry Philip that brought about 100 'Protestant Heretics' being burnt at the stake – as a warning to other heretics of what they could expect from this Queen. The Protestant community was afraid of how Philip might influence Mary and rightly so, as the number of Heretic executions grew in Mary's reign and topped out at 300. Jane Grey was executed alongside the ringleaders of the revolution although she hadn't played any part in the uprising. She was just there and had a claim to the throne. A dangerous position to be in in the sixteenth century. Mary watched from a secret viewpoint when they took Lady Jane Grey to the execution block. She looked pale and very frail and Mary felt genuinely sorry that this had to happen, but she'd only recently heard of a further move to free Jane and put her on the throne. She couldn't allow this now, could she? And Jane went to the block with her husband following soon after.

Mary and Philip married in 1554 at Winchester Castle – she was 37 and he was 27. They had met each other only two days before the wedding, so barely knew each other. The unrest amongst the people can only be imagined. She brought the Archbishop of Canterbury, Thomas Cranmer from the Tower of

London and had him burnt at the stake. She was still angry at how he'd signed a document for Henry declaring the marriage between Henry and her mother to be null and void and never legal in the first place. Cranmer never forgave himself for signing the document and believed he'd betrayed Mary's mother, which of course he had. He even thrust his writing hand into the fire as a gesture of his disgust with himself. This was before the flames completely engulfed him. Mary actually forgave some others who had done exactly the same but in Cranmer's case, she couldn't bring herself to forgive him. She refused to allow him to live and insisted he be burnt at the stake. Considering she herself had signed such a paper for her father a few years before, this seemed rather harsh but then, this was Mary and she had the power. She made sure that a further Act of Parliament was passed, abolishing Protestantism and re-establishing Catholicism in England. All of which her half-sister Elizabeth I, undid, when she eventually came to the throne.

Mary was suspicious of everyone and rightly so. "I suppose we really did have to execute Jane." She had sent for her first minister. "It was too dangerous to let her live, her claim to my throne wouldn't have gone away. Also, whilst we're on the subject, my half-sister must be imprisoned in the Tower of London. There are still people who believe her claim to the throne is stronger than mine although her mother was a whore and an adulteress. It'll be a lot safer with her locked away." The minister agreed this was the best plan and Elizabeth went to the Tower through 'Traitor's Gate' and remained there for many months.

"Just imagine, Philip, a few years ago, I was supposed to marry your father but that all fell through and here we are now. Will you dance with me now husband?" Mary's foot was tapping. She loved dancing and wanted to show off her husband to the court. She was a great follower of the fashion of the day and spent much money on elaborate gowns which were replaced as quickly as they'd been made. She was never a dowdy queen no matter how history has painted her.

"Not just yet, wife, I am still fatigued after my journey here. You must give me more time to adjust." He was looking at his wife with some disdain as he didn't find her attractive, but she was the Queen of England and as such, could be of great value to him, especially as her intentions seemed to be to turn England once more to Catholicism. He was a handsome man and although it took Mary a little while to warm towards him, she came around very quickly and became rather clinging and demanding. He actually told his friend and confident that he had no amorous feelings towards Mary and the marriage was for political and strategic gains only. The marriage was concluded for no fleshly consideration but to remedy the disorders of his own kingdom and to preserve the state of the Low Countries. Philip wrote this to his brother-in-law at home. He made it clear he had little interest in Mary as a loving wife. To elevate his son to Mary's rank of Queen, Emperor Charles V seeded to his son the Crown of Naples as well as his own claim to the Crown of Jerusalem. Mary therefore became titular Queen in these countries as well as her own.

"Shall we retire for the night then, if you are tired? I am quite happy to leave this celebration and begin our marriage together."

"In time, wife, in time. Do not pressure me so." Philip was enjoying drinking and laughing with his own gentlemen and found Mary a poor substitute for them. Obviously, she looked crest fallen, but in order to keep him sweet, she didn't press the point.

She went off with her ladies and ordered that a gaming table was set up in the next room. Mary was a confirmed gambler and was quite obsessive about it. She wasn't particularly good at it and lost considerable amounts of money. Strangely enough, she didn't actually carry money on her person and was known to be a 'borrower' by her ladies. A 'borrower', who always forgot to pay back.

"Oh come on, ladies, share what money you have. I know I'm just about to win and you'll get it all back with interest." Mary was enjoying herself although she would have preferred Philip's company. One of the ladies gave in and gave her some money, which Mary quickly lost and promised to pay back – tomorrow. She was known for forgetting her debts owed to anyone who was foolish enough to lend her money. Records from her Privy Purse at the time showed great losses from her gambling and on one occasion when no one would lend her money, she said she would provide all their breakfasts for the next morning, if they gave her some money. And that is how the debt is recorded in fiscal papers to this day. The Queen paid her debts with breakfasts!

She did fall pregnant a few months later but lost the child – at least a child was never seen. A second pregnancy went the same way as the first. Many people actually doubted she'd been pregnant at all but then with the passing of more time, she declared herself pregnant for a third time. In September 1554, Mary stopped menstruating. She gained weight and her belly swelled and she was sick each morning. The doctors could come to no other conclusion except to declare her with child. There was an Act of Parliament passed declaring Philip as Regent in case of Mary's death in childbirth. In fact, there was a belief that he planned to marry Elizabeth, should his wife die in childbirth and he wrote to his brother-in-law Maximilian of Austria, saying that he actually doubted his wife was pregnant at all. Meanwhile, Elizabeth was released from house arrest and allowed to come to Court just in case the worst happened to Mary. This would also be necessary for when Mary gave birth, as Elizabeth would have to witness the birth of any child her half-sister had.

That evening, the Queen was languishing on a chaise longue in the large withdrawing room with her ladies all around. She was dressed in a black smock-like gown and covered by a fur shawl. She was feeling rather sorry for herself.

"Philip, I've been having very disturbing dreams of late and that bitch, Lady Jane Gray keeps coming into my bed chamber. She stands at the bottom of my bed and points at me accusingly. I fear for my baby – she may harm it. Why should she hate me so much? She was a thief after my crown, wasn't she?" Mary was in tears and genuinely afraid.

"Perhaps if you stopped executing so many people, and her being one of them, you wouldn't be subjected to such dreams, my dear." Philip sniffed on a delicate lace handkerchief and left her alone, still sobbing. He was impatient with her and didn't mind showing it.

"Please, Philip, don't leave me at a time like this, stay by my side. I have enemies all around me and I feel better when you're by my side. Look, there she is now over by the window, staring. Always staring. And if I hadn't had her executed, you wouldn't be here now as my consort, would you?" But Philip took no notice and turned his back on her.

"I'll show him, I'll show them all. I'll carry this child and produce a male heir." She felt her belly swelling; she was sure. In fact, she thought the baby moved. It would be a healthy boy, she just knew. She called for her ladies to comfort her and settled down to play the harpsichord, one of her favourite pastimes. Mary played excellently.

"Ladies, ladies, you must make a fuss of me for I am with child. I was sick only this morning and I feel absolutely exhausted." She was repeatedly sick and her skin had taken on a grey pallor, her stomach had become swollen and distended over the months. She rested as often as she could for the safety of the baby and followed Philip around the palace, pleading for his company.

In April of that that year, bells were rung all over London, then the whole country and over Europe itself, declaring that Mary had given birth to a son. The months of May and June passed and right up to the end of July, the Queen was rumoured to be in labour, but in the end, nothing happened and the whole subject was hushed up and ignored. She felt humiliated and believed it was God's punishment for her allowing heretics to live in her country i.e., Protestants. She had to place the blame somewhere!

Philip left England and set off for Europe where he led his armies against the French. Many of her courtiers noted how heartbroken she was at her husband's departure and spoke of how deeply she must love the man. She loved him so much that she sent an English army to fight alongside the Spanish, against the French and is doing so, lost Calais which was the last holding England had on French soil. This proved to be a disastrous loss and Mary deeply regretted it.

Her father appeared in her dreams that night and accused her of being careless in losing Calais. He had regarded it as a jewel in his crown.

"Daughter, you must think carefully before taking action. You have married a Catholic King and you will live to regret it." Henry was very angry.

"I didn't mean to, father – it was the Spanish who let me down. The French were stronger than they were and my poor army suffered the consequences." She felt so bad about it at the time that she was known to have said, 'When I am dead and opened, you shall find 'Calais' written in my heart.' She felt its loss greatly and knew she had let her country down. Now, she just pulled the covers over her eyes to make Henry go away but he stayed there for a long time plaguing and tormenting her. Next day, she called for her ministers to attend a special meeting and set about restyling the English Navy. She knew this would have pleased her father. It was something her sister, Elizabeth, benefitted from when she later came to the throne. Mary was not all play and attended to the needs of her country as best she could.

She stayed at Court until October and received a letter from Philip advising her that she should marry Elizabeth to his cousin, the Duke of Savoy, who was a staunch Catholic and it would ensure the line of succession after her, was secure in the true faith. Mary, however, on the advice of Parliament, refused this and kept Elizabeth where she could keep an eye on her. Parliament was persuaded to repeal Henry's right to call himself 'Head of the Church of England' and she had issued a proclamation about Henry VIII's decision to reject Catholicism in England. She had it publicly declared that the marriage between her mother, Katherine and Henry had been valid. She also abolished Edward's religious laws. She took this opportunity to re-establish clerical celibacy and imprisoned many leaders who favoured Protestantism. She was very much a pro-active queen, especially on the subject of religion.

She had done much to undo what her father and brother had done to the country and Catholicism was once again, the true 'Official' religion in England. Heresy Laws were again reinstated and Mary appointed a good Catholic, Reginald Pole, as Archbishop of Canterbury.

She also had an Act of Parliament drawn up, declaring that from then onwards, a Queen could reign in a natural line, just as a male heir could. This paved the way for the rules as they stand to the present day.

"Why do my people turn against me and call those heretics I've executed 'Martyrs'? I truly don't understand them, do you?" she asked her chief minister. "Those heretics will surely go straight to Hell, I'm sure."

"I'm afraid, Majesty, there are still many people in this country who favour the Protestant religion, although you have done much to make it impossible." He agreed.

"Well, Minister, I'll just have to do more, won't I?" said the unrepentant Mary. When she had first sat upon the throne, she'd issued a proclamation across England saying she would not impose her own religion onto those of her subjects who didn't want it. This seemed at odds with her burning of many Protestants who challenged her faith. Another of her first acts on becoming Queen however was to release from the Tower of London, those Catholics who'd been placed there by her brother, Edward. Her prejudice was quite clear and she wasn't afraid to make decisions, after all she had the power, although it had been a long time coming. 'Heretics were Traitors' and as traitors, their executions were necessary and she believed this firmly.

Mary had no mother, no baby and no husband. She was a very lonely woman. She stood before the mirror and looked closely at her face. She saw an old, rather haggard woman looking back and yet she was only forty-one. Life had not been easy for her and she'd had to struggle to maintain her place in society. She imagined Philip was standing behind her. He placed his hands on her shoulders and bent to kiss her cheek and then he was gone. She missed him greatly but knew she had to get on with her life. From May 1558, her health weakened and she began to rest more than usual. Her short reign had been subject to severe weather conditions across the country and it had been wet for long periods, making the crops fail year after year. Yet another blow she had to deal with – she drafted a new plan for a currency reform but it wasn't promulgated until after her death, when Elizabeth was given the credit for achieving it. She hadn't rested on her laurels, something of which she has always been accused but rather acted frequently in an attempt to make England a better place.

She retired to St James Palace in 1558 and there she died on 17 November of that year. It was in the middle of an Influenza epidemic in England but Mary died of Cancer. On the same day as Mary's death, the Archbishop of Canterbury, Catholic Reginald Pole also died. He hadn't long been released from the Tower and so had had only a short time of freedom to enjoy. Protestant Elizabeth succeeded Mary as Queen.

Mary saw her mother, Queen Katherine, one more time. A very few moments were left to her but she was delighted to see her mother before her death. "Mama?" she said, "I knew you'd come for me. You've never let me down in my whole life. I'm glad you're here so you can see that I die a good Catholic, just as you did." She reached for Katherine's hand, but of course there was no one there.

As a final gesture, whilst breathing her last, Mary held up her hand to her husband, Philip whom she saw standing by her bedside. She mumbled, "You have come husband to your Mary. I am unable to rise from this bed and welcome you properly but I shall feel better tomorrow." Alone, she breathed her last. Philip however was in Brussels looking after his other interests. He wrote to his sister, Joan, as soon as he heard about the death. 'I felt a reasonable regret for her death.' Not much sadness or pity but then, he'd never professed to have been very fond of her.

In her will, she'd left instructions that she was to be buried alongside her mother, Katherine. But her wishes were ignored and she was buried in Westminster Abbey. The Bishop of Winchester spoke of her at the funeral, saying she'd been a King's daughter, a King's sister and a King's wife and a Queen in her own right. She was the first woman to claim the throne despite great odds at the time and enjoyed support and sympathy throughout her reign, primarily from the Roman Catholics in England.

Mary Tudor was buried in a tomb in December 1558, a tomb she would eventually share with her sister Elizabeth. James I when he succeeded Elizabeth had her body moved to another part of the Abbey and Elizabeth was buried on top of Mary. The Latin inscription on the tomb reads 'Consorts in realm and tomb, we sisters Elizabeth and Mary, here lie down to sleep in hope of resurrection.' James, I had been a strong Protestant but treated Catholic Mary accordingly.

Should you visit Westminster Abbey today, spend a little time thinking of the two sisters whose names are engraved there. Both Queens of England but who left very different impressions of their characters and capabilities.

The verse written about Mary:

Mary, Mary quite contrary

How does your garden grow?

With silver bells and cockle shells

And pretty maids all in a row.

The 'silver bells' were iron thumb screws, the 'cockle shells' were testicle vices and the pretty maids in a row were the guillotine constructions used to execute heretics. 'Maids' soon became the name for guillotines used to execute the aristocracy in the later French Revolution.

You've learned a little bit about Mary Tudor now. Did she deserve this verse or could she have lived her life any differently, circumstances being what they were at the time? Had there not been a man called John Foxe, a heretic who escaped England when Mary began executing Protestants, history would not have recorded her reign as one of such 'Bloody Acts'. He spent his writing career accusing her of bringing about many of the disasters from which England suffered throughout her reign. He pointed an accusing finger at her and earned her the name of 'Bloody Mary – but he failed to mention all the changes she'd made in the country, making it a better place to live – if you were a Catholic, that is! Strangely enough, Mary Tudor had been responsible for around 300 executions in her short reign, but her father Henry, had been responsible for ordering the deaths of between 57,000 and 72,000.

I ask your opinion, who was the real 'bloody' monster? Father or daughter?

Loving Memories Never Fade

Middle Brompton is a sleepy village in the English countryside and Juliana lived in the grandest house there. She lived with her grandfather who was a widower and who doted on his only granddaughter and spoiled her beyond measure. She was the envy of all the other girls at school – the teachers liked her as well, but that may have been because of her rich Grandfather, or it could have been because she was a jolly, nice girl. She'd been called Juliana, after her mother, who'd been killed in a motor accident when her husband was driving. Poor little thing! People were always saying that, but she was actually a happy little girl living with Grandfather, who insisted she attend the posh school in the next village, but didn't want her to become a boarder there or he'd lose touch with her. The arrangement suited them both perfectly.

"Why don't you ask your rich, old Grandfather for more money and then you can give it to us?" The girl, Matilda – she of the carroty red hair – called out and laughed as she collected her tennis racket from the middle locker! "We might let you be our friend then; you never know." And she closed the door with a loud bang. Juliana ignored her and fetched her own racket before going out to the court for a game. Maggie was already waiting for her, swinging her racket, "Hurry up, Ju, I'm waiting for you to beat me again." The two girls laughed and went into an empty court. Matilda seemed to have disappeared. It was quite odd how much she seemed to dislike Juliana – perhaps it was the unusual name, her prettiness, her family money or how highly the teachers regarded her. Who could tell, but she couldn't meet up with her without saying something nasty.

"Good riddance to bad rubbish," Maggie said, "I hate that girl. She always thinks she's so smart."

"Maggie, why don't you come home with me this weekend and meet my grandfather? You'd like him, I know you would – he's so kind." Juliana whacked the ball so hard; Maggie missed it completely.

"Okay, my dear – that would be jolly nice. By the way, is your house haunted – it's so old, isn't it?" She whacked the ball back at her friend.

"Don't be silly – that's just a rumour. I've certainly never seen a ghost there."

And so, the weekend was decided and Juliana went on to beat her three sets in a row.

"Enough! Enough! I need some squash. Let's go back to the Common Room." And Juliana followed her into the school.

On the Friday afternoon, after the last class (Maths – Ug!) the two young girls rode their cycles to Brampton House, where Juliana's Grandfather lived. He was in the study when they got there and immediately called for tea and scones. "You girls will be hungry, I don't doubt – girls of your age are always hungry. Thank God, you're still too young to start worrying about calories and body shapes. Keep your stomach full and you'll never get ill." He really was a nice old man. He held out the book he'd been reading – it looked like architects' drawings and maps. "Now this really is interesting, girls – it's from the time when the house was built and it actually suggests there are secret passages built into the walls – not that I've ever seen them, but then, I've never looked for them." He laughed at the expressions on the girls' faces. "Perhaps you could find them, what do you think?"

Maggie answered, "We can have a jolly good try, can't we, Juliana?" But then, she lost interest in the book when a maid came into the room, carrying a large, silver tray with scones and jam and a pot of tea. Maggie's eyes glittered in appreciation. "They don't feed us at that school, you know – it's disgraceful, when I think about it – with all the money they get from us." Juliana smiled at her, 'It wasn't true' but Maggie had a very healthy appetite.

"Grandad, may I borrow this book tonight – I'd like to learn a bit more about the house's past?" Juliana had only come to live with her grandfather two years before, when her parents were killed. There was no one else to care for her and, as he had just been widowed, he was more than happy to have her come and share his lonely life. They were both content with the arrangement and soon grew close to one another and even learned to love one another. When her parents were still alive, Juliana spent most of her young years travelling around the world with them and so, never saw much of her grandparents. In fact, she never really knew her Grandma at all. She did know, however, that the big house at Middle Brompton had been the Manor house for the local village people – very important

174

at one time. Some people still thought of her grandfather as the Squire. He laughingly played along with it.

"Of course you may, my dear. In fact, I'd like it if you did. My old eyes are not what they used to be and it would be good if you could read some of the library books and tell me if you find anything about this house." Grandad helped himself to another scone and offered one to Maggie, who was happy to oblige. "I'll tell you what I have learned so far – this house is on the site of what was a monastery and the monks lived here until the sixteenth century when Henry VIII confiscated all belongings of religious institutions and grabbed any valuables, he could lay his hands on. The monks were chased off and they scattered around the country with nowhere to go. Some of the walls of the building were demolished and not even one candlestick was to be found in the whole place." He took out his old pipe and packed the tobacco inside before lighting it. "What do you think of that?" He looked at the girl with amusement.

Juliana was very interested "I had no idea the house was so old, but what a history it must have. Are there more books in the library about local history? Mind you, the school has a very good library and I should be able to find some facts there." She turned to Maggie. "Do you want to take a walk whilst there's still light?"

"Oh yes, please, I'd like to look about the garden – especially now I know how old the house is." And the girls left the old man to his pipe and some peace.

"Do you think it's haunted, Ju – have you ever seen anything whilst you've been here?" Maggie looked excited and scared at the same time.

"Wouldn't it be fantastic if it was? I'm going to make it a priority to conjure up wandering spirits."

Juliana just laughed at her friend. "Now you're just being silly, Maggie – ghosts – I ask you!" And they wandered off together out of the garden and into some trees growing in a thick wood just outside. They came across a stone building that looked empty and very overgrown.

"Perhaps, it's from the monastery days and the bad monks were kept there." Maggie said. "Mind you, I'm not sure if monks were ever bad."

"I bet they were no different from other people – good and bad alike, but I don't think it was for imprisoning bad monks. Anyway, it's not big enough to get more than two monks at a time. Think again, young Maggie!" Although Juliana seemed flippant, she was just as curious as Maggie and ventured slowly towards the building. There was a door hanging off its hinges and she turned to

Maggie, "Go on then Maggie, you can go in first, if you like." But it was beginning to get dark and they decided to leave further exploration to another day – well it was as good an excuse as any.

Juliana went to see the school librarian and asked for advice on which books she might know of – in fact, anything about past happenings in the next village and about the Manor house in particular. Mrs Jones was very helpful and sent the girl to the back of the library where the ancient books were kept. "You'll find several books there that might help – but if you don't, I'll do a bit of research to see what I can find for you."

There were two books which Juliana asked if she could borrow and she couldn't wait to show Maggie what she'd found. The monastery that had stood where her home now was, had belonged to the Catholic Order of Cistercian monks and they'd been there even before the village itself existed. So many years that no one really knew. However, in 1534, Thomas Cromwell, Henry VIII's First Minister visited the monks and took an inventory of what possessions they had. Jewels, gold ornaments and goblets, statues painted in gold, even the lead on the roofs was all taken into consideration and with the Cistercians' richness, it was decided to dissolve their monastery and send them all on their way. It helped fill the King's purse very well.

"But what people don't know is that monks, nuns and friars who ended up homeless, were all given a pension – the nuns getting the least of all because they were women. Isn't that so unfair?" Juliana was eager to tell her friend everything she knew but they were both late for history and they had to run.

"Stop, girls! No running in the corridor – you know that." Miss Collins was the Deputy Head and very hot on the rules.

"Sorry, Miss, it's just that we're late for history," Maggie explained and slowed her rush to a walk.

Miss Collins grimaced and tutted at the same time. "You've dropped your book, Juliana – pick it up girl and get along with you both."

That evening, in their shared dormitory, they discussed the book. "Henry VIII must have been a right despot, mustn't he? Imagine changing a whole country's religion because he wanted to marry a particular woman – and then cutting her head off a few years later? God, the Middle Ages were pretty scary, weren't they?"

"Listen to this, Maggie – it says that Sir Walter Raleigh actually stayed at my house once. He was travelling and needed some place to rest his men and

176

horses. The squire at the time was a relative of his and was happy to have his cousin visit. He must have slept in the bedroom Grandfather uses now – imagine – the man who was responsible for starting America, actually stayed at my house!"

"Well, that's stretching history a bit but he was extremely important. There must be ghosts there – we'll just have to find them. Can I come home with you next weekend and we'll do some more investigating."

And so, the ghost hunters found themselves standing outside Grandfather's bedroom. They'd been given permission to look around – anywhere they pleased – he was as interested in their findings as they were. Juliana was holding one of the architect's drawings of when the present house was first built and she had an uneasy feeling that they'd find something soon. She recalled how odd it was that her mother – Grandfather's daughter – had said she didn't like the house when she was young and repeated it when they came to visit both grandparents. Mother could never wait to get away from the place. In fact, she bordered on being rude about the house and Grandma used to get quite upset. Juliana didn't feel like that however, she liked the place.

They both went inside the room and it was a very grand place with wooden panels on all the walls. (Wainscoting it was called, the book told her.) The bed was very big and sat in the middle of the room with curtains down two sides. (To keep out the cold in the olden days, the book also told her.) There were a lot of brass bits and pieces and two big paintings on the walls. Ancestors, she presumed as they looked rather grim. There was a large candlestick on a sideboard-cum-cupboard and a comfortable looking armchair by the window. The window was huge and made of small, leaded panes of glass – it really did look the part of a very old room. The atmosphere and style made the girls think of the seventeenth century, when Quaker fashions were favoured.

"It would have been Charles I on the throne at the time – he pretended to be a good Protestant but really favoured the Catholic faith, like his foreign queen. But they cut off his head in the end – imagine killing the King." Juliana found the thought unbelievable. "Religion really did have a lot to answer for in the old days."

Maggie jogged her arm impatiently. "Light the candle, Ju – there's the matches, and it's beginning to get dark." Maggie was scared but enjoying the experience at the same time.

"It'll look creepier if I do that." Juliana was more practical than her friend.

"So what – that'll be good. Look at these carved panels around the headboard – they seem to be telling a story, don't you think? Sort of biblical really. Hold the candle closer, so I can see better." Juliana did as she was bid and the candle light shimmered across the headboard.

"That bear is growling, I think – look at his great mouth – ferocious! His tongue looks strange through, don't you think." Maggie was squinting at the bear and reached out and prodded his tongue. She jumped back with a start when the panel slid to one side and revealed a brass button. "It's asking to be pressed, Ju – go on, reach up and press it."

At her touch, a full panel slid open and showed another room, hidden from sight. Juliana stood back and turned to put on the electric light – the candle was making things look too spooky. "Listen, can you hear singing, Maggie? It's rather solemn music and it sounds like men's voices." In fact, it was a dirge and sounded religious.

"It can't be, can it? Perhaps someone's playing music next door – or playing a trick on us."

They clearly heard a man's voice calling out, "Make way for Sir Walter, he's ready to retire now." Then silence and suddenly, the bedroom door opened and Grandfather came in. The wall panel slid back into place, the bear's tongue no longer protruded, the men's voices stopped singing and there was no sign of Sir Walter Raleigh. Where had he gone?

"Found anything interesting, girls? Not that there's much to find though. I've come to fetch you – dinner's ready and getting cold. Come on, I'm going to challenge you both to a game of cards after we've eaten. Are you game?" The old man's eyes twinkled and he ushered them from the room.

"Did you hear any men singing, Grandad?" But on being told he hadn't, Juliana decided to say no more just then. There'd be time enough for that.

Next day, the girls visited the village church which was also very old, with lots of memorial stones built into the floor and plaques all around the walls. One name in particular was repeated again and again – it had been the Squire's family name from the 1600s right up until the beginning of the eighteenth century. Many family members' names also adorned the church. The baptismal font had been gifted to the church by the squire in 1710 and many hundreds – if not thousands of children had been christened there. (It said so on a notice on a pillar.) The family name was Howard and the first name that appeared over and over again, was William Francis Howard. The history was laid out clearly for all to see and the Middle Brampton house that was home to Juliana had been the home of many of these Howards for generations.

They heard the low humming voices they'd heard the previous night and both froze on the spot. They could almost see the tonsured heads of the monks walking up the aisle of the church. Fortunately, the vicar appeared from behind a heavy curtain and smiled at the girls. This time, the singing didn't stop and the monk's voices were clearer than ever. The vicar crossed to a small table under the pulpit and fiddled with something there. Suddenly, the music and singing ceased – he had switched off a tape recorder.

"I hope the music didn't disturb you – I like to play it as it gives atmosphere to the place. At one time, there were monks here – Cistercian monks to be exact – and it seems fitting to play their music." He was smiling at the girls – and not in the least daunting.

"Oh no, vicar, it was very pleasant and fitting." Maggie was never lost for words. She turned to Juliana. "Let's go find that funny little building in the woods near your garden – I feel brave enough today to go inside." Both girls wandered off into the woods.

"I've got a torch with me, Maggie – it's quite dark in that building." Juliana was prepared for anything.

"Jolly good Ju – come on!" And she led the way.

It was a scary building and Juliana tentatively pushed open the broken door and pulled out some of the long grass growing around it. No one had been in here for a long time, it seemed. She shone the torch around the walls and realised it was bigger than she'd first thought. Maggie followed her inside and tripped over the doorstep, scaring Juliana as she did.

"Get up, you clod!" No sympathy for her, it seemed. Both sets of eyes followed the torch's beam around the building – there were several scratches, messages from previous inhabitants no doubt. Names and dates and some sort of secret signs.

Suddenly, the vicar from the church was standing in the doorway. He'd obviously followed them. "I heard you say you were coming here and I knew you were intent on exploring. I thought I might be able to help. Do you know how old this place is?"

He didn't wait for an answer. "It belongs to a time when a stone monastery stood where the big house next door stands now. Do you know what happened to it? Let me enlighten you – it was a lovely monastery in the sixteenth century and the monks were happy here, but Henry VIII turfed them out and stole all their worldly goods. The monks were of the Cistercian Order and although some of them lived as best they could, many of them didn't do well and became beggars and even thieves. In fact, following the destruction of the religious houses, stealing and criminality increased a lot – even murder – when people were desperate. The religious orders were treated most cruelly." It was as though he was in his pulpit and was preaching to the congregation. He bowed his head and the girls thought he was going to pray.

"We know some of that, but what was this place?" Maggie was impatient.

This was a cell – see the dents on the wall where chains were hung. It was used to keep a monk inside as a prisoner. He had to have broken some serious rule or maybe spoken out of turn – but he needed to be punished and seclusion in this place was not unknown for the monks. They wouldn't have fought it as when they did wrong, they knew they'd be punished." He stopped talking and looked around. "Can you not feel them here – feel their suffering – it's been absorbed into the walls." He pointed to the far corner and said, "See – see him there. His spirit has stayed here, in fact, he probably died here, so it's only right. When a monk was imprisoned here, it seemed everyone soon forgot about him. Maybe he – and he pointed to where he saw the monk – was imprisoned when Thomas Cromwell finally cleared out the monastery – he wouldn't have known about this place, so it was overlooked by his men."

The girls peered into the corner and Maggie thought she saw something move, but she couldn't be sure.

"We'd best get home now – it must be tea time. Goodbye Vicar, and thank you for telling us everything." Juliana pulled her friend outside and set off for home. The vicar just stayed where he was and didn't follow them this time.

Grandfather was in a jolly mood that evening and told the girls stories about when he was young. "I used to think this house was haunted and I used to bring my friends here from the village, to see if we could find them."

"And did you, Grandad?" Juliana was keen to hear the answer.

"Well, you know I wish I could say we didn't, but it wouldn't be true. On your investigations the other night, I suppose you found the priest's hole behind the bed in my room? It was used for hiding the Catholic priest so he could hear Mass and Confessions from the Howard family, who had to pretend they were actually Protestant, but had always been good Catholics. If they hadn't done this, their estates would have been confiscated by Oliver Cromwell – a later descendant of Thomas Cromwell, who had destroyed all the religious houses in the name of Henry VIII. Ironic that, isn't it? That they were related?" And he lit his pipe before settling back in his chair and raising both eyebrows at the girls' expressions.

"Yes, but what about the ghosts you saw when you were young?" Maggie could hardly contain herself.

"Well, what about them? They never harmed me and I didn't harm them. One I remember in particular though was the ghost of Sir Walter Raleigh. He used to appear in my parents' room – mine now – and my mum and dad just accepted him as well. Ghosts aren't as scary as people think – it's the ones who see them that cause the problems, not the ghosts. Why don't you wander upstairs to my room and see what you can find? Go on – don't be scared – remember, nothing you see will hurt you. Just ignore them."

The girls got up reluctantly and climbed the stairs slowly. And in the bedroom, they pressed the bear's tongue-revealing the Priest Hole which didn't look very welcoming.

"Go on, Ju – you go first – I've looked around and I can't see Sir Walter." Maggie followed her friend into the small room. There were no windows nor much furniture but a very old bureau stood against one wall with two brass candlesticks on it. A couple of drawers were hanging off but another was tightly shut. Juliana pulled at the drawer and it soon opened. "That seemed rather easy, considering how long it must have been closed. She took it all the way out and looked at the back of the space – there was something there and she managed to ease it out. It was an old miniature painting and showed a beautiful face of a young girl, dressed in a nun's wimple. It was only her head and shoulders but the face was so beautiful, with slightly rosy cheeks and vivid blue eyes. Her hair colour couldn't be seen, but she had probably been blond with her fair colouring. It had been painted in oils and the nun's face shone in the light of Juliana's torch.

"She looks too beautiful to be real," Maggie whispered and gently touched the picture with her smallest finger. "I wonder who she was and why her picture was hidden at the back of the drawer."

"I doubt we'll ever know that. Let's go down and show it to Grandfather – he may know something, although I think it's been hidden in that drawer for centuries." They came out of the Priest Hole and touched the bear's tongue – and then they heard it. The same singing voices they'd heard before. Neither girl could discern where exactly the sound was coming from but it filled the room.

Again, it was more like a dirge – a lament or something – probably for the dissolution of the monastery itself. Who could tell?

"Remember what your grandfather said – they can't hurt us and probably don't want to. Let's just leave them here in peace and go downstairs."

"I've never see that before, girls – but what a find! You know there was a Convent in the next village – near to your school – and of course, the nuns lived there in the Middle Ages. I suppose your mystery lady could have been one of them. I tell you what, why don't you take the painting to your school and speak to Miss Collins about it? She's very interested in history and knows much more than I do about the local area – even about past centuries?"

"She's a bit of an old dragon, you know – do you really think she'll help us?" Juliana was sceptical.

"Why don't you ask her, that's the answer?" Grandfather was looking tired and the girls left him and went to bed. It was very late.

"Come in," Miss Collins called out and Juliana and Maggie entered the room. They stood awkwardly in front of her desk and waited for her to look up. She took her time in doing this – part of the protocol was that they must wait until she was ready before they spoke.

"What do you girls want? I'm very busy, you know." She was not an attractive woman. She was about fifty, very thin with steel grey hair, caught in a severe bun that did nothing for her. Juliana took the miniature painting from her satchel and offered it to the mistress.

"Where did you find this? The woman looks familiar – I think I've seen her before." She stared at the painting. "It's very old, but I'm sure I've seen it before." She squinted her eyes behind her horn-rimmed spectacles and took a magnifying glass from her drawer. Looking at it for a while, she asked for an explanation and the girls were only too happy to oblige, butting into each other's speech as they talked.

"Grandfather suggested that we come to see you and you might be able to find out something about it. What do you think, Miss Collins?"

"Can you leave it with me for a few hours and I'll get back to you? I want to look into the school's archives and see what I can find. This building is very old you know and we have records going back for centuries, although they get a bit sketchy the further back you go. Did you know the school stands on the site of a Convent that housed nuns – and I feel there's something familiar about this face. I think I've seen a sketch of it somewhere."

"Did the nuns suffer the same devastation of their home when the Dissolution of the Monasteries took place?" Juliana asked.

"Only partially. Many of their valuables were taken but it wasn't until Charles I's time, that they suffered the most. Again, it was to do with their continuing to practice the Catholic faith. In the end, I think they were worse off than the monks as their pensions were just a few pennies – and suddenly they had nowhere to live either." Miss Collins stood up and gathered her papers. "I have a class now – so I must go but I'll be in touch as soon as I have anything to tell you."

Maggie bravely prolonged the conversation, asking, "Did you know that Juliana's house in Middle Brompton stands on the site of an old monastery and it was destroyed by Thomas Crowell, everything was confiscated – and the monks were chased off their land?"

"I did know that, young lady now you must both leave me to my work." And she showed them to the door.

As they were leaving her room, they bumped into Matilda, she of the carrot hair and obnoxious personality. "Been hobnobbing with the Deputy Head then, have we? I suppose it will do you no harm to keep on her right side – you might benefit from such crawling. I suppose your rich old Grandfather might give the school more funds, if she's nice to you."

"Matilda, are you free next weekend? If so, would you like to come to my house to stay – both you and Maggie – I'm sure my grandfather would like to meet you?" Maggie was looking at her friend with disbelief on her face. This was the most hateful girl in their year. *What was Juliana thinking of?* As they walked away from. "Carrots," Juliana mouthed, "I'll explain later!"

Before school broke up for the weekend, Miss Collins sent for both girls to come to her study. "Well, I've been searching through our archives – there are still some old papers talking about this place when it was a Convent – not many of course, but enough of interest. She produced a large cardboard box tied up with string. It was quite dusty and Juliana wondered how old that dust was. The Deputy Head lifted out some documents and a couple of small books.

She cleared her throat. "Your lady was the Prioress of the Benedictine Convert that stood on this site. Only the Abbess was higher in status. Her name was Prioress Josephine Louise and she had entered the Convent as an Oblate – that is a girl child who is given by her parents, for her to be brought up as a nun. Your lady was such a one – she'd never known any other life than that of the religious order. Her parents would have given the Abbess a dowry for taking in their daughter – in fact, the churches then were richer than the King's Treasury, which was a large part of the reason for destroying and sacking them all. Their power, which was significant, was also taken away and the practice of worshipping as a Catholic was made completely illegal."

She cleared her throat and poured herself a glass of water before continuing. "With the passing of the years, Josephine Louise grew older and more and more beautiful every day and she was unofficially known as 'The Beautiful Nun'. She was also an intelligent and very devoted woman who rose quickly to a higher status in the Convent until she was appointed the Prioress.

"In medieval times, nunneries and monasteries provided shelter and food for travelling folk and helped them if they could. The Benedictine Convent was well known for its generosity to passing travellers and one day, a priest turned up asking for succour. He was a man in his thirties – not much older than Josephine Louise and he had come to the area to meet the Howard family in the next village. The Howards had been Catholics but, in line with Henry VIII's original decision about Catholicism, they quickly turned to Protestantism and built a Priest Hole in their house, so they could continue to celebrate the Mass. To do this, they would need a secret priest. This then, was why the stranger turned up in the area. He only stayed at the Convent for three days, but it only took that time for he and the Prioress to fall deeply in love. It was true love and the very first time, the Prioress had experienced it. They were besotted with each other and met secretly in the woods between the two villages. Josephine Louise had lived her whole life by the Benedictine rules for nuns – she had sworn to adhere to stability, fidelity, poverty, charity and obedience, but after she'd met the Catholic priest, that all changed."

The two girls were mesmerised and hanging on Miss Collins's every word, but Maggie broke the silence, by asking for a drink of water. Miss Collins poured it for her.

"What happened to them, Miss? They couldn't have got together as that wasn't allowed, was it?"

Miss Collins returned the miniature painting of the beautiful nun and said, "Just look at that face and imagine the anguish she must have felt – did she choose Father Angelino or the Convent, after all she was already a bride of Christ." She looked closely at Juliana and took out a box of tissues from her desk drawer, "There, dear, dry your eyes – it was a very long time ago."

"But what happened to the priest? Did he use the special room the Howards built for him – and did he live there?" Maggie was deeply disturbed by the story.

"Girls, I've been talking for a long time – shall we stop now and begin again later?"

"Oh no, Miss Collins, please tell us what happened to them – I'll never sleep again until I know." Juliana was impatient.

"Well, I'll cut a long story short, so that you know what happened before you go home for the weekend. The couple began to meet secretly over the next few months but then, one day, Father Angelino failed to turn up at their agreed time and the Prioress had to return to the Convent, wondering what had happened to him."

She shuffled her papers and lifted a new one to the top.

"This paper was written by Josephine Louise herself and has been preserved in our archives. The Roundheads turned up one day at the Howard's Manor and said they intended to search the property. The captain told the Squire, 'We've had a report that there are Catholics, conducting services here – holding Masses and hearing Confessions. You know that is not allowed under the Law and if it's found to be true, those responsible will be punished.' He called to his men to begin their investigation.

"The Squire at the time was of course a Howard – another member of the family line. He had been taking part in the Catholic services and Father Angelino had been conducting them. When Cromwell's men began to search the house, he escaped into the Priest Hole which wasn't visible to the naked eye – but unfortunately, it was visible to soldiers who had searched many such houses around the country – and the hideout was discovered. The Howard family were all arrested and their Estate confiscated in the name of King Charles I and of the Army General, Oliver Cromwell. Father Angelino was arrested and imprisoned in a stone building in the grounds of the Manor. He was tortured there until he admitted he was a Catholic Priest who had served the Howard family. The experience must have been dreadful – he ended up with broken bones, cuts and lacerations and a broken heart over his beloved nun, Josephine Louise." She held up a faded paper. "All of this was reported by the soldiers who did it – and left in the Convent."

She went on, "The same battalion of soldiers moved onto the Benedictine Convent where the nuns were discovered to still be practising in the Catholic faith and as such, they were thrown out of their home and sent on their way to

God only knew where. Josephine Louise was one of these nuns. She'd searched all over the land in the area but couldn't find her loved one, who was still in the barricaded building, ill, hungry and desolate. He'd been forgotten about – once he'd admitted to being a priest, the soldiers had no further use for him. He was left there to die and with no Howard family member around, no one came looking for him. He died soon of his wounds, but also of a broken heart.

"His beloved nun – as a Prioress – was given a small pension, but she had no home to go to. She'd lived at the convent all her life. She wandered the roads, begging for shelter wherever she could and some people did allow her to stay with them, but only for a few days, as they feared a Catholic nun would only bring danger to their door. She assumed Angelino had run away when the soldiers went to the Manor – and had forgotten all about her and the love he had declared for her. Eventually, she found a position with a local farmer's wife – she became her scullery maid and was lucky because she discovered she was pregnant with the priest's child. Normally, any farmer would have thrown her out but his wife was a kind woman, who pitied the beautiful girl."

Miss Collins was finished. "There is nothing more to tell – you now know about your miniature painting, don't you? It's up to you to decide what to do with it. It has nothing to do with me – and there are no more records to check. The only reason I know what happened to the nun was because she wrote a letter, telling all – and asked the farmer's wife to keep it for her unborn baby. So the child would know who her father and mother had been. The wife was a kind woman and did as she was asked.

Josephine Louise died in childbirth and when she was older, the farmer's wife gave the daughter her mother's letter, so she learned who she was – even from beyond the grave. She stayed and worked on the farm and took the farmer's name which was Collins, by the way."

"But that's your name, Miss Collins – are you a descendant of the nun?" Juliana asked.

"Just coincidence, I'm sure, but I will look into it later when I have a moment." She swept the old papers into the box and stood up. "Good day, girls, have a good weekend."

The two girls left her study in a sort of trance, only to find Matilda waiting for them at the school gate. "Did you forget about me? I bet you did. Typical of you, Juliana."

"No, we didn't, but we've been busy. Come on then if you're coming," Maggie said curtly and the three girls rode to the Manor house on their bicycles.

"Go on, Matilda – go inside – there's nothing in there that can hurt you. Honest, there isn't. Look, I'll go in first, shall I?" Juliana encouraged the girl.

"I'm scared – it looks so creepy." She really was afraid but moved unwillingly towards the open Priest Hole. As soon as she stepped over the threshold, Juliana banged the door closed behind her.

"There you are, madam – that'll teach you to keep bad mouthing me at school – in front of everyone. You can stay in there until you beg my pardon and ask to be released." Juliana was usually a kind girl but Matilda had pushed her too far and she didn't know how to stop herself.

"Let me out, please – there's lots of men's voices singing in here. Can you hear it?" Matilda was obviously crying.

"I hear nothing, Matilda." She lied to the frightened, hearing the singing perfectly well.

"I hear them too, Juliana!" Maggie was rather agitated.

"I know, so do I – but I want her to be even more scared. And remember what Grandfather said – ghosts can't hurt us."

"I remember all right – but I don't like it much." She turned to leave the room when she was confronted by Sir Walter Raleigh in all his finery – a true Elizabethan gentleman. He ignored her and crossed to the desk by the window. He looked out into the garden. "What a lovely day it is, but why are you treating your friend so badly?" He was a very handsome man with a small pointed beard and had a long sword hanging from his waist.

"It's not me, sir – it's Juliana – tell her!" Maggie really was frightened. Sir Walter looked at Juliana and raised an eyebrow. Juliana shouted through the door of the secret room. "Well, Matilda – are you going to ask me to forgive you and promise to stop teasing me so much and bad mouthing my grandfather?"

"Yes – yes, please forgive me. I promise to stop doing it. Please will you let me out of here?" Her upset was obvious. Juliana touched the bear's tongue and the door sprang back, allowing Matilda to fall forward into the bedroom. She did look rather penitent and ran from the house and cycled back to school as quickly as her pedals would allow.

The little housemaid came into the room and Sir Walter disappeared. "Your Grandfather is asking for you downstairs. Dinner is ready."

"Okay, Betty, we're just coming but there's something we have to do first – we'll be only ten minutes." Juliana took Maggie by the arm. "You see why I invited Matilda here. I had a cunning plan." Maggie laughed. "Follow me, Mags, there's something we have to do." She was carrying a small silver box and led the way across the garden and into the woods beyond.

It was beginning to get dark, so they knew they'd have to hurry. The door of the stone building was open and Juliana went in first. She'd brought her torch and a small spade. She bent down and dug a deep hole against the wall, placing the silver box inside before covering it over with soil. "Why are you doing that, Ju?" Maggie asked.

"They've got to be together, Mags. He died here and has been waiting for Josephine Louise to come to him – she of course, thought he'd deserted her. He never knew he had a child and the nun died before she could get to know that child. Now the couple are united again and their love for each other can go on."

The two girls ran all the way back to the house and crashed into the dining room, where Grandfather had some guests – all sitting around the table. To their surprise, one of them was Miss Collins and the other, a man who looked familiar. It was the vicar they'd met in the village church a few weeks before. "Sorry to be late, Grandfather." Juliana was quite breathless and settled down at the table. Maggie thought dinner was especially yummy that night.

"Aren't you wondering why Miss Collins and Mr Howard have joined us tonight?" Grandfather asked with a smile on his face. "These are my good friends, who have been helping me with a little subterfuge I arranged to entertain you both. Juliana, you'd been looking rather sad for some time and I thought you needed something new to occupy your mind. Miss Collins and Mr Howard, who is an actor by the way, agreed to help – you'd have suspected me, I'm sure – but not them, both pillars of society. Have you found the last few weeks interesting?" He waited for their reply.

"Why yes, Grandad – we've been pretty occupied at least but not actually enjoying it – it was a rather sad story about a beautiful nun and a handsome Catholic Priest." Juliana started to explain.

"I know all about it – I arranged it for you. Mr Howard here, is a descendant of the Howard family who lived here until Oliver Cromwell arrested them all. He is also quite an authority on the local church and has been my friend for a number of years. We play chess together as well, when he's not dressing up as a vicar or Sir Walter Raleigh. Miss Collins on the other hand has been a friend and acquaintance of mine for so long I can't remember. Between us, we invented Father Angelino and Prioress Josephine Louise and their unrequited love. Some of the story may have been true but I doubt it. Miss Collins did find some records that helped fill in the missing bits and Mr Howard worked the sound system of the monks' voices."

Juliana looked around the table and Maggie just sat there speechless. "It doesn't seem very kind, Grandad – couldn't you have invented a happier story to entertain us?"

"Well no, you'd have sussed us out. We had to be careful. It wasn't easy, you know – it took quite a bit of digging for information – and careful timing. What did you do with the miniature painting of the nun, by the way?" He re-filled his friends' glasses and asked if they'd mind if he smoked his pipe.

"It's buried in the stone building so that both the poor souls can be together. We really took everything seriously, you know – and believed in the priest and the nun. Also, Miss Collins, do you plan to investigate your family line – the baby born to the nun and brought up to be a Collins, might be an ancestor of yours. Or was everything just a lie?"

Miss Collins had the grace to look embarrassed. "Yes, I may do that, Juliana. One never knows what one may discover."

It was very odd but, from their initial laughter at finding the girls' discomfort entertaining, the group of friends were changing and looked rather crestfallen.

"We're off to bed now, Grandad, and thank you for trying to amuse us. The strange thing is that I don't feel very amused – just rather sad." The two girls left the room and went upstairs.

"I feel very weird, don't you, Maggie? I don't think their trick was very clever." They stopped at the big window on the landing and looked out at the bright moon. "What a lovely night, so romantic – a night for lovers." Juliana's melancholy was apparent.

"I think you're right, Ju – just look over there, beyond the garden towards the trees. Who is that, do you think?" Maggie pressed her forehead against the glass.

There, in the light of the moon, stood a couple with their arms entwined around each other. One was a tall bearded man and the other, a slight but beautiful woman. One was a priest and one was a nun, of that there was no doubt.

Juliana sighed and smiled at her friend. "It's Angelino and Josephine Louise, I'm sure of it. We did manage to bring them together, didn't we? The grown-ups downstairs think they're so clever – but we're the clever ones. We did the right thing.

The girls looked again at the couple in the moonlight and were sure they both turned their faces towards the window, raising hands in thanks and smiling in their contentment with each other. It may have taken a very long time, but thanks to the determination of two schoolgirls, they were together at last.

What the Changing Seasons Bring

She stood in the cottage doorway; her arms wrapped around each other to try to keep out the cold. It was Winter and usually she liked the season but Robert was going away to war today and she could hear her heart making strange sounds, as if it was breaking. He was her only child and he'd been called up to serve his country, something he was quite willing to do, but something she would have preferred never to happen.

He was walking down the garden path, his rucksack over one shoulder. He hadn't quite reached the gate yet and turned to look at her once more. The snow was swirling around him but his heavy army greatcoat seemed to be keeping out the cold. The nearby street lamp made his blond hair shine – and it was already covered by falling snowflakes. He raised his arm and smiled at her. "Bye Mum." He mouthed and opened the gate. Would she ever see him again, she thought, but she'd kept her thoughts to herself since he'd first shown her his call-up papers.

"Bye, my Darlin'." She mouthed back at him as he closed the gate and began walking across the street towards the village bus. It was the last bus of the night and it would drop him – and a few other village boys – at the Army Camp near the next village. She continued to stand at the door until he had climbed onto the bus. She wanted to see him for as long as she could because he was going out of her life, something he'd never done before and she found herself again thinking how much she hated that man Hitler.

She stared into the darkness and saw the sky was full of bright, shiny stars. The snow was beautiful and lay in swathes and piles on every surface, making the shapes of the trees look black and twisted against the whiteness. It looked like soft marshmallows and she reached outside to pick some up. Such beauty shouldn't exist when young men were going to war and possibly their deaths. She stared closely at the snowflakes in her hand and thought how intricately formed they were, like diamonds and crystals all rolled into one. Staring intently at something helped to stop the tears from running down her cheeks, and freezing in the cold night air.

She turned suddenly and went into the warm cottage to sit by the fire, first lifting the parcel that he'd left for her, ordering her not to open it until after he'd gone. "Oh Robert," she said out loud, "you and your secrets." But she loved his secrets and had played along with him since he was a young boy.

She tore at the brown paper and rolled up the piece of string he'd put around it. In wartime, she'd learned everything had to be saved in case it was needed later – even string. It was a heavy parcel and she thought she already knew what it was. Four picture frames rested on top of each other and she lined them up along the mantelpiece. The first one was a snow scene with several figures running around between snow-covered buildings. The second was a grass-covered meadow with rabbits running between 'hosts of golden daffodils' and buttercups. It was Spring in a frame. Number three was of a splendid country house sitting in the middle of a beautiful garden, full of roses of every colour. They were old fashioned, heavy headed roses whose perfume would have filled the air, if only she could have smelt them. Actually, she thought she could smell them and took a deep breath. Lastly, the fourth picture was of a tall Horse Chestnut Tree with conkers lying in little piles on the ground. It stood amongst other trees whose leaves were already covering the grass – in yellow, orange, cream and pink autumnal colours.

Funnily enough, she thought she'd stood them in the right order – Winter, Spring, Summer and Autumn. They were lovely pictures and she went off to make herself a cup of cocoa before returning to the fire and admiring Robert's present. She'd keep them there, she thought, they brightened the room and brightened herself too. It was a little like Robert was still there.

She climbed the stairs to bed and couldn't resist looking into his bedroom to see if everything was as it should be – neat as a new pin – just as he usually kept it. She sat on the bed and wiped the tears from her eyes. She wanted to shake off this sadness but couldn't so she prayed to God to look after her son. She felt so tired and found herself lying down on top of the blanket that still smelt of him. Of course, she fell asleep – it had been a long day that started very early in the morning. She began to dream of the lovely, snow scene in the first picture and suddenly she was in an army training camp with many young men exercising at the commands of a very loud Sergeant Major. She knew no one could see her as they didn't even look her way.

"Right, you lot, move quicker than that unless you want the Gerries to catch you. You there, keep up or you'll go round the square twice as much as the others." They definitely couldn't see her but then it was her dream after all. She moved closer to the figures and saw Robert at the back. She made her way over to him, but he couldn't see her either. "Hey you, Blondie – yeah, you at the back. What's your sister's name? Shout it out so everyone can hear."

"Don't have a sister, Sir," Robert called out loudly. His cheeks were very red and he added out of politeness, "My name is Robert Smedley."

"Well, I think we'll call you Roberta then 'cause you move like a girl. Do you hear that, lads?" he called to the others. "This is Roberta from now on." He then dismissed all the soldiers and went back into the Guard Room. She stood there in the middle of the parade ground with snow falling all around her and thought how cruel the man had been. There was no need to humiliate Robert like that. Her boy was no girl. She went into the low building where the lads had gone and her nostrils filled with a delicious smell. It was the canteen and the men formed a long queue, plates in hand, very eager for supper it seemed. She watched the young men laugh and joke with each other, Robert being one of them.

"Well, I'm not going to call you Roberta, no matter what he says." A cheeky young chappie playfully punched Robert's shoulder – and from that moment, they were friends. It was funny that the Sergeant Major's attempt to push the young blond man outside of the group had actually had the opposite result.

A couple of days passed with a lot of training. She saw Robert for the first time carrying a rifle and realised killing was something he'd have to get used to if he were to survive. A group of the lads were sitting around a small gas fire and holding their hands towards a non-existent heat. Billy, the youngest, spoke up. "Where do you think they'll send us?"

Everybody grumbled a few words and one said, "I heard the sergeant talking with an officer yesterday and saying, "They'd better pick up some Dutch fast. Do you think we could be heading for Holland?"

"Why Holland? I heard there's only skirmishes around the border and that Germany has complete control of the country. Why would they send us there?"

"Maybe to help the resistance – there's always a resistance movement in the occupied countries. They must need help, mustn't they?" Robert joined in the conversation. "What do you think, Billy?" His new friend was sitting across from him. "Well, wherever it is, I hope that sergeant doesn't come with us." And all the lads laughed in agreement, before slipping off one by one to their narrow bunks that only had one blanket.

Billy said to Robert, "I'm scared, are you?"

"Of course I'm scared, you clot! Why wouldn't I be? This time next week, we could both be dead." But Billy was already asleep and Robert felt he was the only one left awake. Molly moved closer to her son and reached for his hand. He was in the lower bunk and she sat down on the edge of the narrow bed. She took his hand, at least she thought she did but he didn't move.

She bent down and whispered in his ear, "You'll be all right, son, I'll watch over you." He sat upright as though he'd heard something, but then slumped back on the pillow. She saw him smile just before he dropped off to sleep.

Next morning, they were all called onto the parade ground and told they were being sent to Holland to help the Resistance movement there. *So they'd been right about the destination.* The parade ground was just like the picture on her mantelpiece, with figures running around and bumping into each other. "Come on, Bill – there's room for a little 'un here." Robert shouted from one of the trucks. Molly was standing at the side and the snow, if anything, was getting worse. She shouted, "The best of luck, lads." But no one heard her although Robert thought he heard something but shrugged it off as the sound of wind. One by one, the trucks started to move and everyone fell silent. This was the start of it for them and they all knew it.

Time passed and Molly found herself standing in a kitchen with half a dozen soldiers. It was built like a log cabin and there were steaming mugs of hot chocolate on the table. The snow outside was falling heavily and had blocked out any daylight, as it piled on mounds on the window ledges. Molly thought it felt safe and cosy, but she knew it wasn't that. One man stood by the fireplace and was dressed differently. He wasn't a soldier but he was clearly in command of the situation. "We're going to blow up a bridge to make things more difficult for the Germans to get about. We've got demolition equipment and an electrical specialist who can oversee things." He spoke good English, but with a strong Dutch accent.

The British soldiers asked some questions and seemed satisfied with the answers. "It's to be the day after tomorrow when we know a battalion of Germans will be crossing the bridge – we'll get two for the price of one – one a broken bridge and no route out of the town and a good number of the enemy taken out of the war forever. Tomorrow night, we'll meet here in complete darkness, wearing all dark clothes and carrying only one torch each. We'll be led to the bridge and three of you will swim under the supporting pillars taking only the explosives and equipment you'll be given. It'll be your job to fix the explosives in place and the engineer will set them to explode at a given time. I'll be waiting just below the parapet with this device attached to each explosive. Once I know you're well clear, I'll flick the switch, and then move faster than I've ever moved in my life before."

Everything seemed like a good plan until Molly saw her son being picked as one of the swimmers. His life would be in great danger and she prayed to God to keep him safe. Next night, three shadowy figures crept out of the log cabin carrying two black bags. Molly followed them to the bridge and watched as, one by one, they slipped into the cold, dark water. The whiteness of the snow gave some light but not enough to make things easy for the soldiers. Twenty minutes later, the first man emerged from the water and quickly made his way up the bank, trailing a long wire behind him. The wire got caught on a branch and Molly reached out without thinking and pulled it free from the tree. She was surprised at herself, as she didn't think she could do anything like that – but she managed and thought it was because she hadn't given it any thought – just did it. She saw Robert and Billy come out of the water then and she breathed a sigh of relief.

Next day, the Dutchman, Billy and Robert waited under the bridge, watching for the approach of the Germans. The Dutch man held the detonator securely in his hands and shifted his position to try to ease the cramp that gripped his leg. They could hear the marching boots coming closer – soon they would be on the bridge. He suddenly fell forward on top of the detonator and for a second, nothing happened. Molly was there watching it all happen and she looked at Robert's face which had gone grey. The marching feet were on the bridge now and it was time to activate the switch. Robert moved forward and pushed the Dutch man to one side, grabbing the detonator as he did so. There were two switches and he didn't know which one to use. The sweat was running down his face and he looked up, desperate for help. Billy didn't know what to do – but Molly did. She moved her son's finger to the right switch and put pressure on his hand.

It only took a second before the loudest bang ever took place. Billy and Robert crouched into a tight ball to avoid falling debris. They lay on top of the Dutch man to protect him. Moving fast and with all the confusion and shouting, they got away quickly and were picked up by the waiting cart, which had been well hidden behind some bushes.

Perhaps it was the loudness of the explosion that woke her. She came out of her dream, afraid and sweating. She looked around and saw she was in Robert's room still. My, she must have slept deeply. Down in the kitchen, she managed to clear her head and calm her thoughts. A pot of tea and some toast later, she realised she'd slept until midday. To her, it was only the day after Robert had left but her dream had seemed like several weeks. She felt sure Robert was safe and alive – but in danger. She made up a fresh fire and noticed the snow had stopped falling but the log pile was still well hidden by a white blanket. Everything looked peaceful and quiet. Fallen snow always made things quiet. She took her third cup of tea to the fireplace and watched the new flames come to life. Her gaze went up to the mantelpiece and she saw the first picture of the snowy scene had fallen forward and lay flat on the shelf. That had certainly been one exciting time; she thought and smiled as she thought of the part she'd played in it all. She stood up the picture again.

A few weeks passed and there was no snow on the ground now. Instead, she could see the first green shoots of the snowdrops peeping out of the still hard earth. She'd heard nothing from Robert, but then she hadn't really expected to with the war escalating across Europe. She hadn't experienced bombing but then she didn't live in one of the important cities or towns. She'd just come back from the village shop where she'd hoped to find at least a little of food which was always scarce. She'd been lucky and smiled as she put away the precious items – she had a little bit of butter, the same of sugar and a whole cup of flour plus two carrots and one onion. That had been a trip worth making, especially in the beautiful spring sunshine. She boiled up a small pot of soup and thickened it with a spoonful of flour, some salt and pepper which she was lucky enough to still have.

Carrying the precious bowl of soup into the parlour, she settled down by the embers of the fire. "Molly. Molly. Are you home? May I come in?" And needing no answer, the parlour door swung open and Mary Stewart from two houses down, came into the room. Mary was on the large side and seemed to fill the room. Molly put her soup on a small table. She liked Mary but not enough to share her precious soup.

"What on earth is it, Mary – you're all out of breath? Sit down and I'll get you a cup of tea?" Molly got to her feet.

"What is that lovely smell? I hope I haven't disturbed your meal." She had already plonked herself in the most comfortable armchair in the room. She wore one of those turbans on her head, the kind all the women were wearing these days. Molly brought the tea for her neighbour.

"Well, what is it, Mary. Have you for something to tell me?"

"Mrs Cooper at the shop forgot to give you this, so she asked me to bring it and to say she was sorry." Mary enjoyed the tea although it was a bit stewed. Molly took the card and reached for her glasses. It said nothing but had a smiling mouth drawn on one side and was addressed to 'Ma Smedley' on the other. "Oh Mary, it's from Robert. He's alive and well. I know it's from him and I know what the smiling mouth means. Thank you for bringing me this, you've put me in a very good mood now. In fact, I'm in such a good mood. I'm going to share my soup with you."

The two women, both of whom had sons in the war, sat in companionable silence and ate the soup, then Mary left as quickly – and as loudly – as she'd come. After the warming meal, Molly felt drowsy and left the washing up 'till later. She nodded off whilst staring at the second picture on the mantelpiece and hoping Robert was experiencing the same kind of weather she was. Spring was coming fast – and she dropped off to sleep with a smile on her face.

She was standing in a field of yellow and white Tulips that stretched as far as the eye could see. There were several people working in the field, all carrying large sacks across their shoulders and gathering the flowers using what looked like very sharp knives to cut the stems. There was a truck waiting on the road, slowly being filled with the baskets and for a moment, she thought she recognised the driver. She moved closer to the truck and saw Robert clearly. There was no doubt in her mind – his golden hair was shining in the sun and he had a healthy glow to his skin. *But it couldn't be Robert, could it? He couldn't be out in the open like this. He was a British soldier and this country was completely occupied by the Germans. They would surely kill him if he was spotted.* She climbed on board the truck and settled in a corner – she would find out where it was going. It seemed again that no one could see or hear her, if she didn't want them to. After a short distance, they arrived at a log cabin that Molly knew she'd seen before – but it had been covered in snow then. Robert went into the cabin, first grabbing a bright yellow Tulip from a basket. She went inside and saw the blonde-haired girl who accepted the flower and gave him a kiss on the cheek as a thank you.

"Well, well," Molly said to herself, "so, that's the name of the game." Another man had taken the truck away to deliver the baskets to a waiting train.

Apparently, the flowers were heading for Berlin and the Germans. The kitchen in the cabin began to fill up with men and women. From the things they were saying, Molly realised why Robert could wander about an occupied country like a native. This was a Resistance meeting and Robert was one of them, dressed in workman's clothes just like those the others were wearing. Whilst the women made hot drinks, the men gathered together around the table. "Let's see your papers again. They're amazing."

Robert got some papers from his inside pocket and twisted his face to one side as he grinned at the questioner in a rather stupid fashion. "My God, you really look simple – you'd fool anyone." They all looked at his papers. "The British army have done you proud, the papers are excellent – even your photo. Do you know how they describe you here? Do you know what that word means?"

The older man in the group said, "They call you an imbecile or idiot. Be grateful to whoever forged the papers, they are good and with that twisted face, you look just what they describe." And he slapped Robert on the shoulder.

"Don't hurt the imbecile, Father." The blond girl laughed and handed Robert his tea. Molly knew who her father was. It was the man who'd been hurt when trying to blow up the bridge. He was a Resistance leader – and Robert was working with him. She hadn't realised that soldiers could be used in this way – as part of an occupied country's resistance but why not – everything was fair in love and war.

"Are we all ready for the drop tonight?" the leader asked. "Speed is of the essence and we have to get the men away as quickly as we can. Robert has the exact location where they're being dropped and he'll lead us there tonight. You can't be told now in case someone here is in league with the Germans." Grunts and boos met this statement and they all laughed.

Robert looked happy enough to Molly and he was obviously playing an important part in the Resistance movement – and he certainly seemed to be getting on very well with the young girl. However, Molly decided she would hang around for a while in case she could be of use. It was very exciting to be here and yet invisible. The girl's name was Sophie and her father called Peter. Robert seemed very much part of the family.

In the very early hours next morning, three dark figures left the cabin, two of them following Robert. They were all well-armed and carried heavy torches. They crossed two fields and Robert suddenly stopped and put his finger to his lips. "They're coming – listen carefully." And all three crouched down, flickering their torches very gently. From the clouds, they spotted dark shapes falling slowly to land. There were six of them and they landed pretty near to the three waiting men. Robert and his friends moved forward and helped to grab hold of the parachutes and fold them into bags. The airmen knew to follow the men on the ground and they did it quietly and cautiously.

Then they heard the sound of an engine and saw headlights on the ground shining through the darkness. Peter said, "I'll take the men away with me. Plan B it is I'm afraid." He beckoned the airmen to follow him and in complete silence, they crawled away from the area. Robert nodded and actually walked towards the approaching jeep, which was full of Germans. He made sure he was seen in the headlights and switched on his imbecile face, looking quite horrific in the headlights. The jeep stopped on a slight hill and all men jumped out. He clearly heard. *"Halt, Halt, auf oder Ich schiesse. Wo sind die anderen geblieben?"* He didn't need a translator for that. He was scared and held up his hands at the first Halt.

Molly found herself standing beside her son and whispered in his ear, "Don't worry, son. I'm here." And she ran up the hill behind the Germans and leaned into the driver's seat. She gripped the handbrake and released it slowly and quietly. The jeep began to creep forward, gaining speed until it rammed into the German soldiers. Suddenly, all was confusion and frightened shouts rang out amongst the sharp sounds of gunfire. The gunfire was the last she knew of the Germans and of Robert. The jeep was big and heavy and sliced into the bodies. She didn't see what happened then but she hoped Robert hadn't been hurt.

The gunshots woke Molly and for a moment, she thought the village had been invaded. Where had she been? Had she really seen Robert? Robert wasn't an imbecile; she was shouting at no one in particular, but she felt very afraid and could still see the hard faces of the German soldiers as they closed in on her son. *I saved him; I hope.* She spoke to herself and started to clear away the dirty dishes. It was dark outside, she must have slept for a long time but at least, she'd seen her boy.

She'd joined the knitting circle in the village and had been talked into joining a baking class as well. She didn't do much baking since there was only her at home now, but the women often baked for the lads at the barracks and she liked the thought of doing this. She was doing her bit, she told herself. Wednesday was the 'Knit and Natter' afternoon and she'd spent the time unravelling one of

Robert's old sweaters – a red one he'd looked good in. Wool was precious these days and it would serve one of the camp lads when Winter arrived.

The days passed and there was no word about or from him. She felt strongly he was still alive – she'd saved him, hadn't she? Well, she hoped she had. Before she'd had her son, she'd been a nurse and when the local doctor's surgery heard this, they contacted her and asked if she could spare the time to help out on a voluntary basis. 'Did she have the time?' That was funny as she had so much time and it would be something else to pass the waking hours when she thought about Robert – always worrying about what could be happening. His birthday had come and gone in May and he was 25 now. Her baby no longer but that didn't stop her calling him that when she talked to herself, something she did regularly. She'd volunteered to stay at the surgery one night a week. It was an on-call duty in case anyone in the village needed help in the night. Molly would get the call and contact the doctor for his advice, but usually she didn't have to ring him as people sometimes just wanted to speak with someone and be reassured. She found the phrase 'Don't worry, this war can't last much longer' was becoming second nature to her.

One Summer's night, she'd been on duty at the surgery and had spent most of the night talking to people on the phone. It was one of the worst nights she'd spent there and she got home next morning feeling exhausted. A nice cup of tea and then she'd sleep the morning away. She mustn't sleep any longer as she was baking with her friends that afternoon. Carrot cake and scones were on the agenda. She climbed into bed and snuggled under the covers, her eyelids already drooping – and was soon asleep.

She could smell roses, she thought – the smell of old fashioned, heavy roses – the sort you couldn't find so easily these days. She sat up in bed and found she was dressed in her Sunday best so she was either going to Church or to visit someone in hospital. She looked around and she was in a beautiful garden with many different trees and shrubs – and some of the loveliest flowers she'd ever seen. It was a large garden, more like the grounds of a country estate and there was a small lake running through it with several young swans chasing their mothers all over the water. Where on earth was she? She really didn't know. It must be a dream. She was due one of her special dreams and that would mean seeing Robert – even for a short time.

She wandered around the garden and was surprised to see a few nurses, some clad in white uniforms and some in dark blue. Some were sitting on benches beside young men who'd obviously been wounded and some were pushing wheelchairs around the lake. The nurses spoke in both broken English and in a language Molly didn't recognise. She crossed over towards the nurses she could understand and asked what was the name of the great house at the edge of the garden. One nurse said, "That is the Convalescent Hospital for wounded Allied servicemen. This country is neutral from the war in Europe and has decided to accept some of the wounded prisoners in an attempt to help the innocents. When healed, however, they must be handed back to the German authorities as they are really prisoners of war and as such, Switzerland must honour the Geneva Convention's rules.

Molly asked, "Are we in Switzerland then?" Molly had obviously chosen a politically minded nurse who'd made that same speech many times before. The nurse nodded her head, before turning away from the mad woman, who didn't even know which country she was in. It was strange but these people could see and hear her – before in her dreams that hadn't happened. Something had to be different here. Maybe it was only when Robert was present that his mother ceased to exist. As she moved away, Molly gently touched the shoulder of a very young man in a wheelchair. She made her way to the main entrance of the hospital. *Why am I here?* she thought. *I know nothing about Switzerland.*

"Can I help?" a very pretty nurse asked her. "Are you looking for someone? What is his name?" Molly told her and was escorted along a warren of corridors in a house that must have been almost a palace in its Heyday. Then she saw him lying on a bed in the corner of a room. He looked grey and haggard and barely alive. She obviously hadn't saved him when she let the jeep run into the German soldiers. She sat on the chair at his side and reached for his hand. He had no idea she was there and she squeezed his fingers gently. She thought she saw a flicker of a smile cross his face but it was just that she wanted to see that. "Robbie, how do you feel? What hurts? It's Mum, son, I've come to see how you are – I've not seen you for such a long time." She just sat there, holding his hand and asking God to help him. What could she do – if she couldn't help? Why had God brought her here at all?

A nurse came into the ward and went to Robert's bed. She took his temperature and bathed his face with a damp flannel. Molly got up and said, "I can do that, nurse. Please let me do it." But no one could see Molly or hear her – when she was with Robert, she became invisible.

The nurse bent down and whispered in his ear, "Robert, there's someone to see you and she's come a long way." Molly thought the nurse could see her now, but realised she was referring to a girl with long blond hair who was standing at the bottom of the bed. In fact, she sat on the chair as if Molly wasn't there and also reached over for Robert's hand.

"Please, Robert, can you hear me?" And this time, Molly really did see a smile cross his face. She remembered now; it was the girl from the log cabin in Holland where he had been living. She was one of the Resistance fighters. Yes, that's who she was. "Please get better, I'm all alone now and I need you. The Gestapo shot my mother and father but I managed to escape and now I am without a country. Please take your medicine and get better – even if it's just for me." And her long hair fell across her face as she bent her head to him – but he didn't stir and she slowly got up from the chair and walked away out of the ward, first stopping at the door for one last look at the young man.

It seemed that Molly had been there for several days. She held his hand and talked of when he was a little boy back in the village. She told him how she worked in the doctor's surgery now and did knitting and baking with the village women. He didn't move although the nurse came to see him regularly and bathed him and talked to him. She heard a doctor talking to the nurse, saying "Well, he's hanging on, isn't he? I wish he'd respond more to the medication. There's little more we can do except be patient." And he left the ward but Molly didn't – she kept right on talking and telling him all the things that happened in the village. One day, she saw his lips move as though he was trying to speak and she felt his hand move too.

"Nurse, Nurse," she called but no one heard her. Then the nurse appeared, carrying a tin tray with his medication.

"Right, young man, let's be having you." And she injected his right arm. He definitely moved then and the nurse called for the doctor. After examining him, the doctor said. "I think he's turned the corner. This could be the change we've been waiting for." And he beamed at the nurse before adding, "Don't let him get well too quickly, or the Germans will claim him."

"I'll be careful doctor, I promise." As she turned, she knocked the tin tray onto the floor with an almighty loud crash. Robert really did move then.

Molly woke up too. It was the alarm clock that did it, not the tray. She felt quite dizzy but happy as she'd seen Robert move his hand when the tray fell. She went baking that afternoon with a light heart and her carrot cake and scones turned out a treat.

On returning home one evening from Choir Practice (another string to her bow these days), she felt a chill in the air, but then it was late Autumn and the red and gold leaves were thick on the ground. There were chestnuts falling from the branches of some trees and forming little piles on the ground. It had been a really lovely season; in fact it was Molly's favourite. Soon she would see Robert she hoped and feeling quite optimistic, she went inside the cottage to the still glowing embers of a fire. She glanced at the mantelpiece and realised it was the fourth picture's turn to take centre stage. It really was a beautiful picture – nature was going to sleep but certainly not dying. In the centre was a huge tree with other trees dotted around and all over the damp grass were the oranges, yellows and reds of the season itself. She squinted her eyes to see better and noticed a small block of stone at the base of one of the trees. She hadn't noticed that before, nor had she noticed the two small figures standing just in front of it. She went to the sideboard and fetched a magnifying glass from the drawer and held it close to the picture. It was a man and a woman. She didn't recognise the man but she thought she knew the girl. It was the girl with the long, blond hair who'd visited Robert in hospital. *How strange,* she thought, *of course it couldn't really be that girl, just someone very like her.* She reasoned. Still, it made a beautiful picture and that was all that mattered.

A cup of tea, she thought, *with lemon instead of milk.* Her throat was a little scratchy from all that singing. She took the drink to her most comfortable armchair and settled there, perhaps enjoy the luxury of a short snooze before making supper. Sipping the tea, she reached for a magazine but only managed a couple of pages before her eyelids began to droop and she fell asleep. Not surprisingly, she suddenly found herself in the small wood in the picture. She could hear voices in the background and realised she must be in Switzerland near to the hospital where she'd visited Robert. The lovely garden was more subdued this time, with little of summer colour to cheer the place, but it was still lovely with the late Autumn leaves and berry covered bushes.

She was in a small cemetery and could see several other blocks of stone, which were gravestones. The man and the girl walked out of the cemetery and she crossed over to the biggest tree. She couldn't bring herself to look at what was written on the headstone. Perhaps she already knew – but if she didn't see it, then it still hadn't happened. It was Robert's grave, but then, she knew that really. He'd lived throughout Autumn and it was not until the middle of Winter when he had a relapse whilst still in hospital – and gave up the fight. She touched the stone gently. Her boy was there – under the ground. Her much cared for and only child whom she'd loved beyond words was under everyone's feet. Hanging from the top of the headstone was a sort of medallion or shiny coin attached to a ribbon. She lifted it down and saw Robert's name engraved on it and the date of that year. It was a Military Medal awarded for bravery in action to a serviceman who showed great courage and who made a positive outcome to the war effort. A great honour indeed. He would then be entitled to have the initials MM after his name. Her heart almost broke with pride and she slumped onto her knees, crying.

When she stood up, she hung the medal back on the headstone. After all, it belonged to him, not her.

She woke up with a start and her cup and saucer fell onto the tiled hearth and broke into several pieces. She had a heavy heart and then remembered why, but she told herself that until she heard from the War Office, she mustn't take her dreams as factual. It had just been a nightmare and was the news that many people believed would reach them sooner or later so she pulled herself together and fetched a dustpan and brush to sweep away the broken china. Tomorrow was another day and she was working at the village surgery all day. The weeks passed and she heard nothing about Robert so she was more convinced than ever that her nightmare about Robert's death was just that – a bad dream. He'd be home soon and she'd be waiting for him. Winter had well and truly arrived and the sky looked very much like snow with a soft pink tint to the clouds. The village shop was decorated for Christmas now and the children were singing Christmas hymns in the local school. Molly had been busy with her baking, helping to provide the sugary treats that weren't available all the rest of the year. The villagers had scraped together their spare bits and pieces of food to make it the party of a life time in the school. She had a good time and tomorrow was Christmas Eve when everybody would be hiding secret presents from each other. Molly had no one to buy a present for, but she had done lots of knitting – little, soft toys, mittens and scarves for the younger children. She would walk around the village on Christmas – after church of course – and hand out the presents.

There was a knock on her door and her heart jumped into her mouth. Most neighbours just opened the door and called out. That knock sounded official. She opened the door and saw the one person she didn't ever want to see – the village post boy. He kept his eyes lowered as he handed her a brown envelope – he knew most people didn't like getting these letters, but Molly smiled at him and gave him threepence. "Snow isn't too far away, is it?" He nodded and went away. She took the letter to her favourite chair by the fire and held it unopened in her hands. Of course she knew what was in it – but she still had to open it. It told her that Robert had died from wounds received in battle and that he'd died bravely. He was awarded the Military Medal for several acts of bravery whilst serving with the Dutch Resistance. She let the letter fall to the floor and wiped her tears with her apron. At last, she knew the worst.

The snow had begun to fall with a vengeance but she got herself warmly wrapped up and went along to the Christmas Eve service. She didn't tell anyone about Robert – he still seemed alive if she didn't talk about his death. The Christmas service was beautiful and strangely comforting for Molly. The old hymns spoke of the old ways and of the Christ Child's birth, born to save the world one day. She left the church with a warm feeling in her heart which surprised her as she knew how she should really be feeling, but for some odd reason, she felt quite optimistic about the future. But she knew that feeling would fade when she remembered she would never see her lovely boy again.

She'd left the lights turned on in the cottage. It was more welcoming that way and the snow was falling even heavier now. She put another log on the fire and filled the kettle for that first cup of tea. She thought she'd imagined the knock at the door, but soon heard a second knock. She opened the door and saw a young, dark-haired man standing on the doorstep. She couldn't help glancing down at his legs and saw that one was missing and that he used two crutches to steady himself.

"I'm sorry but should I know you?" she asked.

"I'm Billy, Robert's friend – we served together in Holland and I promised I'd come to see you if I was back in Britain before he was." The snow was beginning to gather on his shoulders and she stepped back from the door.

"Please come in, won't you?"

He hesitated for a moment and turned round slowly. "I have someone with me who knew Robert too – and she'd like to meet you." Behind him stood a young blonde-haired woman who was carrying something in her arms. Molly realised it was a baby, warmly wrapped up in a lovely, blue shawl.

"Please come in, all of you. I've just put the kettle on." The couple crunched their way up the garden path – through the fast-falling snow. Molly settled them on the chairs nearest the fire and went to fetch cups and saucers – and some Christmas cake. The young woman uncovered the baby's head and removed its bonnet and Molly saw a shock of shiny blond hair above two of the bluest eyes she'd ever seen – except for Robert's eyes of course.

The girl stood up and offered the baby to Molly. "I've brought Robbie home to meet you. I promised Robert I would. Here you are, Grandma." She had a foreign accent but good English. Molly took the baby and touched his cheek gently. She couldn't think of what to say and she looked at Billy, wondering what part he had to play in what was happening. Billy spoke up.

"I served with Robert and we became good friends. I was with him in Holland when he was wounded and I visited him in hospital. I'm not in the army anymore." And he slapped his good leg. "My running's not what it used to be." And he smiled.

"Are you Sophie?" Molly asked. "I feel as if I know you. We've never actually met but I've met you in my dreams." The girl looked confused and Molly added, "I'll tell you all about it later." The two women fussed over little Robbie who could only have been a few weeks old and Billy rose to his feet.

"Well, after that tea and the best Christmas cake I've ever had, I'll be off. I live only a couple of villages away and I have a taxi coming. May I come back to see you after Christmas?"

"Of course you may – in fact I'd be angry if you didn't. You've got a lot to tell me, I'm sure. Sophie and Robbie will be safe here with me. I have plenty of room and we'll empty a drawer for a baby cot." Molly was already on her feet ready to prepare what was needed.

Sophie spotted the brown envelop on the mantelpiece and asked, "When did you hear from the War Office?" and was astonished to hear it was so recent.

"They've been pretty good to me and the baby. They arranged for me to come here – I have no home in Holland now and my husband was a British soldier who died for his country. They have offered me citizenship and the baby has it automatically."

Molly gasped. "You and Robert were married?" How did you manage that?"

"Well, when we knew the baby was coming, we were able to move very past – and my parents helped me a lot." Sophie looked sad.

Molly looked again at the baby and whispered, "This is really my legal grandson then?"

"He most certainly is." Sophie passed Robbie again to his grandmother. "You've had to take in a lot of information today, haven't you? You're a pretty amazing woman, I think." And she came over and kissed her new mother's cheek. Then she fetched a photo from her handbag. It was a happy looking couple – Robert and herself. "This was our wedding day and we really did love each other."

"He was a very loving boy was my Robert. In fact, I realise now that he was preparing me for his death even before he went away. That's what the pictures were for – he kept me informed all the way and helped me to face this day. All the time he was away, I dreamt about him vividly. That's how I feel as if I know you – you appeared in the dreams." She handed the photo to Sophie and told her to stand it on the mantelpiece. It looked good there – if only he'd been there as well.

Having settled her unexpected visitors in Robert's old room and found a suitable drawer to use as a cot for the baby, Molly returned to the small sitting room and plonked herself down on the armchair. The snow was thick outside and it made her feel cosy and safe inside the cottage. Tomorrow was Christmas day and she had nothing to give to Sophie and Robbie. She went through the knitted presents she'd put in her Christmas Box and found a pretty red scarf for Sophie and a knitted teddy bear for the baby. Excellent! She was pleased that she'd done all that knitting and wrapped it in scraps of wallpaper. Christmas paper was in short supply in the war years.

Her hand brushed against an unfamiliar shape and she pulled it from the box. It was small and hard and wrapped in white paper. It had her name on it – well, at least it said 'Mum' in Robert's handwriting. She opened it and pulled out a letter and his Military Medal – she'd last seen it on his grave in Switzerland. The letter was his citation and spoke of his bravery, how he'd died for his country and how proud his country was of him. He'd helped the War Effort by his action in Holland and died a hero in everyone's eyes. She held the medal to her cheek and cried.

She went into Sophie's room and asked her if she'd put it there, but the girl said she knew nothing about it. The last time she'd seen it was hanging on his headstone in Switzerland but she was tired and soon fell asleep again. What a day she must have had, Molly thought, and smoothed her brow.

So, how had the medal come to be in her Christmas Box? There was no answer to that. He'd loved his mother so much and it was Christmas. Somehow, he'd managed to 'magic' the gift through time and space. He'd known she would treasure it and it would be his last gift to her. She put it on the mantelpiece beside the wedding photo and stood back to admire it. She would keep it safe for young Robbie – her son would have wanted that.

Love really knew no bounds – no matter what the season was – and her dear son had proved it. Maybe life would be good again – in time – but never very good – without Robert.

A cup of tea, she thought and went into the kitchen.

Who is Real – And Who is Not

"I lost my two children in that fire. Do you remember it? It happened 20 years ago and I'd had to nip to the store to get some last-minute Christmas presents for the children. It was Christmas Eve and the children were busy wrapping last minute presents in bright tinsel paper." She went on talking although no one was paying attention. "It was four o'clock in the afternoon but it was quite dark already and the town's Christmas lights twinkled on all trees and buildings. They cast a cheerful multicoloured glow on the little mounds of fast falling snow, blown by the breeze to the sides of the pavement. Everyone's cheeks shone rosy red on their happy faces, as I rushed around the stores, collecting all the nice things to help make Christmas especially nice for the children. I remember feeling very happy."

The woman paused there and pulled her collar tighter around her neck. She was standing outside the town bus station where she'd just alighted from the coach. It was the first time she'd returned to the town since her home there had been burnt to the ground many years before. The derelict building still stood about half a mile from the bus station – it sat there between a row of other Edwardian houses, which were all lit up for Christmas. She'd seen it as she passed in the coach – the other houses had every colour shining from the windows onto the snowy street, but the burnt-out home she'd once known, stood dark and forbidding in the darkness.

When she looked around, she saw that all the other people had disappeared and she was really talking to herself. No one listened these days – they were all in too much of a hurry to get where they were going. Anyway, she must have seemed quite mad to them – talking to herself.

Strangely enough, she still owned the derelict house although it was falling to pieces with all the windows broken and glass lying all around. She hadn't been able to make the decision to have it pulled down as it was where her two children had died. She wanted to believe they were still in the house, but knew deep down,

209

that it wasn't so. Still, one never knew and she could live in hope. She lifted her small suitcase and made her way to the nearby hotel where she'd booked a room. It was rather old fashioned with a big street lamp pointing the way to the front door.

"Good evening, Ma'am. Do come in, you must be exhausted." The receptionist said and beckoned over a young bellboy to carry her suitcase up the stairs. The hotel had no lift. As she followed the boy, she realised the hotel couldn't have been decorated for a long time – everything seemed so old fashioned and just a bit musty. The boy placed her case at the end of the bed – a huge bed that filled half the room – and he left quickly, pocketing the coin the woman had slipped him.

He popped his head around the door again and said, "Oh I should tell you, dinner's at eight." And closed the door quietly.

She sank into the big bed and wondered how anything could be so soft. Lifting the case from the floor, the first thing she took out was a framed photo of two children. She put it on the bedside table and smiled. She felt lucky to have had the photo taken just before they died, or she just might have forgotten what they looked like. She knew it wasn't very motherly to think that but she was realistic enough to know it was probably true. Matthew had been only six and Georgina had just reached four. They'd been her lovely little family and she'd loved the bones of them. One day, she had both of them and the next day, she was childless. She'd been left alone with only Peter, her husband, with whom she'd already started to fall out of love. He was so wrapped up in his work; he barely knew she was there sometimes. She'd really felt alone when the children died and she still felt the same now, after all the years. She'd spent the past fifteen years working in America and she'd been reasonably happy there although she'd kept her head buried in her work, never finding time to socialise and meet someone new. When she felt happy on occasion, she also felt guilty, realising she had no right to feel happy but time passed, as time must, and she took each day as it came and got on with her life.

When she reached sixty, she had a sudden yearning to return to her own country and it took only a couple of months to square everything away, to sell her apartment and book a flight to the UK. And here she was, back in the town she'd left all that time ago. She stood up and crossed to the window, pulling back the drapes as she did so. It would soon be Christmas and the town was drenched in sparkling lights with people rushing around as they had been the last time she was there. That was the night of the fire. She'd been in town when she heard the fire engines speeding along the road. *Oh dear,* she thought, *some poor soul's in for a shock.*

When she'd finished her shopping, she caught the bus home and alighted from the platform into the worst disaster she'd ever seen. The flames in the tall Edwardian house were still reaching into the sky and dense, black smoke and ash covered everything around. The whole place reeked of water, damp leaves and smouldering wood. The firemen were everywhere and they stopped her from going into the house, although she tried her very best. There were two ambulances standing by the roadside but she saw one fireman wave them away. They went back to the hospital, empty it seemed. "The children must already be in the hospital," she told herself but a gnawing doubt made her nibble at her lips until she realised, she was making them bleed.

And that was that. The ambulances had returned empty. The fire had been so intense in the sitting room, that nothing and no one was left, except all the ashes from furniture, walls, clothes and children – not enough to distinguish what had been there. So, she never got to bury her children. Like a puff of wind, they'd just disappeared and she was left alone with the husband she no longer loved. He left her soon after it happened and she never saw him again. He'd made it clear that he blamed her for what had happened, but that didn't matter to her because she blamed herself too. Imagine leaving such young children on their own. She'd asked herself a million times, *Why did I do it – I should have known better,* but she had done it and that was that. She'd planned to be only a few minutes, that was all, but the best laid plans of mice and men gang aft agley, or so she'd heard.

Next morning, she breakfasted well at the hotel before starting off towards the area where she'd once lived. And there it stood, completely derelict and blackened even after all this time. Trees and shrubs covered most of it and there was no clear path to the front door. The houses on either side were bright and attractive and the street was coming alive. She stood in front of the house and the memories came flooding back. The next-door neighbour came out of his front door and smiled at the lonely-looking woman.

"An eye-soar, isn't it? 'Fraid, it's been like that for years, although several people have wanted to rebuild it, but the owner has never allowed it." He seemed a nice man so she crossed towards him and held out her hand.

"My name is Julie Sheridan and I'm afraid I'm that dreadful owner – who's just about to find some builders to make the house beautiful again." On saying the words, Julie felt she could move mountains, so building a house wasn't such a huge task after all.

"In that case, we're almost neighbours already. Would you like to come inside and have a coffee? Maybe you'll be able to put paid to all the stories that circulate about the house."

So, she followed him gratefully up the garden path and found herself in a cosy chair in a very comfortable lounge. Two minutes later, the man's wife joined them carrying a tray of cups and saucers. "My name's Ruth and this is my husband, Gerry – I'm sure he hasn't bothered to introduce himself." She was an attractive woman and much younger than herself.

So, the next hour passed easily and Julie felt she may have found new friends. It was a relief to talk about what had happened twenty years before – in America, she'd never raised the subject, as she was too embarrassed.

"Could you advise me – do you happen to know a builder who might be able work for me? I have the money – I had a good job in America – but clearing out the house and rebuilding it, is way beyond me." Julie looked at them with pleading eyes. "I know nobody in this town now – too much time's gone by since I lived here and I never had many friends even when I did."

"Well, funnily enough, I do know of a young chap who lives in a cottage at the edge of town who has a very good reputation as a builder. He lives with his sister, an Interior Decorator, so between them, they should be able to help you. If you're able to wait for a couple of days, I'll be able to show you where he lives."

And so, Julie was started in her quest to rebuild her old house. In the meantime, she hung around the derelict building, but it was unsafe and she knew she shouldn't be poking around. She had gone around the back and saw an overgrown jungle where a garden had once been. She started to pull some branches away from the kitchen window, when she heard the sound for the first time. She thought it could be a baby crying, or perhaps a cat somewhere but she looked around carefully and found nothing. She leaned forward and peered into the empty shell of the room that had once her kitchen and she saw them all sitting around the breakfast table, the two children squabbling as usual. She found herself begin to tell them to behave, but in an instant when she closed her eyes for a moment to catch her breath, they had disappeared. No more children and no mother and father, she must have imagined it but then she heard the child whimpering again. The sound made her move quickly and she darted around to the front of the house. "It's amazing what your imagination can do," she told herself.

Gerry took her to meet the young builder, so she wasn't alone next time she visited the house. This time, she heard no child's voice. The young man was called Bill but his sister was absent when she called, so Julie never got to meet the Interior Designer, whom she might employ to help bring the house back to life. She watched the builder poking around the site and felt there was something familiar about him but she knew she couldn't have met him before.

"Well, Bill," Gerry asked, "is it all possible?"

"Oh yes," he replied and added, "but it'll cost a pretty penny. Once I get some plans drawn up and work out some costings, I should be able to give you a 'very' ballpark figure. It'll take at least a week, is that all right?"

"That's perfectly all right, Bill, I'll wait to hear from you and in the meantime, perhaps I could meet your sister to see how we get on." A meeting was arranged and Julie called at the village cottage two days later.

The girl was slightly built and quite pretty. She must have been mid-twenties and her talents showed in the cottage which had obviously benefitted from her skills. It was very simply laid out with several, tasteful ornaments and items of interest. The colour of walls and drapes Julie felt she could die for. "Your rooms are lovely; did you design everything yourself? I'm surprised I don't know your professional name – you're certainly good enough to have made your mark in the world of Interior Design."

Waiting for her reply, Julie realised the young woman had a speech impediment and was having difficulty in answering. She did manage it however and after a bit of stuttering, she smiled and said, "It's very kind of you to say so. I love what I do and would like to advise you on the décor in your house." The speech was jerky and it took a few moments to get out all the words.

The two women bonded immediately and they discussed a plan for the rest of the afternoon. Julie had brought some doughnuts and chocolate biscuits as a gift and most were demolished before she stood up to leave. She'd noticed how much less Susan stuttered once she became more comfortable with the stranger. They promised to meet up soon and discuss the interior of the house in detail.

Since Bill and his contractors had started work on her house, Julie had taken to walking past the house to check on progress. On her way back to the hotel, she did just this and was delighted to see the project was beginning to take shape. It was late now and all the builders had left for the day so she had the place to herself. She walked up the garden path, through bricks, sand and a small bulldozer until she reached where the front door would soon be. Then she heard it. That same sound she'd heard before, like a child crying and calling out for her Mama. She didn't know what to do. *Had a child somehow got inside the building?* She called out, "Hello – Hello. Is someone in the house? I'm here to help if I can." she was scared now. But there was no sound in reply and she stumbled around to the side of the house to see if she could see anyone there. But there was no one.

"What do you think you're doin', Missus?" A tetchy voice broke the intense silence. "You don't belong around here, do ye?" Julie stared at the old woman, standing on the path. She was small and bent with a grey shawl wrapped around her shoulders and was leaning on a stick to support herself. She was an odd figure – more like someone from the past. She had appeared so suddenly. Julia was quite shocked. She knew who this was however.

She spoke up, "It's all right, Mrs McDougall – you know me. At least you did once." And she stepped closer to the old woman where the street lamp could cast a better light.

The old woman said, "I don't know you. Who are ye and what are ye doin' here?"

"I knew you a long time ago, Mrs McDougall. I was your neighbour many years ago. It's Julie – Julie Sheridan – and I used to live here with my husband and children – but that was before the fire – the one that destroyed this house. Don't you recognise me?" She thought, *Mrs McDougall doesn't look any older than she did twenty years ago, but she'd looked old then too.*

"Julie, is that really you? I thought ye were dead – after ye let those wee bairns die in that terrible fire. Why have ye come back here? But then, they say a murderer always returns to the scene of their crime." She started to turn around but Julie moved further forward.

"I heard a child crying in the house and I wanted to help." Julie tried to explain her presence.

"A pity ye didn't try to help your own children all those years ago." She obviously hated the younger woman. "As for hearing a child crying in the house, I've heard that same cry for many years. I've had to listen to a dying child over and over again. I blame ye for all the unhappiness in this house."

"I didn't mean to hurt anyone," Julie pleaded, "I was only going out for a few moments…" Words she had said so many times throughout the years, whilst knowing that she'd taken more than a few moments to do her shopping. And that was how her children had died.

The old woman disappeared as quickly as she'd come and Julie was left alone in the garden.

Back in the hotel, she felt safe and poured herself a generous gin and tonic that helped calm her nerves. That old woman was convinced she'd neglected her children and that was why they'd died. She couldn't really argue with her because she knew it was true. Another gin and tonic did the trick however and she soon fell asleep in the armchair.

She woke up in the middle of the night and heard the little child crying again. It couldn't be, she knew that but the sound was still ringing in her ears. It seemed so real. She climbed onto the bed and fell asleep again, fully clothed.

She woke up to the sound of someone banging loudly on the door. "Telephone call for you, Madam – it's the second time they've rung – I couldn't wake you the first time." And the young man went back down to the lobby. The phone call was from Susan, arranging to meet up with her at the building project, so she showered quickly and got dressed in a hurry to meet the young woman that afternoon. Bill was there too when she arrived and he'd made mugs of tea on a little, camp stove he'd brought with him. They sat around the stove, comfortable in each other's company. Susan had brought some samples of material as a suggestion for drapes and maybe sofa coverings. She'd brought paint cards too. Bill was working on the house as per his drawings which had been approved by Julie and the two women were perched on a couple of crates with the swatches and paint surrounding them. Julie stretched suddenly and stood up, shouting to Bill as she did so,

"Matthew, would you like another cuppa?" But she had to repeat it and realised Susan was looking at her with a quizzical expression. "He won't answer you, Julie – he'll think you're speaking to someone else. His name's Bill."

"I'm sorry, I meant Bill." Julie looked confused and Susan managed to stutter. "I've always thought of him as Matthew and I don't know why. I use the name sometimes – he knows who I mean." She picked up a crisp, white material covered with small bunches of red cherries. It was very pretty and she explained she'd thought of it for the two spare bedrooms.

"Oh yes, that would be lovely." And Julie pushed the thought to the back of her mind that it was almost exactly what she'd hung in those windows herself about twenty-five years before. Strange pattern Susan had chosen for the bedroom drapes – so like what had been burnt in the fire. Obviously, a coincidence!

The work progressed at a great pace and Bill and his team of contractors had built the insides of the house. There was plumbing now and electricity and Julie was amazed at how similar the rooms were rebuilt just where they'd initially been. Bill told her everything would be ready in a few weeks, then she could say goodbye to the hotel.

Three weeks later, she met up with Bill and Susan in the new kitchen, where the kettle had just been boiled.

She found the experience quite unreal. The whole house felt like the one she'd had all that time ago. The rooms were as they were before and Susan's colour schemes, for both walls and windows, were almost just as she remembered. She felt shocked by all the similarities. As she went around the rooms, she felt even more strange as she imagined family scenes of when the children were little. She had to shake off this mood and she knew it. This was going to be her home again and when all was said and done, she couldn't really be hearing a child crying, could she? The talk turned to money and Bill said he would need some payment soon as the Bank were pressing him. She promised to have it transferred from Boston. "It'll soon be with you, Bill – you can trust me."

Sitting on the newly bought kitchen chairs, Julie asked in a rather disinterested tone. "In all your visits here, have you ever heard a child crying? I've heard one, you see when I've visited the house on my own. I can't tell where the sound is coming from – when I go into individual rooms, the sound stops and I hear nothing until the next time I visit."

"I've never heard anything," Bill replied, helping himself to some biscuits, but Susan looked puzzled and added.

"I've heard a little child crying sometimes, but like you Julie, when I go into the room, I thought it was coming from, the sound immediately stops." Her stutter had been getting better for a while, but now it was as bad as ever.

Bill added to the conversation. "Susan has had a lot of therapy to try to help her stutter and it's getting better all the time, but when she hears that child crying, it seems to remind her of the trauma she suffered as a child." His hand went out to the biscuits again. "She was trapped in a fire once but was rescued just in time. I was a boy, so I was braver." And he laughed at his own modesty.

There was a ring at the newly fitted doorbell although only Bill heard it. Mrs McDougall stood there with a cake in her hands. It looked like a creamy Victoria Sponge and Bill invited her inside quickly. She followed him into the kitchen and put the cake on the table. She stared at Bill and Susan, completely ignoring Julie and asked them how they were.

"We're all the better for you and your cake, thank you." Bill fetched a knife and some small plates. "What made you come to see us today? Not that you're not welcome, 'cause you are."

The cake was beautiful and half of it soon disappeared. She sat on the fourth chair saying, "No cake for me, thank you."

Julie couldn't resist saying, "I remember this cake – you used to make it for me when I lived here. Funny how you can forget some things, but a good taste always stays with you."

"So, you remember this lady, Julie?" Bill asked but it was Mrs McDougall who replied.

"She certainly does, she remembers me well, as I do her. I was here the day she left the wee bairns on their own whilst she went gallivanting to the shops. The kids were petrified when the fire broke out and they tried to get out of the house – but couldn't because she'd locked them in. She said to the police that it was to keep them safe but I had other thoughts about that, I can tell you."

"If you remember that much, why didn't you help the children?" Julie asked.

"I didn't know what was happening next door and it was only later, I learned what the kids had to go through." Her face crumpled as she remembered. "They scrambled out onto the upstairs window ledge and fell to the ground. Little Georgina hurt herself and broke her leg but the boy was okay, tough little boot that he was."

"What happened to the children then?" Julie asked frantically and stood up, moving towards the old woman.

"An old man stopped his car and helped them inside, where his wife was sitting. He drove off with the children and the house continued to burn."

"So, you did nothing to help the children? You let everyone – including me – think they were dead? You let me immigrate to America 'cause I had nothing else here and yet you knew my children were alive?" Julie was screaming now and Bill moved over to her, holding her arms by her sides. He and Susan looked at each other but Susan couldn't get a word out.

She managed at last. "So...we are... Matthew and Georgina? And Julie...is our mother? I sometimes remember breaking my leg and having to wear a plaster for weeks – but that's all I remember." Her head fell forward and she laid her hands on the table. It was all too much for her.

"Is that right?" Bill said accusingly. "I vaguely remember the name Georgina but Grampy Jenkins never used that name – he always called her Susan – and me, Bill. I only remember my life with the Jenkins – Grampy and Nanny – in the cottage outside the town. I don't remember you at all – apparently memories can disappear after trauma – and we were certainly traumatised. They were good to us but told us our mother was dead and we would be staying with them from the day of the fire. It took a few months for us to recover – especially Sus...Georgina...and we were sent to the village school – not the town one." He stopped talking and almost fell onto the nearby chair. He covered his sister's hands with his own.

Slowly raising his head, he looked into Julie's eyes. "So Mother, what do you have to say to that? Did you even bother to look for us and why did you leave us in a big house all by ourselves in the first place?"

"Bill, Matthew – what would you like me to call you?" Julie started.

"Call me Bill – didn't Matthew die in that fire? I think he did and anyway, you thought it as well or you'd never have run off to America." He felt his anger growing towards this woman whom he'd only got to know in the last few months. "Susan had just turned four when it happened. How could you leave a four-year-old on her own?"

"I really don't know why I did it – I was looking for last minute gifts for you and your sister – I wasn't thinking straight. I'm as shocked as you are by all of this. Please forgive what I did all those years ago."

"Stop whining, woman – ye were just a selfish cow of a mother and the children were an inconvenience. I remember ye when you were younger – always thinking of yourself, ye were." Mrs Mc Dougall joined in the conversation and put her arms around the trembling Susan.

The old lay pulled her shawl over her head and went on, "I knew Mr and Mrs Jenkins who lived outside the town and being brought up by them was better than with your own mother, at least they cared for ye both."

Julie jumped to her feet. "I loved my children and what happened to them was an accident. You're just an old witch – you were the same then. You knew my children were alive for all those years and you never said a word. How evil you are, old woman! I hate you." And she made to push the old woman out of the room, but Bill stood in her way and protected the frail figure of the woman.

"Don't try to blame her for what you did. You made Susan stammer all her life and made her too shy to even go out to play with the village children. They poked fun at her for years – she only felt safe when indoors. You're the evil one, not Mrs McDougall." He was standing in front of his mother, daring her to reach out for the old woman. Suddenly, Susan jumped up pushing her chair onto its side. She started screaming and shouting, "Stop this, everybody. I can't stand it." And she ran from the house with Bill a few steps behind her. Julie and Mrs McDougall were left alone in the kitchen.

Julie said, "Do you realise what you've put me through all these years? I couldn't stay here because I lost the children and I spent more than twenty, lonely years in America before I could pluck up the courage to come back here. You can't imagine how much I detest you but you don't even feel any guilt, do you? You think what you did was right, don't you?" And she picked up the knife Bill had used to cut the cake and moved slowly towards the old woman. Mrs McDougall stared her out and didn't move. Julie was younger and quicker and she grabbed the old lady's hair and pulled her backwards. It was easy to hold her in her grasp and even easier to slide the sharp knife across her scraggy throat. Bright red blood should have gushed onto the floor but it didn't and when Julie looked into the woman's eyes, she saw they were smiling and the mouth was doing the same. She took a couple of steps backwards and dropped the knife with a clatter onto the marble floor.

The old lady was either laughing or cackling, anyway she was looking very pleased with herself. "Ye can't kill me, ye idiot – I've been dead for ten years. I've hung around to keep an eye on the two children, but I know they don't need me now. I was just about to leave this world when I realised, you'd come back from America and had employed your own children to put together the house ye'd let burn down. I knew it was necessary to make sure they learned who ye were and to make ye explain why ye did what ye did. They deserved to know and now they do and ye have to deal with that." Mrs McDougall was beginning to fade away – she'd achieved what she needed to do and there was no reason for her to hang around now. Her long skirt and shawl disappeared slowly and only the old face was left staring at Julie, but then it too, faded away into nothing and Julie was left alone in the kitchen. She'd come to the house that day to meet Bill and Susan and celebrate the fact that the house was all but completed – but she'd learned much more than she'd bargained for. She slumped down onto a chair and stared unseeingly at the leftover cake.

Strange for a ghost to come with a cake – it made no sense. She almost smiled at the thought.

Suddenly, there was the sound of a child crying somewhere in the house and Julie shook with fear. *Why was that child still crying?* She knew she had to get out of the house. The old hotel suddenly seemed very welcoming.

Bill and Susan – or Matthew and Georgina – sat closely together on the sofa in their cottage. Neither of them knew what to say, so they just stared, but not at each other. It was too much to take in – they'd missed out on not having a mother and father all their lives – and now, here she was, large as life. They'd both loved Old Grampy and Nanny who'd brought them up as their own and now it seemed, removed them from a mother who cared little for them.

"What…do…we do now, Bill?" Her stutter had got much worse. He leaned across and put his arm around her shoulder.

"We'll be all right, Sis – we've been through worse and lived to tell the tale. A lot of things make sense now – strange broken memories and recurring dreams of a woman and of a fire. We both had panic attacks for years – and that was all thanks to her." He was crying now and ashamed that he was crying. Susan put her arms around him and said,

"She'll have run back to the hotel now and Mrs McDougall will have gone home. Let's just be patient and think of what we'll do. She was a bad mother to us and ran off to hide in America. What a coincidence it was that you were recommended to her as a builder!"

Funnily enough, the girl's speech was getting better as she was getting angrier. She went on, "It wasn't just that she's a bad mother – she's a criminal as well and the only punishment she got was to travel to America and live there for 20 years, without a care in the world – that must have been exciting or she wouldn't have stayed there for so long." She was biting her lips and looked thoughtful before staring defiantly at her brother. "We've got to punish her somehow – and we will." A phrase about the 'fury of a woman scorned' came clearly into her mind. She'd been scorned by her own mother.

Julie Sheridan began to feel calmer and knew she had to move into the house she'd just had renovated – she had nowhere else to go. She moved her meagre belongings into her shiny new home and on the day, her nice neighbours – Gerry and Ruth – arrived on her doorstep with a welcoming bottle of Champagne.

"Good to have you here, Julie." Gerry was a kind man. He knew there had been some sort of mishap concerning the builder, but said nothing about it. His wife, however, tried to get it out of Julie, but she remained tight-lipped and wouldn't discuss the matter. *What would they have thought if they'd known the truth – that the builder and the interior designer were actually her children whom she had always thought were dead. That would have been a surprise for them.*

She began to feel at home but didn't like having to share the house with a crying child and a mad, old woman who spent all her time appearing suddenly at a moment's notice and startling Julie out of her wits. The child cried every night and usually just after Julie had fallen asleep. It was like a nightmare in which Mrs McDougall liked to join sometimes and on one occasion, she spoke to Julie, "Do ye ever wonder who that child is – and why it keeps crying?" Julie sat up in bed, suddenly interested in Mrs McDougall. "That's a baby who died here – the mother lived in this house years before ye did. She wasn't a good mother either." The old ghost smirked, looking uglier than ever. "The baby wouldn't stop crying for her either and so – she grabbed a cushion and pushed it over the child's face and pressed down hard. She stayed that way until the child stopped moving – and of course stopped crying. The mother was taken away but the baby has stayed in the house ever since – and is now choosing you to annoy." Cackling like an old witch, she disappeared and left Julie to her restless sleep.

A series of letters began to arrive – Julie picked them up from the mat but didn't open them right away. She knew what was in them as she'd had many of them before. She'd noticed other things as well – people stopped talking to her, stopped saying 'Good Morning' or 'Good Evening'. It was odd and even Gerry and Ruth had started to avoid her. She learned then that her neighbours had also been getting letters, signed 'A Well Wisher' – and telling them of her involvement in leaving her small children alone at home, whilst she went gallivanting about the town. The fire of course was mentioned and it was said the children had died in the house – which is exactly what people believed. The letters were pretty similar:

'Dear Friend,

This letter comes from a well-wisher. It's important that you know about Julie Sheridan, your neighbour. She's a very evil woman who murdered her own children. She left them to burn in a fire whilst she went shopping for fripperies.

You should avoid her and spit on her if you get the chance. Evil is as evil does. Keep your children away from her!

Yours very sincerely – A Well Wisher.'

The letters addressed directly to her were always pushed through her letterbox at the dead of night – and were even more cruel than what the neighbours received. She was a monster, it seemed.

It looked like everyone hated her. She'd never seen Bill and Susan since that dreadful day in her kitchen. In fact, she still owed them money for the work they'd done for her. Since they'd learned she was their mother, they'd kept well out of her way. She thought her heart couldn't hurt more than when she thought she'd lost her children in the fire, but now she felt even worse, she'd lost them for a second time.

One night around midnight, she was just going up to bed when a brick came crashing through the sitting room window and glass flew all over the place. She rushed to the front door and looked outside – but there was no one there. It was the last straw – she couldn't take it anymore. She'd come from America to curb the nostalgia she felt for her old country – but it hadn't worked and everything had backfired and she'd lost her children again. She pulled on Wellington boots and ignoring the darkness and bitter cold, she left the house and walked down the street. It was almost Christmas and there were already twinkling lights at several of the windows – it reminded her of the night twenty years before, the night she left the children on their own. Mrs McDougall watched her go and laughed. "That's the way to do it, dearie – leave this place. You were never welcome here."

Julie disappeared that night – but no one noticed. No one looked for her or enquired where she was. It was as though she'd never existed.

"Probably gone back to America to live now her dark secret is out. Good riddance to bad rubbish, I say." The neighbours spoke with one voice. And they meant it. Her son and daughter heard how she'd just disappeared and left no trace. They stopped writing the anonymous letters then– what was the point now that she'd gone? They'd done her a lot of harm however and they'd enjoyed doing it. It had been a great way to get their own back on the woman who'd ruined their lives. It was in their interest to keep quiet about still being alive – the story about her allowing her children burn to death was a lot better. The house still stood there – empty now, except for the resident ghosts, of which they knew nothing – and with no prospect of a new owner because of its ghostly reputation.

"Actually, Susan, the house must be worth quite a bit, especially now it's been renovated. Perhaps it's time we told the authorities that we didn't die in that fire and that we're still alive. We are her closest relatives and should inherit the house. She still owes us all that money and boy; did I spend a pretty penny on that. Do you think she ever made a will?" Bill's building business had been undergoing some bad times and the money would be very welcome and it would help pay back what she owed them.

"I don't know the answer to that – but we could enquire of the authorities in Boston where she'd lived – and where she probably is now. In fact, we could first ask if they have an address for her in the city." As always, Susan was the practical one. And so, they drafted a letter and sent it the authorities, local to Boston. It took a long time to get a reply and the letter was first passed from one department to another, as is usual. In the end, however, a rather formal letter arrived addressed to Susan – she waited 'till Bill came home that night and after the evening meal, she produced it.

'Dear Madam,

Thank you for your recent letter, concerning your mother Julie Sheridan and for all the helpful details you provided about her. She did work and live in Boston for about 20 years. She was an upright citizen and spoken highly of by those who knew her.

She did leave a Will with a local lawyer and I attach a copy for your information. She only had a house in England and this was the subject of the Will. Unfortunately, she knew it wouldn't have been worth much, having been destroyed in a local fire, and she bequeathed it to a Boston Charity for Children, saying that, if they ever took the trouble to renovate it, the house would be worth a good sum of money for their charity. They never did this, but now you advise that the house has been renovated, they confirm they will be contacting a local estate agent in England and instructing them to put it on the market. You will soon see a 'For Sale' board going up on the premises but at least, you'll understand why – and the Children's Charity will benefit from the proceeds.

I tell you this as I feel you should know everything and I am building up to my main piece of news. It is my painful duty to advise that your mother died two years ago, here in Boston and has been buried in the town cemetery. I am sorry you had to find this out in this way but she left no names to contact, when it happened.

Again, please believe I am sorry for your loss and hope your grieving will not be too severe.

Yours Sincerely,'

The signature was of course, illegible.

The brother and sister stared at each other. How was it possible? They'd both met her here, talked to her and even argued with her. She'd told them things only she would know – she'd met her neighbours and that old lady, Mrs McDougall certainly seemed to know her. How could she have died two years ago in Boston – and turn up here just a few months ago?

"I don't know what to say, Bill." Susan was confused and disbelieving, "Perhaps we can talk to a lawyer here and find out if we can challenge her Will. We'd have to come into the open and tell we didn't die in the fire – after all, none of it was our fault – and at the end of the day, we are her only children – we must have some rights."

"We can only find out, Sister – and we will." He contacted a lawyer the very next day – and then a second lawyer and then a third. They all advised there was nothing they could do. One of them even spoke with the American authorities who told them that Julie's Will was intact and set in concrete. No challenge of it would be successful. In the end, and after several months of communications, Bill and Susan had to accept they had no case to challenge their mother's Will – and that was that. There was nothing they could do.

"We could always buy the house for ourselves, since we renovated it. It's been on the market for some time – I'm afraid it has a reputation now and people are a bit scared of it. We could perhaps negotiate a reasonable price for it – and then we could move into the centre of town and that would help both our businesses. What do you think?" Georgina/Susan was getting quite excited.

"Yes, we could get a mortgage and buy it – then we wouldn't have to pay rent for this cottage. Mind you, we shouldn't have to saddle ourselves with a mortgage – by rights the house belongs to us." Bill felt cheated.

"Yes, but we can't prove it, can we? She managed to punish us a second time – once when we were little, and now by arranging things so that we can't inherit." Again, Susan was trying to be practical. "What I don't get is who was the woman who employed us to work on the house – and were did she disappear to?"

"In fairness, Susan, she disappeared because we sent letters to everyone – herself included – telling them what she did to us. How evil she was and why they should ignore her. But then, we were only telling the truth, weren't we?"

He stood up. "Let's go buy a house, Sis." He'd made up his mind and there would be no stopping him now.

The house was still available and they soon achieved the necessary mortgage. On an overcast, rainy day, the brother and sister moved into the house. It was still clinically clean, as Julie had only lived in it for a short time. Or had she? They knew she'd existed but wondered in what form. Had she been a ghost – or some sort of supernatural phenomenon? The inside of the house reminded them of when they were children – its renovations had been in keeping with Julie's instructions. Bill, of course, remembered more than Susan.

The evening was darker than usual and the fire had to be lit to make things look welcoming. They sat on the sofa together, surrounded by soft cushions, piled one on top of the other. They both heard the sound at the same time – there it was again – a baby crying and the sound of a woman's soothing tones, as she tried to calm the child.

The room was suddenly cold and the sitting room door flew open. Julie came in from the hall, carrying the baby, wrapped in a soft shawl. "There, there," she cooed to the child, "now stop crying – you'll scare Matthew and Georgina who are going to live with you now. Won't that be nice? Shush, little baby – I'm your Mama now." And they both disappeared through the wall into the room next door.

"For God's Sake, haud yer wheest, ye're giving me a headache. Bloomin' baby! Never shuts up." And Mrs McDougall pulled her shawl tighter around her shoulders, glared at the couple on the sofa and went through the same wall as Julie and the baby had.

Now the couple knew – the house was full of ghosts and was indeed a supernatural phenomenon. Had their mother really been here or had she died in Boston? Either way, they'd just paid good money to buy the house that should have been theirs for free and on top of this, all the renovation costs she'd ordered them to make.

Had their mother played a very clever trick on them? But why? It seemed Matthew and Georgina would never know. Oops – or was that Bill and Susan? Who cares?

Three White Pebbles

The boy walked slowly along the shoreline, kicking pebbles into the sea. The waves lapped against the edge of the beach until his trainers were wet and discoloured with wavy lines of white salt. He suddenly felt very tired and lay down away from the waves, listening to the loud cries of the seagulls swirling above his head. His thoughts drifted back to the schoolroom and he could see the teacher's twisted face as he told him to 'Get out of my class and don't come back until you can behave yourself.' He knew he'd been behaving badly in the class but he didn't care. He was 14 years old and wasn't any good at art anyway and now he had a free afternoon away from school. His one love at school was history, he'd always been fascinated by the past and how everything that happened through time had made us what we are today. He loved it so much that he dreamt about it every night and had decided a long time ago he'd study and become a professional Historian when he left school. But he'd first have to find out what a Historian actually did. He was at a difficult time in his life, falling out regularly with his Mum and Dad, behaving badly at school and having no friends to talk with. His Mum said it was just his age. Either way, Simon was becoming a very disturbed boy.

The pebbles were pushing against his back and he sat up. Suddenly, a sharp crack took his attention away from the horizon and he realised he'd actually seen a seagull drop a round very white pebble from its sharp beak. He reached across, picked it up and looked at it closely. Nothing unusual about it until he spotted some scratches which actually formed a cross, the kind used to say 'mark this spot'. Eyes screwed tightly; he saw a question mark scratched on the other side. Strange or what! He raised his arm and was just about to throw the pebble far into the sea, when something stopped him and he reached for his satchel and placed it in there instead.

He looked around and was surprised to find himself alone on the beach. It was a sunny day but not particularly warm. There should have been some people around however, perhaps walking a dog or allowing children to build sand castles, but there was no one in sight. A few yards away, he spotted the old stone building that he knew had once been used to hold POWs during the Second World War. It was an unusual one because of where it was placed – most such camps were in the countryside, well away from the coast, to stop the prisoners from escaping across the Channel. The authorities must have been running out of possible camps in the countryside and had to come to this unused but 'already built' one by the sea.

He sauntered along the beach, dragging his satchel across the pebbles. He reached the building and was surprised to find the main door ajar. It was very dark inside and not very encouraging to visitors, so he went around the back to see what was there. Old boxes, rolls of very rusty wire netting, some light fittings and lots of pebbles piled up against the walls. He felt like an adventurer and used an old stick to poke around the debris. The land behind the stone building swept upwards towards sand dunes and was covered in thick reeds. Just beyond the dunes, where the earth was more packed and solid, a tree stood all on its own. It was very old and parts of the trunk were shrivelled and dry but the rest appeared still reasonably healthy. It was a Hawthorn tree, a bi-floral because it flowered twice a year – once in Spring and once in Winter. He remembered that from his Botany classes. At one time, it must have been very tall – possibly about six metres high and wide to match judging by the length of the hanging branches, but now it was gnarled and twisted and more bent, leaning to one side more than to the other – an enormous umbrella for the sandy place. Strange though, he'd always believed such trees grew in dense, wooded places – ah well, someone had obviously thought it would do well here. And it had. At present, the healthy part was covered in white four leafed flowers and red berries and he thought it looked pretty – but what did he know anyway, he wasn't a very good Botanist, more a Historian? Something stirred in his memory and he remembered a tale about a Hawthorn tree in Glastonbury in England, but he couldn't remember the actual tale. Something about Joseph of Arithmethia – Jesus's Uncle, but that's all he could remember.

Tree forgotten, he returned to the sandy slope and sat down to have a rest. It was a long way to the road from here and the dunes in the distance were covered with even taller reeds. It was quite a sight and he felt all alone in the world. The sun was lower in the sky now and the clouds had taken on a lilac, pinky hue, with the deep orange of the sun reflected in the sea. It was a very beautiful horizon.

227

He looked down and there was the seagull sitting beside him, rather closer than a bird would normally sit. It made a kind of guttural sound and flew off into the sky. Then he saw it. Another white pebble that stood out amongst the grey ones. He wasn't sure whether to pick it up or not, but curiosity got the better of him in the end and he grabbed the pebble – and there it was. A cross-scratched onto the surface. Just like the one he'd put in his satchel. What on earth was going on here? And it seemed to have something to do with the birds.

He moved his position slightly and felt himself falling down one side of the slope with his feet slipping away from beneath him. The sand was falling down the slope too and turning into an ever-widening hole. It seemed to get bigger as the sand and some reeds slipped inside the opening as well. He stood up quickly as he was about to fall into the hole himself and had to step away from the ever-widening gap in the ground. He waited for a while until the sand was moving more slowly and then actually stopped. The hole was quite wide now and the roots of the reeds were what was holding its sides intact. It looked quite secure now and he tentatively moved towards it. To his amazement, the sand seemed very solid underfoot and before doing anything else, he jumped down towards the stone building, where he'd left his satchel. He had a torch there – he always carried a torch – and then he'd be able to see further into the hole.

Back at the top of the slope, the first thing he did was to put the second pebble into the satchel and then lie full length on the ground and point the torch into the hole. He could see nothing but darkness and he edged more into the hole. Suddenly he felt himself slipping downwards and tried to grab onto the reeds at the side, but it was no use and he slipped very slowly forward. He thought of Alice in Wonderland and the White Rabbit – it must have been like this for them – what would he find? If there was a bottle with 'Drink Me' on the label, he would certainly not do that. He seemed to be in some sort of cavern which opened up for him as soon as he stopped slipping. The ground felt firmer beneath his feet now and there was some light too at the far side of the cavern. That really threw him. How could there be light down here, deep under the sand dunes?

Then he saw the explanation for the light. It was the light from a fire in the middle of the cavern and around it, sat three men. The men looked like Viking warriors, dressed in some sort of sackcloth tunics, and sandals that laced up to their knees. Shiny helmets with animal horns lay by their side and some sort of meat was cooking on and a tripod stretched over the fire. The men were laughing and drinking from horn shaped beakers and spoke in English with a rather strange accent. The tallest man stood up and raised his hand. "Let's drink to the Chieftain we've just sent to Valhalla in his own long boat, surrounded by all the treasures he'll need for the next world. He was a great man and we've done him proud this day." They all drained their beakers and sat back down by the fire cross-legged and all reached for the chunks of meat which they hungrily shared between them.

"We've been sent away from the tribe to sort out between us who is to be the next chieftain – so we'd better get on with it." One man spoke and the others nodded their heads in agreement. The tall Viking suddenly spotted the boy at the side of the cavern and reached for his sword but his friends told him to hold back. It was only a boy and he had no weapons. They beckoned him to join them by the fire – and he did so, but hesitantly

"Have you been sent by one of the Gods? Have you come to help us in our deliberations to appoint the next chieftain of our tribe? We are having great problems with who to pick. Come sit by the fire and rest yourself. You've obviously come a long way – you wear strange clothes and you carry no weapons. How would you defend yourself were you to be attacked by the Saxons?" the tall man asked the boy.

"I'm not very likely to be attacked, am I?" He couldn't help finding it funny to think about being attacked by a Saxon. He sat cross-legged like the others and accepted a beaker, the drink tasted like cider and was very enjoyable. The tall man, who already seemed like the leader of the group asked, "How are you called, boy? I am Eric and this is Gorm and Halfden." He indicated the other men to the boy. "And you are?"

"I am Simon," he replied and tried to smile as he said it. He was very nervous and afraid of what was going to happen next, but he thought on his feet and said, "How do the other men in your tribe regard you? What are you known best for?"

"We are all great Vikings and have conquered much of this land but we always return to our native country each year." One man spoke for the first time. "We would greatly value your opinion as you've been sent from the Gods in this moment of our need, so it is written that we listen to what you have to say." He poured more cider from a stone flagon.

All Simon could think of was how he was going to get out of the cavern alive but he tried to look thoughtful and drank slowly. "First of all, tell me how you're called and that may help me."

The third man said, "I am Halfden and this means I am not wholly Viking, I am half Danish, so I have a good mixture of blood in my veins. This is something our people take seriously and it may mean that I shouldn't be here at all but the tribe voted for me to be included in the final choice of we three."

Then the next man said, "I am Gorm and my name means that I worship the Gods more than my brothers. I honestly don't know what that says of me, but it is my name." Gorm stared at his feet whilst he talked.

"And I am Eric," the tall man said, "my name means 'Absolute Ruler'. I know that sounds like I should be the chosen one but I want our decision to be a joint one, not to be based on what our fathers chose to call us. That is too simple. If you've been sent by the Gods to help us, what can you do?" Simon could only sit there, his mind a blank.

They all stared into the flames of the fire as though the answer lay there. It gave Simon an idea. He reached for his satchel and looked inside. "I must separate from you to think in peace, I shall only be a few moments." And he grabbed his satchel and disappeared to the back of the cavern. He pulled out a pad of white paper and a pen. On the pad, he wrote the name 'Eric' in bold capitals. He didn't care which man was chosen to be the Chieftain; he was much more concerned about getting out in one piece. The swords the men carried were sharp and vicious and Simon had nothing to defend himself. He put the things away, but held onto the sheet which was the one below the sheet he'd written on. It looked quite blank but he knew there would be an indentation on it that read 'Eric'.

He returned to the fire and settled down again. "Are you able to read? I know that's an odd question but it's important that you can because of the way the Gods have advised me to help choose the Chieftain. I have discussed it with them and a way has been suggested that will help you to know who will be the best leader."

Gorm stood up and said, "I have been made the Reader of the tribe because I study what the Gods have done in the past and what they plan for us in the future. What is it you want me to read?"

Simon reached for his sheet of paper and showed it to all of them. "You can see there is nothing on this piece of parchment, can't you?" They all nodded. Simon kicked a few burning sticks away from the main fire and told them to watch closely. He held the sheet over the sticks, careful not to touch them, and lo and behold the paper began to scorch and the edges began to curl inwards. Suddenly, a scrawl appeared. It was quite clear but only for a very few seconds.

Simon told Gorm to read aloud what was written before the paper completely disappeared – and he did.

"Eric. It said Eric. You are the chosen one brother, of that there is no doubt. The Gods have spoken through magic and we must obey." Halfden reached out and patted Eric on the back and Gorm held out his hand in congratulations. Eric looked pleased and, in his turn, held out his hand to Simon.

"Well done, little messenger from the Gods, you were sent here to help us and you have."

As the men lay down by the warm embers of the fire, they fell asleep quickly with the effects of the cider no doubt, and soon Simon was the only one left awake. Cautiously, he gathered his things together and crept quietly in the direction he'd come from. At least, he hoped it was the right direction. It was and soon, he could see a light. Crawling up the side of the hole, he emerged into the sunlight and could have cried with relief. What an old trick that was – but it was enough to make them happy and helped them find a solution to their problem.

That night at the kitchen table, he was enjoying his tea; he seemed extra hungry after his adventure. "Mum, have you ever heard anything unusual about the beach by the old stone POW building near the shore?"

"What on earth do you mean, Simon? Something unusual? No, I can't say I've ever heard anything like that. I shouldn't go too near that building – it's old and falling apart. Probably dangerous." He could tell she wasn't really listening. She was getting Dad's tea ready. He'd soon be back from work. "I'll ask Dad too, when he comes in." Simon wasn't going to let it go as easily as that.

Dad had finished his meal and went over to the bookcase, where he found a book, he wanted. It was a dark green book – a history book of local battles and he slowly read down the index at the front, before exclaiming, "That's what I want." And he opened the book at a specific paragraph. Out loud, he read. "And the battle of Largs was next on the Vikings' agenda. The small town of Largs won its very own battle and a tall stone monument stands on the beach there in praise of the local people, who successfully fought off an attack by several, long boats. The battle came right onto the beach and the locals swung their claymores and swords with abandon, and although many were killed, the Viking ship eventually sailed off in disgrace and at great speed. That's all I can find referring to the coastline where you were today but if you walk about a mile further on, you'll come to the spot where the stone monument stands today."

"I'll do that tomorrow, Dad and tell you how I get on." Simon was eager to go to bed now so the morning would come quickly. Luckily, it was Saturday tomorrow and he could have the whole day to explore.

He went straight back to the beach but walked a mile further than where he'd been on the first day and there it was coming into view, a tall stone pillar. He got up close and read the inscription about the Viking attack, six long boats with many Vikings. They fought on the shore, on the beach and right up to the hills surrounding the cove. The local people, with help from other Scots' clans, forced the Vikings back into the sea, with many left for dead on the shore. Two boats actually sank and the others escaped, never coming to that part of coastline again. Simon walked back to the beach he knew well and climbed up the sand dune beside the stone building. He hoped none of his Viking friends had been in the sunken boats He moved the junk he'd put over the hole and lay down to get a better look inside. What he dreaded was that the three Vikings might still be there, waiting for him. But it wasn't the case.

He slid down the hole into the cavern and walked along to where he'd been before. He'd brought a much stronger torch this time and he searched closely around the ground where the fire had been and spotted something bright and shiny lying half hidden against the cavern wall. On pulling it from the earth, he discovered it was a large bronze bangle, big enough to fit the upper arm of a man and there was something written on the inside with a fine and detailed pattern on the outside. He'd examine it later but for now, he slipped it into his trusty satchel, which he took everywhere with him.

There was the sound of footsteps coming from the deeper cavern. He shrank back into the shadows and held his breath. "Come on, chaps, keep up or you'll be spotted." He saw long leather clad legs coming to where the Viking fire had previously been. There were at least half-a-dozen men and they were all dressed similarly in long suede or leather jackets and pantaloons trousers. They had some sort of cravat around their necks and wore very large hats with feathers attached. The hats were like cowboy hats but much larger. The men carried swords and their pistols were tucked into a leather band across their chests. They all had beards and moustaches. *They're cavaliers,* Simon decided, *but where have they come from – and where have the Vikings gone?*

A man with golden – and very long – hair crouched down on the ground. "Let's rest, gentlemen. I'm bushed, I don't know about you." The others grunted their agreement and sat down.

"Do you think we'll make it out to sea?" one of them asked.

"I just don't know, Peter but we've got a good chance, haven't we? Crossing the border into Scotland was a brilliant suggestion and I'm glad we took your advice. We must rest here and wait for the boat's signal." Just like the Vikings, two men searched around the cavern for old pieces of wood and straw and soon had a good fire. Peter reached for a big sack he'd brought with him and pulled out a very rustic loaf and a block of rather smelly cheese. He cut himself a share and passed it to the others, who grabbed it. They looked starving.

Simon's right leg had gone into a cramp and he fidgeted on his other leg to ease the pain. As with the Vikings, he gave his presence away. The men were immediately on their feet, swords at the ready. "Why it's only a boy," Peter said, "and rather a strange looking boy, at that." The others didn't laugh as they were unsure whether or not the boy was dangerous. Deciding he wasn't, they beckoned him forward towards the fire. Simon moved slowly as his leg was still cramped. "He's wounded. See, he can't walk." And Peter crossed the cavern and took Simon's arm to help him. The boy slowly sat down by the fire and stared at the men. They were very strong looking and their weapons could obviously do some harm, if their owners so wished.

"Who are you and where do you come from?" the golden haired one asked.

"I am called Simon and I come from about a mile from here. I am just a local fisher boy and I stumbled across this cavern by mistake. May I ask who you are?"

"Yes, Fisher Boy, you may ask but before we tell you, we need an answer to this question: Are you for the King or are you for that lowlife Oliver Cromwell?"

Simon was wise enough to know which one to choose and he declared, "I am for the King of course. I have always been a King's man. And the men cheered. He went on to ask them what they were doing here and where they were going.

"We've come from a pretty wild skirmish with some Roundheads and we're here to be picked up by a boat to take us to the South of England. Then, we plan to split up and make our ways home to hide amongst our own folk. Unfortunately, Cromwell with his round-headed soldiers – the Model Army we're told – has won the struggle and King Charles II has left England to return to France, where he can plan his next move to recapture the throne of England – and we'll be waiting for him no matter how long it takes." Everyone cheered at this, but Simon swallowed hard and ventured, "Don't you think your appearance rather gives you away as Cavaliers? If you go down the beach, someone may recognise you and report it to the Roundheads."

"That may be true but what can we do? We are Cavaliers and proud of it? Two of them said together. "Well, perhaps I could make a few suggestions to make you look more like fishermen just going about your business on the beach and when your boat arrives, well then, you're just going fishing." They accepted it as a good idea and piled all their spare clothes and weapons into their big sack. "Tie your cravats around your necks – sort of pirate-like." Simon showed them and soon they were just a group of fishermen ready to go to sea. He took them to the mouth of the cavern, to the spot he'd come in by and everyone was surprised to see how misty it had become. The horizon had disappeared and vision was not good. Simon lifted his satchel onto his lap and fumbled inside, coming out with his Dad's binoculars. The men shrank back at first, thinking it was a weapon and then curiosity got the better of them as they watched Simon put 'the weapon' to his eyes.

"This way, we can watch for your boat hovering off the shore. I suppose they'll be showing a light of sorts?" he asked.

"They will be doing that – one light at either end of the boat they can beach, with the bigger boat not too far away ready to pick us up. If we can conceal what we are, we should be safe to cross the beach without being detected. Do you agree?" One of the men who hadn't spoken so far asked Simon the question.

"Yes, but it depends on the time the boat comes for you. If I were you, I'd rub some dirt onto your white shirts as they're a bit conspicuous and might be seen for miles. The men complied, tied the cravats around their heads and packed everything else into their bag. "Have a go with the binoculars, they'll amaze you." And he passed them to the men who took it in turn to use them. Frightened at first, they thought it was magic and then when nothing happened, they grew braver. To make images so large was truly amazing, and they were soon laughing and passing the binoculars around.

One of them suddenly said, "What's that light I can see out at sea?" Simon grabbed the binoculars and looked at the horizon. Much closer to shore however, he spotted two lights about three yards apart.

"I think they're coming for you. You'd never have seen the boat's lights without the binoculars, it's so misty. They'll reach the shore in about half an hour, so you'd better gather your things together and be ready. I'll come down the beach with you, just in case, but I should think you'll be safe now, the mist will help conceal you." Simon started to chivvy them on. "You can keep the binoculars if you like – they'll certainly impress the people where – and when –

you're going. I'll have to explain to my father that your need was greater than his own. I'm sure he'll understand." He crossed his fingers as he said this.

Peter, who seemed to be the leader took Simon's hand and pressed a large ring into the palm. "This is my family signet ring and my coat of arms is inscribed on the stone. It's in exchange for your magic seeing box. If you hadn't spotted the boat today, it would never have dared to risk come back for us again. We were warned about that so you can see our gratitude knows no bounds."

Gathering their things together, the group left the cavern by climbing through Simon's secret hole in the sand and they all made their way across the beach. The boat was being dragged from the sea and the sailors were helping the Cavaliers aboard. They all shook Simon's hand or patted his shoulder and when he got to Peter, he said, "May I have a word with you just before you leave?"

Peter pushed the others ahead of him. "You will never know grateful we are for your kindness. Is there something you want to tell us?"

"You already know I have some magic powers, so I want to tell you what I see in the future for Cavaliers like yourselves. Bide your time and lie low in your homes or wherever you plan to live, don't try to fight the Roundheads now as their days are numbered and your King Charles II will be invited to return from France and sit on the English throne. When this happens, he will restore your family losses and re-instate any titles you lost. I cannot say more, but I hope you'll listen to me as seeing the future is something I'm blessed with. Goodbye and good luck to you all." And having dropped this bombshell, he ran back up the beach and covered the hole in the sand, before scurrying off home for a welcome tea with his family. The heavy ring was safe in his satchel, lying beside the Viking armband. It was amazing how these adventures had given him confidence in himself and made him feel more like a man. He felt he even spoke with more authority.

On Monday, he returned to school with a slightly different attitude to learning. Now he understood how his learning had helped him through the last few days. He took stock of all that had happened and planned to go to the Town Museum and Records Office to see what he could find out about the old stone building and the beach around it. It had such mystical, magical powers – something must have happened there, he decided.

He now had two white pebbles and he kept them in his satchel. They were all marked with a cross and all found on the beach not far from the building. He came straight to the beach the next free day from school and cleared away the entrance to the sandy hole. Suddenly, he could hear music, strangely familiar music, but he couldn't detect where it was coming from. Then it hit him. It was the French National Anthem written during the Napoleonic Wars, but he remembered it was also known as The Chant *de Guerre de l'Armee du Rhil*, the official song of the Republicans in France. What on earth had he arrived at this time and at what point in history. It was gentle humming at first and then it seemed to get louder with a drum keeping all the voices in time. *Where was it coming from*, he asked himself. There was no one inside the cavern – the sound was more coming from the stone building which had been amazingly smartened up overnight and had new bars at the windows and enormous padlocks on all the doors. He went down to peer in the windows. The place was occupied by a great number of men all sitting around the big room on old benches and a young boy was beating his drum very softly, standing in the middle of the room. There was no way Simon could get inside and there were at least half a dozen British guards watching the building.

Suddenly, he heard the sound of heavy horse-driven carts coming along the back of the sand dunes and stopping just beside his special hill. With what he'd seen so far, he knew he had arrived during – or near the end – of the Napoleonic Wars when the French fought with almost the whole of Europe so that Napoleon could take charge of the whole Continent. One guard unlocked the heavy padlock on the door and gestured with his rifle, shouting 'First twenty of you come out'. They didn't understand him and Simon had to bite his tongue to stop himself saying '*Premier Vingt des Hommes, Vennez vous ici*' – he knew he had only schoolboy French but it was better than that the guards were using. Soon the men began to emerge from the darkness and began to climb the sand dunes and clamber aboard the waiting carts. There were three carts and it looked as if they'd need all of them. The little drummer boy tried to come out with the men but they just pushed him back inside, shouting 'Stay Back'. For some reason, they didn't seem to want him to join them. Maybe it was the way he was dressed.

So many prisoners had gone up to the trucks now, that Simon found it easy to slip inside the building. He found the little drummer boy squatting behind the door. He crouched down beside him and asked, "What's wrong with you, boy? Why won't the others let you go with them?" The boy was crying and Simon reckoned he could only be about twelve.

"Were you in battle in France?" he managed to speak in broken French.

"Oui, I was soldier – but now the others think I'm useless and there is no room for me on the carts. They are all going home now – the war is over and we will be free again – but not for me it seems."

"Come on now, cheer up. What's your name?" Simon tried to stay positive.

"*Je m'appel,* Charles." The boys were doing well between them with broken French and English.

"What if I could go up to the carts and offer one of the men a bribe to take you in the truck as his son?"

"It would be wonderful but I have nothing to bribe him with." Charles looked crestfallen.

"Ah, but I have." And he rummaged in his trusty satchel and brought out the Cavalier's brilliant signet ring which shone and sparkled in the light. "Do you think this would do it?" he asked the drummer boy.

"I think it might," Charles looked hopeful, "but I have nothing to give you for the ring. When I was captured, all my possessions were taken from me."

"I want nothing from you but to help you. The ring was given to me as a gift by a grateful friend and I'm sure, in the circumstances, he'd like you to have it." Simon left the building and followed the last of the French prisoners – the ones who had been seriously injured and had difficulty in walking unaided. The first two men he approached didn't understand what he wanted and pushed him aside, then he came upon a younger soldier who seemed friendlier than the others. He grabbed the ring from Simon and beckoned to the drummer boy to come up the hill and join him. Then he pushed Charles in front of him and forced him forward. Charles turned to Simon and thrust his drum at his new friend.

"Please, you must take this. It's all I have of value and I'd like you to have it." He almost threw it at Simon and then climbed onto the cart alongside his saviour. The carts were moving off and the British guards were hanging onto the backs of them. The year was 1795 and the Napoleonic Wars were over. Wellington had been victorious at Waterloo and Napoleon had been captured. Watching the trucks disappear into the distance, Simon realised that just for a short time, he'd lived in yet another time and had made friends with people from different worlds. He looked at the drum and smiled. There was no way he was going to be able to conceal it in his satchel. He looked down at his feet and saw yet another white pebble amongst the grey ones. The cross was clear and he put it in his satchel with the others. He had three now. They were obviously trying to tell him something and soon he might know what. He left the beach and hurried home.

His mother and father were both in the kitchen when he arrived. "God boy, you've got good colour in your cheeks – that beach is doing you good." His mother put a heaped plate before her son. "Get that down you, Simon, you must be starving." She ruffled his hair.

After tea, they all settled down in the sitting room to examine his latest beach discovery. His dad said, "I've seen some odd things found on the beach but I've never seen a drum." He crossed to his bookcase and brought back another large book. "Let's see if we can find out how old this is." He put on his glasses and began to flick through the pages. Ten minutes later, he shouted 'Eureka' and passed the book to Simon. The drum looked really like the French Revolutionary ones which were in the book. The date was about 1790s and it fitted with the story Charles had told.

"Did you really find this just lying on the beach?" Dad asked.

"Well, not exactly just lying on the beach. It was partly concealed by the sand and some barbed wire coiled around it. It could have been easily overlooked; I suppose."

"If I, were you, Simon – and I'm perfectly willing to come with you – I'd visit the Military Museum in the city and ask what they think of it. We might learn something." They agreed to do this in a couple of days and Simon added that he still had to go to the town's Records Office to see if he could find more about the stone prison building. Plans ahead were exciting! He couldn't tell his Dad about the adventures he'd had in the cavern 'cause he just wouldn't believe him.

A week later, Simon and his Dad returned from the city, Simon with £300 in his pocket. The little French drummer boy really had given him a gift in exchange for the Cavalier's ring, and he hoped everything had gone well for him when he returned to France with the other men.

"Well, my dear, our boy is turning into an entrepreneur. If you're short of cash, go to him for a loan." Dad laughed and kissed his wife's cheek. "Where are you off to now, Simon? Going to look for more drums?"

"No, Dad, but I'd like you to have a look at this Viking arm band that I found near the drum. I think it's Viking at least – look at the decorations." He handed the band to his dad, knowing full well it was from Viking times. "But you're right; I am going beach combing now near the old prison building." And he left the house. It was a blustery day and he wore his anorak so he could pull up the hood. His adrenalin was beginning to flow through his body and he started to run across the pebbles. What was he going to find, he wondered?

The rain had come on heavily when he reached the old stone building and he quickly ducked inside to shelter. It had very quickly turned into a storm and the sea looked wild and uninviting. Outside, the Hawthorn tree had shed many of its leaves in the wind but some blossom still clung to its bent branches. The petals were like a carpet lying all over the ground and inside the building, he sat on a broken stool and threw off his hood. "Pretty wild out there, isn't it?" A boy's voice broke through the noise of the wind and rain. It almost sounded like himself. The owner of the voice must have been sitting in the shadows, as Simon couldn't quite make him out.

"Come out and show yourself." He spoke more harshly than he'd intended, but he was scared.

"I'm just like you – I won't harm you – I'm just a boy about your age, I think." And a figure slowly emerged from the shadow. Simon did a quick intake of breath for he recognised the boy as himself.

"What's going on here?" He shouted. "Who are you?" The boy crossed the room and came to stand in front of Simon. The two boys were identical except they were wearing different clothes.

They were sitting side by side on the bench and then the ghostly boy said, "We're both called Simon you know, and I am your grandfather at the age you are now. I grew up and became a soldier and was sent here as a guard for German prisoners of war – I knew the area you see and that's why they chose me. Unfortunately, I was attacked by one of the Germans and he strangled me. I was only 24 years old and I was dead. I know you've been coming here for some time now and I wanted you to meet me and at least be able to say you'd once met your Grandfather." He patted his grandson on the shoulder and went on, "I bet you've seen some strange things here, haven't you? I know 'cause I used to see them when I was a boy."

"But why have you come here now? What made you do that?"

"I knew you'd be going away soon – perhaps to college – and I just felt we should meet. Has your father never told you how I died in the war? Did you never think to ask that question?" He looked into his grandson's eyes and smiled. "You're going to be all right, you know. You won't forget the things you've seen here but you'll remember them with a fondness. To understand why this place is so special, you'll have to go to the old library in town and ask the librarian if he can show you the ancient book he has under 'Antiquities' written a very long time ago by a monk who lived in the cavern as a hermit. He was the only one who could write in the area and only he knew what had happened here. He had been a young monk at Lindisfarne Abbey when it was founded in 712 AD and the story about this place had been recorded there but the writings were destroyed when the Vikings first came. They couldn't destroy the ones the monks were able to secrete about their persons and they were saved for the future. The cavern was quite an open place when he came here – the land around the sea moves about quite a bit and changes shape with the passing centuries. He hid here and stayed until he died. He had a lot of writing materials he'd brought from the Abbey and he hid them in an old iron box which was found much later and eventually published by the library. I'm not going to tell you its contents – you must read the book for yourself, but believe every word and you'll better understand what this place is."

"You say he lived in the cavern, but how did he know it was there?" Simon asked.

"He was a holy man and much blessed, just as this ground is holy ground and much blessed and as I explained, the cavern was more accessible then and ideal for a hermit's home." He stood up and both boys left the stone building and walked along the beach together. They were just like two friends! The stormy weather had subsided and the calm after the storm made the beach feel like a more peaceful place.

When the boys reached their garden gate, they realised the house had been – and was still a home where they'd both lived and one still did. As he went into the hall, he knew he was alone. His grandfather had disappeared completely. The boy who'd looked just like himself. He was so full of emotion; he couldn't face asking his Dad why he hadn't been told about his grandfather. He just put his head around the living room door and said goodnight. "I'm not hungry, thank you."

The first free moment he had, he went to the old town library and asked the librarian about the 'Antiquities' section. Sure enough, he was shown up some creaking stairs into an attic room and told to wear gloves every time he touched the book. They were thin rubber gloves and obviously kept there for just this kind of occasion.

It took Simon the best part of two weeks to read the book. It was the most fascinating thing he'd ever read and made him even more keen to become a Historian in adult life. He built up all the information he could and made copious notes. He wanted to explain everything to his Dad whom, he knew, would enjoy hearing everything he had to tell him. He was fascinated by history too, just like his son.

"Dad, have you heard of Lindisfarne Abbey in Northumbria, of how the Vikings came there and killed and slaughtered all the monks, and stole all their holy relics and valuables. It was barbaric and very few of the monks managed to escape. One monk who escaped was called Echfrith and he managed to take some of the Abbey's papers to save them from destruction. After wandering far and wide, it was Echfrith who found the cavern on our beach and settled there as a hermit. He had all the time in the world to study the scrolls he'd brought, and time passed for him just as quickly as the years peeled away. He lived to be 80 years and made sure his writings were hidden tightly between the rocks, safe for future eyes to discover."

Simon went into the kitchen to bring back two glasses of orange squash. "Come on, Simon, I'm waiting. Go on with your story." His Dad was engrossed and swallowed his drink in a couple of gulps. Simon went on, "Time passed and nothing exceptional happened for many years and then some children found Echfrith's scrolls. They'd actually been digging for treasure but with no luck They took them to the teacher who taught history in school and were relieved when he said he would be responsible for them.

To cut a long story short, the teacher told the authorities and the museum about the children's find and the scrolls were made into a book that's in the Archives Section of the town museum – and with special permission and wearing gloves, you can see them. There were a lot of details about what happened at Lindisfarne Abbey but there were also even older papers that had been brought to the Abbey prior to its foundation in 710 AD – and the story they tell is fascinating.

Simon's Dad was on the edge of his seat by this time, his eyes like saucers. "Yes – and what did they say?" Simon enjoyed peeling the onion slowly and knew how excited his dad was.

"A few years after the Crucifixion of Jesus, his great Uncle, Joseph of Arimathea set out from the Holy Lands in a boat with a crew and a couple of scribes. He was a businessman and came to England to set up a commercial deal with the locals. His intended location was the South and the West of England, but the sea journey was not an easy one and took much longer than was expected. The wild weather as good as took control of the boat although it was a well-built, strong vessel, they ended up on the west coast of Scotland after many weeks at sea. In desperation, the crew beached the boat on a pebble shore. They had no idea where they were but they knew this safe stretch of shore saved all their lives. A deep cavern gave them shelter and they were able to build a fire inside and rest there. They'd brought blankets from the boat so, for a short time, they were comfortable. The sailors soon worked out where they were and how they should travel to the English South and West coast. They pulled and pushed the heavy boat back into the sea and were soon ready to set off but Jesus' great uncle had a mission to perform before they left the land. He carried a long, wooden staff which had helped him travel over many roads and hills in the old country. He spoke to the crew and to the scribes. "Before we leave this place, I want to leave something in thanks and gratitude for the safety offered when we were at our most desperate. He walked alone back up the beach, carrying his staff and reached the very top of the sand dunes beyond the long sandy reeds and grasses to where the ground was firmer. He pushed the staff deep into the ground and bent his head in prayer. He asked God to allow it to produce fruit in time and to give it longevity as a growing Hawthorn tree and to make the spot there be specially blessed and a place of comfort for people in distress. He left the staff and returned to the boat which set sail immediately and no one looked back.

The twist in the tale however was that he'd brought two staffs with him from the Holy Land – one to use himself – and one to present to the Holy Orders in Glastonbury as a token of good will. It had belonged to Jesus himself and he'd used it on many occasions. Joseph feared he may have mixed up the two staffs and the one he'd left in Scotland might have been the holier one of the two. He was unsure of the staff he'd presented to the Bishop in Glastonbury – was it his own or had it belonged to Jesus? It had been given in good faith and with good intentions and that was that. And Glastonbury would never know that what he'd planted in the ground outside their church building, as Jesus's own staff – might not actually have been that. A practical, wise man Joseph succeeded with his business projects in that part of England and eventually returned to the Holy land and to his home.

Simon had to pause for breath and fetch another drink. His Dad just sat there, staring at nothing. He couldn't speak, so shocked was he. "And the papers that recorded all this are still in the museum? There is no doubt about this story?"

His son came back into the room and just sat there. "I have three white pebbles now, all in my satchel. I must have been one of the chosen few who was given the gift of meeting people from other times and countries, but I can't see the connection to the white pebbles."

"May I see the pebbles?" his Dad asked and Simon fetched his satchel. He spread them along the coffee table and sat back on the sofa. Dad picked them up one by one and turned them all over. "Simon, what sort of crosses do you think these are?"

"They're criss-crosses, aren't they?" the boy said.

Dad placed them on their pointed ends and said, "Look at them now. What do you see?"

"I see three pebbles with a cross on them."

"Yes, but they're not criss-crosses now, are they? They're holy crosses for the three people who were crucified on Golgotha Hill, Jesus himself and the two thieves who died on either side of him, Dismas and Gestas. They're meant to tell whoever finds them that they're special and can help those in distress. It's amazing the knowledge you pick up in life, isn't it?" Simon just nodded and put the pebbles back into the satchel.

"By the way, son – you know how you wanted to go to University but we explained that we couldn't afford it, well I think you may be able to go after all. I took the Viking arm band to the city for a valuation and you'll be amazed to hear how much you'd get if you sold it, and it's not classed as Treasure Trove, I've checked – you dug it up from the cave and it's owner is long gone by about fifteen hundred years, so he's hardly going to claim it any day now."

The boy looked up expectantly. "Go on then." Dad named a sum of money that made the boy blow out his cheeks and whistle loudly. "I don't need to ask you what you'll study at Uni, do I?" There was no need for an answer.

Both Simon and his Dad spent the next few weeks visiting the old stone building. They took several cuttings from the Hawthorn Tree and planted them all around the solid ground above the sand dunes, so one day hopefully, the old tree would feel more at home in its natural habitat in a wooded area. The strange thing however was there was no trace of the deep hole that had led into the secret cavern. They looked and poked at the hill but it was all just sand with no trace of what Simon knew was there. It was obviously lying-in wait for the next person with a troubled mind to come along and then it would spring into action.

Simon grew up and spent very enjoyable years at Uni studying Ancient History which he put to good use and, as an eminent professor, eventually took a year off and wrote his first book. He called it 'Three White Pebbles' and of course, it became a Best Seller. The beach became a tourist attraction and Simon's Dad had to put a strong netting over the young tree saplings to keep them safe from a great many trampling feet. But the saplings thrived and grew. After all, they were growing in a very magical and blessed place.

The old, bent tree is still there if you're ever passing that way. It's rather tired and sad looking – but still there in amongst all the saplings. Look for a group of trees where you'd not normally find them, remember they flower and bear fruit twice a year and are always on the lookout for people with problems.

Catherine the Great – Or Was She?

She was only a young woman, a teenager in fact and she was about to leave her home country and travel to Russia. Her name was Sophie von Anhalt-Zerbst but she would become known to the world as Catherine the Great. Born in 1729, she was the daughter of a Prussian Prince, who betrothed her to a Russian Prince, Peter, who was shortly to become the Emperor of Russia – Tsar Peter III.

On arriving in St Petersburg in 1744, young Sophie travelled to the Winter Palace and asked to be presented to the Tsarina Elizabeth – the Empress of Russia and the daughter of Peter the Great. She hoped she didn't look too dusty after the journey and wiped some mud from the hem of her skirt. She was only fourteen years of age but had been trained at the Prussian court as to how she should conduct herself. Nonetheless, meeting the Tsarina was daunting. When the tall, elegant woman entered the room, Sophie stood up and curtsied. "Good afternoon, your Highness – I am the Princess Sophie of Prussia – you asked me to come and visit you. Are you well?" Elizabeth stared through her pince-nez at the girl and replied "I am well, thank you. And you, Princess, are you well? Please take a seat and I shall ring for coffee – you must be tired after your long journey.

"Not really, Highness, there was so much to see – I didn't notice the time passing," Sophie replied. The Tsarina was dressed in the height of fashion and Sophie felt quite dowdy beside her. A maid came into the room, carrying a tray with coffee and macaroons.

"Help yourself." the Tsarina poured the coffee and handed a cup to Sophie.

"Didn't you wonder why I have sent for you?" she asked the young woman.

"Of course I did, although I was well aware of the great honour the invitation implied. I did wonder why you wanted to see me personally." She sipped her coffee and reached for a macaroon. She had the hunger of a young person – and hadn't eaten anything since early that morning.

"You are aware I have a son, Peter, who will succeed to the throne of Russia, when I am gone? He is a little older than you but still very young. I need to know what your attitude would be if I told you, I have chosen you to be his wife and therefore, the next Tsarina of Russia." The young Princess was shocked. She had assumed the Tsarina was going to offer her a position as lady-in-waiting, which would have been enough of an honour in itself – but to be told she had been chosen for the Empress's son, was all too much. Her coffee cup shook in its saucer and she had to put it down on the table quickly.

She stuttered and felt her cheeks turn pink. "Oh Highness, I don't know what to say. You do me the greatest of honours. I have never met your son, but I would love to do so."

And that was how it all came about and how Sophie – or Ekaterina, as she was now known – found herself standing at the altar in the church at St Petersburg, alongside of Peter III, as he would become.

On the day of the wedding, and in a dress of ivory silk with a rope of pearls cascading down her breast, she stood straight and tall. She was still only 15 years of age. He was in uniform with numerous service medals on his chest. She cast a sideways glance at his profile and realised she didn't find him attractive in the slightest. He looked like a weak person which is just what he turned out to be. He was reasonably intelligent, always with his nose in a book, but he was a most impractical man who usually did the wrong thing in any situation. When the priest nodded to him, the sign that he should place the ring on his bride's finger, he reached for the wrong hand and fumbling to get it right, he dropped the ring on the floor. It rolled away and luckily stopped at the foot of the best man – Grigory Orlov – who picked it up and returned it to the groom. It was like a sign of what was to come, as Catherine chose Grigory as her lover within a few weeks of marriage to Peter.

She chastised her husband as soon as the ceremony was over. "Don't be so clumsy, Peter – what happened could be construed as a bad omen for our marriage. People are probably saying that already." And she turned her back on him in despair. She was no longer the shy, young woman who'd come to Russia to meet the Tsarina. She had blossomed and even seemed to have grown in such a short time, but then she was the wife of the Tsar of Russia in-waiting and his mother could soon be of little importance. Her confidence was growing by the minute.

"I am truly sorry, Catherine, I do have a tendency to drop things – especially precious things. I think it must be nerves." Peter looked crestfallen. It was unfortunate that he apologised for anything and everything. He accepted the blame for things he hadn't even done. In fact, one of his biggest mistakes was when he invaded Denmark with a large army in an attempt to secure the country for Russia – he was ill prepared and it ended as an enormous failure, with a great loss of Russian troops. It didn't cover him with glory and Denmark remained Danish. He was also a heavy drinker and spent much of his time with his drunken cronies, arguing about politics, of which he knew nothing at all, but it did allow him to make the most outrageous statements that often made no sense at all.

However, he would soon be the possessor of the most precious thing of all – the coveted crown of Russia – which hopefully he wouldn't drop. And Catherine would be Her Royal Majesty, Queen Ekaterina The Great – to be remembered throughout history, but mainly because of her romantic entanglements. In fact, from her own mouth, she bragged that she'd had at least twenty-two lovers in her life – if not more. She could never remember them all. She became a proud, haughty woman who strutted, rather than walked her way throughout the court – but she was respected or feared by all servants and courtiers, as she knew exactly what she wanted from them and they were anxious to please her. She had always favoured the culture and politics of Europe and led Russia's reform to the ways of Europe, in line with the work first started by Peter the Great himself. She was becoming even more astute in the world of government, although she saw herself as an autocrat, whose word and opinion were law. She was devoted to luxury and all good things which she ensured came her way.

Strangely enough, when she first came from Poland, she wanted to make the lives of Russian serfs better than ever before. In fact, she wrote a paper on the subject and called it 'Instruction of Catherine the Great'. It was a political document, mainly dealing with legislative issues for the country's internal reform. It was mainly about humanitarian theories and she must have meant it at the beginning of her reign. A few years later, however, she had abandoned the theory as she had learned to enjoy the benefits of the free labour of the serfs and the luxury it produced for herself and her 'noble friends'. Within the court, she was regarded as suspicious and she had to keep herself to herself for a short time, which she passed by reading voraciously and always had more than one book on the go at the same time. The paper she instructed read:

All men should be considered equal before the law
The law should protect not oppress the people
The law should only forbid harmful acts
Serfdom should be abolished
Capital punishment should cease
The principle of absolutism should be upheld

But in Catherine's reign, these things never happened! After many months of meetings, this paper died on the table, as Catherin realised Russia couldn't be manoeuvred as England was, with its flexible control of its people. The Russian serfs were very different from England's people. Anarchic and backward, she realised she must leave her adopted country as it had been when she arrived.

Catherine enjoyed her early days in Russia even when Peter was still alive. "I will drive out today, Peter, and show myself to the people," she told her husband one day.

"Very well, my dear – would you like me to accompany you?" He tried to be agreeable.

"No, Husband – I will take Grigory Orlov as my escort. I believe the people want to see me, not you." As was normal, she showed a high opinion of herself. And with a shake of her feathered head dress, she was off. In the carriage, she flirted outrageously with Grigory and he responded, as she knew he would.

Outside the palace gates, the people lined the streets out of the way of the carriage. They were a motley crew, dirty and unkempt. They looked as if they hadn't eaten for weeks, which many of them probably hadn't. Catherine liked the way they dropped their gazes when she passed and dropped to their knees. "But why must they be so dirty – water costs them nothing and there are plenty rivers and lakes around, where they could bathe."

The Dowager Tsarina, Elizabeth, died on Christmas Day 1761. At the time, Russia was an ally of France and Austria in the Seven Years War – but in one of his crazy moments, Tsar Peter took Russia out of this agreement and formed a new alliance with Frederick II of Prussia. For some reason, he hated Russia – but loved his native Germany. He had a secret plan to remove Catherine from the throne. In 1762, she rallied the army regiments who had supported her cause and marched into St Petersburg where she was proclaimed Empress of Russia and made a total autocrat. At this failed attack on his wife, Peter III abdicated and eight days later was dead. Catherine was crowned in Moscow, which had always been the country's capital in past years.

Catherine the Great always said she deplored the conditions in which her subjects lived – her instruction at the start of her reign (which was never acted upon), proved it! She liked to believe herself to be their benefactress who took care of them. Alas, this was not so. She did like to say repeatedly that conditions in the country must be improved for the people. But she never actually did anything about it. And Peter was oblivious to the people and ignored their plight. Russia was very much a country of 'Haves' and 'Have Nots' – you were either rich and comfortable or you were treated as a slave. Referred to as serfs, they were at the mercy of their employers and landlords and woe betide them if they complained or asked for more. For this, they were either imprisoned, whipped by the 'knout' – a heavy rope – or deported to Nerchinsk for a life of permanent servitude. Catherine always said she deplored such cruel treatment – but didn't lift a finger to stop it. History was to remember her as a despot – she was called oppressive, even by people who liked her. You had to be rich to live in Russia in the eighteenth century.

Of course, there were pockets of people who met in secret to bemoan their lot, but what could they do about it? They had no power, no money and worse of all, no rights. Statistics for the time showed that those serfs who worked down the mines, in the foundries and factories were lucky if they managed to reach middle age. In effect, no serf in Russia ever grew old as their lives were too harsh. There were similarities in France at the same time, with Catherine behaving much as 'Marie Antoinette' in France had done. 'Let them eat cake' was obviously the solution shared by more than one monarch at that time.

But it was the start of a Communist Russia which unfortunately for the serfs took more than another hundred years to emerge. If only Catherine – and Marie Antoinette – could have seen into the future, they might have been more understanding of the plight of their people.

Meanwhile, the Empress of Russia was experiencing many delights in her life. Within six months, she had completely lost patience with her inept husband and instructed the Military to arrest him – with the aid of her then lover, Grigory Orlov – and subsequently, to force him to sign a declaration of abdication and still within the first year of marriage. He was killed by Grigory's brother, although Catherine denied any involvement with that. She had successfully over thrown Tsar Peter in a Coup d'etat and was solely in charge of the whole country.

His mother Elizabeth had little power now that she was a Dowager and could do nothing to help her son, but what she later managed to do was to remove her grandson, Paul from his mother's charge.

Catherine was interested in raising the awareness of well-off members of society – in any and all of the Arts. She wanted Russia to be seen as a leader in the world of social culture. She encouraged female writers and poets to indulge their talents and she herself made sure the Hermitage Museum opened 'for the good of the people' – but of course, only the well-off people could attend. She believed herself to be a Philosopher and had regular correspondence with Voltaire, the famous French Philosopher. She was an admirer of Western European society and culture and encouraged her own countrymen to be the same. She promoted women into the higher echelons of society and was generous in bestowing many gifts on them.

In a strange way, she was an early feminist and yet did nothing to help the plight of the poor people in her country whose backbreaking work sustained the quality of her luxurious life style, as well as that of her richer subjects. She had the power but would never waste it on the serfs.

"Nadia, bring me some bonbons from the dish – in fact, come and entertain me, I am bored. I am tired of Grigory now and need another lover to take my mind off the cold and rain outside. What a dull day it is." She was stretched along a silk chaise longue and covered by a turquoise lace shawl. Her companion went to the dish of sweets but it was empty already.

"Oh, Madam, you've had them all, I'm afraid." She covered her mouth with her hand, realising she'd been impertinent. Catherine glared at her.

"Well, ring for the footman to fetch some more, you stupid girl."

It was a new footman who came into the room and he was sent to fetch the bonbons immediately. On his return, he placed the dish on the side table. "Bring the dish to me – I am very tired today." He did as she bid. "And what is your name, boy?"

"I am called Nicholas, Madam. Is there anything else I can get for you?" He was a tall and well-built young man with bright, yellow hair. He looked spotlessly clean.

"Do you play any instrument? I am in the mood for some music." She didn't sit up but did reach for the dish.

"I play the balalaika, Madam. Would you like me to fetch my instrument?" he asked shyly.

"Fetch it now, Nicholas – and be quick about it – I'm not used to having to wait." She never could conceal her irritation at having to wait for anything.

Ten minutes later and with several bonbons under her belt, she was listening to a sweet melody being played by her footman. The music was so gentle and soothing that she felt good for the first time that day. Then, she began to listen to the actual words and realised they were criticising her government and therefore her. It was a Russian folksong, complaining that the serfs in Russia were being treated abominably and that the government were doing nothing to prevent it.

She jumped from her seat and shouted, "Stop that – stop that. I want none of your anti-government songs here. Have you forgotten where you are – and who I am? Get out – get out of my palace before I call for the guards to take you away." Balalaika in hand, the young man ran from the room, leaving the lady-in-waiting to appease her mistress.

He managed to call over his shoulder, "You should listen, Madam – it's the voice of the people."

Catherine was shocked at the footman having the audacity to sing that song in her presence. She realised there was a movement afoot to try to get better conditions for Russian serfs – but as her ministers told her, they were nothing but troublemakers, whose greed kept them always asking for more. She knew they were right, there was a movement against the government and the monarchy and it was getting stronger every day. The starving serfs were forming groups, under the leadership of one man. An upstart, of course!

Her government heard what had happened with the footman and came to see her. "Majesty, the leader of the movement is an ex-military Cossack, called Yemelyan Pugachev. He is claiming to be your husband, Peter III – and he is offering the world to the crowds – free land and generous handouts – but most importantly, freedom from their landlords and bosses. He has managed to amass great numbers of supporters – if they help him to replace you on the throne of Russia."

This all happened in 1773 and it started in the Ural region and quickly spread through the vast south eastern provinces. By 1774, they were ready to march into Moscow but the war with Turkey ended with a victory for Russia and Catherine's crack troops were available to be brought home to crush the rebellion. Pugachev was beheaded in 1775 – but what he had stood for was never forgotten by the people. This made Catherine realise that, rather than pitying her subjects, she must tighten their bonds. She had no problem with her conscience when she told herself she could do nothing to help the serfs. She now imposed serfdom on the Ukrainians who had been free until then. She worsened the lot of these peasants by taking away their freedom. By the end of her reign, there was scarcely a free peasant left in Russia but there was a severe systematized control over them and their conditions were worse than they'd been before Catherine came to power.

The man who pretended to be her husband and his followers had worked hard to depose Catherine – they'd raided houses that belonged to rich citizens and formed a scarecrow army to march on the gates of the Winter Palace but despite some successes, it all petered out in the end when the leader was executed. But it was the biggest revolution in Russia until the one that toppled the then Tsar Nicholas and his family and turned Russia into a Communist country.

Having successfully put down the insurrection, Catherine turned her attention to the expansion of her empire and this was something at which she was very good. It would please her subjects and silence the voices of the serf's sympathisers. The Polish King, Augustus III died suddenly and on 1763, she appointed one of her lovers – Stanisław Poniatowski to the throne, although he had no claim whatsoever to take it. Poniatowski was one of her favourites and she had no qualms about giving him such gifts, even if they were not actually hers to give. She and Poniatowski however, paid for this brash move as she commanded him to give more rights to Poland's Orthodox and Protestant worshippers – and in so doing, angered and offended the Polish Catholics. This resulted in unrest amongst the people and Russian troops were despatched to Poland to deal with the militant Catholics.

This turn of events scared the countries which were situated close to Poland as they thought this was Russia on the move to take their own territories. The Sultan of Turkey thought the Russians planned to pour into the Balkans and threaten Istanbul itself. He anticipated blood and death for his people and at this point, Turkey declared war on Russia.

The Turkish army suffered great defeats and a Russian naval squadron sailed into the eastern Mediterranean – and so the war was really won. Turkey was forced to sue for peace as they were on their knees by this point and the Russians were jubilant and took whatever they wanted in plunder. Catherine, however, benefitted from all this as she was given the credit for adding many territories to Russia. The Black Sea and the Sea of Azov area were two areas where Russia triumphed. Although it had started badly with Catherine placing an upstart on the Polish throne, it ended well for her and she will be remembered in History for expanding the already great empire of Russia. Her armies also absorbed The Crimea, for which she accepted the credit but of which she actually knew nothing. In fact, her military leader invited her to visit the area, which she did. It was actually vast empty plains with very few properties and buildings of value so he had his men build false walls and buildings of lightweight wood, to fool the Empress into believing the country she'd just won at great cost, was worth much more than it actually was.

The Russian government would regularly meet in St Petersburg and Catherine sometimes attended the cabinet meetings. Although the meetings were political in content, she was the Tsarina of Russia and had every right to involve herself with decisions made about the country and her people. The room used for these meetings was entirely furnished by Catherine herself. The furniture resembled erotic shapes and added to her reputation for having many – and varied – lovers of all ages. She was well known for her promiscuity. Some were very young men and some quite old – but as long as they were men, Catherine was content. She had no interest in women, except to enhance their position in society. She liked to attend the meetings with her government – she was after all the Queen Bee. Mostly talk was about how to enhance their individual fiscal positions and as long as they included Catherine in all their lucrative projects, she was content.

There were a couple of politicians who usually stirred things up – they were sympathetic to the needs of the serfs and how they should do more to help their plight. Catherine thought she recognised one of the men – a man in his forties, tall with blond hair. He was a newcomer to the meetings and had fought to be allowed to attend them. Most of the others attended only to feather their own nests and pass laws to enhance their own fortunes. She thought she recognised the blond man and asked him outright in her best imperial manner, "Who are you – and where have I seen you before?" She leaned forward in her chair.

He stared back straight into her eyes. "I'm told by people that my son resembled me – and until recently, he worked at the palace – you may have seen him there. He was a footman."

"Oh yes, the young man who liked to play the balalaika and sing songs against the government and myself? Yes, that's who you look like. Your son was lucky – I only dismissed him although I could have had him arrested."

One of the other ministers spoke up, "You are always generous to a fault, your Majesty. It was like you not to punish him more." The man was one of her toadies who liked to ingratiate himself whenever he could. That way, he could look forward to one of her generous gifts.

Then she saw him, standing behind his father's chair. He was not dressed as a footman but wore the clothes of a peasant serf. It was Nicholas of the balalaika incident.

"Where is your son now, sir?" she asked, tapping her fingernails loudly on the desk.

"When you dismissed him from your service, he ran from the palace, thinking the guards were behind him and ran straight into a horse and carriage. The horse trampled him and then the carriage wheels ran over him. He died instantly and so, was punished for singing a forbidden song – one about the terrible lives lived by the serfs in your kingdom." Both men were staring at her.

"I am sorry your son is dead – but it wasn't my fault. He shouldn't have been stupid enough to sing such a song to his Empress. I hope you're not here to argue the serfs' case further." She stood up and pushed her chair back. "When I first came to Russia and took the Crown, I was initially supportive of bettering the lives of the serfs, but after a short time here, learning more about them and how dependent they were on their betters' goodwill, I soon changed my mind."

"But, Madam, you must be aware of what is happening in France and how the people have turned on their aristocracy and removed them from power. In fact, the guillotine has never been busier in that country. And it came about because Royalty turned a blind eye to the plight of the ordinary people." The blond man was furious. "There is no reason it can't happen here, you know."

Catherine ignored his outburst. "Good day, gentlemen, I have had enough for one day." And she left the meeting. What she didn't notice was the young, blond chap left his father's side and followed her out of the building.

Next morning, she woke up early and stretched her arms over her head. Her lover was still asleep – but she threw a glass of water over him and he jumped up. She threw him out of the room. She knew she could never marry again as this would confuse the line of inheritance – she had one son, Paul, whose father was claimed to have been her husband, Peter, whom she'd had executed. Many people however disbelieved it had been Peter, as there had been so many possible fathers to date. In fact, so disgusted was the Tsarina Dowager Elizabeth with her daughter-in-law's romantic entanglements and blatant promiscuity, that she took the child from his mother – and raised him herself. History thinks that Catherine may have had at least three more children, but no one ever knew who their fathers were. They were all bastards, with Paul being the only one that may have been legitimate – but a legal heir to the throne was needed for the future of Russia. And that was Paul I.

Catherine really was her own worst enemy – but she enjoyed her life and rarely worried about her future. She had recently taken up with a new lover. His name was Alexander Dmitriev-Mamonov and it was said that she adored him. He was at least one of her favourites, on whom she bestowed many wonderful gifts, which he passed in turn to a sixteen-year-old maid-of-honour who was a servant to Catherine herself. The love affair lasted several months and Catherine adored him, never suspecting he was also involved with a young, sixteen-year-old. The Empress was now 60 years of age and Alexander was many years younger. He made up his mind to run away from court without telling the Tsarina what he intended. He stayed with her one more night and cradled her in his arms, saying how much he loved her. Contended, she let him go next morning, promising to give him a prizewinning stallion from her own stables. Before he left, he made sure that, as well as collecting the maid-of-honour, he also collected the horse, which was worth a great deal of money. So ended many of Catherine's romantic exploits – it was easier when she finished and discarded them, but when the opposite happened, she was a most unhappy woman. No one was allowed to reject her.

She felt better however when she discovered where the couple were living and sent round some of her special guards, dressed as policemen. The men held the young girl and whipped her soundly in front of Alexander, who was tied up in ropes and made to watch the whole procedure. Such punishment implied Catherine was angrier with her maid-of-honour for deserting her than she was with Alexander for stopping loving her. The phrase 'A woman scorned' comes to mind and worse still when that woman has as much power as Catherine had.

As with many Royals at the time, Food Tasters were employed to test meals before it was consumed. Catherine the Great used a sex tester to judge whether or not a new 'lover' came up to expectations. Countess Praskovya Bruce tested any new man by having sex with him before he was allowed into Catherine's private chamber. This continued for some time before the Countess was discovered having an ongoing relationship with Rimsky-Korsakov – a very young gentleman whom Catherine liked. And that was the end of that project.

She had to test the men herself from that moment on. This however, was a story about Catherine which the courtiers liked to spread.

There he was again – the young footman. This time standing at the foot of her bed. She'd seen him several times before but he liked to appear suddenly and startle her. Now he had taken to bringing small children with him. They were stick-thin with bold, staring eyes. Dressed in rags, they looked pleadingly at the Tsarina. Catherine knew they were figures of her imagination – but not of her conscience – as she had no conscience about the plight of the serfs. There was work for them and they were paid for doing it; they could buy food and little luxuries if they so wished. She had no idea of the life they lived – of how they had to bend the knee to anyone in charge, no matter if they were cruel, unjust or vicious. The apparitions who appeared to her kept on re-appearing; hoping her conscience would one day prick and she would do something to eradicate the serfs' – or slaves' – miserable existences. One day, it would come to pass but not for many years ahead and not until the then-Tsar and his entire family lay in a stone cellar and were shot and bayonetted by the Russian people themselves.

She became uneasy about the blond footman and called on the church to remove him from her presence. The priests tried and then tried again but Catherine kept on seeing the apparition. Was it all in her mind? She didn't know. It didn't make her do anything to help the serfs however and so their torment went on.

Catherine was an autocratic ruler and had an excellent opinion of herself. She was also an excellent equestrian and rode her horse very well, something she'd done all her life. In fact, on one occasion, she actually led 14,000 of her military to take charge of her country and she wore armour to do it. A very strong woman indeed, but one who was described as a tyrant by even those who were close to her.

The people didn't love her as she'd done little to earn that love. She was quoted as saying, "If the Russian people could read – they would write me off." She had no illusions about her popularity but she had however helped Russia become an even greater country than when she – as a 15-year-old girl – had come to the throne. She did try to please everyone, but only if it suited her and was to her own advantage. She allowed the Muslims to build many mosques across Russia but this back fired on her as they built them too high – much higher than the churches, so the other religions complained and asked her to tell the Muslims not to build their places of worship so high up into the sky. Her reply was. "I am the Tsarina of the Russian land but the sky is beyond my jurisdiction." And so, the mosques were allowed to reach as high as they wanted. Whilst this decision pleased many of her subjects, it displeased many more. Of course, it didn't bother Catherine.

Catherine the Great was now at the very top and her first dedicated action was to establish a court that rivalled Versailles. To achieve this, she had to find a way to replenish the Russian Treasury, which Elizabeth had left empty when she died. The Clergy owned one third of the country's lands and one third of the serfs and so she stripped them of their wealth and ended up appointing just a few administrators who received a meagre stipend for their labour. Now she had the money and the land. She was friends with Prussia (Russia's old enemy) and again with France and Austria. Poland too benefitted from her plans and this was when she appointed one of her own lovers – Stanisław Poniatowski – as King. A big mistake on Catherine's part!

Being brought up by the Dowager Tsarina, Paul, Catherine's son, didn't regard his mother with any great esteem. He was only eight years old when his father was removed from the throne and subsequently murdered. Although just a youngster, he couldn't rid his mind of the memory that one minute he had a father and the next, he didn't. His mother had never cared very much for him and he knew it, which was why he was quite happy to live with his grandmother. As he grew older and reached adulthood, he didn't trust his mother and he knew she favoured his own son – her grandson Alexander and planned to bypass Paul and make her grandson her successor. She had never made a secret of how she felt. Catherine in her turn, didn't trust her son as she believed he was plotting to remove her from the throne. Mother and son disliked each other and were right to suspect potential treachery – both only interested in their own destiny.

Catherine had instructed her son, Paul to marry a German princess and settle in Garchina, well away from St Petersburg. However, when their son was born, he was quickly removed from the couple and brought up at his mother's court – just as he had been taken to live with his own grandmother, Elizabeth. Being a rather feeble man, Paul had no say in the matter.

Like his father, Paul was always playing with toy soldiers and forcing the local military to parade every morning. He admired the smartness of the Prussian army and made his soldiers dress as they did. They resented being treated like toy soldiers and being drilled relentlessly and regularly on one parade after the other. Again, rather similar to his own father, no one thought much of him.

Catherine was 67 years old and not in the best of health. She had fewer lovers now and didn't like what she'd become. Following a sumptuous dinner at the Winter Palace, she withdrew from the candlelit table and made her way to her room. Her maids of honour followed her.

"You seem weary tonight, Your Serene Highness – is there anything I can get you? A sedative perhaps? It was rather a heavy meal." Olga was always eager to please her mistress.

"I want none of your sedatives, girl – I just need to soothe my tired bones in a warm bath. Go along and draw me the bath now." The girl did as she was bid and Catherine waited on a chaise longue by the fireside. She stared at herself in a giant mirror opposite and leaned forward to look at her face more intently. She was old and tired and rather too full of rich food. She had felt better. Going into the bathroom, she removed her robe and piled her hair on top of her head. She suddenly looked even older. Her face stared back at her and then she noticed some movement behind her back – and there was another face staring at her from the glass.

Nicholas, the young, blond man stood behind her and she jumped. "What are you doing here? You have no right to be here." Then she recognised him – it was the footman she'd met so long ago – the cheeky one, who'd sung a sympathetic song about the serfs.

"I am here, Madam, to bid you goodbye. You have reached the end of your life but not done anything to help your fellow man. With this on your conscience, you are about to meet your maker and may God have mercy on your soul. You had so many opportunities but did little for the serfs in Russia."

"Be gone, you impudent man – you know nothing. Russia is in a better state than when I came to the throne." She was angry.

"But your people are not in a better state – in fact, they're worse." His figure began to waver and slowly disappeared from the mirror. Catherine clutched at the sink edge but couldn't help herself to move. A stroke had forced her to the floor and she tried to shout for her lady-in-waiting – but no sound would come. Her eyes fluttered and closed and Catherine the Great was no more. She sighed and breathed her last, dying on the floor of her bathroom. It was November 1796.

This was actually a story that began to circulate by the people who had little regard for her. They spread the word that the mighty Empress had been sitting on the toilet when she passed away and she had to be carted out of the bathroom.

This story was more damning and insulting to her and it gave her enemies pleasure to smirk and recount it.

It was calculated at the time, that 95 per cent of the Russian people did not benefit directly from the achievements of Catherine's reign – although their forced and free labour did finance the immense expenditures required for Catherine's many projects. With these projects however, she did prove herself to be a good administrator – and could always claim that the blood and sweat of the people had not been wasted. It had served its purpose.

Paul heard his mother had died and he was joyful. She hadn't had the time needed to remove him from the line of inheritance and he was now Paul I, Imperial Tsar of Russia. He immediately began to make his mark – firstly putting his troops into Prussian style uniforms and inspecting them every day in St Petersburg and always at precisely 11 am. The elite officers did not like this, but he was the Tsar.

More importantly, he began to reverse many of his mother's policies and this weakened the influence of the aristocracy. He really did try to lighten the burden of the serfs and this was at the expense of the landowners and aristocrats. He set up a model Civil Service to run local and central government. To stop people from learning too much about the French Revolution, he forbade them to travel overseas and prohibited the reading of foreign books and periodicals. Knowledge of how successful the Revolution had been for the serfs would not have helped his position in Russia. However, he managed to achieve some very practical changes to the country but ruined it all by his frequent bouts of temper and capricious outbursts of an ungovernable rage. He was ignorant of Foreign Policy but still made major decisions that proved to be unwise. All of this led people to believe that their Tsar was insane. Like his mother, but for different reasons, he was not liked by his people.

One wet and cold Monday night in St Petersburg, he hosted a dinner party which included his son, the Grand Duke Alexander. The boy seemed curiously ill at east and ate very little for which his father chastised him. The Tsar retired to his bed and left a small group of diners still drinking at the table. What he didn't know was that they were part of a conspiracy and were led by General Leo Bennigsen and Count von Pahlen, the latter being the military commander of the city. Von Pahlen went to Alexander's chamber (presumably to tell him what was happening) and Bennigsen led a party of guard officers to the Tsar's suite. They were all pretty intoxicated and overpowered two valets, broke down the door and went into the room, which was lit by a single candle. At first, the room seemed quiet and uninhabited which made one of them say, "The bird has flown." Bennigsen, however, crossed to the bed which had rumpled covers on top – and felt the sheets, which were still warm, as though from someone's warm body." The bird has not flown far," he called out to his fellow conspirators – and they soon found Paul I Tsar of all Russia, cowering in terror behind a screen. A struggle ensued, Paul fighting for his life but the guards battered him and throttled him with a scarf. It was one o'clock in the morning and his son, Alexander was nowhere to be seen but there was a strange, blond haired young man amongst the group, whom no one recognised – but Catherine would have, had she been present.

They had brought with them an abdication document for Paul to sign, so perhaps they had not intended to kill him – just remove him from the throne and place his son there. But the struggle had been too intense and Paul had died a very ignominious death. Von Pahlen then asked, "Once Alexander is on the throne, what would we have done with the Tsar anyway?"

And was told, "You can't make an omelette without breaking the eggs first." So, certainly some of them had intended to kill him.

Alexander succeeded his father and became the new Tsar of Russia. He had been his grandmother's favourite and she had prepared him for such a role. The Romanovs were still in charge of the country, but their days were numbered. Tsar Alexander I, who became known as Alexander the Blessed, died 1825 (*Assassinated)* – he was succeeded by his brother Constantine(*Abdicated*)) then by his other brother: Nicholas I (*Died* 1855): next was Alexander II, known as Alexander the Liberator Nephew of Alexander I *(Assassinated):* then by Alexander III known as Alexander the Peacemaker *(Died* 1894): and finally succeeded by Nicholas II Known as Nicholas the Bloody*) Assassinated with all his family in 1918 by the Bolsheviks – first abdicating the throne during the Russian Revolution.*

I make no apology for this lesson in history. I make it to show how deadly the throne of Russia actually was, since Catherine the Great's time (and on many occasions before then – think of Ivan the Terrible).

Catherine had many opportunities and the Instruction she wrote concerning the need for the freedom of man proves that she knew Russia was not perfect. Had she just started to seek a better society for the people then perhaps all those who came after her, may have done just a little more of the same. From acorns, great oak trees grow. She hadn't listened to her conscience which took the form of the young, blond man who tried to tell her. Her line came to a bloody end with a young and innocent family being executed together – and executed most horrifically.

*An Instruction by Catherine the Great, however, still remains in the 'Dead Letters Office' in the Winter Palace. Too little, too late! **Did she deserve the name of Great –well, that depends on your point of view?***

The French Revolution

Louis stayed in the shadows. He hid from the screaming men and women in the streets of Paris. It was easy for him to hide, being small for his age and dressed in rags. He had the same very large, protruding eyes of the hungry and malnourished who lived in the city at that time. He looked frail and brittle as if he could break if you touched him, even gently. No shoes on his blackened feet and only the scrappiest of clothes covering his thin body. A starving child who lived amongst all the other starving people in the Parisienne streets.

His one beauty was his hair. He had a thick, unruly – and unclean – mop of dark-brown hair that grew down his neck onto his shoulders. A nine-year-old boy with no future or ambition, except to find food to keep him going until the next day. His mother had died when he was only five and his father then ran away, as he didn't want to be burdened with his son. Not a good start for the boy. Every day, he sauntered along the streets of Paris, watching for scraps of food that people had either thrown away or dropped by accident. The starving population usually dropped the scraps as throwing food away was a 'no-no' for them.

Louis had been watching a small group of girls who'd somehow managed to find – or steal – a cabbage, which they were ripping apart and stuffing into their mouths. He crept up behind them. "Spare a cabbage leaf, go on, I've not eaten anything for two days."

One of the girls turned to him and said, "Well then, you must still be pretty full up." And all the girls giggled and finished off the vegetable, with nothing to spare for the scruffy boy.

The street was erupting with men waving flags and shouting 'Down with King Louis' and 'Long Live the Revolution'. They were the sons of the Revolution that France was undergoing just then. King Louis XVI and his queen, Marie Antoinette along with their children were living in the lap of luxury at

Versailles, whilst their subjects suffered with malnutrition, no money and no expectation of things getting any better in the future.

"On Friends, on to the Bastille. We'll set free those prisoners, many of whom are there only because they are penniless." A great cheer arose from the marchers at his words and they quickened their pace towards the prison. They reached their goal and stormed the great building. The force of their numbers broke down the main gate – and they were inside. The prisoners began to stream into the streets and all Louis could think of was, *How many more mouths would be looking for food.* There were cries of 'Liberty, Equality, Fraternity' and the year was 1789, a year too many for the French people to endure under the present monarchy. Louis marched alongside the men of the Revolution and suddenly felt as though he might have a future after all. The prison guards soon threw down their rifles and stood aside to let the crowd come into the prison. They were hungry too, just like the people of Paris and all over France itself.

One tall man carrying a flag looked down at Louis and said, "Well done, boy. Follow us and things will get better. In fact, come back tomorrow. We're going to storm Versailles itself and you can come along with us." Louis nodded his agreement but added, "It's 12 miles to Versailles, isn't it? Will we be able to walk all the way?"

"There'll be plenty of carts. I'm sure you'll be able to hitch a ride." The man laughed at the boy's concern. The man's name was Gabriel he told the boy.

Louis left the marching men. He was so hungry; he had to find something to eat. He felt as if he was going to pass out, He crossed to one of the smarter streets where the houses were big and the people looked wealthy and well fed. He crept around to the back of the house – to where the kitchen was and there stood a snarling dog, chewing on a large bone that still had some pieces of meat sticking to it. *These folks are certainly not hungry if they can throw that to the dog,* he thought and lunged at the dog with a heavy stick he'd found. The dog growled and bared his teeth at Louis but the boy was even hungrier than the animal and he managed to get the bone for himself. He hit the dog once more, harder this time and it ran indoors, whimpering loudly.

Louis fell on the bone and ran away with it under his arm. Oh, the juicy bits of meat were lovely and he sucked at it until it was absolutely clean. He found a corner behind some barrels and sat there quite contented until a couple of rats moved him on. Inside the big house, some well-dressed men were having an argument in the drawing room. Some were members of the Government and were enjoying an impromptu meeting in the private house.

One man said, "It's all the King's fault and as for that dratted woman, his wife, she goes on as if the country's not in turmoil. This country is going bankrupt and no one is doing anything about it." He stamped his foot in exasperation.

The others 'Hurrah'd' their agreement and another man said, "The crowds in the street are baying for blood and it should be theirs, not ours." The feelings inside the house were as angry as those out in the streets; everyone wanted to blame the King. "The Monarchy only looks after itself and the affairs of state are ignored along with the needs of the people. Louis XVI regularly sends money to his friends in Europe, just to impress them." One rather pompous man shouted. He was wearing a huge powdered wig which had toppled to the one side, but it didn't look funny, it looked more pitiful.

So in 1789, peasant and nobility had one thought in common. *It's the King's fault. Poor old King Louis*, the boy thought, *all his riches aren't doing him much good.* Louis had no actual home and he slept wherever he could, but he still felt pity for the King. That night, it was under the bar in a small tavern in Montmartre, a bohemian part of the city. No one spotted him slipping in and he was so small, he was able to hide well away from prying eyes. There was, however, another boy hiding in a corner of the same bar and he told him to get lost. Although small and frail, Louis was afraid of nothing and stayed exactly where he was. "Either be my friend, or learn what it is to be my enemy." Scruffy Louis looked as tough as he could and the other boy fell silent.

Next morning, nice and early, both boys crept out of the tavern and joined the huge number of men already on their way to Versailles. Gabriel Boucher was at the head of the crowd and waved at the two boys. They were a mean looking mass but they were starving and knew they had to take the law into their own hands, as there was no one else to help them. It took most of the day to reach Versailles but soon the magnificent building loomed into view. The long drive was lined with soldiers carrying rifles but after a few token shots, which hit no one, they laid down their arms and fled the scene. Very much like the guards in the Bastille had done the day before. They knew how much the people were suffering. They were after all, themselves of the people. Louis and his new friend Pierre came up on the outside of the crowd and because they were so small, they were able to sneak around to the back of the building without being spotted. They were starving and hoping to find an open kitchen. And they did because the cooks and servants were in complete disarray and bumping into one another, unsure of whether to leave the place or hide deeper inside. The smell of cooking food was overpowering and saliva dribbled from the boys' mouths.

The King and his family were hiding in a stone-built cellar at the very back of the huge palace. They'd been warned that the crowds were marching from Paris and they'd been hiding from them for quite some time now. King Louis's Minister had taken them to the cellar and said he would talk to the crowd on the King' behalf. On no account were they to show themselves. The Minister went to the upstairs balcony and the crowd stopped in their tracks when they saw him come out. They were shouting, "The King. We want to talk to the King."

The Minister who was a red-faced, very florid gentleman at the best of times was quite scarlet when he stepped onto the balcony. He had several soldiers with him and they were all carrying rifles.

"I am here to speak with you on behalf of the King. He would be here himself but had to travel to another part of the country." He mopped his brow. "One of you must act as speaker and I shall ensure that what he says to me will be reported to the King."

Several men shouted, "Let Gabriel Boucher be our spokesman. He knows why we're all here." Gabriel climbed onto the balcony and went through the glass doors with the Minister. He stayed there for at least an hour and then emerged to tell his comrades that food and drink would be placed outside the main door and they were to help themselves.

"I shall tell you everything that was talked about but only after we've eaten, and then we must return to Paris and wait to be contacted." The men mumbled but were grateful for the food as being so hungry was making them feel sick and they knew they still had to cover the 12 miles back to Paris.

Whilst this was happening, Louis and Pierre were rambling about the palace. They had complete freedom of movement as all the servants were either in hiding or had fled the palace completely. The luxury and magnificence of the rooms and corridors shocked them very much. "No one should have this sort of wealth," Pierre said, "it's too much."

Louis agreed and picked up a silver dish from a small table. "This dish would feed many, many people and yet here it lies, of no use to anyone." And he looked around at all the other silver and gold ornaments lying everywhere. The two boys ran through other rooms, grabbing bonbons and sweetmeats as they went. There seemed to be food in every room whether people were there or not. They went into the most famous room, called the Hall of Mirrors which stretched as far as the eye could see. It was truly magnificent and enormous and the boys looked more like ants, so small were they under the high ceilings and mirrored walls. There was a War Room and a Peace Room: there was a Mars Room, a Venus Room, a Mercury Room and an Apollo Room – in fact, the rooms went on and on and the boys gave up in the end, there were just too many of them. All of the rooms were as splendid as the first had been.

On reaching a slightly smaller room with a fire burning in the grate, they lay down on a fluffy rug alongside it. The great doors were thrown open and a gentleman and lady came in. He was dressed in a silk jacket and matching pantaloons. She was dressed like a fairy queen with a towering, powdered wig adorning her head. The headdress was four feet high. They were a magnificent pair. Two footmen accompanied them and a maid was carrying a plateful of sweetmeats which she placed on a gold table. The couple had married when Louis was fifteen and Marie Antoinette only 14. It was seven years before their first child was born, probably because they were still children themselves when they married.

The boys were spotted immediately and the footmen made to throw them out of the room, but the king held up his hand and said, "No, let them stay – I would speak with them." The boys stood up and waited by the side of the fireplace. "Why do you hate your King?" he asked and waited patiently for an answer. Louis could think of nothing to say but Pierre had more confidence gained in the streets and wasn't afraid to speak up. He brushed his fringe from his forehead. Marie Antoinette tutted in disapproval and bent over to pamper her two children who had quietly come into the room. She never offered the bonbons to anyone but her own children and herself.

"Well, Your Majesty, it's like this. You take all the riches and wealth for yourself and your people all over the country are starving – they have nothing. They hear stories about the Queen's small village built just for her and her ladies to play in. It has lambs and cows and farms and lakes." He looked towards the Queen. "Isn't that true, *Madam*?"

She stood up and fluttered her fan across her face. "I will not discuss my private life with this urchin." She turned to her husband. "You may do as you wish Louis, I will not stay here."

Young Louis started to answer her but she said, "I was not talking to you, boy." He said he was sorry but explained his name was Louis as well.

"I was named Louis after you, *Sire*." The King looked sad and nodded at the child – many babies had been named after him. The Queen turned suddenly and her tall wig wobbled with the movement.

"You mean my Little Hameaux I suppose," she spoke to Pierre, "and yes I have spent a fortune on it but it's worth it as I've created something great and beautiful. There are lakes, farms and even a water mill where my ladies and I live as milkmaids and servants. It is very amusing. The crowd out there can't say they've ever done that, can they?" She failed to see the injustices in what she'd just described.

"No, *Madam*, they cannot as they don't have the money and what they do have, is for food to feed their children." Marie Antoinette ignored the mouthy boy. Pierre was being very brave.

The King asked the boys if they knew the leader of the crowd outside. They said they did and he went on, "Can I trust you boys? Can I trust you not to let down your King? Will you go back outside and bring him to me? The footman here will show you the secret passage which goes down to the kitchen, it's been used for many, many years." The two boys left with Edward, the footman and Louis XVI watched them go with a very sad expression on his face.

They found Gabriel Boucher easily enough. He'd just come out of the palace front door, having spent at least an hour with the Minister. They sidled up to him just as servants and a cook carrying food and drink emerged and handed all of it to the crowd. "Please will you come with us, Gabriel? We know you'd rather stay here and eat but we have a surprise for you." Gabriel went with them, but first grabbed a chicken leg. He looked uncomfortable and awkward, his tattered clothes looking worse when surrounded by the glittering décor in the palace, but he bravely followed the boys into the secret staircase and up to the King.

"So you are the man who has brought these people here?" he asked the peasant.

Gabriel stood straight and said, "I am Your Majesty and I would be willing to do so again, if the current situation in the country doesn't change." Little Louis spoke up and told the King that Gabriel had had nothing to eat for several days and so Louis himself served the man with some sweetmeats and Burgundy. Gabriel took them gratefully and the King told him to sit down. The conversation went as one would have expected and the boys were delighted that they'd brought about this meeting all on their own. They moved towards the Dauphin and his sister and as children are want to do, they chatted to each other, despite the great differences in their stations.

Gabriel and the King chatted for at least an hour and parted with Louis XVI promising to speak with his government about the problems.

Outside, the crowd did as they were told and Gabriel began to lead them back to Paris but what they didn't know was that they were no longer alone in their quest to make the country a more equal place for everyone – rich and poor alike, because the government too had come to the same conclusion about the state of France. The King's selfishness had to be stopped. He was changing the Tax system so that even more wealth would come to him personally and not to the treasury where it was desperately needed. Louis was greedy and not a good manager of funds. Marie Antoinette was a wasteful spendthrift who cared very little for the people. Her famous quote was uttered in this momentous year. When being told that many of her subjects had no bread, she shrugged and said, "*Qu'ils mangent de la brioches,*" i.e., let them eat cake. It really was an excellent example of what her attitude was towards the people.

Very quickly, things moved on in France, in Paris in particular. The Royal family were imprisoned by the Revolutionaries and kept under house arrest in the Tuileries and had to face much hardship meted out by their gaolers. In fact, it was at this time that the Dauphin first contracted tuberculosis and became very ill. Little Louis tried to get into the Tuileries but was refused admission. He'd brought an orange for the Dauphin but was forced to eat it himself. He stayed friends with Pierre and together they watched as Paris fell apart. It was called 'The reign of Terror' and Madame La Guillotine was erected in the 'Place de la Revolution'. Executions and murders were commonplace now there was a French Republic. Eventually, a French Consulate was established with a man called Napoleon Bonaparte as the leader. The year was now 1792 and Little Louis was twelve years old and fast growing up. He'd had better access to food lately and he looked older than he was. Actually, Pierre had taught him to steal better without getting caught and this was how he looked so much better than when they'd first met.

Four thousand people were murdered and executed in France by 1793 but many aristocrats managed to escape the country and ended up all over Europe. Then it was the turn of King, Louis XVI to pay for being such a 'bad king.' His son also called Louis, outlived his father by two years only and died at the age of 10, still imprisoned in the Tuileries. In fact, many believed that it was the cruel and harsh imprisonment he'd suffered at the hands of the Revolutionaries that sapped his energy and strength and ended his days. Only one daughter of the four children survived her family. Her name was Marie Therese and she was kept in prison until she was 17 years old and then fortunately had a continuously unhappy life, married but not in love, life had not been kind to her. She died at age 58 years.

Pierre and Louis pushed their way to the front of the crowd who'd gathered at the Place de la Revolution to watch Louis XVI losing his head. It was a day of celebration in Paris where the atmosphere was like a festival. The wine was running freely and lots of people were quite out of their heads but Pierre and Louis found a place at the front and waited. They didn't feel like rejoicing as the King had once been kind to them but they knew his death was inevitable. The rumbling sound of a wooden hurdle could be heard on the cobbles. Louis XVI stood in the back, his hands gripping onto the side of the cart. His clothes were in tatters and he'd lost a lot of weight, completely unlike the man the boys had met at Versailles. The hurdle stopped just in front of the two boys, who wanted to cheer for the King but of course couldn't or the crowd would have turned on them. King Louis was pulled down from the cart and stood in front of the people, looking sad and forlorn. Although he was a proud man, there were tears in his eyes. The crowd was jeering at him, shouting 'Down with Louis' 'Cut his royal head off'.

A man came forward and started to push him up a ladder, but he tripped on the first rung and fell to the ground. The man was rough and pulled him up by the hair. "Get up you waster and take it like a man." Little Louis left the front of the crowd and made towards the fallen King. Pierre called him back. "Don't be such a fool, you don't need to help him." But Louis stepped forward and bent down towards his namesake, the King. He took his arm and helped him to his feet. Louis XVI looked at the boy and knew he'd seen him before. For a moment, he smiled and said quietly '*Merci, Monsieur*' before struggling up the ladder and kneeling down, his head resting on the block. The boy shouted, "God bless the King," and suddenly more people joined in the chant until it became a loud cry. It was the last thing the King heard before the guillotine was released and fell with a thud, slicing off his head. His blood was spreading over the straw around the block and he was dragged down from the scaffold onto the ground below.

The two boys scampered in case anyone asked who had first shouted 'God Bless the King'.

So Louis XVI was no more. The French people hadn't really disliked him, he was just useless as a king. His wife, on the other hand, they did dislike very much. She'd always been a spendthrift, not really interested in the people of the country and actively encouraged her husband to do the wrong things. She'd encouraged him to send millions of Francs to help Bonnie Prince Charlie in Scotland and lots of money and frigates to the America's to help them with the defeat of the British in the War of Independence. He liked to dabble in international politics but used the money for such things that should have been spent on his own people and in rebuilding a France that was fast falling into chaos and disrepair. Marie Antoinette on the other hand, thought the money was well spent and increased France's world status in all the royal families in Europe. Unfortunately, this may have glamorised the French court but it didn't put food in the bellies of the ordinary people.

She'd been born in 1755 in Austria in 1755 and married at age 14 to a boy king of 15 years. Her first child was born seven years after the marriage took place. She'd lived a luxurious life as the Queen of France and had wanted for nothing. Now, here she was being bundled onto a wooden hurdle that was to be dragged through the streets of Paris. The people were already gathering at the Tuileries to see her being brought out. They lined the entire route to the Place de la Revolution where they'd enjoy the spectacle of the high and mighty Queen losing her head. A great number of aristocrats had already been executed there.

As before, Louis and Pierre had secured a place by the guillotine, almost exactly in the same spot when they saw the King being beheaded. This time, they didn't feel sad as they'd never liked the woman. Her trial hadn't lasted long and the jury had been all men. She was found guilty of High Treason, sexual promiscuity and of incestuous relations with her son. She was described by the Judge as a 'frivolous, selfish, immoral woman who lived a lavish lifestyle'. Again, the phrase was repeated '*Qu'ils mangent de la Brioche*' was mentioned by the judge and would be mentioned long into the future.

When pressed for her response to the charges, she said, "I have seen all – I have heard all – I have forgotten all. My courage has been truly tested; I have shown it for years – think you I shall lose it at the moment when my sufferings are to end?" Still to the end, she was arrogant and too proud. Her hair had turned white the night before her execution. She was only 37 years old but looked much older.

The hurdle stopped at the ladder leaning against the steps to the guillotine, the very one her husband had stumbled on. She climbed to the top, first gazing over all the jeering people who were throwing rotten fruit and vegetables at her. "Death to the witch," they shouted and the hooded executioner knelt before her as was the practice to ask the prisoner's pardon before releasing the blade. His name was Henri Sanson. The Queen inadvertently stepped on his foot as she bent to the block and her last words were to him.

"*Pardonnez-moi, Monsieur, je ne l'ai pas fait exprès.*" 'I am sorry, sir, I did not mean to do it.' And those were the last words of the famous Queen Marie Antoinette. Did she mean that she was sorry for stepping on his foot – or was it regret for all the mistakes she'd made throughout her life? Who could tell, but the irony of her words was not lost in many in the crowd.

The strange thing was that Little Louis saw a man come out of the crowd and climb the ladder to where the headless queen's body lay. The man was dressed in a silk suit of clothes and wore a white wig tied with a blue ribbon. Louis recognised him as King Louis XVI of France. He put his arms around the queen's body and helped her to her feet. There was no blood around her and her head sat intact on her shoulders. How could this be? The husband and wife seemed to walk off the guillotine platform into the air itself and they looked happy and contented. They disappeared and left the messy bloody body to be cleared away. There was only a nine-year-old Dauphin and his sister left to carry on the Bourbon line. And that situation was soon to change.

The two boys left the scene, Little Louis in a daze, still shocked by what only he had witnessed. His friend took him to a café where they both sat for a long time. "What will happen now, Pierre?" he asked and received the answer.

"Who can tell, Louis, who can tell?

The actual French Republic was established in 1792 and a little Corsican soldier rose quickly through the military ranks of the French Army and created The Consulate, led by himself. He had successfully helped to overthrow the Revolutionary Government, 'Liberty, Equality, Fraternity' continued as the cry of both the people and of the government. The old-style autocratic monarchy had been completely abolished. Louis and Pierre had joined the military although only 14 years old. They looked older and were now strongly built, perhaps living on the streets during the Revolution had toughened them.

They were first employed as clerks in the Army but their street-cred soon helped them achieve promotion. Now they had a home, wages and food and they liked the new man in charge, one Napoleon Bonaparte. They moved heaven and earth to be transferred into his regiment and soon became to be known to him as his messengers. He liked the speed they carried out his orders and were always willing to undertake challenges on his behalf. Sometimes they were trusted to take secret messages to some very important people. Louis even took the trouble to investigate the great man's background so he'd be able to understand the reasoning behind his orders. He seemed to have a permanent seat in the library on the camp so he could study Napoleon's past and this led on to the great libraries at the Tuileries. Napoleon came from a Corsican family and was a member of the minor nobility there. He became an officer at age 16 and worked his way up the ladder of both the military and the French aristocracy but he did also work for the good of the people and for the country as a whole. His own self-interest was part of his whole plan.

One afternoon, he called Louis into his office and asked him if he knew how many battles he had fought so far in his life. He had tried to catch out the young man before as he knew Louis spent a lot of time in the huge palatial libraries, studying his leader's life so far.

"I know, *Sire*, that you've fought fifty battles in your life and only lost four of them. I know you are an incredible general and the people love you." Louis was ready for the questions. Just then, the door flew open and the Empress Josephine came into the room. She was very fashionably dressed in a long muslin gown, lilac in colour and a feather headdress in the same colour. Around her neck and both wrists, were pearls of the most superior class and a large emerald adorned her hair. She paused at the open door and looked around her husband's office, disappointed to find only the young man whom Napoleon had always favoured. Wandering further into the room, she led a very large, fluffy cat on a chain, the chain was studded with several diamonds. Napoleon shrank back into his chair and screwed up his face in disgust.

"Come, come, husband, be a man. It is only a little cat. You have no problem fighting battles and killing people, but you can't face this small animal. Really!" Josephine laughed at her husband's cowardice. It was well known that the great man both hated and had a severe allergy to cats, which is why his wife liked to tease him. It was a standing joke that if you wanted to upset the man who would become Emperor, just throw a moggy at him and he'll run a mile.

Josephine and Napoleon had a strange relationship. They'd been married about eight years and had become rather tired of each other. The fact that she'd never managed to produce a legitimate child was giving him grave concern, although she'd had two children by her first husband – he had been executed during the Revolution. Actually, he had already set in motion legal proceedings to divorce her, although of course, she knew nothing about this. If she had, she wouldn't have changed her luck by bringing the cat into his private domain. Louis looked at Napolean and asked, "Would you like me to take the cat away, *Sire*?" Napoleon just nodded and crossed to the window. Josephine angrily pulled the cat's lead and disappeared from the room. Napoleon sat at his desk again and beckoned Louis to come across.

"Did you see in your research that I was made an officer at 16? I was only a boy but because I believed in myself, I persuaded everyone else to do the same. That's what you must do Louis, believe in your own abilities. At my recent coronation in Notre Dame when they made me Emperor, I snatched the crown from the hands of Pope Pius VII and placed it on my own head. I crowned myself. The old fool was dithering about as though he had all the time in the world, so I hurried him along a bit. I could do that and yet I fear cats for some strange reason. Always be prepared for the unexpected, Louis."

"Yes, *Sire*, I promise I will try to be positive about myself, but I could never reform the Military the way you've done – and most of the countries in Europe are in awe of you. You've created the civil 'Code Napoleon' where all men are regarded as equal under the Law. I know the sentiment will last forever, *Sire*. And there is a document you wrote called 'The Rights of Men' and all the people love it. If only Louis XVI had understood that was what people wanted, he might still have been on the throne today." He paused, realising perhaps he'd gone too far this time.

"You have a good point there, Louis, but as I played a large part in the success of the Revolution, I can't be too sorry that Louis was so ill-informed about his people." He was smiling as he said this. Soon, both Louis and Pierre were promoted to Corporal and Napoleon liked to call them by rank every time he wanted one of them. The two boys became inseparable to the Emperor and even at the time his divorce from Josephine was going through, they were always at his side and ready to do his bidding.

"Do you think we'll be promoted again, Louis?" Pierre asked one afternoon when they were seated at a café in the middle of Paris.

"I do, Pierre, but we must continue to be Napoleon's eyes and ears and support him as we've always done." Time was passing and they were young men now. They could have been posted into the wider army but the Emperor wouldn't let them go. He was to be married again – this time to Marie Louise Duchess of Parma, an eighteen-year-old lady who came from Vienna. He desperately wanted and needed a male heir to secure the Bonaparte line as future rulers of France.

The two had drunk very freely of several bottles of wine and had gone wandering around the streets. They ended up just outside the dilapidated Bastille prison. The great iron door was hanging on its last hinge and the glass in the windows had been smashed to pieces.

"Go on, Louis, I dare you. Go on inside, there's no one there now. Are you scared? You're scared, aren't you?" Pierre was already going inside the prison very slowly.

"I'm right behind you, Corporal." Both men had only gone a few yards when they realised, they were in the open yard. Voices could be heard off to one side, one man seemed to be making a speech to some others. There were shouts of agreement and the two onlookers could see now from the light of some candles. One man was standing on a wooden box and about thirty others were grouped around him. He was speaking loudly, probably feeling quite safe as no one ever came into the Bastille building, probably through fear. Pierre and Louis could hear everything he was saying.

"Right, men, we're all agreed with the principle that it has to be done. He must be got rid of – he's no better than the Bourbon family. He's made himself King – even Emperor – and keeps the country's wealth for himself. He is so conceited; he believes all the people love him." At these words, more shouts of derision could be heard. "Down with Bonaparte. Down with the man who's only interested in what he can get for himself." Some of the men carried wooden clubs and were brandishing them in the air. The speaker on the box held up his hands and the group fell silent. "The day after tomorrow, there's a parade in front of the Army Department's main building near Le Place de la Revolution and the Emperor is to attend. He is to come by coach and watch the parade from the open balcony. Before his carriage reaches the building, the bomb will be thrown through the window and hopefully fall in his lap. It will be 3 pm precisely – everyone be there." Laughter greeted the picture he drew.

As the group began to disperse, the eavesdroppers shrunk back into the shadows and waited in silence. The men were careful when leaving the Bastille and they did it in small groups to avoid being noticed. Not that any innocent person hung around the area – it was considered too dangerous and therefore an ideal place for secret meetings. The two corporals waited for a while after they believed the last of the men had gone, then they came out of their hiding place. They had to pause however as they could still hear voices inside the prison, but it wasn't just people talking, it was moans and groans and even crying. They could see no one, even in the dawn light which was beginning to show, then they realised with horror that it was sounds from the inmates who'd been imprisoned for so long and who'd been given very little food and water – except for the richer prisoners who could afford to bribe the gaolers. The thick stone walls seemed to have absorbed the sounds of their past.

"Let's get out of here." They both said at the same time. "I don't believe I'm hearing this, but you hear it too, don't you?" Pierre added. "That's why no one ever comes near here anymore." And they ran out through the big iron gate, then, first making sure there weren't any stragglers from the group still hanging around, they ran back to the Tuileries as if the Devil himself was after them, as indeed he may have been. They sobered up so quickly it was incredible.

They didn't bother with bed but sat up till they could smell coffee wafting in their window from the army kitchen below. They had a piece of freshly baked baton and then made their way to General Bonaparte's private offices and asked to see him. The clerk in charge said not until the afternoon as he was away all morning at a conference. They looked at each other in despair; the planned assassination was due to take place the next day. They could do nothing else but wait. They asked the clerk, politely, if he could send for them when the General arrived and so, it happened like that. They were sent for at 2 o'clock by an irate leader who hadn't got it all his own way at the meeting, something that didn't happen very often. Napoleon was I a pretty dire mood.

He jumped up and knocked back his chair. "How sure are you that you heard them say all this?"

"Very sure, *Sire*, we weren't far from where they'd gathered and we could hear everything clearly," Pierre said and Louis nodded his head vehemently.

The next day dawned and the General's carriage came round to the front entrance at half past two. Bonaparte came down the front stairs and climbed aboard. A second carriage followed behind and its blacked-out windows hid six soldiers with army rifles at the ready. Napoleon sat very comfortably on the leather seat and nodded and waved to the people who were lining the route. As the carriage drew up at the bottom of the stairs, one of the gendarmes stepped forward and made to open the door, but he was suddenly pushed out of the way by a man emerging from the crowd, carrying a black bag. He ran up to the carriage and raised the bag to window height, intending to thrust it through the opening but was stopped in his tracks by at least ten burly soldiers who brought the man to the ground. A second man came out of the crowd and tried to wrestle the bag from his comrade's hands but was immediately jumped on by two soldiers. Meanwhile, Napoleon climbed from the carriage's opposite side and was quickly bundled away by several gendarmes, who'd been waiting there.

It had all happened so quickly but with such precision that some people were unaware of what was happening and continued to cheer the Emperor. The bag with the bomb was hastily taken away from the square and rushed to the lake in the Tuileries Gardens where it was thrown deep into the water. There was a loud bang and water and debris exploded into the air, completely covering any passers-by. Confusion and panic began to spread through the people, as they realised what had happened. The soldiers and the gendarmes had pulled several men from the crowd near the building steps and they were already being taken away to an army gaol. They still continued to shout, "Down with Bonaparte, the Brigand."

Meanwhile, the 'Brigand' had managed to get away from his protectors and was coming back to where the carriage stood. He gestured to one of the soldiers to place a box on the ground so that he could better see the people. Being a strategist and a politician, he wasn't going to miss this opportunity to raise his profile and show his bravery and courage.

"My friends, everything is all right and your Emperor is safe and intends to remain so. I am here – and always will be – to take care of my people. I had been aware that this was going to happen but nothing could have stopped me from coming to see you today. I shall now go on with my everyday business and inspect my military colleagues, all of whom have behaved brilliantly today and saved anyone from being hurt. Thank you for coming to see me today. I do appreciate it." And he jumped off the box and made his way up the stairs.

The following week, there was a presentation of medals, awarded by Napoleon himself, who was dressed in the most impressive regalia that glittered in the sunshine. The soldiers and gendarmes who were involved were given medals and small pouches of money, leaving them in no doubt that the Emperor was grateful for their diligence in protecting him.

Pierre and Louis were also rewarded for the very important part they'd played in the incident. Napoleon promoted them from Corporal status to that of Lieutenant and made sure the small purses they were given were much fuller than those of the others. He placed their medals on their chests with pride and told them he knew he could trust them no matter what happened in the future. The young men who'd been street urchins, then army corporals and now army lieutenant beamed their gratitude to the great man.

Life went on in Paris and the country flourished under Napoleon who had married again and had a son. His second wife, Marie Louise, was well, he was reasonably contended and his son was called Napoleon the second. This must have been a good time for the emperor with most of the executions at an end and the French Revolution behind the government. He continued to win battles and had conquered a great deal of Europe, changing many of their legal procedures for the better.

He made such a difference in Europe but then he met his 'Waterloo'. In all, he had won sixty battles, only seven of which he'd lost and now he was ready to take on the British and her many European allies. He was going to be the leader of *all* of Europe and not just of France.

He had to be stopped – most of Europe was in agreement with each other on this subject. Under the leadership of Great Britain's General Wellington, the allies were formed, and included Great Britain, the Netherlands, Belgium and Germany. They formed an alliance with each other to thwart Napoleon from dominating Europe. Napoleon had planned this for a long time and had been very successful throughout the years but when he invaded Belgium, it was just one step too much. He had been planning to take control of Europe since 1804 and it was now 1815. His determination became known as 'The Napoleonic Wars', killing over five million people in course, throughout Europe. The Battle of Waterloo was not an easy battle and some of Wellington's quotes sum up the difficulties he had with the French Army. He said of Bonaparte 'He has humbugged me' and 'It was the closest run battle you've ever seen in your life', so Napoleon obviously fought his corner very well, but he was not victorious. His under Generals was also fighting on another front in Prussia and this added to Napoleon's problems.

One of the saddest things he witnessed during the battle was, as his horse Merengo was being brought to him, he saw a young man fall to the ground under the horse's hooves and he was sad to see it was Pierre, his trustworthy Lieutenant.

A crack shot had come right into the camp and found its target in the young man Napoleon had begun to look upon as a son.

Before mounting, he instructed that Pierre's body be carefully removed and taken into the Commander's tent and disposed of with dignity.

On 18 June 1815, the battle was over and four days later, Napoleon abdicated and declared his son as his successor. The allies, however, had no intention of allowing Napoleon II to take over the throne of France, child though he was, and they quickly named Louis XVIII as King. They marched into Paris just a few days after the battle and placed the next in line of the Bourbon family on the throne. Napoleon's son wouldn't have had a very long reign anyway as he died at age 21 of tuberculosis. So ended the royalm but short line of the Bonapartes.

The Emperor was sent to Elba from where he escaped and managed to form a new army, and even proclaimed France a new Republic again, but it was all for nothing. He was captured again and this time, sent to St Helena as his prison. Louis XVIII had been made King twice now – once after Napoleon's first escape and then again after his second. He was placed on the throne by the victorious allies and his coronation took place in Paris. Lieutenant Louis attended the coronation, but only as an onlooker and there he saw someone he recognised from the early days of the Revolution. Standing at the front of the crowd was an elderly man with shoulder length white hair. It was Henri Sanson, the executioner who had cut off the heads of Louis XVI and Marie Antoinette – and many more besides. He kept a low profile. Was he regretting his part in the Revolution and glad to see another Bourbon King regain the throne of France? No one recognised Henri Sanson except Louis.

Louis had made a request in 1859 to go with the ex-emperor to St Helena and help to look after him there. He was now a fully grown man but missed his friend, Pierre. Life had to go on however and caring for Bonaparte was very important to him. He looked upon him as a mentor and almost a friend, but the master/servant relationship had never changed. Louis reported to his master what he had seen in Paris and told him of the irony of again seeing the executioner who'd played a significant part in making it possible for Bonaparte to rule France and much of Europe as well.

A few years passed and Louis stayed with his master, this time on Saint Helena. He played cards with him, read to him and played chess. Bonaparte was very good at games and Louis rarely won. One afternoon, the two men were involved in a game of chess, when Napoleon suddenly asked, "Why have you stayed with me for all these years, Louis? You're still a young man and could make a life for yourself in Paris? You could maybe meet a young lady whose charms you would love? Answer me, Louis – I don't want you to end your days here with me in isolation."

"*Sire*, Paris would not be the same without you and I would be most unhappy. Anyway, I don't think I could trust you on your own, you'd neglect your health." The two had a good relationship; they'd been together for so many years. To change the subject, Louis asked a question, "Why don't you ask for this bedroom of yours to be re-decorated. This dull green flocked wallpaper is so depressing?"

"I need not wallpaper to depress me; I have enough reason to be depressed with all I've gained and then lost in my life. Europe was quite a challenge, wasn't it but I did quite well, didn't I?" And he laughed. But Louis saw no humour in what the great man said.

"You would have won the Battle at Waterloo but for those damned countries forming a coalition. You were a greater General than Wellington – he was just lucky."

"No, my boy, he too was a great General but God was obviously more on his side than on mine. Check mate!" And of course, he won the game.

His health however was failing and he had severe stomach problems. He took to his bed and his two most trustworthy servants, one being Louis, looked after him hand and foot. One night, however, he seemed more tired than usual and his aid-de-camp came to see him, as he had to send regular reports about the prisoner to the governments in Paris and in Great Britain.

"*Sire*, what ails you this evening, you are usually jollier than this?" the aid-de-camp asked. Actually, it had been many years since Napoleon had been jolly but knew the man was just trying to cheer him up. He sat up in bed suddenly and pointed to the back of the bedroom.

"Who are those people standing there? They look like a King and Queen – are they that damned Bourbon couple who were executed? By God, I believe they are. Who invited them here? I don't want them here." And his head dropped again onto the pillow. Louis moved forward and held a cup of water to his master's lips, but the man couldn't manage to swallow. Louis had to dampen a cloth in the water and hold it against the dying man's lips. There was no doubt that the great man had taken a turn for the worse.

Louis leaned over the bed and whispered in the unhearing ear, "Is there anything you want, *Sire*? Just say and I will fetch it.

For a split second, Napoleon met his eyes and said quite clearly, "Look, look over there...I see my good Josephine..." And he fell back on the pillows, half closed his eyes and breathed his last.

It was the 5th of May and the moment was 5.49 pm. Everyone left the room and a priest was sent for but of course, arrived too late to give him his Last Rights. After the doctor had declared the great Napoleon Bonaparte dead, the two most loyal servants took the body from the bed. They washed him with water and cologne and shaved the light growth from his face. They then redressed him in fresh, fine clothes and placed him gently back on the newly made bed. They tidied the room, as there would be people who would want to reassure themselves that the ex-Emperor was dead.

Before leaving the room, however, Louis knelt at the side of the bed and prayed for the greatest man he'd ever known. What Bonaparte had accomplished from the age of 16 was nothing short of a miracle. Now the miracle was over. The little street urchin had remained with his General and had been privileged to hear the last words spoken by the great man.

When Dreams Become an Obsession

The guard almost smiled at her as he turned the key in the lock and pushed open the big, creaking door of the prison. She almost smiled back but thought better of it and stepped outside with her small case in her hand. She took a deep breath and exhaled loudly.

The first day of the rest of my life, she thought and started to walk towards the bus stop which must have been used by many other ex-inmates. At the bus stop, she stood alone and felt very obvious. Anyone standing at this bus stop had probably come from only one place and she looked back at the ominous, grey building that had been her home for the past ten years. The bus came to a stop in front of her and she hesitated, waiting for a guard to tell her to get on board. Of course, there were no guards around. She was free and still had the rest of her three score years and ten to live. She promised herself she would spend the time well and meet the future with enthusiasm.

The bus drew off and she knew she'd have to watch for her stop. She'd been given an address where she could stay until she'd found a place of her own. It was a kind of hostel and housed people from all walks of life. She opened her small handbag and took out an official looking letter given her by the prison governor, just after he'd shaken her hand and wished her luck for the future. She almost whistled as she read the letter again. What a lot of money the State was going to give her and she'd use it to do exactly what she wanted. She did realise though that she deserved it. After all, she spent the last ten years of her life locked behind bars with her only exercise, being a daily walk in the prison yard. And the sick irony was that she'd been innocent of the crime of which she'd been accused. Luckily, some man had come forward to tell he'd seen the murder happen, it was done by another man – and so she was given her freedom. No one knew the name of who'd committed the crime – nor where he lived.

She'd been 25 years old when she was arrested by the police and taken to the station for questioning. Despite her repeated denials that she'd been anywhere near the small corner shop on the night in question, they didn't believe her and after several months whilst awaiting trial, she ended up as a prisoner with a twenty-five-year sentence hanging over her head. Although it had taken a long time, it also seemed like a very short time for her life to change so dramatically. She remembered being taken down the steep courtroom steps to her cell below. She knew she was shouting. She could hear her own voice screaming that she didn't do it, that she wasn't anywhere near there on the night in question. No one listened however and she found herself again a prisoner with no future and probably no life for a very long time indeed.

Jane folded the letter and placed it securely back in her bag. She had been thinking of this moment for many years, it was what kept her going when she felt particularly low. She knew she had an obsession about finding the man who'd actually committed the crime – but that was for the future. In the meantime, the money would help tremendously of course and she smiled, despite her situation. Still, it was a better situation than she'd been in a few days before. The bus driver called out to her, "Your stop, Miss. You get off here." Jane did as she was told, something she'd got into the habit of doing over the past few years. She stood alone on the pavement holding her small suitcase. The building opposite must be the hostel so she crossed the street towards it. The big door looked uninviting but she rang the doorbell anyway and a grey-haired woman appeared and opened the door.

"Hello, dear. You're our new one, aren't you? Come on in and I'll show you your room." She seemed quite nice and Jane thought, *Well, nothing too bad so far* and she followed the woman inside. She had to follow her up two flights of stairs, her case getting heavier all the time.

"This is your room, dear." And she showed Jane into a small room. The room was rather empty but it was clean and she wasn't sharing with anyone else. *A room all of my own,* she thought and thanked her escort by holding out her hand. The woman took her hand and said she hoped Jane would be comfortable here. "Dinner is at eight o'clock and if you miss dinner, I'm afraid you'll just have to go hungry." She smiled and left her alone. Miss Sedgewick was the woman's name and she was the housekeeper of the hostel.

She sat on the bed and put her case on a small table in the middle of the room. She knew it was a cliché but couldn't help thinking, *Tomorrow is another day, a new day.* And she started unpacking the case which only took a few minutes as she had so few clothes. She suddenly felt brave and cautiously went back down the stairs to the lobby. There was the housekeeper's office and she knocked softly on the door.

"Yes?" a voice boomed out and the door was flung open. There stood another woman whose face was covered in a red and very big birthmark. It was quite disfiguring and Jane almost recoiled. The birthmark was pink and purple in colour and covered nearly all of her face. She managed, however, to stutter out a request for a front door and room key, explaining that she'd just arrived, but wanted to go out for some fresh air.

"You're in a bit of a rush, aren't you?" And she turned back into the room, barking out an instruction to someone else. "Give this woman her keys, will you?" And Mrs Sedgewick appeared at the door, keys dangling from her hand.

"Now don't forget dinner at eight. Enjoy your walk." And she closed the door very firmly.

Jane strolled towards the park which was pretty and quite large. Oh, how wonderful it was to breathe the fresh air and know that she need never go to that prison again. She'd been accused of killing a young man who served behind the counter in a corner shop. His name had been Ali and she'd spoken with him several times, as she often popped in to get something she needed. He was very pleasant and always had a lovely and very white smile on his face. He could only have been about eighteen when he died and he'd been serving alone behind the counter one evening. It was about ten o'clock and Jane realised she'd run out of milk and wouldn't have any for breakfast next day. Although the shop was only a few yards from her flat, it was January and very cold outside. She put on her warmest coat and ran down the stairs. The lights were still bright in the shop window and Jane knew she was lucky; she'd just catch the shop before it closed.

She didn't notice the two figures who were already in the shop but when she tried to pay Ali for the milk, he backed away from her and shook his head. She turned then and saw the men with scarves around their faces and one was pointing a large knife at her. She started to talk but found her voice wouldn't work.

Ali said, "Go, Miss Jane. You go now." And he came out from behind the counter and made to push her back out of the door but she suddenly felt a hard crack across the front of her head and she fell to the floor unconscious. She knew nothing after that until a policeman bending over her managed to bring her around. And that was that. That was how she found herself in a prison with a twenty-five-year sentence hanging over her. She had been found with a bloody

283

knife in her hand, covered with Ali's blood. There had apparently been no one else there and she was the only suspect. The case against her was pretty strong and both Jury and Judge found her guilty of the crime. She'd only come out for a pint of milk and her life had changed by 360%.

Sitting on a bench in the park now, she could hardly believe the last ten years had happened, but they had. She looked up to the sunny sky and marvelled at the blueness between the clouds. She'd bought a bag of rolls from a local bakery and she broke pieces off to throw to the ducks in the pond. It really was the first day of the rest of her life and she meant to make the most of it. She shook thoughts of the real murderer out of her head. A very old man shuffled towards her and asked if he could share the bench. She moved over to make room for him and he gratefully sat down. They made the usual small talk about the weather and then, he sighed deeply.

"Are you okay?" she asked him, putting her hand on his sleeve.

"Oh, I'm all right my dear, just rather sad. I don't have long to live now and I've never been on a cruise ship. It's something my wife and I always promised ourselves, but she died two years ago and I know I won't be long behind her." He had tears in his eyes.

"Why don't you go now, you still can? They'll even arrange for a car to pick you up and take you to the port and there'll be lots of people there to help you." Jane thought how sad he looked.

"I can't do that I'm afraid," he replied, "I've no more money now. I had to use my savings to bury my wife and I gave her a good funeral, I really did." He was getting to his feet, perhaps realising he'd said too much to the stranger.

Jane was thinking quickly and she stood up too. "Will you meet me exactly here in a week's time? I've got rather a lot to do over the next few days but if you'll meet me, I may have a proposition for you. Will you be here?" He told her he would and left the park then. Jane sat on for quite a long time, working things out in her mind. She knew what she was going to do, and she'd waste no time setting it up.

She had enough money to last for years and to buy herself a comfortable place to live. She chose a newly built apartment on the ground floor of a large complex, which she would not only have as her home but also use as an office for the business she planned. It was a brand-new apartment, so clean and so fresh and being on the ground floor, so easy for clients to find. She arranged for an advert to be placed in the local newspaper which read:

'Feeling a bit blue and sad and in need of an adventure?

Call this number and make an appointment to come and see me

Between us, we'll make sure you get that adventure

The fee for my services is small, only £20 per person

I'll meet all the other costs.

She placed her new number in the advert and set about furnishing her new home, whilst she waited for someone to call. She made the apartment modern and yet comfortable with one very efficient looking room for her clients. But she knew she mustn't forget to meet the old gentleman, whom she hoped would be her first client. In fact, there he was waiting for her on the bench in the park. She went up to him and sat down beside him. She had a large, brown envelope under her arm. When they'd first met, he'd introduced himself as Edmund Parker and even told her his age and where he lived. Enough information for her to prepare for this meeting with him.

"Well, my dear, and how have you been since we last spoke?" He produced a paper bag of sweets from his pocket and offered her a humbug. She took it gratefully and popped it in her mouth and they sat there for a few minutes in companionable silence. When her sweet had gone, she smiled at him and held out the brown envelope.

"But you can't take it until you've given me £20. You can afford that, can't you?"

"I can my dear but not much more than that, I'm afraid." He fumbled in his pocket and handed her two ten-pound notes. She gave him the envelope which contained cruise tickets, some health insurance and a sizeable fist of money.

She explained, "Normally, I would only conduct business from my office but you are my first client, so I'm making an exception. The cruise leaves the port in two weeks and you must be aboard. You said it was the one thing you'd wanted to do with your wife, but alas that wasn't to be. You will have to go on the cruise on your own. Is that a problem?"

He started to remonstrate with her, saying he couldn't accept such generosity, but she shushed him and went on, "There's only one thing you must promise me. You'll be home in about three weeks and the first thing I want you to do, is to visit me at this address." And she gave him her business card. Edmund was speechless and just kept staring at her. She left him then and waved goodbye, adding, "Now remember you must come to see me on your return." He nodded and walked off in a daze.

On her return to the apartment, she spotted a middle-aged woman sitting in the small waiting room. She smiled at her and told her she'd only be a few minutes before she could see her. The woman just nodded but didn't smile. Jane made some coffee and fetched an unopened packet of Custard Creams – everyone's favourite – then went out of her office and asked the woman to come in. The woman moved slowly, she walked with the aid of two walking sticks and seemed to find it difficult to stand up. Before saying anything, Jane gave the woman the coffee and biscuits. She could sense her client's discomfort at being there at all. In fact, before saying anything, the woman burst into tears. She had sat down awkwardly in the chair opposite Jane.

"I feel such a fool coming to you. I'm sure there's nothing you can do for me. In fact, perhaps I had just better go now." And she made to leave. But she moved slowly and fell back down again on the chair.

"Why don't we have our coffee and biscuits and then we can decide if there's anything I can do for you." Jane tried to be as soothing as she could and sat back in her chair, cup in hand. She asked the woman, "What is your dearest wish, one you've had for a long time? And remember, anything you tell me is in the strictest confidence and only I will ever know what you say."

The woman gulped and said, "My name is Maisie Roberts and I'm forty years of age. I know I look older but I've always looked older than my age, it's these blasted sticks you see, they've always made me look old. I contracted Polio when I was a child and was never able to walk unaided after that. Do you understand what that's been like? All through my childhood, teenage years and adult life I've felt like a freak. You can't do anything about that, can you?" And she almost smiled but the smile didn't reach her eyes. She couldn't hide her bitterness, and Jane completely understood that.

"I may not be able to heal your condition but I would like to try to make you feel better about yourself. That's what I'm here for, you know. I've set myself up as a counsellor cum confidant and my main interest in life is to try to help people. Now tell me about that dream you've always had. You never know, I may be able to help."

And out it all poured, her self-disgust and lack of confidence. Her misery when she has to go someplace new where people don't know her. How she would have liked to be the same as other people and marry and have children, but no one had ever shown any interest in her. Her one big wish and she looked embarrassed at telling this to Jane, was to go to the Edinburgh Castle Tattoo with a handsome, uniformed soldier as her escort. "I know it doesn't sound much but for someone in my position, I assure you it is. I don't have the money and I can't travel on my own very well and I certainly don't know any handsome soldier to take my arm." The tears were different now, not loud but more subdued. They seemed more intense than her initial outburst.

"Well, at least I know what's wrong now. The first thing I'm going to do is make some plans. It'll take me a few days and then I'll either ring you or write." Maisie volunteered that she didn't have a phone but she could always ring Jane from a call box.

"That's okay but I'll need a few details from you so I can arrange things." And Jane set about collecting the information she needed. Closing her office that day and going into her living room, Jane felt very sad for the woman. What a little thing to ask as your big wish. Having her supper, she made plans for the woman and set down her step-by-step plan for Maisie Roberts.

The middle-aged woman was dressed in her favourite, lilac dress and wore a cream jacket on top. She stood by the window in her flat and watched anxiously for a taxi to draw up, but it wasn't a taxi, it was a big blue BMW car that stopped outside and a very smart man got out. He was an Army Captain and was in full military uniform. In fact, he was the most handsome man she'd ever seen. He stood for a few moments, looking up and down the street, before crossing to Maisie's front door and ringing the doorbell. She hesitated inside. Could she find the courage to open the door? There was no option, she couldn't just ignore him. She looked again in the mirror and made up her mind to do it. He really was a handsome man, not too young, perhaps about 35 or thereabouts. Tall and well built, he nodded his head slightly and asked if she was Maisie. He held out his hand and escorted her to his car, where he settled her beside him in the front seat.

"We're on our way to the airport, Maisie, but then you probably know that." His smile showed amazingly white teeth and now that he'd removed his hat, she could see he had well-cut and very blond hair.

"Yes, I've been told that and also that I was to be ready on time for your arrival." She managed to say.

"And so you were." He laughed and touched her hand gently.

She had never flown in a plane before and he had to help her with the boarding procedure. They were travelling 'First Class' although she wasn't aware of it, just aware of how well they were being treated. She'd also received special treatment in boarding the plane because of her use of walking sticks. She felt very privileged, more than the other passengers. They arrived at Edinburgh Airport where another BMW was waiting for Jeremy her escort, and she got into the car as though in a dream.

"We're going straight to the hotel where we'll be staying two nights. The Edinburgh Military Tattoo doesn't end till almost eleven o'clock and Jane thought that too late to travel back the same night," he explained, as he manoeuvred through the traffic.

The hotel was very smart and luxurious and the porter showed them to their rooms. Maisie looked around at the most beautiful room she'd ever seen. It was all silk and brocade with a lovely suite of furniture that matched the décor. Tea things were waiting for her and she poured herself a cup. She felt very special.

After a splendid dinner that night, they both retired to their rooms, Jeremy kissing her hand as he left her outside her door. He really was a gentleman. How had Jane arranged all this, she thought? She must be a magician.

After breakfast next morning, they went out of the hotel to find their car waiting for them and they made their way up The Royal Mile, passed the statue of Sir Walter Scott and arrived at the castle itself. They had the most expensive tickets on sale and were escorted to a private coffee room where they could wait until they were ready for the first demonstration of the Tattoo. Jeremy explained to her that the name of 'tattoo' actually came from the beating of soldiers' drums. He was so easy to talk to, she thought. He had a good sense of humour but also a sensitive and caring side to his nature. Not once had he even mentioned her sticks, just made allowances where necessary. They laughed and cheered as the military bands began to perform. They stopped for a light lunch in the castle itself, only for respected guests of course.

After the Tattoo ended and it was a very long day, the streets of Edinburgh were buzzing with people and he had to help her through the crowds. Nothing was too much trouble for him, it seemed. For a moment, she imagined she was the young girl she once was, with no need of sticks. It had been a wonderful day.

Next day, on the flight home, they sat together like old friends and he told her what a great time he'd had, she'd been a wonderful companion. Again, his car was waiting at the airport and he drove her home. He helped her to her door, carrying her small case and deposited her inside. He saluted her and bent to kiss her cheek.

"Goodbye, Jeremy, and thank you for a wonderful time. I'll never forget it." And she closed the door as he drove off. She'd never see him again; she knew but she'd fulfilled her greatest wish and that was what mattered.

Jeremy called at Jane's office two days later to collect his wages for a job well done. "How did she seem when you left her?" she asked him. He was a very pleasant chap and was happy to take on special acting jobs, such as Maisie.

"She seemed very happy and I played my part of an Army captain to perfection, although I say so myself. At first, she'd been rather sad but soon brightened as the Edinburgh atmosphere got to her. I have to say I enjoyed myself too." He left with his money secure in his pocket.

On his way out, he noticed a pretty, young blond girl in the waiting room and wondered if she would need an acting role from him. Before inviting the girl into the office, Jane quickly opened the day's post and was surprised to find a letter from Maisie, thanking her for arranging the Edinburgh trip. The letter then went on for a couple of long paragraphs.

I hope you'll understand why I have to end it all. I believer in the words of the Bible and I want you to read this list:

After being baptised by John the Baptist, Jesus fasted for 40 days and nights

Following the ten plagues visited by God on Egypt, Moses led the children of Israel out of the country and spent 40 days and nights wandering in the desert

It was 40 days from Jesus's resurrection until his ascension

Lent requires 40 days and nights of fasting

Following Noah's death, it rained for 40 days and nights until the highest mountains were covered by 15 cubits and man was no longer alive on the earth.

I am very religious and the number 40 is of great significance. I am 40 years old and I have no wishes left because I've just spent the most perfect time of my life with Jeremy in Edinburgh – and that's all thanks to you. I'll be dead by the time you read this but don't be sad for me, I'm really happy.

Bless you Jane, I know I do.
Maisie

Jane folded the letter and put it in her desk drawer. If she'd known Maisie was so close to taking her own life, she would have done things differently, but it was too late now. She stood up and straightened her back before going into the waiting room and inviting the blond girl into her office. She was a very lovely girl with long blond hair and the most gorgeous eyes Jane had ever seen. Jane went behind her desk and sat down. Looking straight at the girl, she noticed for the first time that an elderly man had come into the office behind her. She knew him. He was the man for whom she'd arranged a cruise only a few weeks before – he didn't acknowledge her but just stood there, ramrod straight.

"Would your companion like to sit as well? There's another chair in the corner?" Jane asked.

"My companion? Who are you talking about?" I've come to see you because I promised someone I would. And here I am." She shook her hair from her face and smiled at Jane.

"Perhaps we'd better start the beginning and you tell me why you've come here."

"My name is Violet and I'm only recently married. I was widowed only a week later but one of the last things my husband asked me to do, was to come and see you. Apparently, you were very kind to him and he wanted me to tell you how grateful he was."

Jane looked up at the old man and recognised her very first client. He'd been called Edmund Parker but now he was dead, and yet here he was, standing behind the young woman. He nodded his head slightly when Jane was told how grateful he was. The woman took up the story again. "We met each other on the cruise and were immediately attracted to each other. A few days into the cruise, he asked me to be his wife and I agreed. The ship's captain married us in the large dining room and that's where we had our wedding reception. Unfortunately, he only lived for three days after that and I had to bring his body back to this country." She had the grace to let a tear fall from her eyes and slide down her face but Jane could tell she wasn't really upset.

"I am very sorry to hear that, Mrs Parker – I presume that's your name? Edmund was a really nice man and I was glad to meet him." Jane was genuinely sorry, but on looking at the ghostly figure standing in the room, she felt a smile coming to her mouth, as he was already smiling at her.

"He pretended he had money but it turns out, he didn't. Mind you, he did have a big, beautiful house which he owned outright. There'll be a pretty penny coming from that. It's in the solicitor's hands now and I'm just waiting to hear from him. He had no relatives, you know. I was his only one and I'm to inherit the lot." She preened like a cat, which caused Edmund to smile again.

"Well, thank you for coming to tell me, Mrs Parker. I really appreciate it. Where will you live when the house has sold?" she enquired.

"Oh, I'll have plenty of money, don't you worry. It's not as if I knew him well, after all we'd only just met. I feel just slightly guilty as I made him eat lots and come dancing every night until he was exhausted. Some people actually suggested I should let him rest, amazing how cheeky some people can be, don't you think?" She stood up intending to leave.

"I'll be off now as I only came because he told me to. Well, I've done my duty, so Goodbye."

And she was off, with Edmund following behind her, but he stopped at the door and turned to Jane. "I'll soon catch up with her but I'm so glad to see you again. You gave me hope when I was at my lowest and I really did enjoy the cruise and even marrying my new wife. I knew she thought I was well off so I let her believe it. She's got my house now but I don't really care. She's in for a shock 'cause I'm going to stick by her whatever she does or wherever she goes. I am her shadow forever. I've got to go on having fun now and I'll find that amusing. Now you take care and keep up the good work." And he disappeared into thin air.

Jane smiled and made herself a cup of tea. That girl was going to have a difficult time and soon, she'd know that Edmund was with her all the time. He'd enjoy that as he'd spotted her as a gold digger as soon as he met her. Still, he had some fun at the end of his life.

Jeremy turned up early next day with a newspaper. "Have you seen this, Jane? Maisie killed herself. What made her do that? I feel really sad about that. She was a nice woman."

"Don't grieve too much, Jeremy." And she told him about the letter she'd received from Maisie. "You gave her the best time she'd ever had and she decided there was nothing more to live for. You're obviously good at what you do."

Two days later, she attended Maisie's funeral and was surprised to meet Jeremy again, standing by the graveside with a bunch of yellow flowers in his hand. In fact, there were forty of them, he told Jane before quickly departing the scene, obviously upset.

On her return to the office, Jane walked into a bit of a lull in clients. She'd been busy since starting the business and had sorted out a few problems for people, but nothing major nor costly. She felt good about what she was doing and was fully committed to helping people. In the corner of the waiting room was a rather unusual man. He was short and very round with a baldhead and round spectacles with very thick lenses. Jane smiled at him and said, "Now how can I help?" She was still in her funeral clothes and felt rather dismal so she removed the jacket. Underneath, there was a pure white blouse, making her look more cheerful. "Would you care for a coffee or tea? It'll only take a minute to boil the kettle?"

She wanted to make him feel less uncomfortable as that was how he looked. He accepted gratefully and joined her in her office.

He was dressed rather oddly too. His suit was two sizes too small and he had a red spotted bow tie around his neck. They drank in silence and he refused her offer of a piece of sugary shortbread. Again, she asked him if she could help. At first, he had a stutter but as he spoke, it slowly disappeared.

"I want to go to Jamaica Inn in Cornwall and I want to sleep at the pub itself for at least two nights." He was looking at her as though he'd said something quite mad. Jane pointed out that wasn't an unusual request and that people had asked for far more difficult things.

"Why don't you just go to Cornwall? It wouldn't be too difficult; do you drive and have a car?" Jane asked innocently.

"Oh I can't do that, you know, not arrange everything by myself. Your advert said you would help me if I needed help. Well, I need help. Look at me, I know what I look like, people laugh at me and call me names. Names like 'The Wobbly Man' and 'Four eyes pig', I can't face the world by myself. Will you help me? I spent ages plucking up the courage to come to see you and the first thing you tell me is 'go away and do it yourself'. Well, I can't go on my own but I desperately want to spend a couple of nights at the famous Daphne Du Maurier Inn."

Jane came around the desk and put her arm around his shoulder. "Of course, I'll help you if that's what you want." And she immediately picked up the phone and booked a room for two nights for the following week. Then she arranged his train journey and for a taxi to pick him up at the Cornish station.

"You know I can't come with you, don't you? I have to stay here and do my work." He looked pitiful at this and then knew he had to do some of it himself. After all, she was doing everything else for him. His name was Horace Penfold and he gave her all the details she asked for. He was a Civil Servant and worked for the Ministry of Agriculture and Fisheries. "Not very exciting, I know, but there you are."

He climbed down from the train the next week and lifted his small suitcase. Two schoolboys were waiting on the platform and they were sniggering at him but he chose to ignore them and spotted his taxi waiting outside. He was very pleased with himself when he heard himself saying, "Jamaica Inn please." And off they went. The inn was everything he'd hoped it would be, from the great wooden rafters and flagstones in the bar area and outside, there still was the horse mounting block that must have been there since the inn was first built. His room was small with only a bed and a chest of drawers. Someone had put some flowers on the window ledge and they looked welcoming against the floral curtains. He took off his thick glasses and lay down on the bed. *Ah, this was pure heaven*, he thought.

He dined in the bar that night and as he climbed the stairs to bed, the landlord said. "Now don't 'e worry 'bout the tales you've 'eard, Jamaica Inn'baint 'aunted. Well only on some nights, but not all the time." And he tugged his forelock to Horace and said, "G'night." Horace said goodnight to him and for such a big man, went up the stairs at an alarming speed. His room looked cosy and someone had turned down the covers. In his pyjamas, he brought out a book which would help him fall asleep, he was sure. Maybe he shouldn't have chosen one about witches and ghosts. "Bad choice, Horace," he said out loud, just to hear a voice in the room. He did actually fall asleep quite quickly but could still hear strange noises outside the room, so he stuffed his head between two pillows and that seemed to do the trick.

He began to dream of pirates and found himself on board a big ship which was being tossed and turned by the wild waves of a turbulent sea. All the men were running to and fro to try to save the ship and then someone spotted a fire on the land. "A Beacon," they shouted to each other, "it's a beacon to steer us into calmer waters." At least that's what they thought but the fire on the shore was to guide them onto the worst rocks on that bit of coast. It was an old trick and Horace had heard of it before. He tried to tell the other sailors it was a trick but everyone was too upset to listen. A loud crack suddenly seemed to rip the ship open and the sea gushed into the hold of the ship, washing many of the men out to sea where they disappeared beneath the waves. They were getting close to the shoreline and Horace could see many of the local people scrabbling along the beach, waiting to gather what they could salvage from the wreck. Bodies were everywhere and Horace himself was scared to death.

Then he woke up and he was sweating so much that he thought for a moment he really had been at sea. He was gulping for air and sat bolt upright in bed. All the noises had stopped and strangely enough, he didn't feel afraid. He was safe after all. Next morning, he had a sumptuous breakfast before he went walking across the heath. He'd bought Daphne Du Maurier's book about Jamaica Inn and although he'd read it before, he sat down on a stone wall and started to read it again. It really was a good book.

He got back to the inn about six o'clock and went up to his room for a rest. He'd been told dinner was at eight so he had plenty of time for a snooze before he went downstairs. When he eventually woke up, the landlord had a large brandy waiting for him and a wonderful roast dinner. He wasn't the only guest staying there that night but the people didn't engage him in conversation. *Oh dear, his short break was almost over*, he thought and asked the landlord if he knew any stories about the inn. Of course, the landlord did. Every time, he was asked this, the landlord added something more to the tale and made it seem even more scary.

"An' that were the end o' old Peter," he concluded. "Peter was always a trouble maker an' liked to scare folks. One night, 'e overdid it though an' two young fellers followed 'im to 'is home an' slit 'is throat. Well, what do ye' make o' that then?" Horace didn't know what to say so he just said Goodnight and left the bar.

There was such a commotion out in the yard and it woke up Horace. Crossing to the window, he saw several men in the yard, manhandling barrels of what smelt like rum from a horse driven cart. The horses were neighing and rearing up as the shouting got even louder. The men were roughly dressed and looked just like the pirates he'd read about in the book that day. They weren't just unloading barrels but what looked like great boxes with tobacco spilling out of them. One of the men shouted, "Mind what yer doing, Fred, that's good money yer' a-wastin'." Fred took umbrage at being told how to do things and hit the man full in the face. Suddenly, they were all at it, punching, swearing and kicking each other. They argued about who owned what. The goods were only being hidden in the inn until the pirates could sort everything out later. They couldn't do it so soon after the wreck had happened and the excise men were still on the prowl. They were a pretty evil looking bunch with scarred faces, cutlasses and knives hanging from their belts. Horace felt no compunction to get closer to them and see how much stuff they were hiding in the cellars of the inn. It was an amazing thought to someone like Horace. These men had first lured a ship onto the rocks and then ignored the plight of the drowning sailors. It was the next part of his earlier dream and many of the local people had done exactly the same as the pirates.

Now, things had got rather serious and Horace his behind the curtain but could still see everything that was happening. Three men were dragging another one across the yard and covering his head with a sackcloth. They pushed him up onto the mounting block and threw a rope around the top bar. The other end they tied round his head and pushed his body off the high mounting block. The man kicked for a while but then just dangled there. They'd just hanged a man in cold blood before turning and finishing the unloading of the contraband goods. Horace was deeply shocked but too scared to do anything about it. Of course, he'd tell the landlord in the morning but that was when it was safer in the morning light, instead of dark clouds and a frosty moon. He might be a coward but he was a realist too.

After a very few hours' sleep, Horace crossed to the window to see how things were developing in the Inn yard. Nothing looked any different from the day he'd arrived there. There were no pirates nor horses and there was no man hanging from the bar above the mounting block. Where had he gone? Everything had been tidied away and the only thing he saw was the landlord pushing a milk churn into the inn. Obviously, he told the landlord all about what he'd seen going on during the night, but he found the man to be totally disinterested. In fact, he said, "Anybody who stays here always see somethin' strange and t'othe night, t'was your turn."

"They hanged a man after putting a bag over his head. No remorse at all. They were all fighting one minute and then dragging the man along the ground the next. It was a terrible thing to see." But still the landlord paid him no attention. Horace paid his bill with the money Jane had given him and phoned for the taxi to take him to the train station. It had already been prepaid.

Soon he was back in his own hometown and as he'd booked the next day off work, he decided to go see Jane and tell her what had happened. Luckily, she had no clients when he arrived.

"Jane, it was fantastic, the inn was just like I'd imagined it and do I have a story to tell you!"

He then told her everything, just as he'd tried to do with the Inn landlord. "The first night was exciting too, but I think it was only a dream. At least I know now how it feels to be on a sinking ship and somehow managing to live. But the second night was no dream – it all happened right before my eyes. I can't thank you enough for organising things for me, I'll never forget those two nights in Jamaica Inn. I even read Daphne Du Maurier's book in the wild countryside a couple of miles away from the inn. It was amazing and better than the first time I'd read it." He was so excited; he was almost crying and the strange thing was that he didn't look as odd as he'd done before. He looked almost normal.

He went away then, saying as he closed the door, "I have nothing else to wish for now. My dream came true." Jane made herself some tea and then sat at her desk with a quizzical look on her face. She was glad he'd enjoyed it so much but all she'd actually arranged was the transport and the inn itself. All of the dramatic happenings he described could only have been his imagination. Or was it? He was so full of everything, right down to the minutest detail and the horror on his face when he described how the pirates had hanged a man, was quite amazing. He had 'lived it'. He couldn't have described it the way he had if he hadn't been part of the happenings, but who could have arranged it? Certainly not anyone she'd asked!

To Horace, however, it had all happened just as he described it and it would be in his mind forever. His attention wasn't on his immediate surroundings however and as he reached the offices where he worked, he stepped off the pavement in the path of a fast-approaching bus. Poor Horace didn't even see it. His thick spectacles lay in the gutter and his bow tie had got twisted around his neck, almost like a hangman's noose. He was no more. The ambulance came and took him away. All the people from his office block came out to see what had happened but what they didn't know – as they pointed and tutted in sympathy – was that Horace had died a happy man, a man very much fulfilled in life. He'd had his biggest wish granted and then some. To Horace, it had all happened. It was his story and he would stick to it. Jane was sad however and began to think she was responsible for killing off many of her clients, unintentionally of course.

But the next few years passed, happily with no other deaths. Well, none that she knew of. Most wishes were rather mundane. 'I've never played a round of golf: I want to be escorted to a show at the London Palladium: I want to see inside Buckingham Palace and the Changing of the Guard.' These wishes were easy to grant and she thoroughly enjoyed doing it, especially when people came back to tell her how wonderful it had been. She felt she was doing a good job, and she got on with it. Jeremy was very involved with her enterprises and played many parts in her schemes, all intending to make the clients' dreams come true. She paid him handsomely for his efforts but knew she was getting value for money.

She was walking in the park one day when the thought she'd soon be 40 years old, suddenly struck her. Her thoughts immediately moved on to Maisie, her second client and she felt a great sadness, remembering how the woman had taken her own life. She had been obsessed by the number 40 and because her age was 40 when she died, Jane felt rather uncomfortable, but she shook her head and told herself not to be silly. It had all just been a coincidence; she was sure. She began then to think about what her greatest wish was. What did she want more than anything else in life? It had been the same wish for many years now but she could never bring herself to utter the words. It was most unlikely to ever happen.

She came out of the park and bought some pretty flowers from the florists on the corner. They would brighten the office and perhaps lift her sombre mood. She was arranging them in the waiting room when the door opened and a man came in. He was about 30 years of age and looked like a down-and-out with long greasy hair and scruffy trainers. Not her usual kind of client. She smiled at him and asked if she could help him – she knew she mustn't judge by appearance.

"Are you the person who advertises her services to people who need help?" he asked.

"I am she. My name is Jane." And she indicated that he should come into the privacy of her office. He hesitated and then did, sitting on the chair opposite her desk.

"Now tell me about yourself. Would you like a cup of tea or coffee perhaps?" She always felt this put people at their ease, but he refused the drink. To give him some time, she went over to the kettle. "Well I'm having one." Cup in hand, she settled at her desk and waited. She knew he'd start talking soon, and sure enough, he started talking very fast.

"When I was young, about 18, I did something very wrong and it's plagued my conscience ever since then. I wondered about seeking help from the church and after a few months, I finally plucked up courage to go to the Catholic Church where they do confessions. I'm not a Catholic but I didn't think they'd know the difference. One sinner is much like another, don't you think?" And he smiled at Jane.

"Well, I don't think that's strictly true but let's not dwell on that. What happened in the Confessional at the church?"

"Before I could even tell the priest about my sin, I realised I recognised him, older yes, but still the same boy I knew when I was young. I found I couldn't tell him why I was there and left the room quickly, saying I'd come back later. I walked about the streets for a couple of hours and then found myself back outside the same church. The young priest was still on duty and invited me in to talk with him. This time, I stayed and talked my head off, but didn't actually come out with the exact story of what I'd done." The man was sweating now and Jane fetched him a glass of water. She still didn't know what he wanted with her.

"Go on, Brian," she said.

"I recognised the priest as the boy who'd come with me on a job when we were both young. We broke into a corner shop to steal the takings. I knifed the young man behind the counter and then hit a woman over the head when she burst into the shop demanding milk. I hadn't meant to kill the young man but I did. I must have gone into some vital organ; he bled all over the floor. The woman had fallen on the floor when my mate hit her and her forehead was bleeding. It all happened so fast and the irony was that there was no money in the till. He'd already cashed up for the night. My mate and I left the shop very quickly and left the two bodies in the shop. But I did something then that has lived with me ever since... I pressed the knife into the woman's hand and made sure it stayed there. She was arrested for killing the young man called Ali and she could provide no evidence she hadn't done it. She was found guilty at trial and went to prison for twenty-odd years. Me and my mate split then and kept a low profile or many years until last week, when I met him as a priest in the Confessional Box. It was a shock I can tell you." He said all of this in a broken voice and with a lot of stuttering. He was completely exhausted when he'd finished.

Jane had just sat there quietly but knew she had to say something. "What is it that you want of me? What can I do to help you?"

He just ignored her question and said, "I went to the church to make my confession, to see if my conscience would clear and all I got was to come face to face with my fellow murderer. A priest, I ask you! And do you know what he told me – apparently the woman who'd gone to prison had been released after only 10 years because *he'd only gone to the police and admitted what we'd done that night. He didn't know my second name so he couldn't tell the police but based on his evidence, she was released from the prison. He had to serve time in prison but at least his conscience was clear.* And do you know what I did then? I reached across the gap and put both my hands around his neck and squeezed and squeezed as hard as I could. Oh it felt good, I can tell you. I had to do it, you see, I'd given him my name when I first met him and I knew he'd go to the police with it. I had no option but to shut him up." He was really exhausted now and slumped forward in his chair. He looked up suddenly.

"I've come to you for help. I need to speak to the best counsellor in the country and I don't have the money to pay him. He will have to be sworn to secrecy as well. He takes some kind of oath, doesn't he?" His story was over and he looked at her with hope in his eyes. "Can you help me?"

Jane said, "Of course I can help you. Come back here in two days' time and I'll have set it all up by then." She was stunned but managed to remain calm. She sat for a long time after he'd left and thought about him. That man had ruined her life. He'd stolen 10 years from her and she'd never get it back. But then without the money she'd been awarded for wrongful imprisonment, she could never have helped all the people. "But he'd murdered a priest – the very priest who'd handed himself into the police and brought about her release from prison.' She spent the rest of that day pondering over what she should do and finally came to a decision.

The next morning after first dealing with a new client, she picked up the phone and dialled '999'. "Police please," she said and proceeded to tell her story. It was arranged for them to be in Jane's office at 3 o'clock the next afternoon when she'd already arranged to meet Brian. She'd been awake all night, thinking about the last fifteen years and she realised she'd helped a lot of people over that time but never thought about her own wishes and dreams. What would be her biggest wish? It was the same wish that she'd had since she heard her sentence being read out in court, all that time ago. She wished the police had searched more thoroughly for the two men who'd attacked Ali, but she'd been such an obvious perpetrator, she honestly believed they'd given up before they should have done. All these years she'd hated the two men and yet one had just turned up in her office and admitted everything he'd done. But then, he'd gone on and murdered the priest, the very priest who'd given up himself to the authorities and so made her release from prison possible after 10 years. She had no choice but to contact the police, she detested Brian and now realised it had always been her biggest wish, to hurt the man who'd hurt her more.

The next day was her birthday, a day she would never forget. She was nervous and couldn't stop nibbling her nails. She was 40 years of age but spent only 30 of them as a free human being. She knew she'd done the right thing and waited for the police to arrive. They came at 2 o'clock. There were two of them and they hid themselves in the stationery cupboard and kept very quiet. Her hands were shaking, in fact so were her knees. She was a nervous wreck. There was a tentative knock on her door and she called out, "Come in."

There he stood, the man who had affected her life so much and he was here to ask for her help. He'd killed young Ali and the priest and heavens only knew who else. He'd stolen 10 years of her life and had made sure she'd never gone to bed without thinking of him. Maybe after today, that would stop for her.

"How are you today, Brian?" she asked, not really caring.

"Have you arranged for a Counsellor for me – I have to get these thoughts out of my mind and you promised you'd help," he blurted out.

"Yes, I have and I'll give you the details in a moment. First of all though, let me sum up what you told me the other day." And she began to list his killing Ali all those years ago, how he'd also killed his fellow thief, who'd become a priest and was about to give the police Brian's details, which he'd learned in the Church Confessional. The irony was that because he'd heard it in the Confessional, the priest may never have told the police – but Brian didn't know that.

Jane asked him, "Didn't you feel any guilt about the woman who was sent to prison in your place?"

"No, I bloody didn't, silly cow. I've always had to look after myself – she should have done the same." Brian was losing patience.

"Well, you've not looked after yourself very well this time." Jane had waited years for this moment. "You're looking at that woman, Brian. I spent 10 years of my life in prison because of you." She stood up and opened the stationery cupboard and the police jumped out. Brian tried to get away but he was well and truly caught. Jane watched it all with the most enjoyment she'd ever felt in her life

"You Bitch." He spat the words at her as the police hustled him out of the office. A young policewoman came in then to see if she was all right. She made two cups of tea and sat beside the shaking woman.

Later on, she felt better and left the building, locking the door behind her. There he stood across the street, waiting for her. He was taking her for a birthday tea. He really was very good looking she thought and she was very proud to show him off as her companion. He took her hand and squeezed her fingers. "Happy Birthday, Darling," he whispered in her ear.

Just ahead and round the corner, a man was working high at the top of some scaffolding. As they reached the corner, the workman stumbled and fell against a large bucket of concrete he was using to point the wall bricks. It tottered on the edge and crashed to the ground. First it hit Jane on the head and shoulder and completely missed Jeremy. Of course, the man shouted "look out" but it was too late. Jane's head was bleeding profusely and a puddle was beginning to form around her. The builder had already phoned for an ambulance. For one second, her eyes flickered open and the hoarse whisper came out quite clearly.

"Today was my greatest wish...but once I'd had it...there was nothing left to live for... Fate takes over then." And her eyes closed slowly.

Jeremy heard the siren of the ambulance but knew it was too late for Jane, and he held her close for a few moments before she was taken from him forever. She was just about to enter a new phase of her life, but she'd wished too hard for what happened today and it had become an obsession that had never left her. An obsession that had somehow resulted in her losing her life, albeit it in a roundabout way. Fate had been waiting just around that corner!

Bluebells are Beautiful Except When...

She cycled past Bluebell Wood outside the village, wishing she had the time to stop and pick a bunch for old Mrs McCready – but they died so quickly, it seemed pointless. The month of June was always lovely and full of hope for the future – and the sun was high in the sky. She visited Mrs McCready twice a week and always took her a cream horn from the village bakery. She didn't know if the old lady looked forward more to the cake, than to her visit – but it didn't matter, as it seemed to cheer her up a lot. She'd been visiting the old lady for a couple of months now and they'd got to know each other really well. When she got to the cottage, the kettle was always on the boil and the china cups were on the table, waiting for the guest to arrive.

Mrs McCready lived in a small, isolated cottage near the woods. She'd lived there all her life and had shared it with her husband until he died – and then she was alone. Virginia had been given her name by the vicar when she offered her spare time to visit the elderly who lived alone, so here she was, on what must have been her tenth visit, cycling along to see the woman who'd become her friend. As she told the vicar, she'd always known Mrs McCready from when she was younger. She'd been a cleaner for her father and she'd come to his big house at least a couple of times a week to help out. In fact, she'd been known as the 'Village Cleaner', working for several families in the community. She'd had the reputation of being a hard worker and asking only a fair wage for her labour. Now Virginia understood why the old lady suddenly stopped coming to the house – it was when her husband died and she'd obviously decided to retire.

On this bright, sunny morning, she arrived at the cottage around eleven o'clock and propped her cycle against the front wall. It was always such a pleasant ride to the cottage and it only took about twenty minutes. She rang the doorbell but there was no answer.

"Mrs Mac, are you there?" she called through the letterbox. "It's Virginia – hope you've got the kettle boiled." But there was no reply from inside the cottage. She called again. "Mrs Mac, are you all right? It's Virginia." Still, no answer. It had never happened before – the old lady rarely went out, other than to the garden. Virginia was beginning to worry. She peered through the window into the sitting room but could see no one, so she went around the back and knocked on that door, in case the old lady hadn't heard her – she didn't have great hearing. There was still no reply and she was really worried now – had Mrs Mac fallen over perhaps and couldn't get up? She opened the door which was never locked, except at night and cautiously went into the kitchen. The room was chaotic with crockery, books, pots and pans all over the place. The small bookcase beside the fireplace had been completely emptied and all its shelves were bare. There on a rocking chair on the other side of the fireplace, Mrs McCready sat with her head slumped forward onto her chest and her poor, old hands tied behind her back. The rope was strong but slightly frayed. She was quite dead and had dried blood around her nose and mouth, as though she'd been hit on the face. The blood had dripped down onto her white blouse.

"Oh Mrs McCready, what on earth has happened?" And she rushed over to the old woman, who felt rather cold and had very wide-open eyes – almost as if she'd been surprised just before her death. There was nothing she could do to help her friend so she went into the sitting room and used the telephone to call the police. When they arrived, she had stayed behind to answer any questions and to make a pot of tea for them. She used the china cups the old lady had already set out on the table. There was little she could tell them as it had happened before she'd arrived but she agreed to look around the cottage to see if she could spot if anything was missing – but without actually touching any surface, she was warned.

It was odd really but the valuables were untouched, as were her pretty and probably expensive ornaments and paintings, some of which were very old. What had obviously been taken was two or three shelves of books. It was really strange. "Isn't that odd, Inspector? Why would anyone leave all the valuables and just take a few books?" Virginia was rather confused and waited for the Inspector to answer.

"That's something we have to find out, miss. Will you please give your details to my Sergeant so we can get in contact with you again? In the meantime, you can go home and we'll arrange for Mrs McCready to be taken from here. Don't worry Miss, we'll be gentle with her." It was easy to see how upset the girl was.

Virginia left the cottage and climbed onto her cycle but there was no joy in her step now and even the Bluebells were less blue than they'd been before. What a terrible day it had been. She went straight to the vicar and told him what had happened. He was shocked beyond words. "Who would want to hurt that sweet old lady? She'd been the church cleaners for years." And this was the attitude of the entire village – they'd all known her, in fact she'd cleaned for most of them throughout the years. Everyone was surprised and saddened by what had happened.

She went home then, knowing she had several things to sort out before her friend Felicity, came to visit in the evening. Her room was in a proper mess and she got down on her knees to tidy up. She'd scattered books everywhere. 'How strange to be thinking of books again,' she thought. She picked up a book that was lying there and opened it. The fly cover said it had been a school prize her father had won as a boy – she'd never seen it before and, although she was supposed to be tidying up, she sat on the floor and began to read. Before she knew it, two hours had passed and the sky was beginning to darken. Her father's voice drifted up the stairs. "Virgie, dinner's ready – come on girl before it gets cold." She picked her way through the debris on her floor and went downstairs, still carrying the book she'd been reading. She'd sort out the books into piles later – and everything else of course – she thought some of Father's books might be valuable as they were First Editions.

"Look, Dad, I found an old book of yours – from your school days." She sat down opposite him and started to tuck into her food.

"Why Virgie, I've not seen this book for years – I remember winning it but it sat on a shelf after that. I never did get around to reading it." He was too interested in his dinner. He'd look at the book later.

Next morning, the telephone rang early and it was the police, saying they'd like to come and ask Virginia some more questions. "Yes, of course Inspector, I'll do anything I can to help." And she waited downstairs for him to arrive.

"Miss Porter, can you confirm that you reached Mrs McCready's cottage at eleven o'clock?" He had his notebook out and was writing down her answers. She was worried – he hadn't done that the day before.

"Yes, that's absolutely right – I left home just after ten thirty and cycled past Bluebell Wood and arrived about eleven." Virginia felt uneasy and she didn't know why. She was playing with her long blond hair and putting wisps into her mouth. If he'd known her better, he'd have known she always did that when she was stressed. "It wasn't pleasant, Inspector – to arrive and find her dead. I'd been looking forward to our usual chat over a cup of tea."

"I appreciate that, Miss – it's just that a witness has come forward and claimed to have seen you leave your garden at around eight o'clock that morning and get into your father's car before driving off up the road. Could you tell me if that's correct and if so, where you were going?"

She answered without hesitation, "Yes, that's right. My father's car had just been MOT'd and serviced and I took it for a short spin to check if it was running well. I told my father what I was doing – he often allows me to drive it after I passed my driving test. I'm eighteen now and I've been driving for a while."

"Where did you go, Miss?" He was insistent.

"Oh, I just drove to the outskirts of the village and came straight back again – I do remember waving to Mr Jones at the village green. He'd probably been out for his newspaper. Was it he who reported seeing me?"

"Yes, it was. That's fine for now, Miss – but I may have some more questions for you later." He touched his hat and nodded to his Sergeant to follow him. He certainly didn't seem a man with a sense of humour.

Her father, Tom, came into the room then. "If you need me to confirm what you told them, I'd be happy to do it." He sat down at the breakfast table and helped himself to some scrambled eggs.

"Oh, I don't think that'll be necessary, Dad, I'm sure Mr Jones's word will be enough." She was just going to sit down at the table when the telephone rang again – and she went to answer. It was her old school friend Felicity who lived just a couple of streets away.

"Is it still okay for you to borrow your Dad's car tonight? I'm looking forward to it and we won't be able to 'do it' without the transport?" She hung up on being told everything was all right and Virginia went back to her breakfast. She knew how to handle her Dad and got his permission to have his car that night. She told him about the festival in the nearby town and how badly she wanted to go. "With Felicity, Dad, she'll be with me." So, that was all right then. There was always safety in numbers – especially for girls.

She spent some time tidying her room that afternoon. It looked much better when she finished. She did find some other books under her bed and some others she hadn't seen before. These she took downstairs to the library – she would ask her father about them later. She might also take some along to the 'Antique

Shoppe' in town and ask if any of them were worth anything. It would do no harm.

Dressed in jeans and a 'Hoodie', she waited outside for Felicity to arrive. Her friend was on her bike which she hid behind the garage. She too, was dressed in jeans and a dark jacket. They both wore gloves and carried torches. They looked as if they were dressed to burgle someone's house. It was eleven o'clock at night when they drove out of the village and headed in the direction of Bluebell Wood. Cleverly, they doubled back on themselves a couple of times in case anyone was watching. It just felt like the right thing to do and they'd seen people do it on the Telly. They arrived at Mrs McCready's cottage. It was about eleven thirty and both girls felt quite nervous. Obviously, the police had arranged for Mrs McCready's body to be taken away but the cottage still looked scary and threatening in the dark. Luckily, it was rather isolated so their torches probably wouldn't be seen by anyone – at least the girls hoped not. Virginia produced a key to the back door, which she'd pinched the previous day when the Policeman was looking elsewhere. It was quite difficult to go inside, knowing it was the room where Mrs McCready had died but they'd promised each other they would do it. There were still several bits of crockery lying on the floor so they had to be careful where they walked.

It's over in the corner by the fireplace," Virginia whispered and led Felicity across the room. Bending down, she asked her friend to shine the torchlight into the corner and she pushed aside the rug that lay there. Old flagstones covered the floor – they were uneven and very large slabs and she knew it would be difficult to move them. The stones were covered by a sort of mildew that smelt odd – it made them feel nauseous and breathing was difficult. Felicity used a heavy, sharp tool she'd brought with her and levered one slab upwards. It took quite a bit of her strength and she wondered how frail, old Mrs McCready had managed. It took both of them all their strength to move the slab but soon they could see a set of stone stairs inside.

"I knew it was here," an exhausted Virginia said, "the old lady told me it was but I didn't believe her at first. Now we must climb down the steps into the cellar – I know it's daunting but this is where she and her husband put everything. Just think Felicity, we're the only people in the world who knows this is here." She led the way and Felicity followed into the jet-black room. They shone their torches around the walls and were amazed. It was a reasonably sized room filled with gold, silver and precious bits and pieces – objects of all kinds – there were

306

lamps, clocks, jewellery and some beautiful ornaments as well as a few lovely old paintings.

"Oh my God," Felicity said quietly, "where has all this come from?"

"It's all come from the village. I told you Mrs McCready used to clean homes there – she did it for many years and both she and her husband stole this stuff from people. They did it over a long time and although the villagers used to get upset when they lost things, they rarely reported it to the police – and any who did, didn't get anywhere. None of the objects could ever be traced. Mrs Mac would take only one thing at a time – never too greedy she told me – it was how she got away with it for so long – and her husband was always there to help her."

The girls carried some of the items up the cellar steps and laid them on the kitchen floor – two mantelpiece clocks, a handful of jewellery, some crystal goblets, two cut glass decanters and two rather beautiful oil paintings. "That'll have to be our lot for tonight – we really can't carry any more just now." Virginia was exhausted.

Before packing everything into the car, they had to rest on the kitchen chairs. Virginia avoided the rocking chair for obvious reasons. They pushed the stone slab back into place and covered it with the rug. It all looked okay again. Suddenly, Felicity pointed a trembling finger at the rocking chair.

"What's that, Virginia – I thought I saw something move over there." Virginia stared and then gasped loudly. Mrs McCready was sitting there watching them with a grim look on her face.

She spoke quite clearly, "What on earth do you think you're doing? I've been watching you – what do you want those things for?" Her skin was luminous and almost white and her eyes were tight slits, screwed into a very threatening expression. "You're stealing my things. How dare you? She made as though to stand up but fell back against the chair.

Virginia and Felicity were petrified – the woman was dead – yet there she was, large as life.

"She's a ghost, Felicity – don't worry, she can't hurt us. I think we'll have to ignore her and pack the things into the car. She can't stop us!" And that's what they did, they carried the things outside and packed the car. Mrs McCready was still rocking to and fro in the chair when Virginia asked her. "Tell me, Mrs Mac, for how long did you steal from the houses you cleaned – and why on earth did the villagers do nothing about it?"

"I did it for so many years I've forgotten, as for why no one reported me to the police – I really don't know, except that they all liked me and thought I was too innocent to do anything like that. I stopped when my husband died and I've taken nothing since." She looked rather wistful at having to stop doing what she had enjoyed so much. But neither girl felt particularly sorry for her.

Virginia said, "We've got to get back to my house, Felicity. Now, you did tell your mother you're having a sleepover with me? We still need to unpack these things and get to bed." She made sure she locked the back door and started the engine as quietly as she could. Mrs McCready was abandoned, still rocking in the chair and telling them 'What Rotters' they were.

In a shed at the bottom of the garden, the items from Mrs McCready's cellar were piling up. As a second precaution, however, they were also covered by an old tarpaulin. No one had used the shed for a long time, so the girls thought the things were safe there. The police had visited Virginia again and it was to say the old lady had actually been murdered and therefore any information she could give, would be doubly valuable. "For example, do you know anyone who is a Diabetic and who uses insulin injections?"

"Well, yes I do – my father is a Diabetic and injects himself. Why do you ask?" Virginia was feeling rather uneasy.

"The autopsy has been carried out now and it's clear that Mrs McCready was injected with insulin, which of course can result in death for someone who is not a Diabetic – and that is apparently what happened in Mrs McCready's case. "I'll have to speak with your father if he's at home, Miss Porter. My Sergeant here will fetch your father – I don't want you speaking to him before I do." The Sergeant went off to find Mr Porter.

"Before you go, you do realise my father uses a wheelchair, don't you?" she called after him.

"No problem, Miss," he replied. Virginia was told she was free to go – and she did – hurrying over to Felicity's house.

"I'd have thought they already knew that, after all she had her hands tied behind her back – she couldn't have done that to herself. The police can't be that bright, can they?" Felicity was making a birthday cake in her kitchen for her young brother and she was covered in flour. Catching a glimpse of her face in the mirror, she gasped, "My God, I'm the same colour as Mrs McCready's ghost."

"Be quiet, Felicity, stop talking so loud. Someone will hear you. Anyway, when the police first saw her, she wasn't tied up – I removed the rope before they came. I though it made her look so undignified."

"I think you should have told the police that, don't you? The rope might have given them a clue, you never know." Felicity still believed it must have been some passing traveller who broke into the cottage. She put the cake tin in the oven, first making the sign of the cross on her chest. "I always do that when I'm not sure something's going to work."

"I think we should go and get some more things from the cottage? Perhaps tonight?" Virginia asked.

"Oh yes please – I want to see that ugly old lady again; I seem drawn to her. She really doesn't like you now – she's not your friend any more. Aren't you a bit afraid of her?" Felicity had no problem believing in ghosts. After all, they couldn't actually hurt you, she thought.

"I'll have to clear it with my father but he won't mind. I've got to go just now – unless I ring you, I'll see you at eleven tonight. I've got an errand to run." Virginia cycled away from Felicity's house. She had half a dozen books in her saddlebag which she was taking to the 'Antique Shoppe' in the nearby town. She'd already done some digging on the internet and knew two of the books were very old First Editions – so they might be worth money – and some of the others might be valuable as well. It was funny, although the next town was in the opposite direction to the McCready cottage, she passed a second field of Bluebells under some trees, which reminded her of what happened to the old woman. She thought, *Gosh, that flower is certainly in full bloom just now*.

In the antique shop in town, she met a tall, rather distinguished man who asked if she needed any help. As expected, the shop smelt of old books and the air was rather musty and dusty. Virginia took out her books and told him her father wanted to sell them and would he be interested in buying them. He asked if she'd like to take a seat whilst he took the books into the back to examine them more closely. She sat down and began to look around the shelves. The man was absent for at least twenty minutes and returned with another assistant, who was carrying a large ledger.

"Miss, I recognise three of these books which actually have come from this shop. In fact, they were stolen from this shop some years ago – and they are worth quite a bit of money because of their age and condition. May I ask where you got them?" He wasn't as friendly as he'd been at the outset.

"They belong to my father – I assure you, he'd never steal anything. I shouldn't think he's ever stolen anything in his life." She was genuinely shocked. The police were called and the books were confiscated. Virginia would have to go down to the station later, to make a statement. She left the bookshop quickly and cycled home. What had she done? Perhaps she was getting greedy!

That night, dressed in their camouflage clothes, the girls drove along the road – it was later than last time, about midnight. When she used the key she'd stolen, it sort of stuck in the lock, but with some gentle persuasion, the door fell open. They shone their torches into the room and there, standing both together, were Mr and Mrs McCready. They'd never met the man but they were pretty sure it was her husband.

"Come no closer, we're both here to put a stop to your wickedness." Mr Mac was ready for them. "You stole my book collection as well as everything else, didn't you?" Both the ghosts were the colour of parchment, with great staring eyes and tight-lipped expressions. Virginia ignored him and told Felicity to lift the rug – both girls moved the stone slab and stepped down into the cellar. They'd already taken items on a few other occasions and now, were down to the last lot. What was left was mainly ordinary bits and pieces and the girls didn't want them, so really their task could have been over. They had a good hoard under the tarpaulin and it was time to move their plan forward.

Felicity looked up the stairs and said, "Don't look now but we're being watched." Mr and Mrs McCready were peering down the stairs. The girls ran up the stairs and just rushed through the figures. They met no opposition – it was as though there was nothing there, certainly nothing solid.

"Well, we'll be off now, if you don't mind. As a point of interest, Mr McCready, how many years did you spend stealing the books and filling the bookcase? It must have taken you a long time – you must have been very choosy when you took them as most of them are apparently valuable. Your wife must have taken books as well from different village houses, including my father's – I found one of his in your bookcase."

"I did, Virginia, and I'm quite proud of it." Mrs McCready nodded her head.

"Well, your thieving might have got me into trouble – the police want me to make a statement about how I got the books. If I tell them I took them from your cottage, they'll know it was me who burgled you – and if I'm really unlucky, they'll suspect me of killing you." Virginia was very angry with the old woman, who just looked very pleased with herself.

"Tough luck, m'dear – they might just suspect you already. They were back here today and I heard them saying they'd be coming back tomorrow. That Inspector knows you've had something to do with the burglary – he' not going to let it go."

Mr McCready intervened, saying, "You know Virginia – and Felicity – my wife and I are not spirits, bound only to haunt where we died. We can go anywhere we like, and if you're not charged with murdering my wife – and in such a cruel way – we've agreed with each other to follow you both wherever you go. And that goes for you as well, Felicity, although you weren't involved with the murder. You were however involved with the burglary and you're as guilty as your friend."

As the girls were leaving, he added, "If you don't come back here one more time, then we'll come to you and that'll scare everyone around you. Remember, I mean it – you're not going to get away with it. We're not going to let you."

They got home in the early hours of the morning and unpacked the car, putting the last things into the shed and covering them. Early next morning, Virginia's father was waiting for her at the breakfast table.

"What's going on, Virgie – the Police have questioned me – and about my insulin of all things." He was clearly upset. "It's not just about poor old Mrs McCready – it's about a bookshop in town who's had some books stolen – and you told them you found them in this house. For God's Sake, what's going on, girl?" He was very agitated.

"I don't understand either, Dad – I was only involved by finding the old lady dead in her kitchen – but the police keep asking me questions. As for the books, I did find them in this house – maybe Mother bought them before she died." She was a good liar and felt no guilt.

"I think we may have to speak to a lawyer – I don't know what's going to happen next." And he turned his attention to his bacon and eggs.

The two girls met for coffee in the village, where they couldn't be overheard. "I'm getting worried, Virginia – the police have been to my house too, asking if I agreed with your statement. Of course, I said I did and I don't like the way Mr and Mrs McCready seem to be blaming us for her death. We had nothing to do with it, did we?"

"Of course not, Felicity. I knew about the valuables in the cellar 'cause she'd told me about them – and once I knew she was dead, I thought it would be silly not to take them for ourselves. My first thought was that we could give them back to the villagers, who'd lost them in the first place – then I realised we could be rich if we sold them. That's not surprising, is it? When I thought more about giving them back to the rightful owners, I thought it wrong to bad-name an old woman who'd just been murdered and so I changed my mind."

When she said these things, she expected Felicity to agree with her, but her friend didn't, "I think you're just trying to make yourself feel better. I wish I hadn't helped you fetch the things from the cottage. And what if the old couple do what they threatened – and haunt us for the rest of our lives, wherever we are. God, that would be awful."

"I expect it would, but it's not going to come to that, I promise." Virginia was very positive.

"Look me in the eyes – and tell me you had nothing to do with the old lady's death."

Virginia looked her straight in the eye, "I had nothing to do with Mrs McCready's death – other than the fact that I found her."

"I had to ask you because I wouldn't like that." Felicity was a kind girl whereas Virginia was quite positively not. "May I sleep on things – I'm not sure what I feel just now." Virginia said okay, but reminded her that they had to go back to the cottage one more time, if they wanted the ghosts to disappear and' not follow them for the rest of their lives.'

Having slept on the matter, both girls met the next day to discuss it more. They cycled to Bluebell Wood where it was private and a lovely place to sit and chat – and they wanted to see the flowers once more, before their time was over and they all disappeared.

Felicity spoke first. "I think we should return all the bits and pieces to the villagers and if you want to protect Mrs McCready's reputation, we could just put everything on a table on the village Green and put a few posters around the village, telling people to come on a particular day and pick up their items – but warning them that God is watching and they shouldn't take anything that doesn't belong to them. If we do that, our own consciences would be clear. What do you think? I realise we wouldn't make any money from our recent efforts but it just seems the right thing to do. And we do it all at the dead of night 'incomunicado'." She was getting more excited at the prospect of doing something good.

Virginia's face changed as though a dark cloud had arrived overhead and she sneered at her friend. "You really are a Goody Two-shoes, aren't you? Who made you God and able to decide what we should do?" She began to pull the heads off Bluebells and throw them onto the grass. Both were seated on the ground, their bicycles propped against a nearby tree trunk. Virginia was pulling her own hair and slipping it through her lips. She was angry and agitated.

"I'm going to tell you something, Felicity – I wasn't going to tell you but I have no option now – you need to see the whole picture. It was me who killed Mrs McCready. I planned it well, driving Dad's car to her cottage earlier in the morning. I had to admit to that as Old Mr Jones saw me and told the Police" – she shifted her position on the grass – "I was a bit early for meeting the old woman but she was still ready for me – I was her friend after all. She'd already told me about the stuff in the cellar and she'd even shown me the valuable First Edition books – she knew exactly how much they were worth. She was a mean old Shylock and she just loved stealing things, especially things of the greatest value." She walked over to her saddlebag and brought over two bars of chocolate, handing one to Felicity. It seemed such an ordinary thing to suddenly do, especially whilst she was saying such things.

"To go on with my story – the old bitch was making coffee and I crept up behind her with the insulin needle and stabbed her in the arm. She just flinched at first and staggered after a few minutes – it was easy to guide her over to the rocking chair and plonk her down. She was in a faint by then and it was so easy to take her hands and tie them behind her back. Her head slumped onto her chest and blood began to trickle from her mouth. It all worked a treat!" Virginia was smiling and obviously pleased with her own audacity, she scoffed the chocolate and threw the wrapper amongst the Bluebells. Felicity made to pick up the wrapper but her friend stood on her outstretched hand.

"Did you empty the bookshelves then and drive back home – a little later, but still in the morning, you again cycled back to the cottage and 'found' poor Mrs McCready dead. Is that when you untied her hands – although I don't know why you tied her up in the first place. She was hardly strong enough to fend you off."

"For the power, my dear – for the power. Anyway, I tied her up initially because I couldn't be sure the insulin had done its job. No point taking any risks."

"So what do you propose we do now?" Felicity knew her friend wanted to sell all the things and keep the money, but she wanted to make her say it. It was such a mean plan; she needed to hear the words.

"Exactly, my dear – I planned it well, didn't I? I've even found a shopkeeper in town who's agreed to take the things and sell them for me – no questions asked. I've left nothing to chance and my stupid, crippled father has helped by corroborating my stories to the police. It seems I can do no wrong." Her smugness was unattractive to say the least.

Felicity stood up as well. "Oh you've done wrong – and for my sins, I've helped you. What a fool am I? I'm going to see the police now, Virginia – I just can't have all this on my conscience, even if you can." She started to walk over to her bike, but Virginia followed behind her, slipping a long, thin knife from her sleeve and sticking it – with great force – into her friend's back. It was so long, it went right through her slight body and pierced her lung. Blood bubbled from the girl's mouth and she fell on the ground before even reaching her bike.

Virginia looked down at her. "You stupid girl – I was going to let you have some of the money – and now what have you got – absolutely nothing. Well, I'll be going now – I'm going to pay my last visit to the old woman's cottage in case there's something I've missed in the dark and because she and the old man said I must." She left the young girl lying in the Bluebell woods without a backward glance.

The sun was still quite high in the sky and it shone brightly on the body of the girl. Her brown hair hung loosely over her shoulder and the red highlights glinted in the sun. Her pretty white dress lay crumpled around her legs and the whole picture looked rather beautiful and sad. A pretty, white clad girl lying on a bed of blue – but with a bright red splash of colour on her chest. The flowers moved in the slight breeze and gave an unreal look to the scene. A dead girl amongst the beauty of the flowers didn't go together at all. In a couple of days, she would be on the front page of the daily papers – 'Young Female Dies Amongst the Bluebells' – not something Felicity would have liked at all.

Suddenly, she was able to open her eyes and raise her head slightly. She fished a notepad from her dress pocket – it had its own little pencil attached to the spine. It wasn't the best handwriting she'd ever managed, but it was legible and described exactly where the pile of valuables could be found and who exactly had put them there. She dropped the pad and it fell under her dress – but still very visible. Her hand and head fell backwards onto the grass and she could swear she could smell the Bluebells, although she'd always thought that flower had no perfume – beauty but no perfume. But when you're lying surrounded by them, perhaps they do smell pleasant. This time, when she passed out, it was into the arms of the Grim Reaper himself.

In the meantime, Virginia cycled the rest of the way to the cottage. She'd been told by the McCreadys that if she didn't come one more time, they'd haunt her forever. *Best not to tempt fate,* she told herself. The back door of the cottage was lying open. *Had the perfect police been careless?* she thought. Standing in the kitchen, were the old man and woman side by side – the McCreadys – they were almost standing to attention – and as if on cue, they moved to either side and a girl in a white dress appeared. Of course, it was Felicity. She still had the blood stain on her front.

"Well, you don't hang about, do you?" Virginia spat at her friend. "You move faster than a speeding bullet." The sarcasm was bitter.

"Why did you have to kill me, friend? At least, that's what I thought you were. I only wanted to do the right thing, after all the cruel things you'd done." Felicity had a strong voice for a ghost. "I've known you for so long – why didn't I know what you were capable of – why did I agree to help you empty the cellar? I'm so disappointed in myself."

Mr McCready intervened. "What will your father say when he hears what you've done. You certainly don't take after your parents. I wonder who you do take after – I knew your mother and I had many chats with your father. They were a very nice couple but I wonder how they managed to produce you. Perhaps you were adopted – were you?" He put his arm around his wife's shoulder.

"Look. I'm not here to chat with a load of deadbeats – that's rather good – deadbeats! I'm here to check there's nothing still in the cellar that might be worth a few pence." However, Mrs McCready stood in her path and tried to spit in her face, but as Virginia laughingly pointed out. "You have no saliva, you stupid old woman."

"The only time I was stupid where you were concerned, was when I confided in you about the things hidden in the cellar – now, that really was stupid."

Virginia pulled back the rug and looked down at the flagstone. "This is going to take some strength – but I'm sure I can manage it." And she crouched down, took out her steel knife and inserted it down one side of the stone. It moved slightly, but only slightly and she had to quickly slip a couple of rocks under it – rocks she'd brought with her for the purpose. She liked to be prepared, did Virginia. Eventually, she managed to move it and with a self-satisfied look, she smiled at the trio of ghosts. "See you in a couple of secs." And she grabbed her torch and shone the beam into the darkness. She followed the light down the stairs and disappeared from view. The three ghosts moved as if they were one and between them, they managed to remove the rocks Virginia had placed there. The flagstone moved and loudly fell into the gap. A voice floated upwards shouting, "Hoi, what do you think you're doing? You can't do this to me – it's inhuman! Let me out of this hole – now!"

The three ghosts ignored her. She hadn't known, that together, they had the power to move things – only slightly of course, but that was all that was needed. "We're actually being kind to you," the man shouted, "you are a disgusting and evil person and you don't deserve to live. You've probably got away with the murder of my wife and possibly the murder of Felicity and you've stolen all the things we'd hidden here and emptied the bookcase of the valuable ones. You've told lies to the police, to your father and to Felicity. You need to be punished and if this isn't going to happen on earth, then people in Limbo, like us, must do it. And we're more than happy to oblige the Fates. You'll only be down there for a few days – and then you'll fall unconscious before you die. It'll be a just punishment."

And that's how it all happened. Virginia received her retribution from the people she'd hurt most. The police eventually found Felicity's body in the woods and found too, the letter she'd left for them.

"Where has she gone? I've rung around everyone I know, but no one's seen her. She's my only daughter and I loved her. Oh my God, I'm speaking about her in the past tense. She's only been gone for a few days – I know one day, she'll come walking through the door, saying she's hungry. She's always had a good appetite, has Virgie." The police of course, suspected that Virginia had been involved with Felicity's murder, but finding her was proving to be impossible – and they never did.

The girls had been seen leaving the village that day, both riding their bikes and looking as though they hadn't a care in the world. The goods were found under the tarpaulin in the shed, just as Felicity had said they would. There was no reason for them to return to the McCready's cottage – it had already been gone over with a fine toothcomb.

Virginia's body was never found, but the cottage earned the reputation for ghosts. Everyone thought the ghost must have been old Mrs McCready who'd been murdered there – but you, as the reader, know better than that. The strange moans heard by the cottage's new tenants were made by one person, and one person alone – Virginia. And she was truly alone, as Felicity and Mr and Mrs McCready had left their Limbo on earth and enjoyed their belated 'Rest in

Peace'. After all, none of them had ever murdered anyone, unlike the young girl in the cellar.

Should you ever be in that area, especially in the month of June when the Bluebells are in bloom, and you come across an old, isolated cottage just outside the village, spare a thought for what happened there – but don't show sympathy if you hear a girl moaning – yet there's no one to be seen. By all means, gather some Bluebells to take home, but remember they tend not to last for long – just like the young girl in the cellar, who really did deserve what she got!

Flora and the Bonnie Prince

Flora MacDonald stood before the big fireplace in Lady Clan Ranald's drawing room. She'd been invited for tea as the Lady had become her benefactress and liked to keep an eye on the young girl. Their families had been friends for years and Flora was actually a close relative of MacDonald of Milton. Her father had been a tenant farmer and her mother had been abducted by a member of another clan when the girl was young. Lady Clan Ranald had almost reared her to womanhood. Flora was very aware of the recent Jacobite Uprising recently crushed by Government troops at the battle of Culloden Moor near Inverness. Although the Clan Ranalds were besotted with the Young Pretender's right to sit on the throne of Scotland, and therefore on that of Great Britain, Flora herself was not very interested in politics, and having been a Presbyterian all her life was quite disinterested in the Jacobite Cause. She was, however, interested in what would become of the Bonnie Prince himself, who was hiding in the Highland Hills of Scotland.

"Is he really out there hiding from King George's soldiers? He's living wild with no roof over his head? He cannot survive that for long, I am sure." She felt great pity for him. She knew he had landed amongst a small army of Jacobite sympathisers at Eriskay on the Outer Hebrides on 23 July 1745. He had come from Brittany in France and marched at the head of his army into Edinburgh where he waited for Louis XV, his cousin, to join him. Louis was supposed to bring many French reinforcements. It was in Edinburgh that he first gained the title 'Bonnie Prince Charlie' because of his handsome looks. Before the battle, he'd lived in Edinburgh for less than a week but he'd attended many balls and parties, held in his honour and was feted by the aristocrats of the city. He must have felt he was already well on his way to gain the throne. The French, however, let him down badly and failed to turn up with any reinforcements. Things soon turned for him however and he was forced to continue with only his own resources, using all the money he had. In fairness, the French King had sent a ship to Scotland full of money to support his cousin's invasion, but it was attacked at sea by the British Navy and all the money was confiscated. The Battle of Culloden near Inverness was looming ever closer.

"He is out there in the hills – the true King – not that German Usurper George who sits safely in London and sends his son to do his dirty work. Prince William, or Butcher Cumberland as he soon became known." Lady Clan Ranald was seething.

"Our loyal soldiers were massacred by a much bigger army at Culloden, or Drumrossie as its name really is. The English and the traitor clans who fought alongside the Government were armed to the teeth and way outnumbered the Jacobites. It wasn't only that they won the battle but the cruel and malicious way they put our brave troops to death, even those who had already been captured and were helpless" She was so angry that she pushed over the table and smashed several pieces of the valuable crockery. As Flora rang for the maidservant, her benefactress watched her closely and was pleased to see tears in her eyes. She would have preferred to see anger but that would probably soon come.

"If only he could escape to Skye, it would be much easier for him to cross to the Scottish mainland and then flee to where he was safe. If only we had a plan, we could get word to him and his two companions. I am in regular contact with him at his base, you understand," she went on, "Oh Madam, that is incredibly dangerous and who on earth could you get to help him?" Flora's eyes were round as saucers – she had failed to pick up on the Lady's intention at all.

"Why, you yourself are shortly to travel to Skye to visit friends, aren't you?"

"Yes, I am but I have had little to do with the Prince. I'm not like you, you have even sent your cook to look after him while he's living rough. You've always been involved with him and with his Grandfather, the Old Pretender."

"And proud to serve my King I am. He may be referred to as the Young Pretender but I will always regard him as a King." She filled both wine glasses and sat on the sofa beside Flora.

"Don't look at me like that, my lady, I could never do anything so dangerous, and anyhow, what could I do for him?" Flora was getting worried.

"Come with me tonight, I'm going to visit him in his camp at Benbecula." She paused and looked pleadingly at the young woman. "Will you come, Flora? I would like you to meet him and judge the man for yourself."

"I will come, Lady Clan Ranald, of course I will." And the dangerous conversation was at an end. Flora stared into the burning logs in the fireplace and imagined she could see a handsome face staring back from the flames, and she knew exactly who it was.

That night, the two women with one of the Munro Clan as companion, travelled to the hiding place in the hills. It was so quiet; the sound of silence could actually be heard. With the kilted man leading the way, all three suddenly stopped in their tracks. They all strained to hear the soft music of bagpipes and waited there on horseback, trying to stop the sound of the hooves on hard ground from breaking into the melody. The clansman rode on ahead to scout the area in front but soon returned, saying there were no bagpipes ahead, but all three could still hear the soft lilt of the pipes.

They rode on and heard a low whistle leading them onwards. At the mouth of a cave, there were three men all dressed in tartan, and one in particular stood in front, staring boldly at the approaching riders. Flora grasped Lady Clan Ranald's arm and pointed to the top of the hills beyond the cave. Standing there – some of them with bagpipes – were row upon row of Jacobite Highlanders. It was dark but they could clearly be seen by the light of the moon and against the wisps of misty air that hung over them. It was estimated that 2,000 Jacobites had been slaughtered on the field of Culloden, but many more at different places around the country. The ghostly figures must have been the very Jacobites who had fallen at Culloden and exactly in the centre of the group was a slightly built young person, who might have been only a boy. Many young people had been involved in the uprising; the prince was a very romantic figure.

The bold man spoke loudly and welcomed the newcomers to the camp and suddenly, all the Highlanders at the top of the hill disappeared, along with the sound of the pipes. Lady Clan Ranald dismounted and knelt before the man who was indeed handsome and merited the name of 'Bonnie Prince Charlie'. Her two companions did likewise and Flora found she couldn't raise her head to look into his eyes. He bent forward however and raised Lady Clan Ranald to her feet, first kissing her hand. He kissed Flora's hand too and held out his hand to the Munro and shook it heartily. The man, however, dropped to his knees and kissed the Prince's feet. The intentions of the ghostly soldiers and pipers were very clear They still wanted to show their loyalty to the 'Bonnie Prince. He couldn't have been mistaken for anything but royal, standing there in the gloaming of the night. The son of James Francis Edward Stuart and the grandson of James II of England and VII of Scotland. A true direct descendant of the Stuart line. He'd been hiding in the hills and glens for five months by then but still looked every inch a King.

The Jacobite ghosts wanted to show their continued loyalty and support – even after death!

The visitors stayed in the camp for a good two hours. The Prince was so charming and courteous that Flora knew at that moment that she would do all she could to help him escape to the Scottish mainland. Lady Clan Ranald had been right after all. She'd known that just meeting the charismatic Prince, Flora would fall under his spell. They all agreed to meet the next night to discuss what could be done.

Flora was staying in a small cottage near the Clan Ranald estate at Ormacleit which belonged to her brother. She was surprised next morning by a visit from one of the men who had been with the Prince. He was called O'Neil. She invited him in and offered some refreshments. He accepted gratefully and when he'd drained the glass, he held it up to the light and examined its base. "I see you are not perhaps an ardent supporter of the Bonny Prince?" he asked her with a smile on his lips.

"Why do you say that, sir? I came to meet him last night, didn't I? That was not without some danger for me?" She felt insulted and let him see it.

"Madam, I meant no affront. I was just testing your resolve. It's just that many of his loyal supporters have his face engraved at the bottom of their glasses, so that when they drain them, they are actually toasting their Prince in secret." At that moment, a serving girl came in to refresh the drinks. She was a tall and well-built girl who'd been with Flora for many years. When she left the room, O'Neil asked Flora if she knew whether her servant was loyal to the 'Cause.'

"As loyal as any true Scots woman can be. She respects the right of the Young Pretender and feels he should be on the throne of Great Britain and not only Scotland. Is that enough loyalty for you?" Flora was indignant.

"She's a well-built young woman, isn't she? I do believe her clothes would not look amiss on the Prince himself." He leaned forward on his chair and added, "And that's how we could help him escape to the mainland. If he travelled with you as your servant when you set off to visit Skye, and he kept a low profile, no one should suspect anything."

"I suppose it is not impossible, dangerous but not impossible." Flora was already involving herself in the plan to help the Prince. "The girl's name is Betty Burke Sir, so the Prince had better get used to answer to that."

"That will be no problem Madam, leave things to me and I will soon be in touch." He left her then, first bowing and kissing her hand.

On the 27th of August 1746, Lady Clan Ranald, her eldest daughter, a manservant called John MacLean who had served as cook to the Prince in hiding, and Flora MacDonald travelled to a place called Roychenish. They brought with them, Betty Burke's one serviceable uniform, which they'd promised to replace as she only had the one and there they met up with Bonnie Prince Charlie himself. He was in tatters but still dressed in the Stuart tartan. He still stood tall and proud.

Lady Clan Ranald whispered in his ear, "Sir, perhaps you'd better try to walk with a slight stoop or you'll stand out as the great King that you are." Charles nodded his head in agreement and hunched down. The news that was waiting for them at Roychenish was that General Campbell of the Government forces had arrived in South Uist, and that Captain Ferguson was even then just a mile from them. There was no time to lose. They sat up all that night in a shieling called Closchinish. Everyone was too excited and afraid to sleep. All the Prince could think of was how badly the battle at Culloden had gone and how he'd had to leave the field – and his dying men – to safeguard his own person. He had cried many times since then but knew he'd had to leave the battle to keep the Stuart flag flying.

As he was leaving the battle, his horse stumbled over a very young boy who lay bleeding in a crumpled heap on some bracken. He could only have been about fourteen years old. The prince recognised the boy and jumped off his horse, telling his escorts to wait.

Crouching down beside the boy, he said, "It's Jimmy, isn't it? I recognise you from Edinburgh, you played the pipes outside my rooms to awaken me in the morning – and played them very well. You were in Edinburgh all the time I was there and now you've come to Culloden to fight my Cause. I thank you for that Jimmy." And he brushed the boy's hair from his forehead.

Jimmy spluttered but managed to say, "Aye, sir, it's me right enough…and I'd follow you anywhere." The Bonnie Prince knew the lad was finished but held onto his hand. The escorts told him he must resit his horse and flee to safety. Jimmy's little hand fell from his as though on queue and the Prince stood up. "Goodbye, Jimmy, my brave wee man." And he placed the bag of his bagpipes beneath his head. "I'll never forget such loyalty." And he never forgot the lad's face and how he'd given his life for the Cause.

He'd heard from one of his men that the British Government had declared that no man in Scotland could wear the tartan, no matter which tartan it was. If they dared to do it, they'd be arrested as traitors. The age-old tradition of tartan-clad men following their chief and being ready to do his bidding when needed, was abolished from the very day of the battle at Culloden. This heaped shame and bitterness on the Scottish nation and removed all pride they had in their clan traditions. Bonnie Prince Charlie was outraged at what George II had decreed and would have loved to have the opportunity of killing him with his own hands. George had ordered his butcher son to burn people out of their homes, to execute any tartan-clad man they found around the country and to arrange transportation for the others. "Give no Scot any quarter," was what George had instructed his Generals. There were many tricks, however that the Jacobite sympathisers used to pass news from one to another, to know who was loyal to the Cause and who was not. The Old Pretender had for his secret symbol, a single white rose, which evolved into a rose with two buds – one for each of his sons, Charles and Henry. The symbols could be found on lady's fans and gentlemen's snuffboxes and of course engraved at the bottom of drinking glasses. It was a secret but something that made people proud.

The toast to the 'little gentleman in the black waistcoat' was very common in Scotland and the little gentleman was the mole who had left a small hill on the ground exactly where William III's horse stumbled and killed its master. Jacobites were very pleased at the death of that very Protestant King, who had taken the throne from their own Catholic Prince – James.

Bonnie Prince Charlie had a visit that night from his father James Edward Stewart, son of James VII of Scotland. It occurred at the saddest moment of his life when he'd first been told officially how many thousands of his army had died at Culloden. He had spent the last five months moving about the Highlands of Scotland trying to keep away from Cumberland's British troops, who seemed to be everywhere. He was sitting amongst the heather outside his makeshift tent when a breeze suddenly came from nowhere and there stood his father, dressed completely in the Stuart tartan. His voice was thunderous and he said, "Pull yourself together man, you're a Prince and my son. You had no option but to leave the field at Culloden. By doing that, you have the chance to live to lead another revolt in the future." The old man looked every inch a King and he seemed to get through to the Young Pretender, 'cause Charlie jumped to his feet and told his men they must move on again. "I have a strong feeling that Captain Ferguson is close by, and we all know what that means." The men quietly closed down the camp, dampened down the fires and removed all evidence of their having been there. Unfortunately as the time passed, the number of his followers dwindled to just a couple at the very end.

Back in the humble cottage, Flora could see the Prince's sadness and made them both a cup of hot soup, using the still burning ashes of the small fire in the hearth. "Drink this, Sir, tomorrow will soon come and your adventure will continue." He gratefully took the drink from her and smiled his thanks. She placed her finger on her lips and whispered, "Can you hear that Sir, the sounds of the pipes, just as we heard the first night we came to your camp."

"Yes, I can hear the music, Flora, the music of my people, still comforting me with their singing. They're trying to encourage me, I know it, and I will go on until that German Usurper is chased out of Britain." The hot soup was doing its work and he felt sleepy at last. Although he'd swear he never slept that night, he did for a little while.

The next day, only the Young Pretender, Flora and a servant called Donald MacDonald, travelled to Sir Alexander MacDonald's House where Flora stayed the night, having been overcome with a sickness. The Prince stayed there too and was very afraid the others living there or visiting the house would recognise him for whom he was. They hadn't planned to stay there too long and two days was quite long when on the run. There was a reward for his capture now, of £30,000 – enough to tempt most people. It was a cast sum of money at the time.

The second night in the house, the whole company was at dinner and the conversation was flowing, as was the wine. The Prince was now dressed in a gentleman's attire. O'Neil had worked wonders in finding the clothes. Suddenly, a man stood up and pushed back his chair. He was looking directly at the Prince.

"Please excuse my disturbance of this merry evening but I would be most grateful if you would tell me who you are. The face seems familiar but I can't put a name to it." He too was dressed as a gentleman with no sign of anything tartan. Sir Alexander MacDonald, as host and head of the table intervened before the Prince could speak.

"That gentleman Sir, is an honoured guest of mine and travels with Miss Flora MacDonald who is my niece. The gentleman's name can be of no consequence to you and I will not have him interrogated in this way." His rebuke was strong and clear and at first, the man was about to apologise and take his seat again, when something made him change his mind. He went on, "I believe that man is Prince Charles Edward Stuart, who has been the cause of death for many a Scotsman and who is wanted by the British Army as a traitor and a criminal, and who also has a price of £30,000 on his head."

Sir Alexander intervened again saying, "And what exactly does that have to do with you? As far as I'm aware, it is no business of yours."

"It is the business of any man who is not a traitor to the British Crown and as such myself, I shall leave this house now and report his whereabouts to Captain Ferguson who is not but a mile from here." The man made to leave the table when O'Neil appeared as if from nowhere and asked him if he would mind following him into the hall, as someone there is asking to speak with him. O'Neil escorted him out of the room and he was never seen again. O'Neil was very handy with the dagger or sword. He didn't mind which. He came back half an hour later and signalled to Sir Alexander that all was well now.

What the company around the table did then was of great comfort to the Bonnie Prince. A servant had refilled everyone's glass and Sir Alexander asked them all to stand and raise their glasses in a salute to Prince Charles Edward Stuart. Everyone did that – even the Prince himself – and he saw in the bright candlelight, his own face engraved at the bottom of every glass, and the words 'God Bless the True King'. The glasses had to be passed over a bowl of water and a second toast made to 'The King over the water', words that had become popular when the Bonnie Prince was still in France.

He was safe for the time being anyway and he slept better that night than he had done for many a night. A lone piper played outside his bedroom window, but played very quietly, just in case.

The next day had been earmarked as 'D Day' and everyone rose early to begin the great adventure. O'Neil spent all day outside and eventually found a boat that would be willing to take some passengers to the Isle of Skye. No mention was made of the Prince, although at that time in Scotland, everyone was suspicious of everyone else. They had moved to a house called Kingsbury, as it wasn't wise to stay overlong in one place. Flora spoke with the Prince and told him he must change into Betty Burke's clothes whilst travelling on the road to Portree where they arrived at midnight. They met with Donald MacDonald there who'd gone on ahead to make sure everything was ready. At Portree, they met another loyal supporter of the prince, one MacAncran who provided refreshments for them all.

The Prince, looking every inch an ungainly woman went aboard the vessel and got some strange looks from the crew. But they'd been paid what they'd asked for, a guinea was a good price. Flora MacDonald climbed aboard the boat as well and so did Donald MacDonald. They all crouched down and allowed the crew to tend to the boat.

"Well, Sire my Prince, you will soon be well on your way to where it's safe." Flora was exhausted and rested her eyes for a few minutes before adding, "We are heading for Raasay Island where you will be met by other loyal supporters and from there, you will be taken on to Skye. I myself will stay on this boat and go straight to Skye but we cannot risk you being seen in our company any longer. From Raasay, you will be taken to Ullapool, where a boat will be waiting to take you to France." She felt very sad as she said this. She had grown to like the Prince and the man, in fact perhaps to love him a little.

"Flora, I have no words to express my gratitude to you. Without you, there is no way I could have got this far. I intend to return to Scotland one day and you are the one person I will seek." He took both her hands in his own. "Don't give up on me, Flora, because I will never give up, not while there are people like you to support me." There was little doubt he was crying, she could hear it in his voice, but it was too dark to see him clearly.

"Oh Sire, never give up, you are Scotland's true King and one day, you'll be just that." Flora raised her hand and said, "Listen Sire, they've come to say goodbye to you. The pipes were all around them and they were playing the tune 'Speed Bonny Boat, Like a Bird on the Wing, over the sea to Skye'." Of course, there were no words and it was actually in the ancient Gaelic – a rowing boat song that had been used by seamen for many years. The words about Skye and Bonnie Prince Charlie weren't written for more than another hundred years, but the haunting melody said clearly how they all felt.

"Land Ahead, and it's Raasay," One crewmember shouted, "and there is the Lord Raasay himself come to meet us." A very tall, bearded man could be seen on the shore and he actually helped the Prince step onto the beach. Whether he thought it was a woman or not, will never be known. The Bonnie Prince turned to Flora and Donald MacDonald and shook the man's hand. He bent towards and kissed her on the mouth. "Goodbye, dear Flora, and again, thank you for all you've done." He looked down at Betty Burke's dress which was very wet now. "Tell Betty, she has done her Prince a great service." And he made his way along the shore with the Raasay by his side and towering over him. The Lord Raasay would see him all right.

Before leaving the beach however, he turned to watch the boat set off again He waved to Flora and she waved back. She stood there, straight and proud and listened to the increasing sound of the pipes. What an adventure she had had and how wonderful she felt at being able to help her Prince. Raasay to the Isle of Skye only took a short boat ride and the next day, the Young Pretender felt almost free, but he knew he still had to reach Ullapool to get back to France.

Epilogue (First Part)

It wouldn't be right to end this tale here. The characters all went on to other things and continued to shape history. We should know their onward paths as we know their pasts:

Although the Prince did reach France safely, his time there was limited. He lived there for a short time but France and Great Britain had become friends after a number of years of war and part of their agreement was that Charles could no longer be allowed to live in France. Before leaving the country, however, he had to face another crushing disappointment. This was in 1759, at the battle of Quiberon, which was also lost to his Cause. After that, the French abandoned the Prince who was often out of his head with drunkenness which so disgusted the fastidious French that they shunned him. He went to live in Italy, in the very place where he'd been born, Pallazo Muti Papazzum located on the Piazza dei Santi Apostoli in Rome. The building still exists and lies northeast of the Forum. Strangely, neither his birth nor death is acknowledged at this building.

Even the Pope in Rome would give no succour to the Catholic Prince and recognised German George as the rightful King in 1760. The fundamental aim of the Stuart line was all but dead. There seemed no hope of a restoration for the Stuarts at that time. Charles had an illegitimate daughter called Charlotte, the Duchess of Albany whom he refused to acknowledge. She was born in 1750 and spent most of her life in one convent after another; she eventually produced three children by the Archbishop of Bordeaux, Ferdinand de Rohan. The Bonny Prince married Princess Louise of Stolberg Gedern in 1772, but the marriage was a disaster and the couple had no children.

In 1784, Charlotte, left her children with her mother and went to her father Charles, to help nurse him through his illness, but to no avail. The Bonnie Prince died in 1788 and his brother Henry, a Roman Catholic Cardinal was then next in the legitimate Stuart Line, but he was not interested in such things. He'd been receiving a pension from King George III of £4,000 a year (a great deal of money) and had no wish to see this come to an end. He'd actually accepted the payment from the very man whom his father and brother had fought against for so long, so hard and so expensively in an attempt to remove from the throne. The throne they claimed to be rightfully theirs. 'Such is life, it seems.' He died in 1807, a very long time after his brother.

Subsequent investigation revealed three of the Bonny Prince's grandchildren, and in the mid-twentieth century their names became known – Marie Victoire Adelaide (1779), Charlotte Maximilienne Amelie (1780) and Charles Edward (1784) – and one other who remains a mystery. A claimant to the Stuart line was one Count Roehenstart i.e., Rohan Stuart and he and his sister died childless. Nothing was ever proved as to his right and he lies buried at Dunkeld Cathedral. So the actual (albeit illegitimate) Stuart line was almost over, but very recently, a new claimant has emerged – Peter Pininski, who claims to be a descendant of the Prince's eldest daughter (Marie Victoire). It seems the mystery continues.

Charles Edward Stuart was buried at Frascati Cathedral where his brother was the Cardinal Bishop. Sometime later, for whatever reason, his body was re-buried in the crypt of the Basilica in Rome, all except his heart which remains at Frascati. He lies beside his father and brother. An elegant but modest monument designed by Antonio Canova and funded by George IV was erected in 1819 in the south aisle of the main church.

The atmosphere around the monument is sombre and very sad. The words of the Skye Boat song were written around this time and if a visitor listens carefully, he can hear the sweet melody in the air, softly played on the bagpipes and the sweetest tune of all will come from the bagpipes of a slightly built boy piper, called Jimmy.

The words of the song may be quite new – 1890s – but the tune is an ancient song that Gaelic oarsmen sang to speed the boat along with its precious cargo – the oars would dip up and down cutting their way through the waves to this tune:

Speed bonnie boat like a bird on the wing
Onward the sailors cry
Carry the lad that's born to be king
Over the sea to Skye
Loud the wind howls
Loud the waves roar

Thunderclouds rend the air
Baffled our foes
Stand by the shore
Follow they will not dare
Speed bonnie boat like a bird on the wing
Onward the sailors cry
Carry the lad that's born to be king
Over the sea to Skye
Many's the lad that fought on that day
Well the claymore did wield
When the night came
Silently lain dead on Culloden Field
Speed bonnie boat like a bird on the wing
Onward the sailors cry
Carry the lad that's born to be king
Over the sea to Skye

Epilogue (Second Part)

We should also follow the path Flora's life took as well as that of her prince. She risked her life to help save him from the wrath of Butcher Cumberland, Georg II's son, and in so doing must have fallen in love with him a little. Both he and she were only 24 years old when they met at Benbecula. She had been born in Milton in 1722 and had a disjointed and strange young life, but it didn't affect her sweet nature in any adverse way.

She was arrested on the Isle of Skye and taken as a traitor to the Tower of London. Her part in the Prince's escape was public knowledge very soon and the authorities were unsure what to do with her.

"She's a heroine to the people, your Majesty, and it has all happened so quickly," the first Minister explained to the king. "Her name is on everyone's lips and even those not sympathetic to the Stuart Cause admire her courage and strength. She must have come close to death whilst helping him escape, the army having been instructed to shoot first and ask questions later." He was exasperated with the whole thing and truth to tell he was just glad that Bonnie Prince Charlie was no longer on British soil.

"Has she been questioned thoroughly," the King asked.

"Most certainly, sir, and she has given a written statement detailing exactly what she did for him. To be honest, she did nothing against your Majesty or the throne. As a Highlander, she believed in the Stuart Cause but never to the point of harming you. She hid him for a few days, dressed him in her woman servant's clothes and sailed, with him as her maid, to the Island of Raasay. She had been going to visit friends on Skye and they had originally planned to travel together in the same boat – but that was changed for his safety."

The King looked thoughtful. "And you say she's popular with the people? In England and Scotland?" How long has she been imprisoned in the Tower?"

"Yes Sire, it seems she's popular over both countries. It's being regarded as a romantic story and you know how people love that. She's actually been in the Tower for two years now, but apparently never complains."

"I do indeed understand the romance of it all." The King stood up. "I say release her and send her back from whence she came. She is not a threat to me nor to the country. She has already committed the crime and has ended up a heroine. I think it would hurt my reputation if I punished her more, after all she's already served two years in prison. In fact, to show our forgiveness and that we don't fear anything she could do to us, arrange for me to meet her at the next afternoon Garden Party I hold. Then we can get rid of her back to the Highlands."

And it happened thus. She was invited to the party and was treated as a social celebrity. People queued up to be introduced and to shake her hand. The King had been right; it was the best thing to do with her. She was introduced to him and to his son, the Duke of Cumberland, or as she knew him Butcher Cumberland, whose manners were not as good as his father's and he berated her for what she did for the Young Pretender. She thought for a while before she told him that had she met him in the same situation as the Prince, defeated and in distress, she would have helped him in the same way as she did the 'Bonnie Prince.' She spoke very calmly but with conviction. He didn't know what to say but did say that he hoped that day would never come. She also was introduced to Dr Johnson, the famous writer who described her to the press as 'a woman of soft features, a gentle manner, a kind soul and had an elegant presence'. He also wrote her epitaph which can be seen today on her gravestone in Kilmuir the Isle of Skye and there is statue to her in the grounds of Inverness Castle.

On her release from the Tower, she was sent back to her own country, where she married the son of Donald of Kingsburgh. They immigrated to America together and he quickly became a Captain fighting in the American War of

Independence. Of course, he fought on the British side in the war but was captured and imprisoned for several years. When he was finally released, he returned to Scotland where Flora had gone ahead to wait for him. They both stayed there for the rest of their lives and had seven children – Ranald, James, John, Charles, Ann, Frances and one other son (name unknown). On her return from America, the ship on which she was travelling was attacked by privateers and Flora refused to go down to the safety of the hold. As a result, she was wounded in the arm but the sailors cheered her bravery.

When Flora breathed the fresh air of her home country, she cried. The smell of heather filled her nostrils and it was more beautiful than any of the exotic flowers she'd seen on her travels. All the memories of what had happened with the Bonnie Prince came flooding back to her. "I am home at last, dear husband, and have once more heard my Gaelic name spoken in the tongue. Fionnghal Nic Dhòmhnill – music to my ears."

The couple and some of their children lived happily on the MacDonald Estate on the Isle of Skye. Flora MacDonald died in 1780, aged 68 years. Engraved on her monument there, Dr Johnson's words read:

'…a name that will be mentioned in history

And, if courage and fidelity be virtues, mentioned with honour…'

The two people whose lives had crossed for only a short but significant time died within two years of each other and if you were to travel to Kilmuir on the Isle of Skye, you will find her grave there, not far from the very spot where she first landed with 'the lad who was born to be king'. And as with the Bonny Prince's grave in Rome, if you listen carefully, you can still hear the sweet melody of the Skye Boat Song. And if you stand very still, and search the skyline, you might even see the ghostly figures of the Jacobite soldiers who died in the Battle of Culloden. Some will be playing bagpipes – and if you spot one shorter than the others, say 'Hello' to Jimmy.' He'd like that!

Before you dismiss this suggestion, perhaps you should travel to both sites and hear and see for yourself. I can guarantee it would be worthwhile.

Peter, the Wild Boy

"Husband, I can no longer care for the boy – he is impossible and gets no better with time passing. I can't continue to neglect my other children because of him – they suffer because he needs so much attention." She was crying and holding her head in the folds of her apron, whilst her husband stared into the garden, seeing nothing except his son crawling around the yard on all fours and pulling up weeds, some of which he ate.

"Wife – wife – he is but seven years old and could get better with time. We have no option but to go on caring for him – he is our son after all – and he has no one but us." His clenched fists were resting on the window ledge and suddenly, he banged it and swore softly. "I work all hours God sends and earn enough to support my family – can't we just go on as we are at present and keep our son hidden from the rest of the world?"

"No, Husband, we can't. I am no longer fit to rear him. Look at him out there in the yard – he can't even stand up but moves about like a dog. He can't speak – even to say his own name – let alone those of his brothers and sisters. He doesn't play with the others, just rolls about and eats the grass and leaves. He can't even hold a spoon or a knife – but eats everything with his hands, no matter how many times I tell him differently. He relieves himself anywhere and everywhere – and now his brothers and sisters try to get away with the same. He is holding them back and teaching them all the wrong things. He is an idiot and you know it." She had been waiting to say this to her husband and knew how he would react. He was a soft man, more sensitive than she was – and she knew he would not take this well.

"I have spoken to the village's wise woman and she has told me that God created him and God should therefore be left to look after him. He is a creation of God's and he is His responsibility – not ours. We have done our best – I can't take any more."

"And what does she say we should do with him so that God can look after him?" Her husband waited for her response impatiently. He too had had enough of the child, who was barely a child and more like an animal and of course, he wasn't the one who was with him day and night, so he didn't have to suffer as much as his wife did.

"She says we must take him deep into the woods just outside Hameln – to Hertswold Forest – and leave him there to fend for himself. If God means for him to survive, he will help him – and if he doesn't mean that, then he will take him into his strong arms and care for him much better than we can. She reminded me that God says, 'Give me the child until he is seven and I'll give you the man.' Our son is all the man he can ever be. She made it quite clear what we should do." She knew how awful her words must have seemed to her husband but she believed in the wisdom of the old woman, who understood how serious the situation with the boy was.

It took a whole week for her husband to be persuaded that it was the best thing to do – but in the end, she managed it and he was given the dreadful task of taking the boy away from his home and into the woods. Father and son set off together on a horse borrowed from the farmer next door and travelled for a whole day and night into the very centre of the forest. He gave his son a bag which contained something to eat and drink and a rough blanket to sleep on. That was to be his lot. He covered him with the blanket and the child fell asleep on the soft ground. As he moved away silently on the horse, the boy stirred in his sleep, but luckily never woke up. As he rode away, the tears were running down his father's cheeks but he knew he had to do it – the boy was really impossible. He was simple, incapable of speech and on occasion, could be quite bad tempered – not fit to live with other people. He knew his wife and the wise woman were right – but that didn't make deserting his son any easier. He stopped in the middle of the night and slept till morning. At first, he was tempted to go back and see what the boy was doing, but knew that wouldn't work as he would be tempted to bring him home again – and his wife would berate him for that. She was made of sterner stuff than he was and he knew she was right.

The man and woman never saw their idiot son again – he did wake up the next morning and, crawling about on all fours, examined his surroundings. He ate the bread and cheese his mother had put in his bag and scooped some water from a nearby pool. In fairness, he didn't realise he'd been taken to the woods to live and just got on with things as usual. The first problem he had was the cold at night. After all, it was northern Germany and the nights could be very cold but the young boy quickly learned to wrap himself in the old blanket and lie tightly rolled in a ball under the trees and fallen leaves. The dry leaves were like another blanket.

As the time passed, he became used to the environment and, although very skinny, he managed to live off berries, acorns and some edible foliage. If he didn't like the taste of anything, he just spat it out and looked for something different. He watched the small animals and the birds in the woods and ate what they ate. He learned that was a good way of learning what was safe – and what was not. Of course, he made some mistakes but soon regurgitated what didn't sit well in his stomach. He had never been big but now he was almost skin and bone – but he didn't know that, so it didn't bother him. Strangely enough, he felt quite comfortable with being unable to stand and liked to crawl around with the animals, who couldn't stand either.

He had one nasty accident when he fell headlong into a river and his arm was caught under a big rock. The water was cold and the current strong and he had to tug at his arm as hard as he could but the arm wouldn't become untangled. He kicked at the rock but only ended by cutting his feet. He rested for a bit but the cold made him almost freeze to death – so he pulled all the harder and eventually the arm came unstuck. His hand was bleeding badly but as he'd seen the wounded animals do, he licked his wounds and kept doing it until the blood eventually dried up. He was pleased and knew he'd done the right thing – but after some time, his fingers in his left hand seemed to fuse together and he had one hand almost like a duck's webbed foot. Once healed, the hand gave him no trouble and he used it just as he had before – although now its use was limited.

He could hear the sounds of the forest and the sounds the birds and animals made and he attempted to copy them. It came out like a series of grunts, but the animals seemed to understand and avoided the new animal when they could, although on occasion, he would wake up to find a couple of squirrels or rabbits cuddled against him for heat. He didn't mind it, in fact he liked it – they were the only friends he had after all.

Not many people ever came this deep into the wood and therefore he never saw anyone. He'd met a bear a couple of times but had an inner sense to keep away from it. He may have been skinny but he knew the big animal would happily have him as a snack if he were hungry enough. He'd seen the way a bear could rip a small animal apart and he didn't want that. He learned – especially from the squirrels – how to steal any titbits from another hungry animal and became quite adept at sneaking up behind them and silently relieving them of their treasures.

He didn't realise, but he was growing all the time. He didn't get any taller but he definitely became hairier and stronger. In fact, he found if he tied back his long, bushy hair with a strong reed, he could see everything better. He became very dirty with the filth of the forest attaching itself to his body like a thick crust, but it only served to help him keep warmer than before.

Then he heard them coming. They weren't quite like the other animals but noisily crashing their way through the trees. He climbed a tree, something he'd become very good at and hid himself in the branches. Although he didn't know how long he'd been in the woods, he knew it was a long time. He didn't have an understanding of time, so wasn't upset. He was about twelve by this time and had been on his own for about five years. He saw the strange men on horseback and vaguely remembered seeing such animals before – but the memory was buried deep in his mind and he didn't know what they were. They weren't furry or hairy like other animals but sat upright on the horses and looked very white to the boy. He didn't know where the animal stopped and the rider began. The riders were fashionably dressed although he didn't know this and they were led by one man in particular, who was even more fashionable than the rest.

He stayed in the safety of the tree and watched what they were doing. They were hunting for animals – and most likely for him, if they could catch him. He had to make sure they didn't do that – and he made no sound whatsoever. He took his cue from the animals. The men on horseback turned and galloped in another direction – he watched them go and then slid quietly down the trunk of the tree, but making sure he kept hidden in the long grass. However, one of the men had seen him in the tree and spoke about it to the others – another had spotted him as well.

They came back next day, making as much noise as they had before. What were they, these strange animals – obviously, the boy didn't know but he sensed he should keep hidden – that probably meant him no good. But he was wrong, they'd only come back to see if they could help him. To them, he looked like a wild animal but he had human form and they knew they must do something. Two of the men dismounted and walked towards his tree – they looked up at the branches and spoke soothingly, "Come down, Lad, we won't hurt you." The boy did and said nothing. In fact, he didn't move a muscle. The men looked back at the others and the one in charge spoke up, "If we get a net, perhaps we can persuade him to jump into it. Have we got such a thing?"

One man came forward and he brought a net which he had to capture wild animals – and that's exactly what he did – they caught a wild animal. He and some of the others shook the tree and shook it so hard that the boy lost his hold and tumbled onto the ground – and into the net. The group of men tied him up and took him back to Hameln to the palace where King George the First of Great Britain was temporarily living. Discussing their catch, the men decided the boy had belonged to someone at some time as he still had tatty remnants of a collar around his neck – no other clothes, just a strip of cloth. Someone must have abandoned him in the forest and they talked about the kind of cruel person who could do something like that.

For three weeks, the wild boy was put into a House of Correction to see if he would calm down and behave less like a wild animal, but it didn't really work and he behaved as before. He was given into the care of one of the ladies of court and for a fee, she tried to look after him – but it proved too much for her and she told the King so. "He is impossible. He hates wearing clothes and it takes two footmen to force the clothes on him every day. He refuses to use cutlery but eats everything with his hands. How we managed to bathe him was a nightmare and washing his hair was a terrible struggle – but not as bad as when we cut his hair – no, he did not like that one bit. And as for his table manners, he eats like an animal too – and crams as much food as he can into his mouth – only vegetables and fruit, mind you, none of our good nourishing recipes. He will eat some meat but it has to be so undercooked it's still raw. Mind you, he does have a very sweet tooth. He can't get enough of sugar!"

The King laughed at all this and told her to bring him to the dinner table that evening and he would judge for himself. "He is to be called Peter and we'll soon train him to behave normally, or I'm not the King." And so, Peter was brought to the royal dining table. He didn't like it and shrunk back against the gown of his keeper, keeping his eyes lowered. The diners spoke about him as though he wasn't there – but then, as he didn't understand them anyway – it didn't really matter. King George offered him some sweetmeats and Peter grabbed them with great speed, stuffed some in his mouth and the rest he hid inside his jacket.

"He eats like an animal," one of the ladies said, "how quaint." And she covered her face with her fan. The other ladies at the table laughed and threw more titbits at the boy, who cleverly caught them, even in his left webbed hand.

In fact, he thought he was doing well and pleasing everyone in the room so he dropped down from his chair and crawled about the room on all fours, looking as though he might dance, but of course, he couldn't do that. He did crawl back to the table and used the tablecloth to pull himself upwards – he was so short in stature that his head barely reached the table. He reached over and snatched one lady's sparkling bag and shoved it inside his jacket. Everyone laughed more so he moved onto a man and grabbed his gold-topped walking stick which was leaning against the table – and to show his strength, he broke it in two. He was so adept at picking peoples' pockets that he soon had a little store of trinkets in front of him and he looked daringly around the table, making sure no one was going to steal any of them. He had obviously learned the trick from the squirrels in the forest and he was good at it. The laughter stopped and the King told Peter's keeper, "Take him away. He is becoming overexcited."

"He likes to steal I fear and doesn't he do it well? It must have been how he lived in the forest – taking whatever he wanted and even fighting over it with some other animal. It must have been a hard life – and yet he lived. I wonder how long he spent in the forest – and who put him there. Very sad – very sad. Poor lad." The King felt very sorry for Peter.

The boy definitely encouraged the court's sympathy and each night, they began to vie for his attention as their entertainment. So odd was his appearance that the courtiers would laugh just to see him react. He still had a great mop of curly black hair that stood on end and a small pouting mouth that formed a perfect cupid bow; his lips were very full and drooping and he was incredibly short of stature; he had heavy hooded eyelids and of course a webbed hand. He was always dressed in a green velvet suit which was a struggle to make him wear. He couldn't speak and didn't even try. He did grunt regularly however. The King had one of his medical specialists try to teach him how to speak, but despite repeated attempts, the doctor failed and told the King he had to give up trying. One thing, however, that Peter the Wild Boy was good at was picking up a tune and humming it, even if he'd heard it only once. One evening, he sat quite still and listened to a violinist playing beautiful music. It was the most silent the court had ever seen him – he was mesmerised. When the violinist stopped playing, the boy crossed the room and picked up the instrument. It wasn't a masterpiece but it was rather sweet – he held the violin awkwardly but managed to make music – not like the musician had done of course, but a reasonable attempt.

He was allowed as much freedom as he wished and he ran around the grounds of the German Palace with gay abandon. The grounds were so big, there was no danger of his wandering off and getting lost, so he had little to complain about and could climb trees and sleep under hedges as much as he liked. Strangely enough, when he came upon anyone in the gardens, he darted over to them and stole a kiss – whether it was a man or woman. It may have been how he had associated with the little creatures in the forest, so he just continued to do it with the courtiers. His kiss was his way of saying 'Hello'. They had no problem with it and positively encouraged him to do it.

King George was to return to England. He would have preferred to remain in Germany but his new realm would have thought that odd, as he had gained much wealth when he was offered the throne. So he had to return. Peter the Wild Boy was left with his keeper in the Palace at Hameln and if he noticed how the court had shrunk in number, he gave no sign of it. He continued as before – a treasured pet with total freedom. But that's all he could ever have been – he had no conversation and didn't seem to understand anyone, but he had his food – his nuts and vegetables and his rare meat and his sweetmeats. However, in order to get them, he had to allow himself to be dressed in his green suit every day. The thing they couldn't make him do however was to sleep in a bed. He was put there and covered up every night and every morning, he would be found asleep in a corner of the room. This too was something he'd done in the forest and it had served him well. He'd learned that keeping his back to the wall was the safest way of sleeping.

"Peter, where are you? You must come immediately – I have something to tell you." His keeper searched the garden, looking for him, but he was so good at blending into the foliage, it was always difficult to find him. He knew his name however – but he couldn't pronounce it – he would just grunt as usual. Marie did find him however and led him back into the palace, where she tried to make him understand that he was a very lucky boy who was going to live with the King in Britain. Peter didn't care and was not impressed – he had food and cover here so what more could he want? He just scrabbled around the floor not allowing her to catch him. He grunted a laugh however, so she'd know he was just playing.

In Great Britain, the Princess Caroline who was the daughter-in-law of George I, demanded that Peter the Wild Boy be brought to Kensington Palace to live. Her father-in-law had painted a very sad picture – and she felt sure she could help the wild boy. Arrangements were made therefore for him to be brought to

Great Britain and as Peter never knew exactly where he was at any one time – the different palace didn't phase him at all. There was a great garden there as well and that pleased him. Princess Caroline took control of the boy and engaged a tutor to try to educate him. For a very long time, it didn't work but after a while, he was able to utter some sounds – but certainly not recognisable words – but after the lessons, he seemed to understand much more than before. He would never be normal, but with Caroline's care, he was just a little better. He was still inclined to wander off and disappear into the big garden and the servants had to go and find him – not an easy task as he was used to camouflaging himself, as he'd done in the forest.

George I had died and his son George II, now sat on the throne with his wife Caroline as Queen. Peter didn't notice any difference and Caroline continued to oversee Peter's well-being.

Word had spread around the country and the Satirists in London began to write about Peter the Wild Boy – people like Jonathan Swift, Daniel Defoe and John Arbuthnot, the latter having been his tutor. They all produced pamphlets about the idiot from Germany who lived with the royals at Kensington Palace and who crawled around and grunted. Satirists were always rather cruel but it was really the Georgian royalty they were highlighting as buffoons, and not Peter himself. Nonetheless, it was a cruel time by London's society writers and many laughs were had at the expense of the monarchy. They used the boy's presence at court as the basis of their prejudice against the German King and his family. It was a time after all when ridiculing the Georgians was very popular and many writers (and cartoonists) took the opportunity to do just that. They used the fact that the Wild Boy from Germany was entertained at court, dined in the royal presence and slept in his own room at Kensington Palace, where he was waited on hand and foot. Of course, with the passage of time, this wasn't true. He was looked after and fed but he no longer was part of the court and the family – he was just too wild and couldn't be trusted to behave himself. In fact, he was positively uncivilised – yet was often heard humming snatches of songs that people recognised – and when he could get his hands on a musical instrument, he could produce pleasant sounds. The Satirists weren't always right.

The existence of Peter was also discussed by Theologians of the day and it was debated as to whether he was actually human, or not. For example, the question was asked, "Does the boy have a soul? After all, he can't walk, he can't speak and he could never win anyone's trust." 'The Theory of Evolution of the

Human Species' often contained references to the King's Wild Boy and so, awarded him a place in history.

The famous painter and interior designer, William Kent, painted a large portrait of the royal court and in it, he included Peter, looking as he normally did and wearing his green velvet suit. In his right hand, he held an acorn and oak leaves to remind people of the life he'd lived in the forest. The great painting was hung on the East wall of the Kstillstilling's staircase at Kensington Palace – and still hangs there to this day.

When his tutor, Dr Arbuthnot, stopped his training, the care of Peter was passed to Mrs Titchbourn who was one of the Queen's bedchamber women. She was paid a handsome pension for taking care of her charge and she was allowed to take him when she took short holiday breaks from the palace.

Therefore, Peter went on holiday with Mrs Titchbourn and arrived at Axter's End in the parish of the yeoman farmer, Mr James Fenn. Mr Fenn took a liking to the boy and gave him some simple and menial tasks to do, all of which Peter thoroughly enjoyed. In fact, he loved his new life at the farm – the freedom to run around with the animals and the good fresh air reminded him of his time in the forest. It was agreed that Mr Fenn was paid the pension Mrs Titchbourn had received and the £35 covered Peter's maintenance and support. So, everyone was happy with the new arrangements and Peter stayed on the farm.

"Come on, Peter, get yourself moving and fill that cart wi' the cows' dung." The farmer watched him as he worked, never sure what he might do next but the cart was soon full of dung and the boy grinned, pleased with his efforts. When the farmer went across the yard to fetch a couple of drinks, he couldn't see what Peter was up to, so when he came back, he was astonished to see the cart was once again empty and the dung spread all over the yard again. The boy was still grinning, proud of his work, but Mr Fenn was not smiling.

"What am I to do wi' you, Peter?" Mr Fenn wasn't pleased and he knew he'd done something wrong, but didn't know what it was. That night – in late summer 1751 – he ran away from the farm. Everyone looked for him and covered a large area, but there was no sight of the youngster. The search went on and, in the confusion, Mr Fenn suddenly passed away and so there was no home for Peter. His care passed to Mr Fenn's brother, Thomas, who lived on a different farm in a place called Broadway. The pension of £35 passed to him as well – and the searching continued, but no one was able to find Peter. Newspaper advertising was placed all over the area – even in London, offering a reward for his return – but with no results.

On 22 October, a fire broke out in the parish of St Andrew's in Norwich. The fire spread quickly and the local jail became engulfed in smoke and flames. The inmates, petrified with fear, were released for their own safety. One of those prisoners aroused great curiosity amongst the milling crowds – primarily because of his strange appearance and the odd sounds he made. He had a very strong build and was covered with a great deal of shaggy, long hair – so much hair in fact that some of the people described him as an orangutan. A few days later, he was identified as Peter the Wild Boy by a reader of the London Evening Post, who recognised the description given in the pamphlet. Soon, Peter was back at Thomas Fenn's farm and in an attempt to keep him safe, he was fitted with a special leather and brass collar, which he wore for the rest of his life. Some people thought it was cruel but it was done for the right reason as he could easily have run off again in the future. The collar was inscribed with his name and address and is still preserved at Berkhamsted School in that area.

Thomas spoke in serious tones to him, saying, "Peter, you must never run away again, or next time, we might not be able to find you. It can be a dangerous world out there – not a nice place at all." He knew the boy understood what was being said from the sad expression in his eyes. He knew he'd done something wrong. Although he could barely speak, he could understand. He grunted at Thomas and the farmer knew his words had hit home. He didn't run away again although he'd really lost his way rather than run away – and he just couldn't find his way home again.

He lived until his early seventies and became a part of the community in Northchurch – and they were happy to have him amongst them. From such a bad start, Peter the Wild Boy had been lucky. How many of us could say we've lived in a palace and more than one as well? In Georgian times, people had a character flaw we'd describe as cruel today – and misfits such as Peter sometimes found themselves as an exhibit in a sideshow at a fairground, not treated well and made to suffer – just like an animal. This hadn't happened to Peter.

He'd dined with Kings and was looked after by a Queen – he'd been protected all his life once George I had brought him from the forest near Hameln. When Thomas Fenn died, another farmer took over the farm and took on Peter too – in fact, other tenants came and went, but Peter remained in their care and still on the farm. His government pension paid to his carers continued until he eventually died. Just before his death, however, a dignitary called James Burnett visited Peter in 1782 – he was a Philosopher and a Judge – and he had long been interested in the boy's story. He described him as looking robust and healthy with a good complexion and a thick mop of white hair. He also believed Peter knew everything that was said to him, but he couldn't converse in return.

He spoke two words, the eminent Philosopher said – one was Peter and one was King George. He even hummed a couple of tunes for the visitor. His own name is understandable but why 'King George', above all the people he'd met throughout his life? Perhaps in his mind, he knew that without his saviour King George rescuing him from the forest, he wouldn't have met any of the other people. There was some intelligence there and he was not an idiot.

He died on 22 February 1785 and is buried in Northchurch. His grave can be seen in the churchyard of St Mary's Church – it is directly outside the main door of the church. Fresh flowers continue to be laid on his grave, which was paid for and erected by the village. If you go there sometime, perhaps you'd take some flowers of your own – for Peter the Wild Boy.

In 2007, a blue Heritage Plaque was placed at the Wild Man Pub in Bedford Street, near St Andrew's Church in Norwich to commemorate Peter and his association with the area.

In 2013, it was announced by the Department for Culture, Media and Sport that the grave was to be given Grade 11 listing on the advice of English Heritage.

Not bad for a boy who once lived in a forest – walked on all fours, couldn't speak and had a deformed, webbed hand. It could never be denied that he'd made an impression on everyone he met and what would his parents have said if they knew – Peter the Wild, their once-idiot son.

Author's Note:

It was concluded in 2011 that the condition that afflicted Peter the Wild Boy was suspected to be the chromosomal disorder, Pitt-Hopkins Syndrome, a condition identified only in 1978, nearly 200 years after Peter's death. Various physical attributes of Peter's which are evident in the Kensington Palace portrait have been matched to the condition, such as his curvy 'Cupid Bow' lips, his short stature, his coarse-curly hair, drooping eyelids and thick lips.

The Burning of Joan of Arc –
And For What?

The year was 1425 and France continued to be an 'occupied' country – occupied by the English was how the French saw the situation but it could be argued that after the Battle of Hastings, William Duke of Normandy never gave up his rights to his home when he became King William the Conqueror of England. He continued to keep one foot in the French camp. Through him, the English believed they still had a strong claim to the country, and were supported in this by Burgundy, which had remained English to all intent and purpose. In effect, the English King in the fifteenth century governed not only England, but much of France as well.

A village in northern France is where this story begins – it was called Domremy and the family with whom we are primarily concerned is the d'Arc family – a mother, father, three sons and two daughters. They were a well set up family and the father, Jacques, was highly thought of by the other villagers and ended up as one of their public figures able to oversee the collection of taxes and organise the local defences. He was, however, a farmer by occupation and both he and his entire family had to work hard to earn an income on which they could live – but they were comfortable and lived reasonably well. They were of the peasant class however but very loyal to the Dauphin, who had yet to be crowned King of France.

In Domremy, a young girl had just finished helping with the milking and she knelt down to lift the wooden shoulder pannier – it had a pail of fresh milk hanging on each side. It was heavy but she was used to it. She lifted the pails and walked slowly across the farmyard, splashing milk onto the ground as she went. Her mother – Isabelle Romee – called to her from the kitchen door, "Straight into the dairy, Joan, and leave it there for Sebastian to start the butter churning. I hope you've not drunk as much as you did yesterday – you're personally creaming off our profits and leaving us with less butter to sell." Although it sounded like a scold, Isabelle was smiling – her daughter had always had a good appetite and although not of a big build, she was strong and straight of limb.

She was a healthy fourteen-year-old farm girl if ever there was one. She had never learned to read or write and had no formal education, except what the local church and her religious mother had given her. When she was young, she was a happy girl however and often played with the local children, dancing around a 'fairy' tree in the woods, calling out to the fairies whom they all believed lived in the tree. In fact, Joan used to believe she could see them and even have conversations with them on certain, special days. This innocent tale would be ultimately used against her at her 'Trial'her, claiming it had been an admission of her indulgence in magic and occult dealings and not just a young child playing make-believe. She would be accused in later years of tempting the other children into questionable games and believing odd and talking about strange things. In fact, it was probably just innocent children at play.

Her father, Jacques d'Arc, was the tenant farmer of a piece of land about fifty acres in size. He, his wife, three sons and two daughters all worked on the farm together. Joan was the most devout of the children and spent a lot of her time in prayer or meditation. In this, she was encouraged by her mother, who was equally devout and had actually been on a pilgrimage to the Vatican in Rome – a very great achievement at the time – but the woman had persevered and eventually reached the holy city. The trip must have been fraught with many difficulties yet this peasant woman managed it. She was a strong woman, as was her daughter and the two were the most religious of the family – if not of the whole village. Joan's sister, Catherine, was not as robust as her sibling and had several health issues – she was also not such a devout, practising Catholic as the other two women were.

The d'Arc family had just experienced a traumatic experience. The village of Domremy was close to Burgundian lands and the English collaborated with Burgundy, both wanting to get rid of the Dauphin of France. The d'Arc family – and the village itself – were known to be anti the Anglo-Burgundian forces – and against the presence of the English altogether. They were quite vocal in their condemnation of them, especially the d'Arc family who were especially strong supporters of Charles the Dauphin and regularly spoke out in support of his claim to the throne. The opposing side had many open ears in the local taverns and market places and knew exactly what the village thought. Unfortunately, this knowledge led them to punish the villagers by attacking and burning the whole area, as well as driving off their cattle. This caused the village great losses which took them a long time to recoup. Jacques d'Arc's farm suffered badly in the attack and his farm was left in great upheaval with all his animals dead or chased off.

Joan had experienced this with the rest of her village and of course, became naturally 'anti the Anglo-Burgundians' – and who could blame her? She had always listened to political debates and was very aware of France's position. The farm eventually did recover and Jacques was building up his stock once more – with the help of his sons. The village pulled together and helped each other – it was that sort of community.

In the early morning of the day in question, Joan had left the milk in the dairy for Sebastian and was in her own little bedroom, kneeling before the self-made altar in front of the window. Statues of Christ and the Virgin Mary stood on the altar and the glow from a smoking candle gave both of them a creamy and translucent look. The room was plain and looked like a nun's cell. The young girl remained on her knees in prayer until her mother called her to come down for breakfast. "Coming, Mother – shall I call Catherine and my brothers as well?" Everything was quite normal – so far.

"Please do, daughter." And as she replied, the church bells in the village began to ring, telling people to hurry or they'd be late for Mass – and the Priest would not like that. Something made Joan remain in her room and move towards the window, which she pushed open.

The day was beautiful, warm and sunny but the atmosphere around her window was heavy and she felt something unusual was going to happen. She sensed a presence at first but could see nothing – then the most beautiful face she'd ever seen appeared in the light breeze. It was a man with long, golden hair and wearing a soft blue robe, which shimmered in the haze. The haze itself was surrounded by a brilliant white light. The sound of church bells had softened in the background and she waited expectantly for the figure to speak and explain his reason for being there.

"I am God's Archangel Michael and He has sent me to speak with you. Firstly, I must remind you to always be good, not just a good Catholic but a good person." His deep voice boomed loudly in Joan's ears and she clearly heard him telling her to help Charles the Dauphin to wear the crown of France – and also, and more importantly to chase the English out of the country. "You could be of great help to Charles in attaining his kingdom – God has spoken on this matter and has chosen you to be the one to help." The beautiful vision smiled at the girl before disappearing and fading upwards into the bright sky and onwards into the Heavens.

Joan was in a state of shock and returned slowly to her own time. She hadn't uttered one word to the Angel – but she hadn't had to, as he'd come to her with a specific message from God. There was no need for words from her. She knew she had always been a good girl, living by moral and religious codes, instilled in her by her mother.

She didn't know what to do next so she joined her family for breakfast. She told no one what had just happened, for fear they wouldn't believe her. Isabelle could see her daughter was upset but she just put it down to her age and poured gruel into the breakfast bowls. After eating, the family left for the church as they always did – the bells still ringing and summoning them to Mass.

Time passed and Joan continued to hear voices and sometimes, see visions. It wasn't always the Archangel Michael who visited her, but also Saint Catherine and Saint Margaret, (both Virgin Martyrs) who brought the same message as he had. All claimed they were speaking for God and she must listen and obey what she was instructed. 'She must save France from the invader and help put Charles of Valois on the throne. She must help bring this about and so remove the English Henry V and his son, Henry VI from ruling France.' This was the clear message the Angels brought to young Joan – and hopefully, it would bring to an end the 100 years War between England and France, which had been a long and bitter struggle between the countries.

She became reclusive as she heard the voices more clearly when there was no one else there, so she steered away from company as much as she could. When she was younger, she sewed and baked and did all the things girls of her age did, as well as helping on the farm, but now she spent many hours in meditation – always waiting for the angels to come. She was liked by people and the local Priest once described her as 'the most devout young woman' he'd ever met. She attended Confession daily – sometimes twice a day – but couldn't have had much to tell the Priest, as she did so little out of the ordinary. Strangely enough, she told very few people about the spiritual visitors – but her religious mother, who'd always though her daughter special, made sure the word spread as widely as possible.

Joan's reputation soon spread – locally at first and then into the wider country. People talked about 'The Maid' and her visions – some people considered her mad, but not her family and those who knew her well – they continued to support her in her claims. The visions still appeared to her as usual; they came in a blinding light and spoke the words of God. 'The English must be exiled from France and this would take many battles and skirmishes.' Unfortunately, the Dauphin's supporters were not as successful in battle as were the English-Burgundians, whose foothold in France was very secure.

When 'The Maid' was 16 years old, her father chose a suitor for her. It was in the same year as her sister, Catherine died of consumption. Obviously, Joan took the death very hard and on top of it, she had to contend with her father's decision about a bridegroom. Joan was a maid and a virgin – she had no interest in marrying anyone – and intended to remain a virgin all her life. To her thinking, the virginal state was something demanded by her religion and she was adamant that she would not marry. She explained to him that she'd accepted the holy mission that God had set her through his angels, and she would defeat the English for the good of France. He wouldn't listen and tried to force her to marry but she went to the local Court and explained everything to them. An amazing step for a simple country girl. The Court issued a statement saying that Joan of Arc was to be allowed to remain a virgin – until she herself decided differently. This was an unusual act on her part as such a thing hadn't happened before, and her father had to accept the ruling, However, he called it clear evidence of wilful disobedience and not a typical attitude from a girl who claimed to be a simple, moral and obedient person. Jacques had a repeated dream about his daughter and in it, he saw her riding away from him, accompanied by men on horseback dressed in armour – and no matter how loudly he called after her, she would not turn back. The dream may have been why he wanted her to marry so much and begin leading a normal life, but it was not to be.

Some of her village friends thought she was becoming a strange person as she grew older. She refused even to dance with them at village celebrations, something expected of all the young girls. Her attitude to things was changing as well and she was heard to reprimand the church bell ringer, if he was ever late summoning the people to church. Apparently, she had been over heard abusing him for his failing. Again, a big change in her attitude.

She was 18 years old when the Archangel Michael came to her again and told her it was time, she went to see Charles of Valois and tell him he must put her at the head of his troops and warn him that if he didn't do it, he would never wear the crown of France. She did question St Michael as to how much help she would be able to give the Dauphin but he just repeated what he'd just said. She now actually had conversations with her angels and there was nothing she could do, but obey their instructions.

"Mother, Father, I have something to tell you and I hope you'll understand." She knew she had to broach the subject with her parents and the moment had come. "As you know, I've had many visits from the Archangels and heard their voices, no matter where I am. They now instruct me to go to the Dauphin and ask that I be put in charge of his army, as only that way will we manage to evict the English invaders from our country. France would then be a free country again with its rightful ruler." As she spoke, she was sitting on a stool by the fireplace and supping a bowl of bread and milk. She kept her eyes lowered as though submissive.

Her father jumped up from his chair saying, "Good God, girl, what are you saying? You are a mere girl who could never lead – nor fight in an army. This nonsense has to stop once and for all. Who do you think you are?" He was very angry.

Isabelle intervened. "Hush, Husband, let the girl speak, you know she has always been special. Just because we don't hear or see holy visions, doesn't mean she's been lying. God may have chosen her to be his emissary and has great plans for her. I for one, believe the Angels have visited her as she says – and given her instructions. Remember, the orders come ultimately from God himself."

Jacques continued, more angry than ever, "But you Wife, are a religious zealot and can't see the wood for the trees. She is still grieving over our Catherine's death and is confused and upset. I fear she is bordering on madness and you are not helping her. I think we should talk with the Priest and send her away to a Nunnery – that's what I think. It's either that or a mad house. You know the dream I have over and over again where I see her being taken away by men-in-arms as a prisoner. If that were ever to happen, I would wish I had told her brothers to drown her years ago – or I should have done it myself." There were tears in his eyes and his head fell onto his chest.

Isabelle shouted back at her husband, "Nothing would please me more than to see out daughter become a Nun – but it seems God has other plans for her – and you will have to accept this." Isabelle was quite angry – something that didn't happen very often.

Joan finished her supper but said nothing. Her father could not be persuaded and insisted she stay at home and behaved like a normal young woman, helping on the farm.

Two weeks later, she told them both that she was needed by Angelique – a friend – who was on the point of giving birth to her first child. The two girls had been friends since childhood and Joan's presence at the birth was important to Angelique, as she believed Joan to be a very devout and religious person who would ease the birthing. At least, that's what Joan claimed her friend had said. She was telling blatant lies to her parents and showing a wilfulness she couldn't control. But then, God was driving her and it was only a little white lie after all. She had to do His work and if a lie meant she could, then it was acceptable. Jacques and Isabelle however, believed their daughter and told her she was free to go to her friend's house.

"I'll see you both later – but it may be very late, if not in the morning – as I don't know how long the birth will take." And she left her parents' house, knowing she had the guilt of the lie in her heart. She set out for the fort at Vaucouleurs and managed to convince the captain-in-charge that it was imperative she be taken to the Dauphin immediately. Her earnestness was impossible to ignore and, in an attempt, to humour the young girl, he made preparations to accede to her request. On 13 February 1429, Joan and a small military escort travelled to the Dauphin's castle at Chinon. Joan now wore the clothes of a man and had her long hair cut short in the style of an urchin boy. On her journey, the disguise would help keep her safe, as the country through which she travelled, was controlled by the English and its Burgundian supporters.

At first, the Dauphin refused to see her, as all his ministers and advisers were against it, but two days after she'd arrived, he agreed to allow her an audience. As part of his security, he hid himself amongst his courtiers and kept a low profile when she was brought into the room. Although, she'd never seen Charles before, she walked straight up to him, having weaved her way through a large crowd. She knelt before him. Charles was taken by surprise but began to understand why this maid was special. Dressed in men's clothes also surprised him and he knew he must tread carefully – she could be a Heretic or a Witch, for all he knew.

"I pledge to help you defeat the English and chase them out of France. I pledge too to ensure you are crowned at Reims as France's true King." She spoke with such conviction that he was inclined to believe her but just in case, he had Ecclesiastical experts interrogate her for three weeks at Poitiers – before he would even consider her request. She also impressed the Duke of Alençon so much with her logic, conviction and ability to debate, that he finally persuaded the Dauphin to agree to her proposition. She was given a military unit of her own – she was the equivalent of a knight with her own squire – Jean d'Aulon – and she was given a Crest and Banner, which would become an inspiration to the Dauphin's forces in the following two years. She was also given a sword which her 'voices' told her was a holy and magic sword which would be of great value to her. When she left with her troops, she was dressed in a white suit of armour and rode a white horse. From Blois, on 27 April 1429, her unit went to reinforce the Dauphin's troops at the Siege of Orleans – a Siege which had been going on for over a year. Some of the other French leaders wanted to wait until more reinforcements arrived before they tackled the English, but Joan's 'voices' told her to attack immediately. The Archangel Michael came to her and repeatedly told her not to listen to the others, but to push onwards and attack the English, who would not be expecting it. The others were aware that reinforcements were expected to join the Dauphin's army and thought the attack would take place when they arrived, so they disagreed with Joan's wishes.

However, the 'Maid of Orleans' obeyed her 'voices' yet again and personally led the attack on the enemy. Although the attack was successful, it resulted in her being injured in the shoulder – and quite seriously. Joan's name was now spoken of as 'the wounded hero' at the Siege of Orleans.

"You were right it seems – immediate attack was the right thing to do and the Dauphin will be pleased with this outcome." One of the other commanders spoke out in her praise and the name of 'The Maid of Orleans' was born and has never gone away.

The only location where surely a Dauphin could be crowned in France was at the Cathedral of Reims, where the sacred anointing oil was held for safety. The English and the collaborating Burgundians held the whole area surrounding Reims – so there would be many future battles to be faced by the Dauphin's forces before he could take his rightful place on the throne. However, Joan was ready to fight by his side – the battle at Les Tourelles 7 May 1429, the battle of Patay 18 June 1429 were both successful. Under the escort of Joan and her troops, the Dauphin arrived in Reims on 17 July 1429, having forced their way through enemy lines – and he was crowned King of France – no longer the Dauphin, but a fully-fledged King. Before retreating to Loire, he paraded around the region, accepting allegiance and praise wherever he went. He had followed

Joan's suggestion and travelled to Reims and success and the crown were his reward.

Joan's father must surely have forgiven her for disobeying him because he now instructed her two brothers to travel to Reims to see her. Also, as a token of his regard, Charles issued the following statement:

'That on behalf and at the request of our much beloved Joan the Maid and for the great and notable and profitable service which she had rendered to us, and each day renders in the recovery of our dominions, we have granted and do grant, of special grace by these presents to the peasants and inhabitants of the towns and villages of Greux and Domremey in the said district of Chaumont in Bassigny, that they be now and hereafter free, quit, exempt of all taxes, aids, subsidies and subventions placed and to be placed on the said district.'

Her father and the people of the district now had much reason to respect and believe in her – or at least be grateful to her, considering many of them had once considered her to be quite mad.

Soon after, the French and English had a skirmish at Senlis whilst Burgundy and France signed a four-month truce between them. Things were changing in France. Joan was a strong leader of men and accepted no failings on their part. As it had always been in the past, Scotland and France were close and loyal to each other and respected their 'Auld Alliance', so Scotland had sent soldiers to fight for the French King. These soldiers were under Joan's command however and she constantly reprimanded those who drank too much or were too loud in their profanities. She spent a lot of time instructing them in morals, especially where the camp followers (women) were concerned. Even whilst in the midst of all this, she was as devout as ever and still received messages from her 'voices'. They told her to struggle on and fight for the sake of Charles. She really was proving to be an exceptional leader.

On 8 September 1429, the French assault began on the English – they held Paris and of course, Joan was in the thick of the battle. She was wounded in the shoulder again – but fought on valiantly. One month later, King Charles VII raised Joan, her parents and her brothers to nobility status in society – what must her father have thought of that? Joan now had the status of a military Knight when she arrived at Compiegne on 14 May 1430 and the King ordered her to confront and deal with an assault on the town. It was noticed that her men's apparel had become more flamboyant of late and almost flashy. Now she was a Knight, she felt she should dress as one. Flamboyant or not, she fought long and hard to defend the town of Compiegne and its citizens but in a wild skirmish of confusion, she was thrown from her horse. She lay – wounded – on the ground outside the town gates which were soon closed. The Burgundians captured her and made a spectacle of her arrest, parading her through the streets in celebration of having captured such a prize. She was taken as a prisoner to the castle of Bouvreuil which was occupied by the English Commander from Rouen. And so her troubles began anew. News of Joan of Arc's capture quickly spread to Paris – it was a triumph for the English.

King Charles discussed her capture with his Ministers. "Yes, but I mustn't become involved with her trial – it has nothing to do with me. Yes – yes – I know – she helped bring about my coronation but it would have happened anyway without her involvement. As you know, I am at present, attempting to forge an agreement with the Duke of Burgundy – and must keep a low profile as regards Joan and her voices." His Ministers looked at each other but said nothing. Joan's part in his coronation had been significant and there was no question about that. Their newly crowned King however had to be placated, so they said nothing. He had his crown for a short time only and didn't want to be involved with the 'Maid', so he kept a low profile as her Trial progressed. History was forever to frown upon him for his lack of support for one who had served him so loyally – and at such misfortune to herself.

The Duke of Burgundy was ecstatic that he had captured the infamous 'Maid' who had given both him and his English compatriots so much trouble. He put Joan and her squire – Jean d'Aulon – into a cell at his castle at Vermandois, but after Joan tried to escape, she was moved to a more northern castle – further away from the French lines. At this castle, however, Joan made an even more daring escape attempt, leaping sixty feet from the top of her prison tower into the moat. Although she ended up unconscious and covered in bruises, Joan was not seriously hurt. Again, Burgundy moved her to an even more secure prison in Arras. She was proving to be as difficult as a prisoner, as she had been as a fighter.

Paris now had a say in what was to be done with 'The Maid of Orleans'. The year was 1430 and it was in the month of May that the University of Paris – which was then very pro English – suggested that Joan be turned over to clergymen for inquisition. Pierre Cauchon, the Bishop of Beauvais would lead the interrogation as she had been captured in his diocese. On 3 January 1431, she came under his control and he paid the authorities a price of 10,000 francs for her – so the church bought the 'Maid of Orleans' from the State and she was transferred to Rouen to stand Trial. England's Earl of Warwick had control of Rouen at the time.

And so, on 13 January 1431 Joan of Arc's Trial began. Bishop Cauchon, along with the Vice Inquisitor of France served as her main judges. They asked for and studied statements from people regarding her reputation as a witch. They believed she met the standard description – she behaved strangely, she heard mysterious voices in her head, she liked to go off by herself for long periods of time, she had had unusually good luck in her battles, she usually wore men's clothing, she had assumed 'manly' characteristics, she'd bravely commanded armies and advised many male authorities like Charles VII. The claim 'witch', seemed based mainly on the fact that she had chosen to adopt male characteristics and appearance.

On 21 February, Joan herself was summoned into Court where she took the oath to tell the truth. They had dressed her in a sackcloth dress and if she was asked anything that might reveal something about Charles VII, she held her silence and refused to speak. This happened on a great number of occasions. She had been kept in a dank and damp cell and she looked and felt ill, but no sympathy was shown to her. The Burgundians didn't want her to die before the Court had declared her a witch – but they did nothing to help her. Joan herself feared she was dying but she insisted she wouldn't change her statement, which had asserted her innocence. She did so well in defending herself and standing up to interrogation, the original 70 heresy charges had been dropped to 12 only. They allowed her to receive Communion and attend Confession – but it seemed they could not shake her and on 23 May 1431, the Court prepared to transfer her to secular authorities, who were not associated with religious issues. They really didn't know what else to do with 'The maid.'

"What are they going to do with me now?" she asked her new warden, John of Luxembourg, who actually had shown her some kindness and even held conversations with her. It was pitiful but she was grateful for this and spoke at length with him. "Can't you release my squire at least – he has done nothing wrong but he is made to suffer as am I?"

"Are you saying that you have done wrong, Joan?" One of her more cunning Burgundian jailers was quick to ask.

"I have done nothing wrong. I obey God, that is all." Was her quick reply.

"But if you are a witch – and a heretic – surely it would be easier to admit it – and then this might all be over." He was persistent and looking for praise from his superiors – if only he could trick her into saying the wrong thing. Burgundy and England wanted to prove the charges against her were valid. The French nation admired her, had great sympathy for her and held her high in their esteem – something that scared her captors. They needed her to admit the charges against her so the French supporters would turn against her – after all, who would want to support a convicted witch? As things stood, whilst she was still being interrogated, they couldn't risk executing a young, convincing and holy martyr without her confession. Only after she admitted her guilt, could they burn her at the stake – and so finally be rid of a dangerous and troublesome French fighter such as Joan. It also helped their case against Charles VII after all he had chosen to support her – how wise was he? Had he allowed himself to be controlled by a witch? The English and Burgundians wanted the church to condemn her and so discredit her in the eyes of the French people. Their plan was cunning – but proving what they wanted was difficult.

Politics were being played out in France, using the nineteen-year-old 'Maid' as a pawn in their game.

"If you say I am a witch, then it is God who has made me so – and you must ask him for his reason. I am what God has made me and I have no guilt about obeying him." She looked tired and frail and ill. She was so young and facing her own execution. The inquisitors couldn't budge her in this assertion or they'd be accused of blaming God and not her. Her arguments – when she chose to make them – were very clever. Any questions about Charles, she refused to answer.

"You hear voices who tell you what to do, don't you?" one judge asked.

"I always obey the Archangels' commands – as they speak with the voice of God." Was her repeated response to such questions.

"So, in obeying your voices, you go against your church – you are a blasphemer as well as a witch and heretic. What do you say to that?"

Joan repeated that they must ask God his reasons for making her what she was. "You prefer to wear man's clothes and this in itself, is indecent. Why do you do that? You have also committed the sin of trying to take your own life – when you jumped from the tower at your last prison. You couldn't really have thought you would live – why did you do that?"

Joan thought for a while and said, "I jumped from the tower, not to kill myself, but so that I could continue to obey the Archangels and therefore God himself." She always managed to turn the argument around and say they should ask God why she did what she did. The judges were becoming increasingly frustrated and threatened her with torture when she refused to change her statements. Joan showed no fear at the mention of torture, saying it would not look good for them when people learned that she'd confessed under torture. She also pointed out that anything to which she admitted whilst under torture must surely be regarded as pain talking rather than herself. They found it too difficult to deal with her clever and evasive responses to their questions. Now they could only question her on twelve charges, with 58 charges having been dropped already. Torturing her was dismissed, as they knew it would be futile.

Two guards remained in her cell and she begged again to be allowed to attend a service of Mass. It was very important to her but she was refused. Her treatment was harsh and because she had already made several attempts to escape, they used iron chains fitted to a wooden block. The guards watched her all the time. She was never allowed any moments of privacy.

Both the ecclesiastical and secular authorities had met their match with the simple farm girl from Domremy, who did nothing worse than defend her King and obey her God. Under intense pressure, chained in irons and constantly watched by her jailers, Joan became even more ill. She was visited by two doctors in the month of April, who were under orders to ensure that she didn't die – certainly not before she was found guilty of blasphemy, heresy and witchcraft – and Joan lived on, albeit very ill and weak. Her main judge – Bishop Cauchon and twenty of his assessors visited her in her cell and tried to convince her it would be best if she admitted to the charges and if she stopped evading certain questions. On their visit, the 'Maid of Orleans' thought she was dying and signed her 'X' to a statement recanting all she had said at the trial. She did it with hesitation and impressed on those around her, that she did it with 'the Lord's Approval'. Strangely enough, the form had already been prepared and readily available for her to sign. Bishop Cauchon was extremely pleased and arranged for her to be taken from her prison to the church of St Ouen where she was preached to by theologians, for many hours. In the tirade, Charles VII was criticised and his character viciously – and perhaps fairly – attacked.

Joan spoke up, "Please desist from speaking so about a good Christian such as the King of France. It is unfair and untrue. If blame is to be imposed, place it on my head and not his." Even at this point, she continued to protect Charles who still had not intervened on her behalf – she did not once consider her own predicament and gave no thought to trying to save herself. However, she was wise enough to request that the Pope in Italy be asked to consider her case and intercede on her behalf – but the chief inquisitor chose to ignore her.

"You are no longer under the judgement of the church but rather of the State and the sentence passed on you is one of 'perpetual imprisonment'. You will be incarcerated in a place commonly used as a prison. You are also instructed to desist from wearing men's clothing and don that of a woman." After this announcement, she was returned to the prison from where she'd come. However, her next visitors to the cell found her dressed again in a man's clothes. She told them she had done this of her own free will, which didn't help her case.

This marked the inevitable end for the Maid of Orleans, especially when she spoke again of hearing her voices – of hearing both St Catherine and St Margaret, both accusing her of 'treason' after putting her 'X' to the confession she'd made to her jailers. The secular authorities saw this as a relapse by Joan and 39 of her ecclesiastical assessors agreed she should again be handed over to the State officials. The very next morning, she was allowed to make Confession and to receive Communion, whilst accompanied by two Dominican Priests. She was then led to the 'Place du Vieux Marche' where she was forced to hear again yet another long sermon before being declared to be a prisoner of the English and their Burgundian collaborators – and no longer a prisoner of the French church. This was read out before all her judges and before a great crowd of people who had come to witness the burning. The executioner stepped forward and led Joan to the high stake recently built in the market, and without more ceremony, put fire to the stake. The pyre was lit and a Dominican Priest stepped forward and tried to console the dying woman.

"Please, raise the crucifix high – so I can see it as I die. Shout loudly the word 'Salvation' – so I can hear it above the roar of the flames." She twisted her body in agony and cried out, "My Lady…St Catherine and my Lady St Margaret – I see you clearly and I am shortly to join you." She was near the end and her head sank forward onto her chest as she shouted one last word 'Jesus'.

The news of Joan of Arc's death reached Paris and quickly spread throughout the country. The news pamphlets read simply:

'French patriot and martyr tried for heresy and sorcery. She was burned at the stake in a market place of Rouen, France on 30 May 1431.' And that's all that was said.

They may have burned her body but they never even dented her spirit. She spoke at the end with the same conviction she'd shown from the moment she left the farm in Domremy – when she left her parents in the kitchen and went to help a friend deliver her baby.

Joan of Arc's name will never die, she was an inspiration to all who met her. And even to those who weren't lucky enough to meet her, she is still an inspiration. She lives on and teaches us to separate wrong from right. She died for what she believed to be right – and did it with great bravery and stoicism. She most certainly did not die in vain.

Author's Note

In 1456, there was a Rehabilitation Procedure when witnesses of Joan's death were interviewed and they swore they believed she died a faithful Christian. A few days after these interviews, her two brothers travelled at their father's instructions to see the King – they asked for the case against their sister to be reviewed and freshly investigated. Charles took no action at this request, but almost twenty years after her execution, he ordered an inquiry into Joan's Trial. Too little, too late! Cardinal Legate Guillaume d'Estouteville made a thorough investigation into the case, resulting in Pope Callixtus' own intervention. He had been petitioned by the d'Arc family for proceedings to be instituted against the decision in Joan's case – and the results of the trial were revoked and annulled.

On 16 May 1920, Joan of Arc or Jeanne d'Arc was canonised as a Saint by the Roman Catholic Church. Pope Benedict XV in his bull Divina Disponente, which concluded the canonisation process, in that the Sacred Congregation of Rights, was instigated after a petition of 1869 of the French Catholic Hierarchy.

St Joan's Feast Day is still celebrated in France on 30 May – the same day in the month when she was burned at the stake. She is the official Patroness of soldiers and of France itself. She was a truly amazing woman.